Rise Like a Phoenix

by

Tammy Lowe

The Acadian Secret Series

Rise Like a Phoenix

Cover Art by *Jennifer Greeff*

The Wild Rose Press, Inc.
PO Box 708
Adams Basin, NY 14410-0708
Visit us at www.thewildrosepress.com

Publishing History
First Edition, 2023
Trade Paperback ISBN 978-1-5092-5303-6
Digital ISBN 978-1-5092-5304-3

The Acadian Secret Series
Published in the United States of America

When Crooked Nose punched, David blocked. Then, with a quick elbow movement, he smacked the man's face with the end of the rope before stepping back. The effect was rather comical.

Crooked threw another punch.

David pounced, wrapping the rope around the man's wrist. Yanking the tied arm back made him double over. His eyes turned cold and hard. "Who sent you?"

The man's breath sawed in and out. "You've no idea whose daughter you've run away with, do you?"

He pulled Crooked's arm straight back some more. "Enlighten me."

"Make *her* tell you," he hissed.

David swallowed a lump in his throat. "She hides nothing from me." He then snapped the man's arm at the elbow, and grabbed Elisabeth's hand, pulling her to a run.

Her breath hitched, and the colorful bouquet of wildflowers dropped.

"By the gods!" David led the way through a field of grazing sheep, toward a grove of trees. "Your father is here?"

"No..." She shook her head in denial. "No, he can't be...can he?"

"You tell me!"

Elisabeth let out an uncontrollable whimper.

If Dad found out she was time-traveling—she was so grounded.

Acknowledgments

I have an enormous thank you to Diana Goodwin. Her knowledge of life in the medieval days is incredible. Walking the streets of Ghent, Bruges, and Brussels with Diana was like stepping back in time and meeting a new friend there. That entire world came to life all around me as she pointed out countless details, answered every single question I could possibly think of, and told exciting tales of days gone by. Any historical inaccuracies or artistic license in Rise Like A Phoenix are no reflection upon Ms. Goodwin.

Special thanks to my awesome editor, Lea Schizas, whom I absolutely love working with. Thank you for all your hard work.

And last, but certainly not least, a huge thank you to Gord and Quinton for their endless love and support.

Chapter One

"Trousers!"

"Aquarius…" Elisabeth confined her laughter to a snort while adjusting the leather belt around her hips. "Will you stop complaining and come down?" She attempted to navigate the ladder-like staircase without tripping over her long dress.

"I look ridiculous."

"But that loincloth you were running around in didn't?" With a huge grin, she waited for him in the passageway at the bottom of the stairs. "I'm sure you look fine. Perenelle went through a lot of trouble to find clothing for us so quickly."

Sunshine poured in through the front and back doors. Both were propped open to create a cross-breeze, allowing the smoky smell of a nearby campfire to fill the air. Elisabeth bounced on tiptoes to the threshold, peeking outside while fiddling with the laces of her fitted bodice. She paused to admire the vegetable patch behind Balinus' house before returning to the corridor, running fingers along the grooves of a carved sideboard.

The floorboards creaked when David began pacing at the top of the stairs. "Promise not to laugh?" he mumbled.

"No." Unable to keep still, Elisabeth danced in a circle, admiring the flare of her burgundy gown and the way the long, tight sleeves came down to her wrists. Bands of white fabric, attached to her upper arms, floated in the air as she twirled.

When David cleared his throat, she twisted around to find him standing tall at the bottom of the staircase. Legs planted wide apart, hands on his hips, he looked like he'd just been cast as Robin Hood.

Elisabeth did a double-take. Her dark eyes widened, and she burst into laughter.

David's shoulders slumped as he trudged closer, his face partially hidden by a dark hood. "I feel like a fool in these trousers."

She covered her mouth with both hands, trying to regain her composure. "Well, if it's any consolation, those aren't trousers. They're tights."

"This is humiliating."

"No…no… you look good." Elisabeth shook her head, inspecting his leather shoes, brown hose, and green hip-length tunic. "Very handsome. I especially love…" Her voice became high-pitched while grabbing the long tail from the back of the hood he wore and wrapping it around his neck like a scarf. "I especially love this ridiculous hat," she blurted out before dissolving into a fit of giggles.

"Oh, you are a wicked girl." With a smirk, he put his hands on her waist, pushing her against the pantry door.

After pulling the absurd hood off so she could see his face, they stood together in the passageway, hidden from the main living area by nothing more than a wall made of carved wooden screens. She heard a clatter of plates, followed by the gentle sawing of a knife. Elisabeth took a deep breath, enjoying a sugar and spice

2

scent that drifted through the house. "I still can't believe I found you," she whispered to David with a smile so big, it couldn't be contained. "I mean, it's the wrong century, but…"

His lips parted while brushing a hand through Elisabeth's dark hair. Perenelle had styled it into a simple half-up crown braid—the finishing touch to her fairy-tale ensemble.

With a feeling of breathlessness, she nestled against him and raised her head, anticipating a kiss.

At that moment, a girl of about ten, burst through the front door, completely out of breath.

"Nellie, have you seen Beau-Beau? I've looked ev…" She froze. A toothy grin then spread across the child's adorable face at having spotted the lovebirds—just as Perenelle cleared her throat while shuffling into the passage as well.

Heat rushed to Elisabeth's cheeks as she ducked under David's arm to step away, and began plucking at her dress.

"She…" David chuckled, fidgeting with the rope sling hanging from his hip. "She had something in her eye." He shot the little one a mischievous look that caused her to burst into giggles.

The girl's blue eyes widened as her attention turned back to Perenelle. "Where's Beau-Beau?" she asked in Latin, enunciating each word. "I cannot find her anywhere."

"I've no doubt she's hiding from *you*, Colette." The old woman's buttery yellow dress fluttered in the cross breeze while pulling her closer. "I swear I just plaited your hair." Perenelle's pleasant voice was strong and deep as she brushed her fingers through the girl's blonde locks.

Elisabeth's mind raced.

Perenelle's granddaughter?

Colette still wore a huge grin, her gaze darting back and forth from Elisabeth to David. "I'm Colette. I already know who you are." Both hands flew excitedly to her chest as she spoke in a posh, yet charming manner. "You must have been exhausted because I was starting to wonder if you were *ever* going to wake up. I once slept for two entire days, and Nicolas banging on pots and pans didn't even wake me."

"That's because you decided to eat a dwale cherry and almost joined your mother in Heaven, God rest her soul," Perenelle said with a heavy sigh.

A flush crept across Colette's cheeks as she giggled into cupped hands. "I didn't know that's what it was."

"I know, darling. I know. Scared everyone nearly to death, though."

Turning her attention back to David and Elisabeth, Colette fiddled with the cloth belt wrapped around the waist of her floor-length mustard tunic, worn atop a linen-gray dress, all while trying to keep her head still as Perenelle braided her hair. "I was *so* careful not to wake you this morning." She glanced over her shoulder, trying to look at Perenelle. "You haven't seen Beau-Beau?"

"She's probably gone for a little walk," Perenelle said, turning Colette's head back in place so she could finish the braid.

Elisabeth's brows squished together. "Do you want me to help you find Beau-Beau?"

"Thank you." The little girl waved her hand. "But

it's all right. She'll eventually show up."

Perenelle gave Colette a loving pat on the head when finished and then bent down, lifting a rush doormat from the compacted earth floor. "Why don't you show David and Elisabeth the way out of the village? Nicolas is going to meet them at the city gate and take them to the bookshop."

She gasped, clasping both hands beneath her chin. "Please, Nellie…can I go to the bookshop too?"

Perenelle shook her head. "Not this time, dear. Take them as far as the main road and come straight home again." The woman looked up at David. "You two take the main road to the city gate and wait for your uncle there."

With a wide grin, David leaned closer, clumsily giving Perenelle a peck on the cheek. It proved difficult due to gray coiled braids pinned up like two cinnamon buns, and a veil that swooped under her chin, attaching to a decorative headband above each ear. "We will, aunt."

"Go on now." She smiled and patted his arm before walking outside to shake off the woven doormat. "All of you. You don't want to keep him waiting."

The half-timbered houses lining both sides of the dirt road were straight out of a fairy-tale, right along with a cast of busy townsfolk. As the villagers scurried about dressed in a brilliant display of color, Elisabeth half expected them to break into song and dance. It looked more like a movie set than real life.

Flowers and herbs overflowing from planter-boxes hung beneath windows. Shutters were thrown wide open to let the sunshine and fresh air inside. A heavy vine wound its way up Balinus' house. Across the street, over a door stained blood red, a white climbing rose bloomed, filling the air with its delicate scent. Recalling last night's cooler temperature when they'd first arrived, the warmth of this morning's sun, and the fact nature seemed to be in its first flush, Elisabeth guessed it was probably June.

With a slow, disbelieving shake of her head, she eyed two men bickering at the side of the road over the sale of a chestnut-colored horse. For some reason, she'd imagined the medieval days to be dark and gloomy, but from the vibrant wall-coverings inside Balinus' house to the crayon box of color on the street, it was anything but dull.

Countless birds chirped and sang. Somewhere, a cow mooed. Elisabeth glanced over at Colette as she skipped alongside them. "So...are you Perenelle's granddaughter?"

"No," she said with an amused snort. "Not *really*. After *maman* died, she promised to take care of me and Beau-Beau."

Elisabeth stared down at her hands. "I'm sorry about your mother," she said in a gentle tone as a puppy yapped in the distance. "And...Beau-Beau's your dog?"

Colette stumbled slightly before regaining her composure. "Yes. Beau-Beau's my dog and I love her so, so, much."

"What's the old girl look like?" David asked.

"Well..." Colette wiped at her mouth and bounced a few steps ahead. "She kind of has auburn-colored hair?"

"Are you sure you don't want us to help you look for her?" Elisabeth asked again.

"Oh no. She goes for walks by herself all the time.

I'm not in the slightest bit worried. Really." After they turned a corner, Colette pointed down a hill at the road leading away from the village. "Keep going straight until you cross the bridge. After that, turn left and head to the city gate. Nicolas will meet you inside." She then turned, bouncing away.

"Good luck finding Beau-Beau," David called out.

Colette spun around and waved, bursting into laughter before running back home.

Elisabeth stopped to pick a handful of poppies growing wild alongside the road, listening as a rooster crowed. "I don't know about you, but I already love it here. It feels like we've stepped into our very own fairy-tale."

With a silly grin on his face, David nodded. "I don't know what fairy-tale is…"

She looked at him with a bemused smile.

"But I'm glad we stepped in it."

Elisabeth let out a hearty laugh before linking her arm through his. "Me too," she said with a satisfied sigh. "Me too."

"How, in the name of Jupiter, did we end up here?" David asked, staring off at a pasture dotted with grazing sheep. Over the crest of the next hill, the walls of a fortified city appeared in the distance.

"It seems the crystal is controlled by thoughts." Her pulse raced as she glanced at David, knowing he'd almost been lost forever—somewhere in time. "You quoted a certain *wise old sage* in an attempt to keep me calm."

David's blue eyes widened. "Balinus?" He then averted his gaze by grabbing a handful of stones from the ground and dropping them into his belt pouch. "It's my fault we're here," he muttered.

"No, it's not your…"

Having reached a brook that trickled and splashed over rocks, their attention turned to an imposing man who lingered near the stone bridge, waiting as his dark brown horse drank from the water. The stranger made eye contact, examining them for a moment before looking away again.

"It's not your fault we're here," she continued in their accustomed Latin after crossing the bridge.

David offered Elisabeth a weak smile, looking more like the lost teenage slave he was, rather than a Roman gladiator.

"Hey…" She leaned in closer, her voice quiet. "Since you already exist in my time, I think maybe it's a good thing you ended up here instead. This could actually work out for the best."

He raised an eyebrow.

"As long as we're together, I don't care where we are." Elisabeth's cheeks flushed with heat. "Because you're my favorite person in the entire world, you dork."

David bit down on a smile. "Dork?"

She pressed her lips together to keep from grinning. "It's a term of endearment in the future."

He let out a spontaneous laugh. "Liar!"

"Look, if I was willing to hang out with you in Ancient Rome, even though I hated it there, I think I could have handled dressing up like a princess and being with you here."

David squinted in amusement. "Could have?"

Her posture slumped while pointing at his pants. "You said yourself only barbarians wear trousers." She gave a melodramatic shrug before marching off.

He stood in place, shaking his head while chuckling, waiting as Elisabeth wandered away to add wild purple bellflowers to her bouquet of poppies. As she turned around to wave him over, a man on horseback cantered toward them–the man from the bridge.

David glanced up, running a nervous hand through his hair, watching as the horse slowed to a trot when nearing Elisabeth.

Although daunting in size, the rider was kind of old; probably in his forties. Dressed in tanned leather rather than bright colors, his brow furrowed, which made deep lines appear on his forehead. He had dark hair, weathered skin, a short beard, and a crooked nose that looked like it had been broken in the past. The man dismounted, walking toward her with hesitant steps.

"Elisabeth?" he asked, his voice low and husky.

She did a double-take, wondering how he knew her name. "Yes…?"

"Your father has sent me." He spoke in Latin. "You're to return with me immediately."

Elisabeth's brows squished together.

"He knows you are here instead of where you should be, but—"

"My father knows I'm here?" she repeated in an uncertain tone. *Had Dad found out about the crystal? About Aquarius?*

"Milady…" He forced a smile. "If you cooperate—"

"*Cor meum…*" David's voice was calm as he drew nearer, reaching for his sling. "Walk toward me, love."

With clenched fists, the man shot David a

cautionary glance. "She isn't yours to take, boy."

Her head flinched back slightly, trying to figure out what was going on.

"Elisabeth…" David warned with a steady, low-pitched voice. "Now."

Her posture went rigid, sidestepping toward him. She'd learned to trust his survival instincts.

The man turned toward David. "Are you really that naïve or just stupid?"

The moment Elisabeth was within reach, David pulled her behind him. He grabbed a stone from his pouch, positioning it in the middle of his rope sling. "I believe this to be a case of mistaken identity." He raised his sling to shoulder height and moved into his archer's stance, taking aim. "I suggest you return to your horse and leave now, for I do not wish to harm you."

With a throaty chuckle, the man with the crooked nose unsheathed his sword. "I've vowed I'll not leave without her."

"Unfortunately for you…" David rotated his sling, faster and faster. "I've made the same vow."

Crooked Nose flashed a bemused smile. "Then I fear one of us is going to be disappointed."

David lunged forward, releasing one end of the rope. The rock shot out of the sling like a bullet, smashing into the man's hand, causing the sword to drop. He then sprinted closer, kicking it out of reach. "Stop. I do not wish to kill you over an error."

With eyes narrowed, the huge man planted his feet wide apart, raising his fists.

"Are we *really* going to do this?" David asked, draping the rope between both hands.

Elisabeth's chest tightened. "Don't hurt him *too*

much, Aquarius," she whispered.

When Crooked Nose punched, David blocked. Then, with a quick elbow movement, he smacked the man's face with the end of the rope before stepping back. The effect was rather comical.

Crooked threw another punch.

David pounced, wrapping the rope around the man's wrist. Yanking the tied arm back made him double over. His eyes turned cold and hard. "Who sent you?"

The man's breath sawed in and out. "You've no idea whose daughter you've run away with, do you?"

He pulled Crooked's arm straight back some more. "Enlighten me."

"Make *her* tell you," he hissed.

David swallowed a lump in his throat. "She hides nothing from me." He then snapped the man's arm at the elbow, and grabbed Elisabeth's hand, pulling her to a run.

Her breath hitched, and the colorful bouquet of wildflowers dropped.

"By the gods!" David led the way through a field of grazing sheep, toward a grove of trees. "Your father is here?"

"No..." She shook her head in denial. "No, he can't be...can he?"

"You tell me!"

Elisabeth let out an uncontrollable whimper.

If Dad found out she was time-traveling—she was *so* grounded.

Chapter Two

They crossed a bridge over a moat and entered the city through the base of a stone watchtower. The quaintness of Balinus' village was immediately replaced with a vibe of excitement. Elisabeth paused, listening to numerous conversations—a dog that wouldn't stop barking, and someone nearby who hammered metal repeatedly. Perhaps a blacksmith? Carts bumping along stones caused her to look down; noticing cobblestone streets within the city replaced the dirt roads outside its walls.

"Is this where we're supposed to meet Balinus?"

David answered with a quick nod.

She held her stomach as if pained. "This is bad, Aquarius...*really* bad. If my parents know I'm here, I'm never going to be allowed to return."

His head jerked back.

"I've no idea how they found out." *Did Mrs. Waters accidentally say something to Dad? Had Mom found the box of treasures hidden in the closet and done some more digging?* Elisabeth's gaze darted around, searching for Crooked Nose. "That man knew my name."

"I thought nobody knows you're here?" David asked in a frantic whisper.

Elisabeth twisted the bracelet around her wrist. "*Technically,* just you and I know. But...I guess it's possible my parents found out."

He swallowed hard. "What are we going to do?"

"I don't know." Her hands trembled. "Avoid the man my father sent…at least until we figure out what's going on?"

"Ahh, there you are," a familiar voice called out. "I was beginning to think you went to another gate."

She turned, watching as Balinus approached. Dressed in an orange jacket with green hose, her favorite part of his outfit was the close-fitting white hat. It tied under his bearded chin like a baby's cap. Elisabeth had to clamp her lips together to keep from laughing.

"Good-morning-and-how-are-you-today?" His sing-song voice always made it sound like one extra-long word.

She reached out, hugging the old man. "I still can't believe it's really you."

"Apologies for our tardiness." David leaned in. "Do you know how unreal all of this seems, Balinus? I mean, look at you. I cannot help but wonder what has become of our old friend."

"Rest assured, your timeworn friend is still here." He paused, taking in a deep breath. "But let us not forget," he whispered. "I am called Nicolas in this…this *life*. Nicolas Flamel. And you are henceforth my nephew—"

"David." His gaze darted toward Elisabeth. "David Perrier."

She flashed a strained smile, unable to shake the feeling that history was repeating itself, despite her best efforts to change it. "We just met Colette. She's adorable."

Balinus let out an appreciative sigh. "That child is a breath of fresh air…and my greatest teacher," he said with a wink. He then clapped his hands together while looking their outfits over, nodding in approval. "Alrighty. Let's introduce this whole new world to you, shall we?"

David scratched his cheek as they followed the old man into the city, his posture stiff while trying to take everything in. Elisabeth wrinkled her nose at the stench in the air. Balinus ushered them along at a quick pace. Hearing the clip-clop of horse hooves, she suddenly felt like they were being watched. Swallowing hard, she peeked behind.

David glanced at her as they weaved through the crowds of people. "You're still looking for the man your father sent, aren't you?"

"I can't help it."

"Rest assured, until we know what to do about your parents, I will shield you from this…bounty hunter." David flashed a strained smile. "He'll be unable to get by me."

She snorted in amusement. "If my father sent him, it's bad enough you probably broke his arm."

"We were unaware of what was going on. I needed to be intimidating."

Elisabeth clamped her lips together to keep from smiling.

"What?" He chuckled. "You don't think I was intimidating? I was a victorious gladiator only yesterday."

She looked at him wide-eyed. "Victorious?"

"Well, it's true I nearly bled to death, but…" He winked at her. "I did beat Soran in the arena."

With a small yelp, she stopped walking. "He stabbed you. I saved your life."

David's eyes sparkled with mischief while playfully pulling her along by the hand. "Well, that is also true, but—"

"Twice!"

He stared at her with a grin before his expression softened. Elisabeth's smile quivered as she gazed down at their entwined fingers.

"It's going to be all right," he said in a soothing voice.

She answered with a small nod.

Hand-in-hand, they followed the old man through the city. The pungent odor intensified, smelling like a combination of spoiled meat, rotten eggs, and an unflushed toilet.

"By the gods—" David made a choking noise. "What is that horrifying smell?"

"You become accustomed to it." Balinus peeked back at them. "Over time." He then pointed at the sewage-filled gulley flowing down the center of the street. "Avoid the runoff as best you can."

Elisabeth covered her mouth with a hand as her stomach churned.

The old man pointed to the left. "The cemetery is close so the stench is worse the nearer you get to the mass graves. Ever since the plague…" His voice trailed off while Elisabeth and David exchanged nervous looks. "But, I find the smell does lessen once you reach the Seine."

The Seine?

Elisabeth's hand dropped from her mouth and she squealed dramatically. "Are we in Paris?"

"Indeed, we are." Balinus stepped onto a wooden board used to cross the open sewer running down the center of the street.

"We're in Paris." Her wide eyes followed David as he stepped in front of her to cross the gully. "This is one of the most romantic cities in the entire world."

"Clearly." He turned around, wiggling his eyebrows while offering his hand. "The odor in the air and dung in the road are terribly romantic."

With a smirk, Elisabeth took hold of David's fingers, letting him guide her across the crowded street. "I do miss your stepping stones," she said after hopping off the wooden board.

"I've *always* longed to hear you say that."

She found it impossible not to smile.

Sighing, he placed a loose fist against his heart. "Aquarius, I miss…your stepping stones."

While laughing, she tried to give him a playful swat.

David grabbed her arm, touching the Hercules love knot he'd tied to her wrist before they'd been sold. "Why are there no aqueducts, old man?"

"That is a long story, my friend. A large city compared to others and there is but one sewer here, built eight years ago. Meanwhile, the underground quarries expand at an alarming rate."

"Quarries?" He edged closer to the old man. "Beneath the city?"

"And below the surrounding countryside."

David flinched.

"The limestone found beneath our feet is used to build the city's churches, castles, monasteries…"

When his grip on her hand tightened, Elisabeth

paused to examine him before leaning in. "The quarries aren't mined by slaves," she whispered in a gentle tone. "And on top of that, you're not a slave anymore. Not here."

David's eyes locked on Elisabeth, and then with a slow smile, he turned his attention back to the old man.

The narrow street ended at the bank of the Seine, opening onto a busy port where the wind picked up. Seagulls cried overhead as waves slapped against the wharf. Boats lined the river while men loaded and unloaded cargo from their barges. Elisabeth took a deep breath, welcoming the smell of fish over the previous stink.

A man's angry shouts were followed by a loud crashing noise, which caused a flock of pigeons to take flight, their wings flapping in unison as they took to the sky. As a bell clanged, Elisabeth's gaze darted to an island in the middle of the wide river. A fortified castle of creamy gray stone took up nearly half of it.

"Is that where the king lives?" she asked, eying trees that peeked over walls, hinting at a garden beyond them.

"No." Balinus shook his head. "It's mostly for prisoners now. King Charles moved into the Louvre after—"

A wide grin spread across her face. "The Louvre?"

"Right behind you." With a gleam in his eye, he pointed over her shoulder.

After spinning around, Elisabeth sucked in a quick breath. Complete with turrets and towers, it looked nothing like the photographs she'd seen of the present-day museum with the glass pyramid in front. The Louvre that stood before her was a medieval fortress with defense towers lining the wall. She let out a spontaneous laugh.

David took a step back, eyes widening as he stared at the dark gray spires shooting up from numerous towers.

"The King spends most of his time at Saint-Pol's." Balinus leaned in closer. "Because he doesn't like the smell in Paris."

"*That* I understand," David said with a chuckle as they began walking toward one of the wooden bridges. Lined with houses and shops, it connected the island to the rest of the city.

Balinus pointed across the Seine, to the middle of the island, where even more timber-framed houses and shops dotted the streets. "Our destination."

Elisabeth's mouth snapped shut, noticing stone twin towers beyond where the old man pointed. "That's Notre Dame, isn't it?"

Balinus looked at her with a beaming face. "It is."

Although she could only see the top of the cathedral from across the river, the color is what stood out. Bright statues of kings, dressed in robes of yellows, reds, oranges, bright blues and greens, with golden crowns upon their heads, stood in a neat line beneath the stained-glass window at the top of the basilica.

"To see it like this…painted…it's more beautiful than I could have ever imagined. In my time, it's still standing, but it's plain stone. It's not colorful like this." She angled herself closer to David. "That will be our meeting place."

He gave her a blank look.

"When I was little, whenever my parents took me somewhere new, we'd always pick the tallest building or monument to be our meeting place in case we became separated. See…" She pointed up at the cathedral. "It's easy to find if one of us gets lost."

With a grin, David tilted his head closer. "I have no intention of ever losing you again," he whispered into her ear.

She glanced up at him with a shy smile before looking away to hide her flushing cheeks.

They followed Balinus across one of the bridges, continuing to make their way along the crowded cobblestone streets. Tables, donkeys, and carts cluttered the roads while colorful banners hung over shops. Wooden shutters propped up on posts acted as awnings beneath which craftsmen displayed their wares: breads, cheese, pottery, fabric, and ribbons. But, the most common merchant in this area near Notre Dame seemed to be bookmakers and scribes.

Balinus unlocked the front door of a shop located on the ground floor of a three-storied, half-timber building. Once inside, he opened shutters to let light pour in through a pair of street-facing windows made with what looked like the round bottoms of glass bottles. The space had tall ceilings, and walls made from wooden beams and milky plaster. In the middle of the room was a long table with two portable writing slopes placed at opposite ends. Elisabeth skimmed her hand along feather quills, jars of ink, scrolls, and various objects that surrounded each work station.

David picked up a palm-sized leather-bound book from the cluttered table. He then became still while admiring the brightly painted pages; its gold edges glistening thanks to a sunbeam reaching into the room. "Are you a scribe now, old man?"

Balinus nodded. "A bookmaker. Mostly of something called *The Book of Hours* for patrons, but…" With a satisfied smile, he held up a massive rawhide folder stuffed with parchment. "…I spend much of my days transferring ancient scrolls I've saved into this one codex."

Elisabeth stifled a gasp as she scanned the workshop, her hand involuntarily covering her mouth. At the back left-hand side of the room, a half flight of stairs led to a platform behind an ornate wooden railing. It created a low loft area that held a small writing desk. She eyed three full burlap sacks pushed neatly against the wall. Across from the desk was a closed wooden door—probably the entrance to a storage room or maybe access to the upper floors of this building.

The remaining rear wall, on the shop's ground floor, contained a long counter with cupboards and drawers below, and shelves and cabinets above. Parchment, unlit candles, more books and scrolls, mortars and pestles, and stacks of clam shells filled every nook and cranny.

To her right, wall-mounted shelves were lined with enormous books. Some were bound in what looked like velvet, others adorned with buckles or gilded pages. None were placed as you'd find in a library today; upright with their spines facing out. Instead, they lay flat in neat stacks.

She glanced over as David put the book down, making his way toward a long sideboard of slatted compartments stuffed with hundreds of scrolls.

Balinus climbed the loft steps and placed his leather folder on the desk. Its top was an organized mess of paints, powders, and brushes. "When Perenelle has time, she likes to work on illuminations here." He flicked his thumb across the bristles of a clean paintbrush before turning an hourglass over to watch the grains of sand tumble. He then cleared his throat, glancing down at David and Elisabeth. "I want you both to know that when my codex is complete, my time here will be complete as well."

Elisabeth jerked her head back, giving him an incredulous look. "What do you mean by that?"

"I mean, when my work is finished...my life as Nicolas Flamel will...*eventually*...be finished as well."

She frowned, fiddling with her belt. "Are you saying you plan to leave this life?"

"Yes." His voice was warm and caring as he descended the stairs again. "I suppose that is what I am saying."

"Are you kidding me?" Elisabeth's tone deepened while lowering her voice to a whisper. "Balinus...? Did you even tell your wife you were immortal? That you don't allow yourself to age? Why...?" She shuffled back a step, feeling a sense of déjà vu. "Why'd you drag poor Perenelle and Colette...and the *dog* into this if only to break their hearts in the end?"

Balinus rubbed his eyebrow and glanced at David.

Elisabeth's heart pounded in her chest. "So, what...are you planning to fake your own death and leave a grieving family behind? I don't understand how you, of all people, can play games with other people's hearts like it's—"

"*Cor meum...*" David shook his head while walking toward her.

She swallowed hard. "You've changed, *Nicolas*."

"You're right. He has changed." David's eyes were

bright as he exchanged a knowing smile with Balinus. "But not in the way you think."

Her posture picked up. "What do you mean?"

"Look at him." He took hold of her fingers. "He's aging."

Elisabeth's mouth fell open as she turned back to Balinus, now noticing the heavier lines etched into his charming face. Although his beard was always snowy white, his once dark brows were lighter. She buried her face in both hands, realizing her mistake. He didn't plan to walk away from his life or a family who loved him. He'd chosen to live out the remainder of his days *with* them. Her stomach felt hard as she looked up at him again. "You've stopped taking the elixir."

Balinus nodded.

With a pained expression, Elisabeth shuffled closer to the old man. "I'm so sorry," she whispered, wrapping her arms around him into a hug. "I should never have said what I did."

"Oh…well, alrighty then." He patted her back. "Apology accepted, my dear."

Elisabeth stepped away, fidgeting with her long sleeves.

"'Wise old sage', they say." With a heavy sigh, Balinus lowered himself onto a wooden stool. "If they only knew it's taken me longer than most to learn what the important things in life *truly* are." He cleared his throat, turning his attention to David. "But enough about me. I'm afraid it seems the one we need to discuss is you…*Aquarius*."

Chapter Three

David grabbed a stool, slid it close to the old man, and sat.

Balinus' eyebrows furrowed, then released. "Can you tell me of your plans for the future?"

"If only I could. Everything has happened so quickly that I have been unable to give the matter much thought." David's posture stiffened as he glanced at Elisabeth.

"I think you have to stay here," she answered in a too-quiet voice. "It's impossible to return to your time now. We'll arrive back in Pompeii at the exact moment we left, which means—"

David's posture sagged. "Death."

"And if I try to bring you home with me again, there's a chance I'll end up losing you somewhere in time...forever." When Elisabeth started to tremble, he reached over, pulling her onto his knee. She looked at Balinus. "The thought of that terrifies me."

David opened his mouth to say something, but stopped short, slipping an arm around her waist instead.

"Even if it did work..." Elisabeth cleared her throat while staring down at her hands. "Aquarius already exists in my time."

Balinus gasped. "What do you mean he already exists in your time?"

When she gave a hard, obvious swallow, David let

out a deep breath. "Apparently, I become immortal like you, old man," he whispered.

Balinus leaned forward. "My dear girl, I think you need to tell me everything."

"I only know bits and pieces myself," she said with a dejected sigh.

"It's all right, *cor meum*. Tell him what you told me."

Elisabeth softly shook her head as she and David held steady eye contact. His face was still full of hope and wonder. "Your name is David," she whispered. "David Perrier." Her gaze drifted to a curl that fell across his forehead. Elisabeth brushed it aside with her fingers, noticing the longer his brown hair grew, the more sun-bleached it became. Her chest ached knowing that someday all of that playfulness etched into his features would be replaced with unspeakable torment. "You don't look much older in my time, Aquarius."

His eyes widened.

"That must mean you begin taking the elixir to stop aging in the next year or so." Elisabeth turned to Balinus. "The first time I met Aquarius wasn't in the Roman Empire." She glanced at David, trying to read his expression. "But it wasn't in my time either."

He slowly nodded.

"It was a previous time I time-traveled." Her posture relaxed. A slight smile formed on her face. "We only met in passing, really. It was the year 1652 in a place called Stonehaven, Scotland. I was twelve years old. I think you were there to watch over me to make sure events unfolded according to some plan we must have."

David's eyebrows rose.

"When I returned home from Scotland—after nearly being burnt at the stake I might add—I vowed to never time-travel again." Elisabeth looked at him with a soft expression. "I hadn't seen you or time-traveled in five years until one day you showed up outside of my house."

Balinus shook his head while listening.

She glanced over at the old man again. "Aquarius was there, urging me to travel back in time to save his life. I assumed he meant to the seventeenth century in Scotland, but—"

David took a deep, pained breath. "But you ended up outside of my cell in the arena, moments before I was to be fed to the lions—or so we thought."

Elisabeth let out a shaky laugh. "To make matters worse, you had no idea who I was yet."

"Believe me…" The old man's eyes twinkled with mischief. "I'm positive Aquarius would have followed you anywhere."

David rubbed the back of his neck while chuckling.

Balinus' smile then faded. "But why does Aquarius take the elixir in the future?"

"Because…" Elisabeth's voice became quiet. "Because he's waiting—for centuries—until the day he can right some terrible wrong."

The old man sat with his hands folded neatly in his lap as he continued to listen.

"I have no idea what it is, but I think it has to do with me since we're…I mean…in the future…Aquarius and I are…" She stood up and began pacing, unable to bring herself to say anymore in front of David. "Never mind."

Balinus started to giggle. "Ah, I see…"

As heat rushed to her cheeks, Elisabeth picked up a book from a nearby shelf, attempting to hide behind the tanned leather cover. "That's all I'm saying. Nothing's written in stone, you know."

From the corner of her eye, she stole a glance at the old man. He was looking over her shoulder at David while clamping his lips together in an obvious attempt not to smile. From behind, David could be heard stretching in an exaggerated manner, trying to draw attention to himself. When he started to chuckle, Elisabeth put the book back and buried her face in both hands.

"*Cor meum...*?"

"Hmm?" Too flustered to turn around, Elisabeth kept her back to him and smoothed down her dress as her ears became impossibly hot. She then swallowed the lump in her throat, forcing herself to face him.

The moment she turned around, David flashed a mischievous grin. He leaned back on the stool, putting both hands behind his head.

With a groan, Elisabeth threw her arms up in the air as Balinus dissolved into laughter. "Fine. All right. Apparently, *you* are the lucky guy I marry." Her lips pinched tightly together as she crossed her arms in front of her chest. "And you're going to be absolutely insufferable now that you know."

David reached out, grabbing hold of her skirt.

"Can we please just change the subject?" Elisabeth asked as he playfully dragged her toward him.

"I've not said a word."

With a shaky laugh, Elisabeth shuffled closer. "Well, if you—"

All three then flinched when the front door flew

open.

"Good morning." Perenelle strolled into the bookshop with a wicker basket hanging from the crook of each arm; one filled with eggs on a protective layer of straw, the other holding items wrapped in faded blue cotton. "Or I suppose I should say good afternoon now."

As Perenelle marched straight to the work table to put the baskets down, Elisabeth leaned forward, unable to take her eyes off the woman's outfit. Except for the sleeves, her buttery yellow dress was now covered with a sapphire blue outer gown that looked like heavy silk. Matching buttons ran down the bodice, stopping at the waist of the full skirt. She may not have been nobility, but Perenelle Flamel appeared to be no pauper.

"Somebody made your favorite tarts this morning," she said in a sing-song voice.

Balinus rubbed his hands together while licking his lips. "I know."

While unpacking fabric-wrapped items from the basket, a wide smile lit up her face. "I swear, there are enough fig tarts in here for half of Paris."

Elisabeth stepped closer. "Can I help with anything?"

"It's all right, dear." Perenelle flitted about the table, clearing up space and unwrapping little blue bundles to reveal wedges of cheese, a wooden bowl filled with blackberries, and several mouth-watering golden-brown tarts. "Nicolas, have you yet spoken to David about…?" Perenelle paused to look up from the makeshift picnic setting. She then scrunched her nose while staring at her husband. "Why do I feel I've interrupted an intense conversation? Have I come at a bad time?"

The old man pursed his lips in amusement. "I do not know. Have you?"

Perenelle put a bowl on the table before leaning back. Her gaze wandered from David to Elisabeth and then back to Balinus. The warmth of her laughter filled the room. "I do believe I have."

"No…" Elisabeth quickly glanced around the room. "No, we were just discussing whether or not…the paints are—"

"My dear girl…" Balinus plucked at his clothes, trying not to laugh as he made his way toward the food. "It is of no use inventing a fanciful tale." Hovering over the pastries, he wiggled his fingers while trying to decide which one to take. "Nellie is quite aware of your circumstances."

Elisabeth lowered her head to hide a smile. It was hard enough getting used to the fact the old man was married, let alone hearing him call his wife by her pet name.

"Believe me…" Balinus' eyes widened in mock amazement before taking a bite of his fig tart. "The woman has an infallible ability to know when someone is telling an untruth."

Perenelle looked at Elisabeth with a thoughtful expression while walking closer. "I'm afraid it's true, dear. After you both fell asleep last night, I pieced it *all* together; where you are from, why David was dressed in naught but a loincloth—"

"Oh…" Elisabeth rubbed her forehead. "So, you know that—?"

"I know exactly what happened and where you are from."

She sagged against the table. "That's a relief."

"I imagine it must be, dear." Perenelle's voice was like a soothing lullaby. "For, I, too, was educated in a convent school as a young girl. I've seen this *exact* situation play out before: your lack of experience in the outside world, stolen glances with a particular young man, falling in love, your family's opposition to the union, resulting—inevitably—in an elopement."

When Elisabeth's eyes widened, Perenelle reached over, lightly touching her arm. "My husband didn't have to utter a word. In fact, the entire village is already buzzing with the news of your arrival, if not all of Paris by now."

Elisabeth nodded her head, pretending she wasn't completely flabbergasted.

Balinus offered her a bemused grin while shuffling back to his stool. "My wife can detect a falsehood like none other."

David clamped his lips together, trying not to smile.

"Where were you two sweethearts headed before being ambushed by bandits?" The woman stepped back. "Ghent?"

Elisabeth shot David a dazed look. "Ghent?"

With a playful grin, he tilted his head back and nodded. "Yes, Ghent."

Elisabeth did a double-take, causing him to press a fist against his lips to keep from laughing.

"I thought so," Perenelle said with a furrowed brow. "Nicolas may have been reluctant to share all of the facts, but ten years he and I have been wed. As you can imagine, I know what he's going to say before he utters a single word."

Elisabeth sucked in a quick breath, eager to change the subject. "You two have been married for *ten* years?"

"Yes. I remember the day we first met as if it were yesterday." Perenelle looked up with an unfocused gaze. "I was walking out of the Hôtel-Dieu after feeding the poor and saw this incredibly handsome man on the street." She paused to flash Balinus a cheeky grin. "And there he was...right behind the handsome man."

David and Elisabeth both groaned before bursting into laughter. Balinus shook his head while smiling as Perenelle excused herself from the room. She climbed the stairs to the nook and then disappeared through the door. All three listened to the sound of footsteps fading away as she climbed an unseen staircase.

Elisabeth scrubbed a hand over her face, leaning closer to the old man. "Seriously? Perenelle thinks Aquarius and I were eloping?" she whispered frantically. "Why didn't you just tell her the truth?"

"How can I tell her the truth? That you are from the future? That he is from the past? That I have been alive for over fourteen hundred years?" He let out a deep sigh. "Elisabeth, most people are not equipped to handle the truth about the world around us. It would turn their lives upside down—if it didn't drive them mad. My wife is a good woman who knows nothing of my...*longevity*. Nellie has a deep-rooted faith in what she was taught to believe. It's part of who she is. When you two showed up last night, disheveled from surviving Vesuvius, I thought it best to let her draw her own conclusion."

Elisabeth's brow furrowed while listening. "Which was?"

"Well..." Balinus bit down on a smile. "While trying to elope, you were ambushed by bandits and robbed of *everything*...hence Aquarius' loincloth."

David snorted. "You have to admit, her version of events is more believable."

Elisabeth gave a half-hearted shrug.

Balinus clapped his hands together when they heard Perenelle's shoes on the wooden staircase once again. "I have a sort of proposal to make myself." The old man's eyes sparkled. He leaned in closer to David, pausing to listen as the floorboards in the backroom creaked. A drawer opened and closed. "Tell me, nephew...what do you think about the notion of becoming my apprentice? I would teach you everything I know about the bookmaking business. It will take years, but you'd live in our home, and become part of our family. An adopted son, if you will."

Elisabeth noticed David's posture stiffen as her own heart raced. When the shuffling in the backroom stopped, she knew Perenelle was eavesdropping.

"After you've learned all I have to teach...well...you can take over all of this. It will be yours. Business is quite good. This little shop will give you the means to support yourself...and a family of your own...quite comfortably someday."

David brought a shaky hand to his forehead. "To a slave, you offer all this?" His voice was barely a whisper. "Surely, you jest?"

The old man leaned closer, speaking into David's ear not to be overheard by Perenelle in the backroom. "You are no longer a slave, Aquarius, and I have never been more serious in my life." He leaned back again, speaking at a normal volume. "Nellie and I have no

children of our own, so to you, my orphaned nephew—
we offer a home, a family, a future."

David ran a shaky hand through his hair.

"Your aunt and I spoke at length last night. We are
more than happy to open our hearts and our home to
you." He glanced at Elisabeth. "To *both* of you."

David's mouth snapped shut. He looked down,
struggling to hide his emotions as Perenelle returned to
the workshop with a wide grin on her face. Elisabeth's
own chest hitched knowing the thought of belonging
somewhere, becoming part of a family, overwhelmed
him.

"All right, all right..." Perenelle's voice choked
with tears as she shut the door and walked down the
steps. "I see your uncle's spoken to you. Let's not get
all sentimental over an apprenticeship. It's naught but a
practical solution seeing we're your only living relation.
The only condition is..." She grimaced. "...you will
have to delay your elopement news. It must be kept
secret from the guild since apprentices are to be
unwed."

"That won't be a problem," Elisabeth blurted out
with a shaky laugh. "At all."

David took a deep breath before looking up at
Balinus with an enormous grin.

"Is that a yes?" the old man asked.

"Yes! Yes! A thousand times yes." David jumped
to his feet, extending his hand in thanks.

Balinus stood up, pulling him into a hug instead.
He clapped his back several times. "First, we shall
register you with the guild and then we need to get you
a..."

Perenelle waved Elisabeth over, handing her the

now empty wicker basket. "Come with me," she whispered while picking up her basket filled with eggs. "We'll leave the apprentice to his new master."

Elisabeth nodded and grabbed one of the fig tarts on the way out the door. She practically bounced through the crowd, swinging her basket as she bit into the little pastry before giving a small yelp. "Oh my gosh, this tastes amazing!"

Perenelle flashed a knowing grin. "They're delicious, aren't they?"

Her eyes widened as she polished it off in two quick bites. "I want to say thank you for what you did for *David*. That was awfully kind of you both." The hum of people socializing and children laughing filled the streets. "You can't even begin to imagine how grateful he is. I mean, did you see him? He was completely overwhelmed."

With a warm smile and an easy walk, Perenelle weaved her way between three people in a row carrying pies. "I did notice," she replied, walking up to a merchant's table, giving an older man a dozen eggs from the basket. He winked at her before exchanging them for a waxy, fabric-topped pot of what might contain jam or honey. "Nicolas thought an apprenticeship would be in his best interest," she said, placing the item into the basket.

They crossed the bridge over the Seine and were heading toward the city gate when Elisabeth spotted him ahead— the man with the crooked nose.

"Also, I thought you might…" Although Perenelle continued talking, the sound of Elisabeth's heartbeat pounded in her ears, drowning out the old woman's voice.

Crooked Nose held the reins of his horse in one hand; the other arm stationary in a makeshift sling.

Their eyes locked.

His posture straightened.

He then handed the reins off to another man and moved toward Elisabeth.

Chapter Four

"Perenelle…" Elisabeth swallowed hard. "We need to go back to the shop."

"Go back to the shop?" The old woman's voice rose in pitch. "What's wrong?"

From behind, Elisabeth heard the whinny of a horse. Hooves stomped along the cobblestone as jingling bells kept time. A hush fell over the crowd, and everyone turned. That's when Crooked Nose let out a piercing wolf-whistle, gesturing to someone who'd obviously been trailing her.

"I need to warn David that…" As Elisabeth glanced over her shoulder, people all around cleared the way for two dark stallions pulling an ornate carriage.

Made of dark wood, inlaid panels on the door, and thick lattice covered windows; it was clearly the Rolls Royce of the medieval era. When the driver signaled a reply to Crooked Nose, the color drained from Elisabeth's face and she handed the basket to Perenelle.

"Oh, I see." Perenelle let out a heavy sigh. "Your father's found you. To be honest, I was hoping true love would win the—" The old woman's eyes widened, staring at the coat of arms inscribed on the carriage. "Whose daughter are you?"

Elisabeth's gaze darted all around.

Crooked Nose was closing in from ahead.

The horses came to a stop behind her.

"Chin up, dear. What's done is done," the old woman said calmly. "It'll all work out in the end, however it's meant to. Your father may be furious now, but perhaps he'll come around. David seems like such a nice boy."

Elisabeth shook her head in denial—and then bolted, running erratically with no destination in mind. She needed to get away from her dad's henchmen in order to buy more time here with Aquarius.

Trembling, she pushed people out of the way, trying to turn down a narrow alley. Her legs were weak and shaky while dodging carts and vendors blocking the path. Rounding another corner, she glanced over her shoulder. Crooked Nose and another man were getting closer.

A wooden ladder resting against a building caught her eye. Yanking it over to block the street bought precious moments as the men scrambled around and over it.

Down another street she sprinted, spotting an open door this time.

Elisabeth ran through, slammed it shut, quickly locking it. She held back a cry, pacing while her eyes adjusted to the darkness.

A table!

Heartbeat racing, she shoved it against the entrance to stop Crooked Nose and his partner from getting in.

After hearing a quiet cough, Elisabeth gasped and spun around.

A frail old man sat in the corner, wide-eyed.

"I'm really sorry," she whimpered as someone outside began body-slamming the blocked door.

With the aid of a hand-carved walking stick, the

old man pushed himself out of his chair and shuffled toward a dark hallway. He said something inaudible, waving Elisabeth over.

Her hands trembled while following him at a painfully slow pace down a dimly lit corridor, listening as her barricade began to fail.

When the old man reached the back of the house, his unsteady hand grasped a doorknob.

Come on, come on, come on...

It seemed to take all his strength to open the door. He then gestured with his cane, pointing at a shuttered window.

Elisabeth let out a shaky laugh. "Oh, thank God."

He gave her a crisp nod followed by a thumbs-up sign.

She flung the wooden shutters wide and climbed through the open window, jumping down onto a cobblestone street.

"There she is!"

Crap.

She kept running as indistinct shouting went on behind her, narrowly avoiding a collision with a donkey before turning down another crowded street. Out of breath, she dodged behind a huge wooden post to hide.

Several men kept running straight ahead.

Wringing her hands, Elisabeth needed to find her way back to Balinus' bookshop to warn David. She'd completely underestimated what her father would do to bring her home if he discovered she was time-traveling.

With a deep breath, she stepped out of her hiding spot and into the crowd. Heart pounding in her chest, she forced herself not to run.

So far, so good.

Ahead is the Seine. I think.

Elisabeth gently bit her lip, hoping she was heading in the right direction.

Once I make it—

Without warning, two men appeared and yanked her arms, their mumbling voices full of irritation. She struggled in vain while being dragged around the corner, back to the main road where the horses waited.

Elisabeth squared her shoulders. "Who sent you?"

"Your father," one said, shoving her inside the carriage.

"Where is he?"

"We're taking you to him now."

The door slammed shut.

"Wait…!" She tried forcing it open, but the door was either locked or jammed from the outside. When the horses began to clomp along the cobblestone streets, Elisabeth slumped onto the upholstered seat. She pushed a thick tasseled curtain aside to look out the lattice-covered window. Sunlight filtered in. The parting crowds stared in awe when she rode by in her gilded prison, as if a member of a royal family. Crooked Nose rode beside, escorting the carriage on horseback.

With a dejected sigh, Elisabeth threw the curtain back over the window to shut out prying eyes.

She knew they'd left the city when the sound of horse hooves on cobblestone quieted, although the jingling bells on the horses continued. Forcing herself to focus, she pushed the curtain aside once again to watch the direction in which they traveled.

On her left was the way back to Balinus' village. Elisabeth spotted the dirt road she and David had strolled along earlier. She scooted across the luxurious bench to look out the right-hand side of the carriage. They traveled beside the city wall, next to the moat. When the carriage eventually turned left, Elisabeth's brow furrowed. She had no idea where they were heading, but if Dad was here, Sissi Waters was probably involved.

Elisabeth gasped.

Had Mrs. Waters *brought* dad here?

The old woman orchestrated events every step of the way so far, from Scotland to Rome. The fact that Aquarius was now in the fourteenth century with her proved it was possible to bring someone. If her parents had learned about the time-traveling, there was no doubt they'd do anything to find her and bring her home—by force, if necessary.

Elisabeth slumped her shoulders and covered her face with both hands, feeling completely defeated. Somehow, she'd messed up a detail along the way and got caught. This timeline was already different, since Mrs. Waters hadn't met her future self. Tears welled behind her eyelids. The adventure and romance were coming to an end. What responsible parents wouldn't make their teenage daughter come home? Elisabeth's heart thudded in her chest as the reality of having to leave Aquarius behind sank in.

The city walls now in the distance, the horses continued down a wide, well-traveled road dotted with houses and churches. They crossed a small bridge that seemed to be the gathering place for a handful of beggars. Elisabeth's posture stiffened as men, women, and children swarmed the carriage, pleading for scraps as she rode by.

Eventually, any signs of city or village life disappeared. A predator bird screeched while circling overhead. On a hill in the distance, Elisabeth could see a huge monument with numerous human remains hanging from different sections; a morbid display of power and warning. Perhaps it was more like barbaric Ancient Rome here than she first thought.

They rode through the forest. It must have been an hour, perhaps a little longer, when the carriage finally emerged from the woods, now traveling through a park-like setting. Birdsong filled the air and a soft breeze rustled through the trees. The occasional twig snapped as they drove along. To her right was a peaceful river with a lone swan floating beneath the branches of a weeping willow. Downstream, a mother duck and her babies paddled beneath a quaint wooden bridge that connected to a walking path before disappearing into the trees beyond.

Elisabeth moved to look out the left-hand side of the carriage. Her eyes widened, spotting a magnificent stone castle situated on an island surrounded by a shining lake. Turrets and towers peeked over curtain walls while swans and waterfowl swam or sunbathed on the shore. Her posture stiffened, noticing a black swan amongst a bevy of white ones. As the carriage rolled along the curved road, a snow-white peacock suddenly spread his tail feathers wide, parading back and forth.

Staring out the right-hand side again, she now noticed the gable entry of a limestone mausoleum with carved architectural details along the top. Because the entrance was built into a hill, no sides, back, or roof were needed. A heavy oak door was flanked with luxurious purple-red pillars polished to a shine.

Elisabeth's hand covered her mouth, captivated by a majestic bird sitting atop the entryway, whistling a high-pitched song. It looked almost mythical, like something found in the misty mountains of an Asian folk tale. The bird was white with long, flowing tail feathers, a velvety black underside, and a bright red head and legs. As Elisabeth drove by in the carriage, the bird spread its wings wide, gliding down to the ground where it began foraging about, much like a chicken.

Ahead was a crumbling gatehouse with raised portcullis; a coat of arms carved into the stone. The weeds and dark pink flowers growing atop the structure led Elisabeth to believe it was the romantic ruins of an even older fortified gate. They drove beneath the arch and the road continued around the lake, leading to a tiny hamlet.

Adrenaline rushed through Elisabeth's body when, instead of continuing along the road, the carriage turned toward the castle. The horse hooves clopped across the stone bridge over the moat, making their way through massive wooden doors adorned with iron studs, brackets, and horizontal straps.

By the time the carriage came to a stop, Elisabeth's mind was racing.

A moment later, the door to her prison opened.

"Welcome home, *milady*," a footman said with a bowed head as he helped her out.

Welcome home?

Elisabeth rubbed her forearms while wandering away from the covered portico toward a grand archway. She stepped out into an enormous courtyard and her mouth dropped. An ornate water fountain, with a statue in the center, was positioned straight ahead. Gravel paths were edged with short hedges, roses, fruit trees, and cottage-style flowers.

Behind her, to the left, was a service door into the castle, in front of which sat the prettiest stone well. Its decorative metal frame held a pulley and bucket. She resisted the urge to run to it and make a wish. Her gaze darted to a pair of chipmunks scampering around the base of the well before chasing each other up a potted orange tree.

Elisabeth's breath caught in her chest while taking it all in, and then a slow smile started to form. If she ever built a fairy-tale castle, it would look *exactly* like this.

An adrenaline rush coursed through her body. Sissi Waters definitely had something to do with whatever was going on here.

She *had* to.

The old woman always carried herself with such an air of elegance that Elisabeth grew up half-convinced she was a long-lost royal. One could easily imagine her living here while visiting the fourteenth century.

With a slow, disbelieving shake of her head, Elisabeth reminded herself once again that *she* was Mrs. Waters.

Stress and slavery filled the time spent in Ancient Rome. With a little forehand knowledge, couldn't the experience here be one of leisure and luxury? Elisabeth's posture stiffened, remembering that Castle Ealasaid in Scotland had been prearranged as a sort of safe haven for her.

Maybe everything here was going to be all right after all.

At that moment, a woman appeared from around a

corner, her shoes scuffing quietly over the gravel. The rough fabric of her blue-black dress led Elisabeth to believe she was a servant. The way she trudged along carrying a basket of garden produce solidified it.

Her eyes widened when she spotted Elisabeth. "Oh!" Shaky fingers adjusted the white wimple on her head. "Welcome home, milady," she said, clearly uncomfortable speaking in Latin. After a quick bob, she disappeared through the service door.

"Welcome home, my lady," Elisabeth repeated in amazement to herself. "Welcome *home*."

Had Mrs. Waters and David Perrier somehow arranged all of this? They needed her on this timeline as much as she wanted to be here, so maybe it was in everyone's best interest to convince Dad to let her stay. It drove Elisabeth crazy how Sissi and David were always so mysterious about everything, but this might be a welcome exception.

From here in the inner courtyard, the ivy-covered castle looked more like an enormous manor house, with rows of windows made from tiny diamond-shaped panes of glass. The building was composed of two wings; the one she entered through, and one on the right, forming an L shape. The section that joined the two wings was obviously a tower from the outside, but inside the courtyard, it appeared to be almost decorative in nature.

With a slight shake of her head, she wandered to the fountain. The statue of a Roman-looking woman poured water from a pitcher into a large basin over which she stood.

"I'm home!" Elisabeth whispered to two birds splashing at the woman's stone feet.

Heartbeat drumming in her chest, she couldn't wait to share the latest turn of events with Aquarius. Between Balinus' quaint village and this enchanting castle, it felt more and more as if she'd escaped from Pompeii and landed right in the middle of a storybook setting.

A wide path caught her eye and Elisabeth followed it. She left the courtyard, winding around the outside perimeter of the castle, taking in the picturesque views of the lake beyond. While strolling along the parapet, the tops of perfectly spaced trees peeked over the ledge.

A slow smile built when she came upon a stone stairwell. An iron gate at the bottom was open, so she descended the stairs, ending up in the middle of a walkway at the water's edge. This reinforced the notion that this entire fortress was built on an island. Elisabeth turned left, strolling along the wide gravel path dotted with the trees she'd noticed from above. Ducks were fast asleep on the grassy bank, or primping and preening in the water. The only thing missing was a bench to sit and reflect upon.

From here, the width of the moat was the size of a river, widening into a small lake as she neared the rear of the castle. The walkway eventually ended at what looked like a cellar door.

Accompanied by a flittering butterfly, Elisabeth turned and walked back along the path and up the stairs, returning to the castle courtyard. Feeling like a queen surveying her land, she stood at the parapet, admiring the shining lake below and the forest beyond. As beautiful as this place was, it was first and foremost a fortress. No doubt it was the safest place in all of medieval France.

Surely, a father could be persuaded to let his daughter hang out here...under the circumstances?

Movement beneath the arch of a nearby doorway caught her eye and Elisabeth turned, smiling as two gray-haired men strode down several steps, walking toward her.

Her new butler or footman, perhaps?

One was dressed in the black cassock of a priest.

The other wore tan boots, black trousers, and a belted, knee-length brown jacket of some luxurious fabric. Perhaps it was suede or velvet, she couldn't tell. It was edged in royal blue. A white ruffled collar peeked out, giving him a clean, sophisticated appearance. As Elisabeth looked at his handsome, line-etched face and graying hair, her mouth dropped.

She glanced around in confusion and then heat rushed through her body while trying to piece together what was *really* going on. Her brow furrowed as her mind raced back to yesterday.

Mount Vesuvius.

Pompeii.

Aquarius dying in the arena after Cato left him for dead.

Her heart pounded in anger, mostly at herself for being so naïve.

The elixir.

Cato had stolen the elixir from her.

"Hello, *Father*," she called out in a scathing tone. Only when both men paused to glance at her did Elisabeth realize her mistake. "Sorry...not you, Father," she said to the priest with a weakened voice.

After looking at Elisabeth with sad smiles, goodbyes were exchanged between the two men. The priest then headed toward the main gate, taking his leave.

"I had no idea you were still alive, you murdering scu—"

"Elisabeth…" Cato said softly as he made his way toward her. A multi-colored bird, about the size of a peacock, strutted closer, seemingly out of nowhere, following like a pet dog. "I bring you here in peace."

"In peace?" Her eyes widened. "Your men dragged me here." There was a tightness in her chest, heart pounding.

This place…? This beautiful place was Cato's?
Cato's!

She crossed both arms over her chest.

Cato reached into a belt pouch, handing the strange, colorful bird a treat. "It was out of necessity and for that, I am truly sorry."

Elisabeth shook her head. "What do you want?"

When he moved closer, the bird made a cooing sound for attention. "Forgiveness."

She felt light-headed, staring at this middle-aged man. Just yesterday he was a healthy young gladiator, not yet twenty years old.

"As you can imagine, gossip travels faster than wildfire. When I heard a young nephew of Balinus'…" He paused, correcting himself. "Of *Nicholas Flamel's* had arrived suddenly, dressed in 'naught but a loincloth', along with a young woman in a tattered ice blue gown…I realized what had happened. Am I correct in assuming you two have *just* left Pompeii?"

Elisabeth nodded and stepped back, trying once again to push the haunting memory of the eruption away. "Yesterday."

He scrubbed a hand over his face. "I can scarcely believe it. Are...are you both all right?"

"Fine," she snapped.

Cato's hands locked together. "And you brought Aquarius with you? Using the crystal?" His eyes began to water. "You saved my brother's life."

"No thanks to you."

His posture stooped. "I understand your anger. You cannot possibly hate me as much as I hate myself for what transpired between us that fateful day. But...you must realize that for me, more than a thousand years have passed. Believe me when I tell you that I am a changed man."

Her eyes narrowed. "I doubt it."

"Then I shall prove it to you," Cato said quietly. "Name your price. Anything."

"Let me go."

"You are not my prisoner. There is the door."

She jerked her head back, not expecting that answer. "See ya," Elisabeth said with a shaky laugh, starting toward the exit.

Cato let out a long, low sigh. "I want only to make amends and help you. Help both of you." With that, he turned and walked away, making kissing noises to call the bird to follow.

Elisabeth's breath hitched. This had not gone as expected. Straight ahead of her was the front gate. To her left, Cato walked toward an entrance of the castle, followed by his loyal bird.

"Wait." With a theatrical groan, she shuffled after him. "What do you mean you're trying to help us?"

As he continued walking, his posture straightened, and he held both hands loosely behind his back. "Dine with me. I will explain everything."

Chapter Five

Elisabeth twisted her hands together while watching Cato walk back to the doorway. "Actually, no. I'm leaving."

He lowered his head. "Then you are breaking this old man's heart."

She drew in a slow, steady breath and started toward the exit again. "We don't need your help. We already have a plan in place, so whatever you're offering, we're not interested."

"Elisabeth…" Cato's voice cracked as he turned to face her. "I am begging for forgiveness."

She smoothed down her dress but kept walking.

"Please, allow me to right the sin I've carried for far too long. You're a sensible girl. I'd hoped you would hear me out and in turn…help Aquarius forgive me."

With a soft shake of her head, Elisabeth looked at him. "How on earth could you ever make right what you did?"

A nearby squirrel began chattering, scolding Cato as well, before rustling through a nearby bush.

"I can't. But will you not let me try to make amends?" he asked with a heavy sigh while walking closer. "I am no longer the young slave you both knew. As you may have guessed by now, I'm in a…*unique* position to help you. Whatever either of you wants, it is yours. The finest—"

Her eyes widened. "You think you can *buy* our forgiveness?"

Cato stepped back, head bowed. "It's much more than that. I offer you protection from the world you've found yourselves in. I'm the only other soul here who knows your secret...other than Aquarius and Balinus, of course." His eyes welled up with tears. "You know...I always aspired to be just like him."

"Like Aquarius?"

"No. Balinus."

Elisabeth's brow furrowed while studying him. "Then why hide from him all this time? He has no idea you're even alive, does he?"

Cato took slow, jerky steps away and crumpled onto a stone bench. "No."

Elisabeth reluctantly crept over and took a seat. An ornate chessboard was set in the middle of the bench between them, its opposing armies positioned for war.

"After escaping from Pompeii, I searched for Balinus along the road to Rome with the other survivors. Finally, when I happened upon the old man, he was traveling with a young child and the gladiator..." He paused, moving a pawn on the chessboard. "I cannot remember his name, but—"

"Soran. His name was Soran."

"Ah, yes. That's right." Cato's shoulders hunched and he looked away. "Soran."

As they sat in silence, Elisabeth picked up a chess piece. She noticed it was intricately carved to look like an actual person, and her eyes widened. She bit her lip, glancing closely at the board. All the pieces appeared to be creepy little marble statues of characters with facial features. She put the bishop back and slid a pawn two squares.

Cato watched and then stared down at his feet. "I'd been so consumed with jealousy and rage…it was only after I saw the old man that I realized what I'd done. The monster I'd become. I felt too humiliated to face either Balinus or Soran. I knew they'd see the truth in my eyes."

Elisabeth frowned while listening.

He looked up at her again. "But with the ambrosia—the elixir, I had a chance to start over. To begin a new life."

She let out a quick, disgusted snort. "You mean you had the chance to live like a king."

Cato gave her a pained stare. "Ironically, the wealthier and more influential I became, the more people I could be of service to. Why help four when you can help four thousand?"

Elisabeth held her hands in her lap. "And how do you propose to help Aquarius and I?" she asked while glancing around uneasily.

"Have you not guessed by now?" He moved another pawn on the chess board.

Her head flinched back, but then her eyes widened as she pieced together his plan. "By telling everyone I'm your daughter."

Cato nodded. "The seed has already been planted. None will doubt my word."

She rubbed her brow. "What does that accomplish?"

"Since you arrived out of thin air once before, I'm under the assumption that's how you ended up here. By agreeing to play the role of your father, this not only gives you a history none will question…but a future here for Aquarius. I know his dreams better than you ever will. Remember, he and I share a kinship by milk."

"A what?"

"His mother died giving birth to him."

She crossed her arms over her chest. "I know."

"And so, my mother nursed him. Babies nursed by the same woman have a bond close as blood siblings."

"You *used* to." She grabbed a pawn and slapped it down on the board.

He snorted, as if amused. "Tell me…do a person's basic desires ever really change? Ironically, Aquarius' are the very things you can never give him: security, stability…"

Elisabeth slowly shook her head but said nothing.

"Forgive me. I mean no disrespect." Cato looked away. "But imagine the life Aquarius could have. The life you could both have. I am a kingmaker and you'd want for nothing."

"If it sounds too good to be true, it probably is," she muttered.

He scraped a hand over his face. "You need not decide this very moment—"

"I'm sorry, but Aquarius won't be interested and neither am I." With a soft shake of her head, she uncrossed her arms and stood up. "I'm leaving before he arrives with villagers carrying pitchforks."

"Elisabeth…" Cato rooted through his belt pouch as if distracted. "I strongly advise you to consider my offer."

A cold chill ran up her spine.

He stood. "I will give you time to think it over," he said in a deeper tone. "Time to come to your senses. If you truly care for him, you will not be a stubborn girl."

Elisabeth's body tensed. "*You* left Aquarius for dead. I don't need time to think it over. We don't want or need anything from you. Ever." Elisabeth's voice was shaky as she started toward the front gate. "And that's common sense, not stubbornness."

A footman opened the door to the waiting carriage.

"Thank you, but I'd rather walk back to Paris than accept help from my *father*," she snapped.

That was stubbornness.

With a bewildered look, the man glanced behind her at Cato. "Sir...?" He then shut the carriage door and opened the front gate.

Elisabeth stomped along—across the bridge over the moat and beneath the ruins of the ancient barbican. Gravel poking through thin shoes made the march uncomfortable as she walked by a statue of a man mounted bravely on a steed. She hadn't noticed it before.

It resembled Cato.

"You're bloody well terrified of riding horses!" she yelled at the statue before letting out a frustrated groan and kicking the stones beneath her feet.

She followed the lake, and then the river. The wind rustled through the leaves along a wooded lane. Unhindered by anyone, Elisabeth released a long, inaudible sigh. Cato was right. As much as she loved Aquarius, security and stability were something she would never be able to promise him. She belonged in a different time.

With a fluttery feeling in her chest, she continued the long trek back to Paris, grabbing handfuls of flowering weeds while trudging down a deserted road.

A streak of cloud in the otherwise blue sky covered the sun for a few minutes. Elisabeth wiped sweat off her brow.

Her heart sank after rounding another corner.

A fork in the road.

She tossed the colorful blooms aside in an attempt to concentrate, the same way Mom turned down the car radio whenever trying to find a particular address.

Neither option looked familiar.

With a shake of her head, Elisabeth chose left, praying it was the correct decision.

Ahead of her, a wide-open road ran through the rolling countryside, where even more wildflowers nodded on a gentle breeze. Onward she marched, seemingly toward the horizon, collecting a bouquet of purple bellflowers and sunny yellow weeds resembling Queen Anne's lace along the way. The grasses brushed against her skirt as she took a shortcut across a field, listening to songbirds softly chirping.

Elisabeth stumbled out of the meadow and back onto the road. While glancing behind, her eyes narrowed at the sight of men on horseback galloping over the crest of a hill she'd already climbed.

They had to be coming from Cato's estate.

Her posture went rigid as she watched.

All alone, in the middle of nowhere—the hair lifted on the back of her neck knowing any rescue would be coming from ahead, from Paris.

The road in front was empty.

Elisabeth looked behind at the riders again. Whether Cato sent them or not, she decided to hide until they were gone. With a pounding heart, she leapt back into the meadow alongside the road, wiggling into a spot where the underbrush was extra thick.

All around, wind feathered through the tall grasses and weeds, providing cover.

Her breath burst in and out as the thunder of hooves grew louder.

Elisabeth's grip tightened around the wildflower stems in her hand when the first two men rode by, their horses kicking up dirt and debris. She tried desperately to stifle a cough as dust settled all around.

While peering up through the grass, the remaining horses trotted along.

Elisabeth's shoulders tightened, waiting as the last three men rode by.

She let out a sigh of relief when the road was clear, wriggling her way back out of the dense undergrowth.

As she climbed from her hiding place, Elisabeth gasped, yelping in pain. She tossed the crushed bouquet onto the road, wincing while checking her hand to see what was wrong. It felt like a thousand tiny ants were biting it. She rocked back and forth, watching welts and blisters forming from fingers to wrist. It looked and felt like a painful burn.

With a sinking feeling in her stomach, Elisabeth turned around. It was a stupid idea to try and find her way back to Paris by herself. She needed to return to Cato's for help...and first aid.

A few strides later, she stopped, softly shaking her head. "What are you doing?" she muttered, turning around once again, pressing ahead on her own. "Cato is the last person to go to for help."

Eventually, the road curved into a forest. Her head kept jerking around as dappled sunshine caused dancing leaves to play tricks on her mind. The wind rustled loudly through the trees and the tapping of a woodpecker could be heard nearby. Elisabeth rubbed the back of her neck with her good hand, no longer certain she was heading in the right direction.

Should I go back to the fork in the road?

Elbows pressed into her sides; Elisabeth continued. With hesitant steps, she followed the twisting path deeper and deeper into the forest. Twigs and pine needles crunched underfoot.

No...this has to be the wrong way.

Nothing seemed familiar.

Go back, the voice in her head warned.

She stopped mid-stride and turned around, gasping when a man on horseback came galloping around a bend in the road, almost trampling her. The sounds of the forest had muffled his approach.

When the horse reared up, neighing, Elisabeth screamed.

The man atop looked about twenty, with dirty blond hair and a short beard. "She's here!" he yelled in Latin, trying to calm his horse at the same time.

Elisabeth's posture went rigid as her eyes scanned the forest floor, looking for a makeshift weapon. With rasping breaths, she lunged for a nearby stone and whipped it at him.

"Whoa!" Blondie ducked, avoiding being hit. "Easy, *ma donna*...easy."

A moment later, two more horses tethered to one another came cantering around the bend—David in the saddle of one.

Her eyes widened and she ran to him as he dismounted. With a huge sigh of relief, he wrapped Elisabeth in a bear hug.

She cried out in pain and squirmed away, cradling her fingers. "My hand's all burned and blistered. I think I touched a poisonous plant."

Acting fast, David grabbed a canteen and poured cool water over the injury. Elisabeth's breath sawed in and out as he pulled the decorative band of white fabric off her sleeve to use as a bandage. When finished, it resembled an oven mitt.

"Listen…" He drew her aside for privacy. "I will talk to your father…or your father's men. I'll explain that—"

"It's not my father," she said with an incredulous look. "It's Cato. He's alive, but—"

David's posture stiffened. "What do you mean Cato's alive?"

"He's older, but he's been taking the elixir he stole from me in the arena to stay alive all these centuries."

David's head drew back sharply. "And you escaped?"

"No. He let me go."

"Everyone's speaking of how Lord Cathon's runaway daughter was grabbed off the street this afternoon by her father's men." David's brows squished together. "When Perenelle returned to say *your* father's men had taken you…I thought for certain—"

"Cato obviously goes by Lord Cathon now. He lives in a huge castle and begged forgiveness for leaving you in the arena. Told me to name our price to prove he's a changed man."

"No…" David shook his head and backed away. "I don't trust him." His voice seeped with anger and suspicion. "Why didn't Balinus say anything?"

"Apparently, he has no idea he's alive." Distracted,

Elisabeth looked over at Blondie as he dismounted. She then gasped loudly. "Oh my gosh…" Her hands cupped her mouth. "I'm sorry. I am *so* sorry I threw that rock at you. I thought—"

"Under the circumstances, it's quite all right." He flashed a shy smile. "Besides, you missed."

She held up her bandaged fingers. "My good hand."

"Aha." He squinted in amusement. "In that case…I shall consider myself fortunate indeed."

David's brow furrowed as he walked to his dark horse and untied the lead rope. "While I have words with your *father*…" He led the mottled gray rider-less mare toward Blondie. "Giovanni here will return you to—"

"What? No. Leave it be. My *father* is nothing to worry about anymore," she said through gritted teeth.

"*Cor meum*…" David's jaw clenched. "Your *father* had his men grab you off the street."

"Yes, and I took care of it. As you can see, he let me leave. I'm clearly on my way back to Paris. Let's quit while we're ahead."

His face reddened. "He let you leave unaccompanied, unprotected…"

Elisabeth's mouth fell open. "Seriously? I'd have made it back *just* fine."

Giovanni took the lead rope from David and looked at Elisabeth. "*Ma donna*, you are in a forest, heading completely in the wrong direction."

Her body tensed. "Then how'd you find me?"

David's shoulders pushed back. "By following a trail of wildflowers you inadvertently left behind. While en route to *Lord Cathon's* castle, we backtracked to a fork in the road."

"Really?" she asked, her tone softer.

"Had I not taken notice of you doing the same thing countless times, we'd not have found you so quickly." When her eyes widened, a slow smile spread across his face. David then strode over to Elisabeth, placed his hand on the small of her back, and nudged her toward the waiting horse. "While I deal with you know who, Giovanni will see you are returned safely to Nicolas and Perenelle."

Elisabeth planted her feet in a wide stance. "No. Just leave it be."

Blondie cleared his throat. "Giovanni di Bicci de Romano, at your service, *ma donna*," he said with a melodramatic bow. "I've one question though." He rubbed his chin, looking back at David. "If you're trying to run away with Cathon's only daughter…here she is. Why continue to the castle? I mean no offence, but her father is the one wronged. Be glad he hasn't hired Guglielmo Tartare and his men to hunt you down."

"See…" Elisabeth made strong eye contact with David. "Listen to him. He's right."

"Giovanni…it's a complicated story."

Elisabeth marched over, taking the lead rope from Blondie. Moving to the horse meant for her, she placed a foot in the stirrup, grabbed the saddle with her good hand, and pulled herself up and over, long skirt and all. She then looked at David with a close-lipped smile, shocked to have mounted the mare so gracefully. "Are we going or what?"

Giovanni snickered while David gave her an incredulous stare.

When the horse became restless, Elisabeth swallowed the lump in her throat, fumbling around with the rope in her hand. "Aren't there supposed to be two reins?"

David threw his arms up in surrender before marching over. He tossed the rope over the horse's neck and knotted it to the halter, creating makeshift reins. "Do you have any idea what you're doing?"

"No," Elisabeth replied with a nervous laugh, taking hold of the rope, trying to remember how she rode Dandy all those years ago.

Giovanni cued his horse to start walking.

She gently nudged the mare's sides with her heels. It started moving…in the opposite direction Giovanni was heading. She managed to turn it around while David sprinted back to mount his own horse. A moment later, he was beside her again.

"Once we get back to the main road, you are to go with Giovanni." He gave her a pained stare as their horses walked side by side. "I will continue on to—"

Elisabeth let out a heavy sigh. "I'm tired, Aquarius. You must be too."

"Look, for once will you please—"

She slowly shook her head. "Let's just go home. Balinus and Perenelle are probably worried sick about us."

For a moment, David's posture stiffened. He then raised his eyebrows. "Say that again?"

"Balinus and Perenelle are probably worried sick about us."

"No…" He cleared his throat. "The, uh, the other thing you said."

Elisabeth's lips twitched, only now realizing she

was about to get her way. She'd inadvertently said the magic word. "Let's go *home* now."

When David nodded rather than speaking, Elisabeth released an appreciative sigh. "Everything is going to be different here. You'll see."

His face seemed to shine. "Giovanni, change of plans."

Blondie glanced over his shoulder.

"I'll storm the castle another day."

"A wise choice," he called back with a smile.

After making their way to the top of another hill, Elisabeth recoiled. The enormous structure, with numerous bodies hanging from it, appeared in the distance. It had a square stone base from which sixteen huge pillars were erected, in four rows of four. Across the top, and in the middle, were giant cross beams that formed an imposing, two-story tall gallows.

At least they were heading in the right direction.

"David…" Giovanni called out. He then pointed at the gallows while shifting around in the saddle.

With a furrowed brow, David nodded.

Elisabeth sucked in a quick breath, eying the predator bird circling overhead. "What's wrong?"

"Nothing for you to worry about, love."

Two black crows, perched atop a tree branch, cawed at them as they rode by.

"Clearly there is," she said as the horses all sped to a canter.

"*Ma donna…?*" Giovanni shouted over his shoulder. "He warned you about the wolves, yes?"

Her eyes bulged. "Wolves? No."

David cursed under his breath.

"The Gibbet of Montfaucon." He pointed at the

dead bodies hanging from different sections. "The wolves feed on the corpses so they are—"

"Enough," David said in a carefully controlled tone." You are going to frighten her."

Giovanni cleared his throat and pulled at his collar. "My apologies. Worry not, my lady. It is still daylight. We should be fine."

Should be fine?

Elisabeth felt the color drain from her face while glancing all around. "Oh, dear God, we're going to be attacked by wolves next?" she whimpered. In a panic, she pulled the reins to stop her mare.

It snorted in disdain.

David's head jerked back. He then struggled to turn his own neighing horse around, watching wide-eyed as Elisabeth suddenly dismounted.

The fabric from her skirt whirled about her legs when she turned, grabbing onto the crystal necklace and thinking of home.

Home.

****

In the middle of the study, David Perrier gasped and shuffled back a step. "I'll never get used to that." A nanosecond earlier, Elisabeth had been sobbing before him, wearing an icy blue Roman gown, having just survived Vesuvius, to this—bulging eyes, wild hair, and a burgundy medieval dress.

"Wolves?" Her heartbeat raced. "Freaking *wolves* now?"

"Did…" David swallowed hard. "Did you find…*me*?"

A slow smile spread across Elisabeth's face. "Of course."

Sissi Waters pressed a palm to her heart. "Oh, thank God."

Chapter Six

"Let me see your hand," David said, stumbling closer.

"It really hurts."

The old woman's eyes widened. "I completely forgot about that."

"Should I give her the elixir?" he asked Sissi while removing the makeshift bandage.

With a yawn, she nodded. "Definitely."

"Why don't you go to bed, Mrs. Waters," Elisabeth said in a soothing tone. "It's been a long day for all of us."

David's brow wrinkled and he nodded while uncapping the vial. "She's right. You should get some sleep."

"But I don't want to miss anything."

With an appreciative sigh, he looked at the old woman. "Elisabeth, considering you've lived all this before—"

"All right." Mrs. Water's eyes filled with tears while nodding. "All right." She walked over to David and Elisabeth, giving them both a kiss on the cheek. "Good night, my dears."

"Good night," they answered in unison, watching as she made her way out of the library with slow, cautious steps.

"Here you go." David placed a minuscule amount

of the red powder onto Elisabeth's tongue.

The elixir of life, ambrosia, nectar of the gods, the philosopher's stone—they were one and the same. It was capable, not just of giving the user immortality, but of turning lead into gold. The thumb-sized bottle in David's hand was the most sought-after treasure in the history of mankind.

Seconds after taking the elixir, Elisabeth could feel it surge through her body. She glanced at the blisters on her hand and gave a small yelp, watching as they disappeared. "That is amazing." She stared at him wide-eyed while taking a seat on the couch before looking down at her hand again, now unable to see where the blisters had been.

"Not being a life-threatening injury, the result is instantaneous." He cleared his throat. "Well…it's getting late."

Elisabeth's body tensed.

"I'll take you home."

Her shoulders dropped, but she propped them back up again. "Great. Thank you." She pushed herself up out of the couch, avoiding David's gaze while leading him out of the library, and down the stairs.

He kept his face blank as they stood in the foyer. "Do you want me to drive you or…?"

"Do you want to walk?" Elisabeth held her breath. "I mean…it's a beautiful night. I can borrow one of Mrs. Water's coats."

"Sure," David said with a hesitant nod.

She pulled a trench coat out of the closet, intending to cover her medieval dress during the walk home. "Good thing it's dark out." Elisabeth made a funny face while cinching the belt at her waist. "I'm not very inconspicuous in this, am I?"

He lowered his gaze, chuckling before looking up with a grin. "Well, it's almost Halloween."

When David opened the door, Elisabeth stepped onto the porch, stuffing her hands into deep pockets to keep them warm. The lamp-posts lining the brick walkway cast a warm golden glow as crickets chirped in the night. Russet and amber colored leaves blanketed the road, filling the air with their earthy scent. It felt like they were walking into a sepia-toned photograph.

"Isn't fall a pretty season?" She took a deep, savoring breath as they sauntered down the quiet street. "I always crave crispy red apples this time of year. The tart ones." She playfully nudged him. "I like to polish them on my sleeve until I can see my reflection."

David shot her a shy smile. "I know."

"So...like..." Elisabeth fumbled over her words. "The elixir. Do you take a tiny bit every day?"

His walk was unhurried. "Yes."

"Is that how you stop yourself from aging?"

David nodded. "It rejuvenates and heals everything internally. A fountain of youth you might say. The tiniest bit taken daily stops the aging process."

She tilted her head to the side. "It must also keep your memory sharp. You seem to remember everything, even though centuries have passed."

David gave her a pained stare. "It's both a blessing and a curse to remember every little detail."

"Yeah." Elisabeth swallowed a lump in her throat. "I guess it would be."

The moon came into view when they turned the corner. Her house was at the end of the road. Walking down the quiet street, she continued to shuffle her feet through the crunching leaves. David turned to look at her, a sad smile on his face.

"Aquarius...?" A million questions buzzed through her mind, but she didn't know where to start.

"Hmm?"

She took a deep breath. "What happened to us? What's this terrible wrong you must right?"

He cleared his throat while rubbing the back of his neck. "That's for me to worry about, *cor meum*."

"Why won't you tell me?" She shook her head repeatedly. "This is so frustrating. I'm trying to help but—"

His shoulders pushed back. "Elisabeth, please..." His voice was barely a whisper. "Stop."

"No...don't tell me to stop." She threw her arms up in the air in frustration. "I'm a part of this, but you won't even tell me what's going on. You won't tell me the full story. I'm tired of all these..." She scrubbed a hand over her face. "Of all these little breadcrumbs. Just, please, assume I can handle it?"

David gazed at the ground.

"There are two of you for crying out loud." Elisabeth closed her eyes. "And you're the exact same person."

He remained unnaturally quiet.

"You're here with me now. Am I supposed to suddenly forget all about the *other* you? Won't history just repeat itself?" Elisabeth's shoulders tightened. "But if I leave all this behind and stay in the past...*this* you would have wandered the earth for centuries—for nothing." She stopped walking, shooting him a long, pained stare.

Although his features looked barely older than

hers, his eyes seemed ageless; dark and serious as they searched hers.

"Why won't you say something?" With a theatrical groan, she stomped her foot and then stormed away.

Eyes clouded with tears, Elisabeth marched past her house, across the street to the town's white gazebo. She slumped onto the bench, sniffling, staring out at the bay. A frog croaked and waves gently lapped against the shore while she waited for him.

A few minutes later, David sat beside her, holding out a tissue.

"I knew I was supposed to save your life in Pompeii, but I don't know what I'm supposed to do now." Her chest caved in. "Thank you," she mumbled, taking the tissue from him to wipe her nose. "Am I supposed to make a choice between you, David Perrier, and him, Gaius Cornelius Aquarius? Is that what this is about? Either way I choose...one of you is going to get hurt. I don't want to hurt either of you." She sniffled and wiped her nose again. "You're the same person."

"Are we?" His voice was devoid of emotion.

With a fluttery feeling in her stomach, she turned to look at him. "What?"

David's eyebrows gathered in. "Are we still the same person?"

"Of course," she said, not realizing she softly shook her head. Elisabeth then cleared her throat and looked away, shoving the tissue into her pocket.

He stared down at his fingers. "I'm waiting to *fix* something, not...*complicate* matters even more. Yes, we were once young and in love, but I..."

She squeezed her eyes shut.

"I haven't been Gaius Cornelius Aquarius for a

very long time."

Heat rushed to Elisabeth's cheeks and she covered her face with both hands while groaning. "You said…and I thought…"

"It's my fault." David's tone was soothing. "I should have realized…" His voice trailed off and they sat in silence until he let out a heavy sigh. "That cuckoo clock in the house? Remember I said it reminds me of you?"

Elisabeth frowned while nodding.

"Think about why." When he pulled her into a side hug, she sagged against him. "Right here, right now…me…you…Sissi…we're like the hands spinning around and around, passing by one another." He paused to examine her. "But what happens when the hands are in the exact right spot, at the exact right moment?"

"The clock springs into action?"

"And…?"

"The cuckoo bird pops his head out of the little alpine cabin and the mechanical couple begin to dance."

"Now, let's say you and your Aquarius are the four o'clock couple. At four o'clock, like magic, the gears click into place and you two are reunited."

Elisabeth's posture perked up.

He took a deep, satisfied breath. "Sissi and her Aquarius were…eleven o'clock."

"And you and your Elisabeth?"

His smile quivered. "We were seven o'clock."

"So, when you and I are together now…" Her voice was soft, full of wonder. "It's like…only four thirty-five."

He let out an amused snort. "Yes. And that

means?"

"No dancing couple. No cuckoo bird. No music." Elisabeth let out a sigh of relief. "Okay. I think I get it. It kind of makes sense." She felt her cheeks flush while looking at him. "I mean, when I'm with you, it's not quite the same as when I'm with my four o'clock Aquarius." She chuckled. "Four o'clock Aquarius. I'm going to call him that."

David lowered his chin while raising an eyebrow. "It's still better than Aquari."

Elisabeth gave him a playful swat. "I couldn't figure out why you—seven o'clock Aquarius—why you and I don't click the same way here."

"I think it's because we're at different points on our adjoined timeline. The points need to align again in order to move forward together. For instance, I absolutely adore that old woman asleep in her bed right now, eleven o'clock Elisabeth, Sissi Waters, but...I'm not *in* love with her...not in the romantic sense. She's too far ahead on her timeline of us."

"Wait—" Her eyes narrowed. "What happens in a few years from now? Won't I catch up to you here and become seven o'clock Elisabeth? I mean...that's what's going to happen, right? Am I not going to eventually have *two* seven o'clock Aquarius'? It doesn't fix anything."

David lowered his gaze, saying nothing for several seconds. "Let me worry about that," he muttered.

"Whatever you're thinking about right now, that's what you're trying to fix, isn't it? I can see it in your face. Just say it. I'm sure you'll feel better once you get it off your chest."

David rested his head in his hands.

"Whatever it is…" Elisabeth touched his arm. "Together, we can fix it."

David let out a long exhale. When he finally looked up, his eyes were watery. "Come on, let's get you home."

She let out a heavy sigh as he pulled her up. Arms linked together, they left the gazebo and crossed the street to her Wedgewood blue house with the white gingerbread trim.

"Well…" David cleared his throat as he climbed the porch steps, walking her right to the door. "Good night." He tipped his head and started to move away.

"Wait—" Elisabeth grabbed his arm. "Am I wrong to go back?" Her bottom lip trembled.

"There's no right or wrong choice. Only *you* can make that decision."

"Be honest," she asked with a tearful voice. "Do you ever wish I hadn't come into your life and…and basically ruined it?"

With an incredulous stare, David pulled her into a hug. "You were my greatest joy," he whispered into her ear. "And I would do it all again, *cor meum*. Remember, I would do it all again." He then smiled at her, but in his ageless eyes, the torment showed.

Her shoulders curled over her chest after David turned away. He walked down the porch steps and disappeared into the night.

Elisabeth's limbs felt heavy while climbing the stairs to her room. She flopped onto the edge of the bed, staring down at empty hands.

Trembling, Elisabeth knew what must be done. She adored Aquarius far too much to ruin his life, despite what he may have said to the contrary. She crumpled on top of the blankets, pulling both knees to her chest.

Her Aquarius—in the fourteenth century—must be forgotten.

She let an uncontrollable sob before burying her face in a pillow.

Elisabeth had to let him go.

Chapter Seven

"Remember…test next Tuesday!" Mrs. Mackenzie yelled as the class piled out the door after the bell rang.

It felt strange being back at school. The familiar sounds of shoes squeaking across the floor and clinks of locks opening made Elisabeth realize how long she'd been away. Technically, she hadn't missed a single day, yet she'd been gone for months.

As she walked by walls of dented lockers, listening to voices laughing and shouting around her, Elisabeth knew it was time to try and get back to her normal life.

She gripped her plastic binder, trying not to think of Aquarius.

That was impossible.

She'd lost her best friend.

Doors slammed and someone's aftershave wafted along the hall. If she never returned to their timeline in the fourteenth century, would she disappear without a trace? Vanish into thin air?

Was she making the right choice?

She had to be. Whatever David was trying to fix hadn't happened yet.

Aquarius deserved the best life possible.

Not only was he a free man now, but with Balinus and Perenelle he had a family, a promising future. Heck, he even had a little sister in Colette and a family dog named Beau-Beau. It was ideal.

As she fiddled with her combination lock, Elisabeth's eyes clouded with tears wondering if he'd eventually fall in love with some pretty village girl and live happily ever—

"Hey, Chickie." Anna blew a pink bubble with her gum. "What time you want me to pick you up?" she asked after it popped.

With a slow smile at the sight of her friend, Elisabeth opened the metal door and grabbed her backpack. "For what?"

"Very funny."

She flinched when Anna snapped her gum loudly.

"You okay?" Her friend's blonde topknot flopped over when tilting her head to the side.

"Yeah, I'm fine." Elisabeth cleared her throat, trying to remember what they'd planned. She grabbed her leather jacket, pulling it on over a crisp white Oxford shirt before shutting the locker door. "It's just—"

"You're still coming to Halifax with me tonight, right?" Anna clasped her hands under her chin. "Pleeease?"

Shopping! Anna needed a new dress for her cousin's wedding. Elisabeth quietly exhaled as they walked outside. "Yeah, of course. I'll let you know as soon as I'm done work."

****

Like always, Elisabeth arrived at Sissi's grand old house at the top of the hour. She dropped her backpack and leather jacket on a chair, listening to the whirring sound of the clock in the foyer as the gears clicked into place. It still made the house feel slightly magical; like a spell was momentarily broken.

The bird popped its head out and cuckooed three times.

The music box melody played while the mechanical couple danced.

Then, everything stopped.

The magic replaced by a somber tick-tock.

Felis traipsed closer, meowing while rubbing against the door frame. He weaved his way between Elisabeth's feet as she pulled Sissi's folded coat out of her backpack and returned it to the closet. Instead of marching straight to the kitchen to put the kettle on, she walked into the living room. Elisabeth wiped sweaty palms on her jeans, only now realizing how much she longed to see David—for it was a way of seeing Aquarius.

"*Salve,*" Elisabeth called out, at this point out of habit.

Sissi appeared in the doorway of the sunroom, beyond both the living room and adjacent dining room, waving hand pruners in the air. "*Salve. Quomodo te habes?*"

"*Satis bene.*" Elisabeth bit her lip while walking to the back of the house, glancing around. "Where's David?"

Dressed in a silver sweater over a soft white blouse with gray suit pants, Sissi looked elegant as always. She stood at a table making flower arrangements for the house. "Can you believe these roses are in their third flush?" She snipped the stem of a blush pink rose and tucked it into a vase amongst wispy foliage.

Elisabeth leaned forward, breathing in their intoxicating fragrance. "There's something extra romantic about the roses of autumn." Her gaze then darted through another doorway, out into the hallway. "Where's David?" she asked again.

"He left this morning." Mrs. Waters added another rose to her arrangement.

Elisabeth's head flinched back. "What do you mean he left? Where'd he go?"

"Darling, he only arrived yesterday morning so we could set the events in motion. We needed you to travel back…"

Her heart felt like it was shrinking. Elisabeth averted her gaze, blinking away the tears threatening to spill. "I thought he'd be around all the time now," she muttered. "He didn't even say goodbye." Her shoulders hunched.

"Oh, honey." Sissi put the hand pruners down. "I know. I know." Her voice was soothing as she walked to Elisabeth, wrapping an arm around her shoulders. "As you can imagine, it's just too painful for him to be here. But…" She exhaled. "…we're one step closer."

Staring down at her hands, Elisabeth realized she had neither David nor Aquarius now.

"Why don't you take the evening off? Go out and enjoy yourself tonight. If I recall correctly, we promised to help Anna choose a new dress?" With a wink, she linked their arms and ushered her toward the front of the house. Mrs. Waters' face seemed to shine as she made strong eye contact. "You need to remember not to get so wrapped up in one world that you neglect the other."

The words tumbled around in Elisabeth's head as she paused to examine the old woman.

"Think back to that carefree summer in Scotland when we were twelve."

Elisabeth's posture perked up. She grabbed her leather jacket from the chair at the front door. "But—"

"When you're old like me, your biggest regrets are the things you *didn't* do." Mrs. Waters shuffled closer, tapping the crystal necklace Elisabeth still wore. "That is a precious gift, my dear. Don't waste it."

Her heart pounded. She opened her mouth to say something, but no words came out.

A knowing grin spread across the old woman's face. "See you tomorrow?"

"Definitely." With wide eyes, Elisabeth bounced down the front porch steps, wondering why on earth hadn't she thought of it before.

Chapter Eight

Elisabeth's mind raced, imagining all the possibilities.

Time stood still in one reality, while she played in the other. She'd learned that in Scotland when she was twelve, traipsing about the seventeenth-century Highlands with Quinton and Fiona. Didn't that mean she could live two lives simultaneously and solve the problem *for* David? He'd waited centuries to fix something. She could continue as normal here: go to school, be with her family, and some day—maybe they'd be together again. Here.

But—she could also be with Aquarius in the fourteenth century. That would stop him from taking the elixir and causing this cycle.

It wasn't perfect but it solved the problem.

Didn't it?

Elisabeth's hand covered her mouth while walking home as fast as possible. Her mind raced. How would she do it? Alternate each day? Devote twenty-four hours to each timeline? She bit down on a smile knowing she'd figure out a way to fix all of this herself.

****

The evening was spent in high spirits. After shopping with Anna, she babbled excitedly through dinner with Mom and Dad about school. Elisabeth had been gone so long, wrapped up in the adventure (and misadventure), she only now realized how much everyday life here was missed. Mrs. Waters was right. For this plan to work, you couldn't get so wrapped up in one world that you neglected the other.

She felt twelve years old again, discovering the crystal for the first time. It was better than Christmas morning, and now she had her best friend to share it with—Aquarius. While scooping mashed potatoes onto her fork, an appreciative sigh escaped at the very thought of him.

Mom paused to examine her. She then wiped her mouth with a napkin in a clear attempt not to laugh.

Elisabeth blinked. "What?"

"Nothing," she replied with a bemused smile.

"What's so funny?"

"It's just…" Mom flashed a knowing grin. "I recognize that look."

Elisabeth could feel her ears turning red while fidgeting with the cutlery. "What look?"

Dad got up slowly, clearing his dishes from the table. "The same look I'm sure your mother had when she met *me* for the first time."

Mom leaned closer. "It's a boy, isn't it?"

With a theatrical groan, Elisabeth pushed a green bean around her plate, avoiding the question. "Oh my God, you guys…"

Anna had asked the same thing earlier.

****

After dinner, Elisabeth tried to study for her calculus exam, but she kept moving around, unable to keep still long enough to focus. Finally, she closed her books, slipped into the burgundy gown, and pulled the crystal necklace over her head. A schedule regarding how to split up the time could be figured out later.

She held the crystal in her hands. Right now, the only thing on her mind was how she longed to be back, riding a horse through the outskirts of medieval Paris—with Aquarius.

****

David's eyes were wide as he pulled his horse's reins to stop. "What's wrong?"

"Oh, I…erm…" Her cheeks burned while grabbing her mare once again, embarrassed she'd run home when frightened. "A bee," she yelled, climbing into the saddle. "I thought a bee flew up my skirt!"

He did a double-take, spotting the crystal necklace she'd forgotten to tuck away. "I see." When David's gaze drifted to her un-bandaged and healed hand, he swallowed hard. His brows then drew together as he glanced over his shoulder at Giovanni. "We'll catch up," he shouted and waved at him to continue. He then turned to Elisabeth, rubbing the back of his neck.

"Aquarius…" she whispered in a soothing tone while slipping the chain behind her dress. It fell below her collarbone, hidden safely once again. "My hand really hurt, so I took some elixir to heal it. Don't look so worried. Everything is fine." A slow smile started to build. "*Especially* with you," she added softly.

He jerked his head back before looking down to hide a grin.

Judging by the sun, it was late afternoon. As their horses kept at a steady pace to catch up with Giovanni, Elisabeth glanced over at David, smiling. Her mind was filled with a million scattered thoughts, and she was too excited to think straight. All she knew was that it felt good to be back here.

They cantered along a road unlike the one she'd traveled by carriage—one that brought them closer to the gallows.

And closer to the wolves.

Despite her better judgment, Elisabeth leaned forward in the saddle, trying to get a better view of the huge monument.

"*Cor meum...*" David warned, his voice low-pitched. "Look away."

Her eyebrows furrowed while trying to figure out what she was seeing.

That couldn't be a person—?

"Hey, hey..." Moving quickly, David positioned his horse closer, attempting to block her view. "You don't want to see that, love."

Too late.

Elisabeth's posture went rigid.

Decaying, half-eaten corpses hung from their necks, most with missing limbs. A hanging head and torso was all that remained of another as crows devoured what was left of the flesh. Below it, several gray wolves gnawed on bones.

She clutched the rope in her hands even tighter. "They let the bodies just hang there and rot?"

Somewhere in the distance, a wolf howled.

Elisabeth's eyes bulged while her gaze darted all around. "I thought wolves only come out at night?"

"Look at that." David scraped a hand over his face before pointing straight ahead, attempting to change the subject. "Curious place for a village."

Elisabeth gently bit her lip, welcoming the distraction.

The roof of a chapel and numerous houses peaked

above a stone wall that enclosed a tiny settlement. A large main gate seemed to be the only way in or out.

"It's kind of adorable," she muttered, imagining medieval families fleeing inside the protective walls to escape the nearby wolves.

Giovanni glanced behind at them, slowing as they caught up. "A leper colony," he shouted out.

Elisabeth's shoulders slumped. "Of course it is."

This fairy-tale better not turn into a Grimm one.

****

They rode in silence; the gallows and leper colony now in the distance. Hopefully, the wolves were too. Eventually, her eyelids became heavy; the rhythmic gait of the horse lulling her to sleep.

When strong hands gripped her waist, Elisabeth gasped, realizing she'd nodded off. They were outside Balinus' house.

David grinned while helping her dismount. "Tired?"

Before she could answer, Perenelle appeared in the doorway holding a basket yet again. With a bark of laughter, she ambled straight toward them. "You're back."

"They're back?" Colette yelped in a high-pitched voice while racing out the door after Perenelle.

"We are, *amita*." David pulled the old woman into a side hug. "Did you find your dog?" he asked Colette as she bounced on tiptoes in front of him.

Perenelle's brows squished together and she turned to look at the little girl. "What dog?"

Colette clasped both hands over her mouth and broke into uncontrollable giggles.

"What dog?" Perenelle repeated.

She mouthed something inaudible, barely able to get the words out, before running back into the house.

Perenelle shook her head. "I don't even want to know." She then turned to Elisabeth, still chuckling. "As I live and breathe...Lord Cathon's daughter."

Elisabeth twisted her long sleeves, hating that, at this point, it seemed easier to let her believe the ever-growing web of lies.

"You must be quite persuasive for your father to allow you to return to David. Did he give his blessing?"

"Oh..." Her heart raced. "He agreed I could stay with you and Nicolas...not to a marriage. I told him I...I hated the convent school and that's why I ran away." She swallowed the lump in her throat while stealing a glance at David, unsure if any of this sounded believable.

Perenelle leaned in closer, lowering her voice. "You didn't mention you'd run away *with* David, did you?"

Elisabeth stared at her feet, unsure how to reply.

"Well, my lips are sealed, as long as you don't expect any special treatment." The woman's brows squished together. "I don't understand why, but if your father's going to allow you to live with us for the time being, you'll not be some high and mighty lady here. You'll sleep with the girls and do chores along with everyone else."

Girls?

Elisabeth let out a huge breath as she looked up, nodding.

Perenelle then handed her the basket she'd been holding. "You can start by fetching some saponaria, sorrel, and raspberries from the garden for me. I trust you can prepare sorrel sauce?"

She replied with a hesitant nod. "Of course."

"Excellent. Come inside when you're finished, dear, and you can help Beau-Beau."

Elisabeth's eyes narrowed. "*Help* Beau-Beau?"

"Yes. Colette's older sister, Isabeau."

"Wait a minute…" David's lips clamped together in amusement. "So…Beau-Beau is *not* Colette's beloved auburn-haired dog?"

Perenelle shuffled back a step. "Is that what she told you?"

"Yes!" David and Elisabeth both burst into laughter.

"Oh Lord, that child. I'm not certain whether she keeps me young or ages me." The old woman then glanced at the others, a bemused smile still on her face. "David, bring the horses to Percy in the stable, if you please. Giovanni, you'll return and join us for a meal later, won't you?"

Blondie cleared his throat and ran a nervous hand through his hair. "Many thanks, *ma donna* Perenelle. I'd like that very much."

"Good. That's settled then." With a crisp nod, she started back toward the house.

Giovanni nodded a farewell before riding off. David led the horses down an alleyway beside the house, toward a small thatched-roof stable."

Elisabeth frowned while walking beside him. "What did Perenelle say I need to gather?"

"Saponaria, sorrel, and raspberries."

"Oh yeah."

He flashed a bemused smile "You've no idea what you're looking for, do you?"

She shook her head. "I've never even heard of them. Except for the raspberries. I'll be able to find those."

"I'm not so sure about that." He swallowed his laughter.

"No...I eat them all the time."

"Well, you just walked right by the raspberry patch, love," David called out while continuing with the horses.

"Shoot!" Heat rushed to Elisabeth's cheeks as she whipped around, backtracking to find the bush. After gathering as many ripe berries as possible, she wandered down the lane leading to the rear of the large property.

She placed a hand over her heart and chuckled when passing a little wooden wagon, most likely abandoned by Colette. A wooden sword, a homemade rag doll, and a pile of sticks awaited their young owner's return.

Just beyond the back door, a series of garden beds were laid out in a geometrical pattern. Each section was edged with a knee-high fence made from branches and twigs that had been woven together. Leaves of various shapes and sizes poked out of the rich earth, and bean stalks climbed teepee-shaped trellises.

Elisabeth's brows squished together while examining a row of mounding plants with lance-shaped leaves. Frowning, she stepped over the fence and looked down at the other herbs and vegetables growing, trying to guess what everything was. The frilly circles were cabbage, but what about—

At her feet, a rabbit froze. With a smile, Elisabeth stood perfectly still, watching as the bunny feigned invisibility. "How you doing, Flopsy?" she whispered.

At the sound of her voice, the rabbit panicked.

Elisabeth laughed, watching Flopsy's cotton tail and furry back paws zip away, out of the garden.

"Any luck, *cor meum*?"

With a slow smile, Elisabeth turned around. "You're back." She pointed at the questionable plant. "Do you know what those are?"

"I do." David's posture relaxed as he walked closer. "That is sorrel. The leaves are edible."

"I told Perenelle I know how to make sorrel sauce," she whispered frantically while harvesting a bundle of leaves, adding them to the basket before making her way out of the vegetable patch. "I've absolutely no idea what I'm doing."

"You'll be fine." David held onto her arm, helping her over the knee-high fence. "Use a mortar and pestle…"

Elisabeth's head flinched back. "A what?"

"It's a bowl…" He lowered his chin while raising an eyebrow. "And a small…club."

She let out a sigh of relief. "Oh, I know what you mean."

"Put some leaves in the bowl with a bit of salt and mash them together until you have a paste. That's it."

With a grin, she sagged against him and raised her head. "Thank you."

His eyes were bright while staring down at her. "And the saponaria?"

Elisabeth's nose wrinkled. "No idea what that is either."

David grabbed her hand, leading her further down the lane, away from the house and garden. "I think it's this way."

With a small laugh and a fluttery feeling in her stomach, she followed him over the hill, down toward a wooded valley. "Why do I have a feeling you're lying?"

He flashed a mischievous grin.

At the edge of the woods, in the dappled sunshine, David walked toward a wild-looking bush. After picking a handful of stems, he handed her the leafy bouquet. "Saponaria."

Elisabeth let out an appreciative sigh while adding it to her bounty. "Thank you. Again."

David reached into her basket, popped a raspberry in his mouth, and tore off a sorrel leaf. "Try it."

Lips pressed into a grimace, she took the leaf from him and tried the tiniest nibble. "Oh, it's not bad. Sort of like…sour apple."

He then held up a saponaria stem, its unopened buds tinged in pink. "I used to have to pick these for Domina." He clamped his lips together, attempting not to laugh. "Try it."

"What's it taste like?" she asked, lifting a leaf to her mouth.

"No, don't." David chuckled, pulling her hand away. "I'm teasing. Those aren't for eating, love. You put the leaves in water and it makes lather."

"Soap?" She gave him a playful shove and he pretended to stumble backward. "You tried to get me to eat soap?"

When he flashed a wide-eyed look, she burst into giggles.

Her heart pounded as he staggered toward her drunkenly. "Oh, no," Elisabeth said with a high-pitched voice, holding up a hand as she backed away.

David squinted in amusement.

Elisabeth managed to take several steps before he gave chase.

With a shriek, she turned and ran into the woods, off the path, through the soft underbrush of ferns, still laughing as he drew nearer. The musty smell of moss hung in the air and twigs snapped beneath her feet. The light faded, leaving them surrounded by shadows.

Ahead was a large boulder.

She ran straight toward it.

David detoured closer to the hillside, attempting to catch her from the other side.

Suddenly, a thunderous sound, like falling rocks, caused Elisabeth to stop mid-stride. Her brows squished together in confusion. "Aquarius...what was that noise?"

No answer.

With a heavy feeling in her stomach, she turned, staring at the hillside where David had been a moment ago. Her posture went rigid and she dropped the basket from her arm. "Aquarius?"

All that remained was a cloud of dust.

David was gone.

Chapter Nine

"Aquarius?" Elisabeth's heart raced as she sprinted to where he had been seconds earlier. "Aquarius!"

"Down here."

"Oh, thank God."

His muffled voice was barely audible. "Watch your step," he warned.

Hands trembling, Elisabeth's gaze darted across the forest floor. "Where are you?"

When David began belting out a Roman marching song, she spun around. Her eyes widened while listening to the raunchy lyrics before bursting into laughter. Clearly, he was alive and well.

Elisabeth's breath hitched, noticing the narrow cave-like opening in the earth. It was tucked into the base of the hillside, hidden by underbrush.

At least twenty feet underground, David's silhouette was barely visible in the darkness. He leaned against a steep slope of rocks, inspecting his hands and arms for cuts and scrapes while singing the ridiculous tune.

She could see he'd made a slight gully of dusty gravel when sliding into the hole, clearing away larger stones as he fell.

Elisabeth dropped to her knees at the edge. "Are you all right?"

"I believe so," he said nonchalantly while looking

up. "Care to join me down here, love?"

"Thanks, I'll pass."

"It's probably not long enough, but..." David removed the rope sling from his hip. "Catch."

Elisabeth lay flat on the ground, her head and shoulders hanging over the pit. After catching the rope, she wrapped one end around her hands and lowered the other end. She then slowly shook her head. "Yeah, it's definitely not long enough."

"I cannot see much for want of light..." David's voice filled with wonder. "But I think there is space down here. Tie your end to the closest branch. I'll make a run for it."

She glanced around at the underbrush, but nothing close seemed thick enough. "There's nothing here to tie it to." Elisabeth tightened her grip on the rope. "I'll hold it."

"*Cor meum*," David warned. "I think it unwise—"

"Don't worry," Elisabeth replied with a curt nod. "I got you."

His eyes widened as he stared up at her. "But who's got you?"

"Seriously? I may not be a gladiator, but I'm not a weakling."

David cleared his throat and the darkness swallowed him up as he stepped back. "I am unsure this plan is—"

"Ready when you are," Elisabeth interrupted. Her brow furrowed, anticipating David's weight.

A minute later, he came sprinting toward the rock slide, momentum driving him upward. Elisabeth held her breath, watching his hands reach for the rope.

He missed, mumbling as he slid back down.

She let out a theatrical groan. "That was so close. Try again."

After a delayed response, he let out a long exhale. "Fine. Tell me when you are ready."

In order to give David some additional rope, Elisabeth positioned her body to hang over the hole a bit more. While wriggling into place, her leg brushed a thick vine growing on the forest floor. She glanced over her shoulder, hooking one foot around the tendril for extra support. Her muscles tightened; hopeful the extra inches would make the difference. "Ready when you are."

David stepped back into the darkness. A moment later, he sprinted toward the rocks again. Arms outstretched, he reached for the rope, desperate to catch it before sliding back down.

With a grunt, one hand grabbed the rope.

Lips pressed together; Elisabeth nodded. "Hurry…"

The moment David grabbed the rope with his other hand, Elisabeth let out a primal scream when she was dragged forward. Now, her entire torso hung above the pit, teetering over the rock slide.

"Aquarius…" she whimpered, unable to move. The leafy vine around her leg was the only thing holding her in place.

David gasped and immediately let go of the rope, trying to keep his balance as he slid back down the rocks. "All right, *cor meum*…" His voice was steady and low-pitched. "Here's what I want you to do. First, put your—"

At that moment, the vine snapped.

Unable to stop, Elisabeth pulled her outstretched

arms protectively around her head into a diving position.

Gasping for air, she slid head-first down the rock slide—gaining speed, bracing for impact.

Instead of crashing into the ground, she felt David's arms reach under her arms, lifting her before they tumbled together. He fell onto his back, cushioning her fall when she landed on top of him with a thud.

As the dust settled around them, Elisabeth buried her face in his neck.

"It's all right." He hugged her tighter. "I've got you."

Heartbeat racing, tears streamed down her cheeks—but they were happy tears. Elisabeth's body trembled while attempting not to laugh. Other than feeling a little bruised and battered, she wasn't in much pain, thanks to the thick fabric and long sleeves of the dress she wore. Her chin felt a little scraped up, but she mostly wanted to be held a while longer as the relief sunk in.

"You're trembling."

"I can't believe you caught me as I slid head first down a…?" Unable to hold her giggles back any longer, she lifted her head to look around, noticing bones from a small creature. "What is this? Some sort of pit?"

Elisabeth could feel David's muscles stiffen beneath her. He gave her an incredulous look. "You're laughing?"

"You have to admit, for a bad idea…" She squinted in amusement while staring down at him. "That was pretty fun."

He let out a huge breath and flipped her over. She

was now beneath him, her head cradled in the crook of his elbow. "Your chin is scraped, but you are otherwise unhurt?"

"Yes—" When he moved his head closer, she met his lips with hers. "I'm surprisingly fine," Elisabeth said between kisses.

A slow smile built. "What about here?" He kissed her forehead.

"Surprisingly fine," she said with a grin.

"And here?" He kissed her gently on the nose.

"Also…surprisingly fine."

David's eyes twinkled with mischief as he took her hand. "Here?" He kissed her wrist.

Elisabeth clamped her lips together, trying not to laugh. "Surprisingly fine."

"I found them, Nellie!" Balinus shouted overhead. "Both appear to be…*surprisingly fine*," he added with a snort. He then cleared his throat, leaning his head over the pit. "Though I am not certain they wish to be found yet."

David and Elisabeth both jumped up, whooping loudly in the excitement of being rescued already.

"You're a sight for sore eyes," Elisabeth said with a shaky laugh.

"Oh, thank God." Perenelle popped her head over the hole and let out a slight moan. "You'd both been gone too long." She clutched at her stomach. "We came to look for you…and then we heard a scream…" Her voice choked with tears. "Ohhh…you nearly scared me half to death."

"Apologies for having frightened you, Aunt," David said. "We had no idea this hole was here. We fell in."

Perenelle looked at Balinus. "Did I not tell you this would happen to someone?" she said with a raised voice. "I told you they didn't fill it in properly and someone was going to get hurt—or worse. What if Colette fell in?" She then looked back down at David and Elisabeth, her tone soothing again. "Are you both all right?"

"Yes, we are unharmed." David's posture perked up. "Uncle…?"

Balinus leaned over the pit.

"If you bring me a longer rope, I was thinking—"

"David?" A bemused grin spread across the old man's face. "A wise sage once said, 'Stop thinking, and end all your problems.'"

David clamped his lips together, attempting not to laugh while holding up a hand. "Say no more."

"Good," Balinus said. "We'll have you out in no time."

"Come, Husband," Perenelle mumbled. "They're losing daylight."

She was right. The tiny amount of light filtering down into their pit continued to fade as the sun set. David picked up his sling and selected stones from the base of the slope. Elisabeth watched dust particles around him sparkle in the waning sunbeam, giving off an ethereal feel. She wrapped both arms around her torso, trying to stay warm while breathing in the cold, damp air. "You know, this kind of reminds me of the Money Pit."

"Tell me…" he paused, adding the stones to his leather belt pouch. "What is a money pit, love?"

"It's a super famous treasure hunt that's been going on near my house for more than two hundred years. My dad's been obsessed with it since he was a kid and—"

What was that noise?

Elisabeth glanced at the black void on the dark side of the hole. The hair lifted on the back of her neck and she rubbed cold hands together before tucking them into her armpits.

"Come here." David reached out, pulling her against him. "I'll keep you warm."

She cuddled against his chest and closed her eyes, savouring the moment. When he suddenly slipped a hand behind her knees, scooping her off the ground, Elisabeth let out a belly laugh and threw both arms around his neck.

"We'll sit while we wait." With a bemused smile, David sat, resting against the rough rock wall.

Elisabeth nestled between his outstretched legs, leaning back against him.

"Where were we?" With a content sigh, he wrapped his arms around her, their body heat warming each other. "Ah, yes, the money pit. Tell me your tale."

"I shall tell you my tale." With a deep voice, she imitated him, before confining her laughter to a snort.

"I amuse you."

Elisabeth twisted around, smiling at him in the fading light. "Constantly."

David brushed a strand of hair behind her ear.

"All right. Remember I told you about the seaside town where I live?" She leaned back against his chest again, making herself cozy. "Mahone Bay?"

"I remember," he whispered, wrapping an arm around her neck.

She tilted her head back, resting it on his shoulder. "Well, several hundred years ago…"

David chuckled. "Do you mean several hundred years from now?"

"Good point," Elisabeth said with an unforced laugh. "I guess I should—"

His lips brushed the tip of her earlobe, causing goose-bumps on the back of her neck. If he was going to say something, he didn't.

She couldn't help smiling at nothing in particular. "So, it's 1795, and three local boys decide to explore a tiny island that's supposedly haunted. Out of hundreds of nearby islands, it's the only one with oak trees growing on it, so everyone called it Oak Island." Elisabeth pulled both knees up to her chest, tucked the dress around her legs for added warmth, and melted into David. "The boys, who were actually our age—"

"So they were not boys, but men," he said with a throaty chuckle.

After giving him a playful nudge, Elisabeth found David's hand and laced her fingers with his. "One summer day, the young men are exploring the island, following an old trail. They stop beneath a tree and one of them points up at a huge branch. The end has been sawed off, but a rusty old pulley is still attached. You know, for lifting heavy things?"

"Mm-hmm."

"Well, when they look down at the ground, they discover they're standing in a depression, as if a long time ago someone dug a hole and filled it back up again. They start digging and within a few minutes, their shovels hit something. Of course, they're super excited, convinced they've just found gold and silver and jewels."

David took a deep, satisfied breath. Although they

now sat in complete darkness, he seemed as content as she was to wait for Balinus and Perenelle.

"They throw their shovels down, hooting and hollering as they clear the dirt and debris away by hand. It's a circle of flagstone they've uncovered." Elisabeth spoke more and more rapidly. "After they pull the stones out and toss 'em aside, one of the boys notices old marks from a pick-axe. So, they're even *more* convinced there's something buried there. They spend the entire day digging and then come back the next morning to continue. I mean, the hole is so deep now only their heads are sticking out the top. At the end of the second day, when they're just about to quit for the night, the shovels hit something again, but...this time it's wood."

When a sudden gust of air blew through the pit, David turned his head, staring into the dark void.

Elisabeth stopped to listen intently. "What was that?" she whispered.

"Just the wind, *cor meum*." David glanced up to the top of their hole. "The old man should be back soon."

When Elisabeth felt David's posture relax, she leaned back and continued. "So, the young men move all the dirt away, only to discover the wood isn't from a treasure chest. It's a floor made of oak logs. They try to haul the logs out but they've been caulked in place with putty. Do they give up? Noooo." She shook her head for emphasis. "After attacking the floor with pick-axes, the logs are finally lifted out of the pit, one at a time. Eventually, they dig so far down they have to go in and out using the pulley and sitting on a bucket. And then guess what?"

David chuckled and kissed the side of her head.

"What?"

"Every ten feet they hit another floor made of oak logs."

His breath hitched. "Wow."

"I know, right? Anyhow, the men eventually decide they need more help so they talk two friends into joining them, promising to split the bounty. However…" Elisabeth let out a heavy sigh. "One of their fathers finds out. He shows up at the pit and makes them all stop digging and fill it back in before someone gets killed."

"Hopefully they did a better job than whoever filled this one in," David whispered.

Elisabeth nodded in agreement. "A couple of years go by. One of the guys gets married and decides he's going to purchase the piece of land where the pit is. It's not expensive because nobody in their right mind wants to live on a supposedly haunted island. So, he moves there with his young wife, who—while in the middle of childbirth—talks the doctor into financing the treasure hunt."

"What?" David couldn't hold back a bark of laughter.

"It's true. The doctor's fascinated. He puts together a team and they come in to continue the hunt using much more sophisticated equipment. They quickly dig down: sixty feet, seventy feet, eighty feet…it keeps going. They eventually start calling it the Money Pit because of all the money they keep investing in the excavation. They dig all the way down to ninety feet."

"*Nonaginta pes*? By the gods…"

"Here, they discover a…tablet." Elisabeth paused. Her brow then furrowed and she sat up straight. "Wait a minute…" Her voice filled with wonder. "Could it have possibly…?"

David tilted his head closer. "What's wrong?"

"Everyone thinks it was nothing, but…oh my gosh…maybe it *was* something. Maybe it *was* the treasure." She sucked in a quick breath and stood up, pulling David to his feet. "What if the treasure was found all those years ago but they didn't realize it? The pit kept going. I mean…they dug and dug, but it was booby-trapped. It flooded; they drained it. It flooded again and they—" She gasped. Eyes bulging, Elisabeth stared at David's silhouette in the darkness. "Whoever built it had knowledge of ancient Roman aqueduct systems that caused the flooding…"

"Slow down, *cor meum*, slow down. What are you trying to say?"

"Aquarius…" Elisabeth's hand covered her mouth. "Whoever built the Oak Island Money Pit had an insane amount of time on their hands, knowledge of ancient aqueducts to flood the pit, and hid a green tablet with strange lettering on it at the ninety-foot level. Nobody really knows what the stone said because it eventually disappeared without a trace."

"Are…?" His tone was uncertain. "Are you saying that I have…or…I *will* have something to do with this money pit?"

"I have no idea what I'm saying." With a slow, disbelieving shake of her head, Elisabeth moved closer, wrapping both arms around David's waist. "But on an island, practically outside my front door, someone with knowledge of ancient aqueducts spent years and years building an elaborate pit. The only significant thing ever found in more than two hundred years of searching was a green colored tablet with strange writing on it."

He cleared his throat. "You've hidden the tablet Balinus gave you safely, right?"

"Of course. It's under my bed. Maybe the—" She stopped, feeling David's posture suddenly become rigid while staring into the dark void of the pit.

With calm and focus, he grasped Elisabeth's arm.

Her eyes narrowed in confusion as he forced her behind him. "What's wro—?"

"Shhh." David planted his feet in a wide stance, reached for his sling, and grabbed a stone from his belt pouch.

Elisabeth's breath burst in and out.

"We're not alone, *cor meum*," he whispered.

Chapter Ten

Elisabeth's pulse raced while staring into the darkness, listening to the sound of boots—or paws—scuffing over rocks. She felt the color drain from her face and glanced up, willing Balinus to return.

How long does it take to run back and grab a freaking rope?

David positioned the stone in the middle of his sling and raised his arms to shoulder height, taking aim.

When Perenelle's muffled voice bounced around their pit, Elisabeth let out a sigh of relief. She looked up, biting her lip, expecting to see the old couple smiling down at them. But, the forest above remained dark and quiet, except for the distant hoot of an owl. She stared back toward the void. A dim light seemed to emanate from it, now casting shadows on the rough walls.

Elisabeth gasped, realizing they weren't in a pit. With a shaky laugh, she stepped out from behind David. "I think…I think it's an echo we hear."

He glanced around as if looking for answers. She could see his head flinch back slightly when the faint light continued to grow. David lowered his arms but kept his stone and sling ready.

Where the dark void had been, the faint outline of a doorway appeared. "Follow me." With a sudden giddiness, Elisabeth rushed toward the growing light.

"We're in a mine. Watch your head. The ceiling's low." She walked out of the pit and into a dark tunnel.

"I'm coming, I'm coming," Perenelle grumbled, holding a candle lantern up as she drew nearer. "Somebody misplaced the key to the mine."

"Told ya," Elisabeth called back to David with a satisfied smile.

He let out a huge breath and tucked the sling away.

"We had no idea we were in a mine," Elisabeth said with a disbelieving voice when they reached the old woman. "I thought we fell into a pit...or maybe a cave." Her eyes then widened realizing Balinus wasn't with her. "You're in here by yourself?"

"Safety precaution. We have a system. If anything unforeseen happens to me, stay put and wait for help. Now..." Perenelle turned around. "Keep close and under *no* circumstance are you to wander off," she instructed over her shoulder, leading them single-file down the passageway. "The mine was owned by my second husband, God rest his soul, so I know these parts of the tunnels better than most."

Elisabeth raised her eyebrows and glanced behind at David.

He ran his fingers along the rough, dusty walls while hunched over, trying not to hit his head. "Your husband owned the mine?"

"If you own the land, you also own everything under the land." Perenelle turned left, then right, seeming to head deeper into a maze of cold and damp, pitch-black corridors. "I reopened it about five years ago. It's a nice supplemental income for the farmers during the winter months."

"*Amita?*" David asked. "Does anyone ever hide in

here, from raiders or—?"

The old woman stopped walking and turned around, brows drawn together as she held up the candle lantern, looking at the two of them. "Listen…you are never, under any circumstance, to come in here by yourselves. Do I make myself clear?"

Wide-eyed, they both nodded in reply.

"I thought it best to bring you out this way in order to satisfy any curiosity you might have, rather than have you snooping around on your own. These mines go on for miles and miles and you will *never* find your way out. Even I dare not venture beyond this well-traveled route. Several years ago, we lost two local boys who snuck in to explore. Their bodies were *never* found. Nicolas says where the mines end, the real passageways begin."

David crossed his arms while observing Perenelle. "What do you mean?"

"I shouldn't be saying this, but…" She let out a dejected sigh and lowered her voice. "Years ago, Nicolas acquired several ancient scrolls. The scrolls are maps of an enormous underground…web." The old woman paused, pressing a hand against her chest. "There are endless passageways connecting all of the lands—from here to Cappadocia, from the North Sea all the way down to the Mediterranean."

Ancient tunnels beneath Europe? Elisabeth moved closer, hanging on to Perenelle's every word.

"Nicolas doesn't know who built them, but says they've probably always been here, beneath the earth." She released an appreciative sigh while smiling at David. "So, to answer your question, yes…your uncle once read that some early Christians in faraway lands knew about the tunnels and hid in them from persecution."

"But they're not mines?" he asked.

"According to the scrolls, some locations are entire underground cities, able to house thousands of people and their livestock indefinitely. Nicolas says some have lovely, smooth walls, unlike a mine…such as this one." Perenelle held the candle lantern up to illuminate the wall. "See all the rough layers here?"

David ran his fingers along a small section of black stone dotting the lighter limestone. "Is this part flint?"

"Yes, you will occasionally find flint amongst the limestone." The old woman pulled in a deep breath and smiled at David. "I have a nagging suspicion you're going to be as wise as your uncle someday."

Elisabeth's smile wavered as she nodded in agreement. Immortality does that to a person.

David rubbed the back of his neck. "I'm quite certain none will ever be as wise as my *patruus*, Aunt."

"True," Perenelle said with a gleam in her eye. "He's the most learned man I've ever known. Knows just enough about every topic to be quite annoying." She then let out a belly laugh. "Let's go home, shall we?"

When David looked down to hide a grin, Elisabeth knew his smile wasn't because of the old woman's joke, but because he was still getting used to the fact he had a home to return to. His happiness caused her own heart to race.

After following Perenelle around another corner, the corridor grew wider and taller, allowing David to walk beside Elisabeth.

"Mind your feet. There are some holes in the

ground here in the entrance tunnel," the old woman warned. "And keep minding your head, David."

"It's kind of scary when you turn around." Elisabeth glanced over her shoulder, feigning horror at the pitch-black void. "But isn't it amazing?"

David answered with a wide grin.

Ahead, another candle lantern shone brightly.

"Ahh, you've made it safely out," Balinus called from the exit.

"We have," Perenelle replied.

Elisabeth could see the night sky behind the old man. She breathed in the warm, fresh air after they exited the tunnel through a door built into the hillside, waiting as Perenelle locked it.

Balinus leaned closer, holding up his lantern. "What did you think of the mine?"

David reached out, touching the old man's shoulder. "Amazing, yet at the same time…terrifying."

"Good," he said with a crisp nod. "And Nellie warned you—?"

"Yes. We promise to never go in on our own."

"Good. Good. Shall we go home and eat then?"

"What do you say?" David's eyes seemed to dance when he grabbed Elisabeth's hand. "Shall we go home?"

"I'd like that." Warmth radiated through her chest. "Because I'm starving."

"You're always starving," he said with a chuckle.

The old couple led the way along a moonlit path, back to the main road. When they neared the house, Elisabeth smiled as David squeezed her fingers, his happiness contagious.

Colette paced outside the front door. "They're

back!" With a squeal, she ran straight for Balinus' outstretched arms. "I absolutely dread it when one of you has to go into the mines."

"I know," he said, wrapping her into a hug. "But everyone's safe now."

Colette took his hand, leading the party through the screens passage and into the large main room, or what Perenelle referred to as the great hall.

Inside, Beau-Beau swayed absent-mindedly, sweeping the stone floor in the flickering candlelight. She wore a sleeveless floor-length tunic of blue, atop a linen-gray dress. A pale red apron accentuated a tiny waist and her nearly waist-length auburn hair was pulled back in a thick braid.

"Isabeau, my dear," Balinus called out in a bubbly voice. "We've returned."

Isabeau spun around. She then leaned the broom against a table, fidgeting with her apron while politely awaiting an introduction. The young woman appeared to be no more than eighteen years old herself. She had bright playful eyes, a wide but attractive nose, and a smile as mischievous as her little sister's.

Elisabeth liked her already.

Balinus asked her something in some sort of French.

With a rich, fruity laugh, Isabeau pointed at the open fire pit in the middle of the room.

Although Elisabeth had spent the night sleeping next to the indoor fire, she only now realized the house had no hearth; no fireplace. A covered pot hung from an iron tri-pod above the embers as smoke drifted up to the blackened rafters, escaping through a hole in the roof.

The structure of Balinus' house was similar to that of a barn, with a soaring two-story high ceiling. The rooms she and David had dressed in this morning were built over the buttery and pantry on the right-hand side of the house. Because the second-floor chambers were larger than the storage rooms below them, they jutted out to create a section with a lower ceiling downstairs. Here, the addition of wooden panels served as a decorative wall. It separated the service area from the great hall and created the cozy passageway between the front and back doors.

"Isabeau still works to improve her Latin," Perenelle said with a crisp nod.

"But I will try my best." Her pleasant voice was deep and strong.

A brightly painted cloth hung on the wall behind Isabeau, illuminated by a flickering candle. Elisabeth stared at the image of a young boy plowing a field. Around the large room, other painted cloths were positioned as artwork, bringing color and personality into the space. Beneath them were random pieces of furniture: chests, benches, wooden chairs with cushions, and a hutch holding pewter dishes.

Like the opposite end of the house with the screened-off passage, the great hall also featured rooms built atop of rooms, but here they were focal points. Pressed against the back wall, a wooden staircase rose to the second floor, leading to a loft-like balcony that overlooked the entire space. In the center was the entrance to Balinus and Perenelle's bed chamber—where Elisabeth had arrived the previous night. Directly below, back on the ground floor, a door had been left open. She could see a desk tucked beneath a shuttered window. The entire house had a rustic elegance. While it was far from a castle, it certainly wasn't a crofter's cottage. It seemed the Flamels were the medieval equivalent of the middle class.

"…met yet, but this is David." Perenelle's voice brought her back to reality. "Nicolas' nephew from Rome."

"David Perrier." He introduced himself with a polite nod before shooting Elisabeth a playful grin.

"And his…*betrothed*, Elisabeth, from Verona."

Elisabeth's brows pulled together. *Verona?*

"But don't tell too many people," Perenelle continued in a hushed tone. "We don't really want the guild to find out about their secret engagement."

In unison, Elisabeth's smile went stiff. David pressed a fist to his mouth to keep from laughing, and Isabeau stepped back to curtsy. She'd obviously heard the plight of Lord Cathon's unfortunate daughter.

Elisabeth's eyes bulged. "No…really…don't—"

Perenelle gave Isabeau a dismissive wave of her hand. "Not necessary."

"Oh…" Isabeau's eyes narrowed in confusion. "A pleasure meeting both of me," she said in Latin.

Colette giggled quietly. "Oh, Beau-Beau…"

Elisabeth cleared her throat. "If you're the one who made the fig tarts…they were absolutely delicious."

Isabeau's face lit up. "Oh, thank me. I make them for both of me. Something special, yes?"

Balinus wiped at his mouth and then walked closer, whispering into Isabeau's ear.

She laughed, covering her face with both hands before looking back at Elisabeth. "Thank *you*. I make them for *you* today." She then smiled at David.

"Something special for both of *you*."

Balinus pointed at the long dining table. A bouquet of wildflowers was arranged in a tin jug. "It looks extra lovely in here today, Beau-Beau." The old man winked at her before turning to Elisabeth. "Isabeau is excited at the prospect of having new people to cook for. She absolutely loves it."

She smiled while nodding. "Also, I happy gown fit...*you*."

Elisabeth grimaced. "This is yours?" She ran her hands along the shredded fabric. "I'm sorry...it was ruined when I fell. I'll replace it."

"After what you go through? Plus robbed by bandits who take even clothes?" Isabeau gave her an incredulous look. "No need replace. I have this one," she said, smoothing down her apron. She then looked at David's outfit and let out a content sigh. "Your clothing from *Giovanni*."

David jerked his head back. "Giovanni? He failed to mention that. Well...he has fine taste." With a smirk, he stared down at his trousers, whispering, "for a barbarian," to Elisabeth.

She elbowed him, trying not to laugh.

"Giovanni from Rome. Like you." She looked at Balinus and started to rattle off various questions in their form of French. "No...Florence. Giovanni born in Rome but move to Florence when he boy."

"Oh..." Elisabeth leaned toward her. "Are you and Giovanni—?"

Isabeau's mouth fell open. "What? No. Eww, no. Giovanni?" Her ears turned red and she hurried out of the room, through the screens passage, out the back door.

Colette burst into giggles, clutching Balinus' arm for support. "She is, isn't she?"

Perenelle shot her husband an exasperated look, letting out a heavy sigh while tying an apron around her waist.

"So, Isabeau's in love with Giovanni," Elisabeth said in between giggles of her own.

"Yes." Perenelle added a log to the fire. "And he with her."

"I do wish someone would tell them," the old man added with a chuckle before pointing at his study. "Would you like to see some illuminations, nephew?"

David's posture perked up. "Of course." He touched the small of Elisabeth's back, excusing himself to join Balinus. Colette yawned and wormed her way into the study as well.

A moment later, Isabeau marched back into the great hall, to the large work table, carrying a handful of leaves. "Elisabeth...you can make sorrel sauce, yes?" She pointed to a spot beside her where the mortar and pestle were already laid out.

"Yes," Elisabeth replied with a quiet voice before making her way over. She hoped the task was as easy as David described.

A loud knock at the door caused all three women to look up.

"I wonder who that could be?" Perenelle exchanged a knowing glance with Elisabeth. "Why don't you answer it, Beau-Beau dear?"

Isabeau jerked her head back before biting down on a smile. She then dashed toward the front door while smoothing down her dress.

After disappearing behind the screened wall,

Perenelle and Elisabeth grinned at each other, both straining to hear the song and dance between two lovebirds.

The door squeaked open.

"*Salve*, Isabeau."

"Oh…" She let out a deep sigh. "You again."

Chapter Eleven

"Well…" Giovanni's voice rose in pitch. "I do apologize for being the cause of such disappointment."

"No…no…come in. I just hoping for other man to visit. Better looking one," she added with a snort.

Elisabeth gave Perenelle an incredulous look.

When the front door slammed shut, the old woman looked down at the work table and began humming.

Isabeau rubbed both hands on her apron while walking back into the great hall.

"Good evening," Giovanni said with a shy smile as he stepped into the room.

Perenelle's humming stopped and she looked up, a grin on her face. "Giovanni, what a nice surprise. I didn't know you were here yet." She pointed toward the study. "Why don't you join Nicolas and David? Supper will be ready shortly."

Isabeau's eyes widened. "Giovanni staying for supper? Again?" She let out an exaggerated groan while filleting a fish. "He always making extra work for me."

Perenelle gasped and Elisabeth clapped a hand over her mouth, trying not to laugh.

"Isabeau! Where are your manners?"

"What…?" She looked at Giovanni with a raised eyebrow, offering him a questioning gaze. "He knows I only tease."

"Beau-Beau…apologize at once."

Blondie chuckled while shaking his head. "It's fine. Ridiculous as she is, I actually enjoy this wretched *rascaile*."

Isabeau squealed. "*Rascaile*!" With a wide grin, she picked up a thick slice of bread and whipped it at him.

He reached up, caught it, and took a bite. "Better aim than Elisabeth," he said with his mouth full before walking into the study.

Isabeau exchanged a confused look with Elisabeth, which caused them both to burst into laughter.

Perenelle's lips pressed together. She grabbed a heavy frying pan before marching back to their work table. Elisabeth quickly looked down, tearing sorrel leaves apart.

"Beau-Beau, you are never going to find a suitable husband if you continue to act like that," she whispered with a firm voice, slapping pieces of salmon into the pan. "It's unbecoming. After your mother died, I told your father I'd—"

Isabeau began rambling on in their form of French.

"In Latin, if you please," Perenelle scolded. "You must improve your Latin if you expect to properly run a household someday. It is not just the language of the church, but of the educated."

"Nell-eee…" She jerked her head back. "It fine."

"With your dowry, you will never find an advantageous match if you continue in this manner. And believe me, for *you*, Giovanni would be an advantageous match in *every* way possible."

Isabeau let out another loud groan and added a piece of salmon to the pan. Perenelle threw her hands up in the air, shaking her head while walking away. In the center of the room, the pot hanging over the open fire began to bubble. The old woman grabbed a wooden spoon, stirring the contents. Isabeau soon joined her, adding the skillet of salmon to the hot embers.

Elisabeth put the sorrel into the little bowl with some coarse salt and began to grind the leaves. Before long, it turned into a mushy paste. "Does Giovanni travel this way often?"

Perenelle looked up. "Oh, yes. He's a journeyman butcher, soon-to-be master." The old woman tilted her head back and stared at Isabeau. "But his father is a well-to-do *banker*," she whispered, theatrically enunciating each word.

Isabeau snorted while turning the salmon over. "That make him son of a usurer…thus *me* advantageous one in a match."

Perenelle let out an exasperated moan and then poked her head into the study. "Supper's ready," she said before returning to the cooking fire.

Balinus walked out, followed by David and Giovanni.

"I'll get Percy," the old man said as he walked out of the great hall.

A sleepy-looking Colette staggered out last. Her hands curled around her head and, while yawning, she stumbled into the wall.

Elisabeth let out a small laugh. "Awwww, you're exhausted."

"*Noooo…*" Colette replied, giggling as her cheeks flushed.

Giovanni inhaled a deep breath and sat at the table. "It smells wonderful."

With a slow smile, Elisabeth looked at David.

When he raised his eyebrows into a questioning glance, she nodded, holding up the little cup of sorrel sauce for him to see. "Thank you," she said, mouthing the words.

With a gleam in his eye, he sat on the bench opposite Giovanni.

A few minutes later, Balinus returned, followed by Percy, who looked no older than fourteen. He ran a shaky hand through his jet-black hair and kept his head down while walking across the room, sliding onto the same bench as Giovanni, next to Balinus, who sat in a chair at the head of the table.

Isabeau fluttered around the work table, assembling their meal, which consisted of a piece of rustic bread, topped with salmon. She then strained Elisabeth's sorrel sauce over top of the fish. Perenelle added mushy peas that had been cooking in the pot before delivering the bowls to the table.

"Percival's seen a unicorn before," Colette randomly announced. "Haven't you, Percy? Tell everyone what you—"

When a flush crept across his alabaster skin, Perenelle walked over, squeezing the young man's shoulder. "This is Percival, our groom," She sat in the chair opposite her husband. "You already know Giovanni."

They both nodded.

She pointed at David. "This is—"

Percy nodded again. "We met earlier."

"And that is Elisabeth."

When he cleared his throat and looked her way, Elisabeth smiled and gave a small wave.

With a satisfied smile, Perenelle watched everyone pile around the table together, talking and laughing.

Elisabeth slid across the bench, squishing in beside David, making room for a sleepy Colette, who rested her head on the table. Isabeau climbed over the bench, squeezing in between Giovanni and Percy.

Elisabeth then bit her lip, pushing peas and sorrel sauce around the dish. "What's it taste like?" she whispered to David.

"Amazing." After shoveling a spoonful into his mouth, he glanced at her and then did a double-take, chuckling. "You're not scared to try it, are you?"

Elisabeth stared at him wide-eyed and gave a small nod.

"It's not *rat*." With a bemused smile, he reached over, taking a huge spoonful of mushy peas from her bowl. "But if you're not going to eat it…" He licked the spoon clean before turning his attention to Giovanni, who was asking him something.

Elisabeth shook her head, trying not to laugh while discreetly scraping the remnants of peas off the salmon.

"Who wants more peas porridge?" Perenelle called out.

Elisabeth's lips parted as she looked up.

Peas porridge?

Like the old nursery rhyme?

Peas porridge hot, peas porridge cold…

"What…?" Giovanni shouted. "You two did *not* fall into a mine after I left!"

Percy's eyes widened and his gaze momentarily darted to David.

"No, it's true." David shoveled more peas into his mouth before leaning in to tell of their misadventure.

Almost bouncing from the bench, Isabeau reached across the table, grabbing Elisabeth's plate. "You eat peas already? You like more?"

"No!" She gasped, trying to take her dish back, but it was too late. "I mean…thank you. They were delicious, but—"

"Don't be shy. I get you more." She gently bit her lip. "One day I hope be good enough to cook for king…or someone like your father." She exhaled while looking up. "To cook like Taillevent himself."

As Isabeau made her way to the porridge pot for more peas, Elisabeth let out a quiet whimper, causing David to confine his laughter to an amused snort.

****

The evening progressed with much merriment, although shy Percival couldn't leave soon enough, preferring to return to the horses in the stable, where he also slept. Colette had already retired upstairs to bed, followed by Balinus and Perenelle, when Giovanni stood up, taking his leave.

"Wait…" Isabeau hurried after him, moving into his personal space.

Elisabeth watched in amusement as Giovanni licked his lips, smiling. Isa's thick braid had long ago come undone, and her hair now hung in long auburn waves—that he couldn't keep his eyes off of.

"You owe me ivory comb still."

"You cheated!" he said with a bark of laughter.

She grabbed a drawstring bag from a nearby cupboard and slapped it on the table.

"Fine." His face seemed to shine as he sat back down on the bench, opening the bag and dumping what looked like clay checker pieces onto the table. "But what will you give me when I win?"

Isabeau spread the bag out flat, revealing a square

game board painted on the leather. "I bake you pie."

David leaned in closer, an incredulous look on his face. "Merels."

Elisabeth yawned, rubbing her eyes. "You know this game?" she mumbled.

"Amazingly…" He pulled her into a side hug so she could nestle lazily against him. "I do."

Isabeau and Giovanni took turns placing their pieces on a grid of lines with dots.

"If I lose…" Blondie studied the board. "You want an ivory comb."

"No. You *already* owe me comb." Isabeau placed a piece on a dot. "I like new *belt* as well. And perhaps pretty purse."

He let out a long, low whistle. "The stakes are quite high this evening."

Isa pinched her lips together to keep from smiling.

As the two-player game advanced, Elisabeth's eyelids grew increasingly heavy. With the fire softly crackling, and a cricket chirping outside a shuttered window, the soft noises were lulling her to sleep.

Isabeau glanced over. "You very tired," she said in a soothing voice.

Elisabeth shook her head while yawning, secretly hoping Blondie would leave so she could go to sleep on the floor, next to the fire again. "No, I'm fine."

"Follow me. You also," Isa said to David while grabbing a candle.

David looked at Giovanni with raised eyebrows. Curious looks on both their faces.

"No cheating," Isabeau called over her shoulder, lighting the way through the screens passage and up the steep staircase. At the top, she pointed to the door on the right. "That room mine and Colette's." The door creaked as she opened it slowly, careful not to wake her sleeping sister. "Colette kicks like donkey so I make you pallet over there," she whispered, showing her a spot on the floor. "It not castle, but believe me...it better than sharing with Colette."

"Thank you," Elisabeth said softly, eyeing the fluffy bedding piled into a cozy corner. "It's perfect."

Isabeau then tiptoed out, walking into the room on the left—the storage room David had dressed in earlier. "I move crates out, clean, and make bed chamber for you here," she said to him. "Since you stay, it more comfortable than floor downstairs."

David's eyes widened. "I, uh...I..."

"Room was Nellie's late husband's...when he boy," she said with a dismissive wave before handing David the candle and leaving them in privacy.

Elisabeth looked around as the flickering candle lit the space. The small bedchamber had wooden beams with plain plaster walls. Straight ahead was a small shuttered window, cracked open a wee bit. To the left, the head of a narrow bed was pushed against the wall. It held a lumpy mattress nestled within a wooden frame. A warm-looking blanket and a flat pillow decorated it. Beside the bed was a rustic side table.

David put the candle on the nightstand and glanced around, shaking his head repeatedly.

Elisabeth released an appreciative sigh. "You've never had a room of your own before, have you?"

He cleared his throat. "I've not had *anything* of my own before." He then playfully reached for Elisabeth's arm, drawing her into a hug. "If this new life here is only a dream, do not wake me," he whispered.

"It's completely real."

David raked his hand through her hair, letting it linger there as they held firm eye contact. "I have something important to ask you," he said quietly.

Elisabeth swallowed hard. "What is it?"

A silly grin spread across his face. "Who do you think will win at merels? Isabeau or Giovanni?"

"Isabeau," she replied with a small laugh.

In the glow of the candlelight, David took a deep, savoring breath, causing Elisabeth's heartbeat to quicken. He murmured something inaudible before their lips met in a series of slow, gentle kisses, leaving her weak in the knees.

She eventually pulled away and, with a giggle, reached behind her back, feeling for the door handle. "All right, I should probably get going." A shy smile spread across her face.

David looked down to hide a grin before glancing up again. "Sleep well," he whispered as Elisabeth slipped out of the room.

While pausing outside the door, she closed her eyes and held a hand over her mouth as warmth radiated through her body. She then crept into the girls' bedchamber, which was bathed in darkness. Elisabeth removed the burgundy dress, leaving the shapeless white shift on. It was cozy as a nightgown. She curled up on the little bed, wondering if David was comfortable in his, and drifted off to sleep.

****

Sometime in the night, Elisabeth woke, gasping for air as Mount Vesuvius' avalanche of ash and debris raced toward her and David all over again. She trembled, unable to get the image out of her mind. It was a tidal wave the size of the Manhattan skyline, destroying everything in its path. She brought a shaky hand to her forehead.

The top of the mountain exploded, going off like a nuclear bomb again.

The air rippled around her again.

Aurelius was dead.

Despite the warnings, that charming, unpredictable old man had stayed behind, along with all the others.

Aurelia, Marius, and their unborn baby were dead.

The room was spinning.

Walls came crashing down.

They were in the arena—David bleeding to death in her arms.

She clamped a hand over her mouth, but a quiet sob escaped.

Wide-eyed, Elisabeth stared over at the bed. Colette and Isabeau were sleeping peacefully. With barely a sound, she crept out of the room...and into David's across the hall.

Her throat and chest ached as she gently shut the door and stumbled across the floor to him. "Aquarius...?"

David sat up quickly, startled, and breathing quickly. "What's wrong?"

"Whenever I close my eyes..." Her voice choked with tears. "I'm in Pompeii all over again."

In the darkness, he reached for her and she crumpled onto the bed next to him, needing to be held. "Everything is going to be all right, *cor meum*," he whispered soothingly while wrapping her into his arms and pulling her close. "It's over now."

Curled up in his protective embrace, Elisabeth felt

all the tension melting away.

****

David's movements stirred Elisabeth from sleep. A moment later, she felt the blanket nestle against her body. Her eyes fluttered open. Through a gap in the shutters, a moonbeam now filled the room with smoky light. David, wearing a loose linen shirt and knee-length shorts—obviously undergarments—lay down on the cold, hard floor beside the bed.

Elisabeth's heart felt full knowing he'd do anything for her. "Aquarius…?"

"Hmm?" The floorboards creaked as he adjusted the pillow between his arm and head, trying to get comfortable.

Elisabeth pressed a fist to her lips to keep from laughing. "Can I have the pillow too?" she whispered.

When it flew up, hitting her on the head, she burst into hushed giggles. "I was only joking," she said, throwing it back to him.

David's breathing deepened as he stretched out, putting both hands behind his head. "Tell me an if?" he asked with a quiet voice.

Elisabeth cleared her throat, trying to be serious now. She rolled onto her side, gazing down at him on the floorboards. "If…if you don't mind, can I stay in your room tonight? You keep the nightmares away." She felt her cheeks flush. "But you don't have to sleep on the floor."

"I *do* have to sleep on the floor." David closed his eyes. "Because you 'kick like a donkey.'" He then began to snore softly, pretending to have fallen asleep.

Elisabeth placed a hand over her heart as a slow smile spread across her face. "Liar," she whispered to

122

him.

****

Outside the window, a choir of clucking and chirping awoke her.

"Here chicken, chicken," Colette sang out. "Heeeere."

With a yawn, Elisabeth rubbed her eyes, blinking when realizing she was alone. The shutters had been thrown wide open. Fresh air and morning sunshine flooded the room. She rose from the bed and peeked out the window, pausing a few moments to watch Colette feeding the hens.

Fluffy clouds dotted the sky and, in the distance, sheep grazed the rolling hills. In the small orchard to her left, a rope swing with a wooden seat hung from the limb of a fruit tree, swaying softly in the breeze. Elisabeth smiled, wondering how she'd missed it yesterday. Her thoughts drifted back to that magical summer in Scotland, where she'd spent many-a-day beneath the old beech tree with Fiona and Quinton.

She let out a dejected sigh knowing it was time to return home and go to school. For this to work, one timeline couldn't be neglected in favor of the other.

But…

Isabeau poked her head into the room after tapping on the door. She wore the same sleeveless blue tunic, linen-gray dress, and pale red apron. "You in here, I see." She wiggled her brows. "It all right. I keep secret."

A sudden warmth flushed her cheeks. "Oh. No, it's not like that. I was having nightmares…about the ambush…"

A wide grin spread across Isabeau's face. "Well,

123

they find your trunk."

Elisabeth's eyebrows squished together. "They found my trunk?"

"Yes!" She bounced on her toes. "They recover your trunk stolen by thieves. It downstairs."

Elisabeth nodded slowly knowing there was no trunk to be found. Her posture then perked up. "They found my trunk!" She dashed through the door, pulling Isabeau's hand as she ran past. "Come…"

Chapter Twelve

At the bottom of the stairs, a large trunk had been plunked down. Elisabeth dropped to her knees in front of it, immediately recognizing Cato's coat of arms engraved in the wood—a wolf, and what looked like either a falcon or a hawk on either side of a shield, with a ram on top.

Her pulse raced. After seeing Cato's fairy-tale castle, there was no denying the man had exquisite taste. Whatever was in here would be beautiful. Fingers traced decorative wrought iron leaves, felt the orange-tinted leather covering the wood. The trunk itself was a work of art.

No!

Don't open it.

Cato's trying to buy our forgiveness.

She shook her head as conflicting emotions took over.

When Isabeau knelt beside her, Elisabeth's lips pressed together into a grimace, weighing the pros and cons of looking inside—of accepting Cato's gift.

"Ohhh…" Perenelle gasped after walking in the back door. "I heard your trunk was found." The old woman lowered her veiled head, studying the chest. "It's still perfectly intact?"

"It appears to be."

Her eyes narrowed as she maneuvered around the

girls, making her way into the pantry. The door creaked as it opened. "Do you think it's possible your father sent a new one? That looks untouched, let alone damaged."

Inside the storage room, Elisabeth eyed rough wooden shelves holding platters and pots, grain chests, fresh bread, cabbage, and a bowl of eggs.

"Well, go on, open it," Perenelle urged as she walked back out of the pantry. "It's the only way to find out."

Elisabeth's gaze drifted back down to the trunk; her posture rigid as she raised the lid.

Isabeau leaned closer and then squealed dramatically.

An attached wooden tray filled with delicate items lifted with the top when you opened it. Tucked neatly beneath appeared to be every fine gown available from Paris to Milan.

"Just as I thought." Perenelle let out a deep, satisfied sigh. "You know, I met your famously elusive father once."

Elisabeth's head jerked back. *She'd met Cato?* "When?"

"About seven years ago at the Hôtel-Dieu. The hospital was in desperate need of repair and your father financed the entire project. I was there, feeding the poor...as was he. He'd come in to see how things were progressing and stayed to help."

Elisabeth listened with a focused gaze.

"I don't recall ever hearing an unkind word about him."

Unable to restrain herself any longer, Isabeau pulled a blue velvet and silk dress from the trunk, her eyes wide while holding it up. "*Biauté*."

Elisabeth glanced at the beaded detail and handmade buttons, nodding in agreement. She then sucked in a quick breath, reaching for a green velvet gown trimmed in fur. "Look at this one!"

Isabeau answered with a wide smile, and then held up a silk headpiece covered in pearls. It almost looked like a crown. "A tressour crispinette." She gasped, reaching for another item. "And velvet tippets."

Perenelle cleared her throat. "Girls…"

They both looked up, frowns on their faces at the interruption.

"Madame Chauderon is ill—"

Isabeau's shoulders slumped. "Yvonette?"

"Yes." With the basket handle looped over her arm, she opened the front door. "It's not serious, but she is confined to bed rest. Now, don't faun over these kirtles and cotehardies too long. There's lots of work to be done. Isabeau, I also need you to deliver the rue and buckthorn to Nicholas as soon as possible. He forgot his—"

"Yes. Yes, Nellie. Go," she said in a soothing tone. "I take care everything. Not to worry."

After Perenelle left, Elisabeth let out a shaky laugh, staring back down at the trunk. Cato had sent more dresses than anyone needed in a lifetime: red linen with long sleeves, ivory with beading at the neckline. The trunk was stuffed with beautiful fabrics, veils, headpieces, belts, cloaks, hoods, and undergarments— all fit for a princess. Her brows rose, curious that there was nothing made of lace, which she adored.

She checked again.

Nope. Not a single inch to be found. Elisabeth's

breath hitched realizing it probably hadn't been invented yet. Her posture then stiffened, holding up a gown that caught her attention. The entire left side was dark blue, the right side light blue—with light blue buttons running down the dark blue half. She stood, one hand clutching the dress, the other hooked casually on her hip. "I'm going to wear this one." It's not like she had anything else to wear here. "Pick whatever you want to keep."

Isabeau's head jerked back. She glanced over her shoulder and then back at Elisabeth. "Me?"

"Yes, you," she replied with a laugh. "I ruined your dress, remember?"

"But…" Isa opened and closed her mouth.

"Isabeau, seriously…take anything you want."

She fiddled with her apron. "No…I couldn't—"

"Move over," Elisabeth said with a good-natured shove. She dropped to her knees, rummaging through the trunk before holding up a velvet emerald green dress. "I think this color would look *amazing* on you. Do you like this one?"

"Of course. It beautiful. They all are." She gave a half-hearted shrug "You forget I cannot wear velvet."

Elisabeth's head flinched back slightly. "Why not?"

An incredulous look spread across Isabeau's face. "Sumptuary laws…?"

"What's that?"

Isa's mouth fell open. "Velvet only for people like you."

"Like me?"

"Lord Cathon's daughter…?"

Elisabeth's body tensed. "Oh…." This gave a

whole new meaning to the term *fashion police*. "Well, there has to be something in here you can wear."

She caught Isabeau's gaze wandering to a particular garment. Her hazel eyes softened, betraying her emotions.

"Ah-ha!" Elisabeth put the green velvet one back and reached for a garnet red gown with white trim made of linen. "You like this one, don't you?"

She bit down on a smile and nodded.

"It's yours." Elisabeth playfully shoved it at her.

As Isabeau broke into spontaneous laughter, Elisabeth slipped the parti-colored dress over the white shift she wore. Her body was in constant motion while looking down in admiration—from the scooped neckline and fitted bodice, to the long tight sleeves and flare of the skirt. "How do I look?"

"Oh!" Isabeau waved her arms before digging through the trunk. She pulled out a brass pendant belt, attaching it loosely around Elisabeth's hips. "Almost perfect...but one more thing." She grabbed a comb from the tray and sat on the bottom step. "Sit."

With a wide grin, Elisabeth sat on the floor while Isabeau combed and twisted part of her hair into a romantic braid.

"Your father very powerful man," she said, attaching the finishing touch—a pearl-encrusted headband.

"Lord Cathon." Elisabeth let out a dejected sigh and rose to her feet. "Yes."

Apparently so.

As Isabeau returned the comb to the trunk, there was a knock at the front door.

Elisabeth's posture perked up and Isa quickly

opened it.

"The Flamel residence?" asked a nondescript man in a brown tunic.

"It is…"

He placed a wooden box into Isa's arms. "From Lord Cathon," he said before disappearing into a waiting carriage.

Isabeau's head jerked back and she turned, giving Elisabeth a wide-eyed look. "Is this what I think it is?"

Gold? Priceless gems? Exquisite jewels fit for a royal?

As Isabeau sniffed the box, Elisabeth crept closer. It was a long, rectangular chest, about four inches thick, and appeared to be made of oak and iron. A shiny key waited in the tiny padlock.

"What do you think it is?" Elisabeth asked in an uncertain tone as Isabeau gently placed the item into Elisabeth's arms and closed the front door.

"Open carefully," she said, leading the way into the great hall, past the cooking fire, and straight to the work table. She then bounced on tiptoes; hands clasped under her chin.

With a wide grin, Elisabeth turned the key, removed the lock, and lifted the latch, leaning forward to see. Inside were eighteen square wooden compartments stuffed with spices, plus an oversized section at one end for larger items. Her shoulders drooped. "Spices?"

"Isabeau's hand covered her mouth and she moved in closer. "*Mon Dieu*…this cost king's ransom." She picked up three little nuts. "Nutmeg."

Elisabeth's head jerked back. "That's nutmeg?" She'd only ever seen it ground in spice jars her mom bought at the grocery store.

"Yes. Each one worth more than twice their weight in gold."

Elisabeth's mouth fell open. "Wait...what?"

Isabeau gave her an incredulous stare. "Yes. Spice a luxury for us simple folk not raised in castle. This like a dream." She gave Elisabeth a playful nudge before picking up several thin crimson-red threads. "Saffron called red gold." With a wide smile, she pointed at papery-looking, light green seeds. "Cardamom pods...cloves...pepper..." She held up what looked like cinnamon sticks. "...cassia..." Isabeau then squealed dramatically, inspecting an ugly brownish cone-shaped item, roughly the size of her palm. "Sugar cane?" Her eyes bulged. "This sugar?"

Elisabeth's voice rose in pitch. "*That's* sugar?"

"Yes. I think it sugar. I don't know. I only ever sweetened with honey." She closed the chest, locked the lid, and handed Elisabeth the key. "Keep locked and keep safe. Taillevent himself would covet this."

"Who?"

"He famous cook for King Charles. I dream one day cook as well as him."

Elisabeth's posture stiffened realizing Isa was basically the fan of a medieval celebrity chef. "You *really* like cooking, don't you?"

A radiant glow spread across Isabeau's cheeks as she nodded. "I feel like artist when preparing meal." She covered her face with both hands. "I know, I know. It not sensible, but in dream world, I'd own bakery in Paris."

"It's a perfectly wonderful dream." She handed Isabeau the key to the chest thinking of all the spices and exotic ingredients her mom easily used at home, no matter the season. "Use all the spices you want. I can get more of anything you'd like…from my father." She swallowed hard, realizing Cato was right. Pretending to be Lord Cathon's daughter gave her a back-story none would doubt. Elisabeth looked down. She adjusted the light blue sleeve on her left wrist, and then the navy sleeve on her right, attempting to steer the conversation to a different topic. "Did you win the game of merels last night?"

"Actually…" Isabeau's face beamed as she attached the spice key to a key ring on her belt and picked up the spice chest. "Giovanni win."

"Giovanni, huh? Guess you've got a pie to bake now," she said with a smirk, following Isabeau to the pantry. Inside, the small room smelled of fresh herbs and ripening berries. "When did David and Nicolas leave this morning?"

"Just after sunrise." Isabeau carefully placed the locked strong box on a shelf and then grabbed a large bowl, filling it with vegetables from a bushel. "Can you carry hair for me?"

"What…?" Elisabeth chuckled, holding a bundle of dried lavender to her nose, breathing in the soothing woodsy fragrance. "Carry *hair* for you?"

"Sorry, my hands full." Isabeau gestured at the wall beside the door before walking out, heading back into the great hall.

Elisabeth turned to look and then shuffled back a step. Hanging from their hind legs above a table were three dead rabbits. "Oh…" She put the lavender back down. "Carry a *hare* for you." Her brow furrowed, realizing if she was to make a life here it was time to suck it up.

"Flopsy...?" Elisabeth whimpered, reaching up, struggling to unhook the bunny. Her breath burst in and out as it fell from the hook, making a loud thud when it hit the table. Her shaking hand moved closer, grabbing hold of the velvety ears. With jerky steps, she kept her arm extended, carrying it into the great hall before dropping it on the work table. "Here you go."

"I teach you how make hare stew for supper," she said with a wide grin. "Good idea, no?"

"Yeah, great idea," Elisabeth said while walking slowly to the wash basin to scrub her hands. *Rabbit stew?* Her stomach rolled. So much for sucking it up. There was no way she could eat poor Flopsy. Couldn't they have chicken instead? Bought from a butcher, like Giovanni, and already prepared?

Isabeau handed Elisabeth a sharp knife. "You skin and debone rabbit while I—"

She responded with an accidental bark of laughter to that instruction.

Isa's head jerked back. "What? Oh..." Her voice became soothing. "Lord Cathon's daughter never skin rabbit before."

"It's fine. I can do it." Elisabeth cleared her throat, staring down at the dead bunny. She needed to focus on the task at hand instead of freaking out. This was part of life here and any intention to stay meant learning to do these things.

How hard can it possibly be?

Elisabeth's lips pressed together, wondering where to make the first cut. Her gaze wandered from the little cotton tail, to long adorable paws, and then over to floppy ears. "Do I cut the stomach first?" She backed away while extending her arm, trying to flip Flopsy over using the tip of the knife.

Elisabeth held the blade against its fur with a trembling hand. "Wait…" She looked up wide-eyed. "Isn't blood going to start gushing out?"

Isabeau burst into laughter and grabbed the knife from her hand. "Here, I show you. First…" Isa held a hunk of fur with one hand and carved a slice along its belly. "Make cut here. Careful though. You don't want guts cut. Then, put hand inside and pull."

As Isabeau skillfully pulled the entrails out, Elisabeth recoiled and looked away. "Hey, I…uh…" She wiped her brow. "I was thinking…do you want me to bring Nicolas' things to town for you?" She held still in expectation.

Isabeau's posture stiffened. "But, it long walk."

"I *really* don't mind." Elisabeth hands curled into tight fists as her gaze darted around the room, glancing anywhere but at the bunny being dissected and skinned. "That'll give you extra time to bake Giovanni's pie too. You know what they say; the way to a man's heart is through his stomach," she added with a nervous laugh.

A wide smile spread across Isabeau's face as she continued skinning the rabbit. "Very funny. I never hear that before. You very overdressed for preparing meal, anyhow."

Elisabeth let out a deep breath. "I'll leave to see Nicolas right now so he gets his things as soon as possible."

Isabeau made a beeline for the study. "You remember route? How to get to bookshop?" she asked over her shoulder.

"Yes. Totally. It's right by Notre Dame."

****

Elisabeth stepped out into the bright sunshine and slipped a fabric cord over her head. Across her body, tucked safely in a blue drawstring purse she'd found in the trunk, were additional supplies for Balinus that Isabeau had gathered: dark berries, dainty green leaves, a handful of feathers, and a bunch of unknown balls that looked like a cross between nuts and crab-apples.

With her chin held high, garbed in the most awesome dress, Elisabeth strolled through Balinus' picturesque village, feeling like a million dollars. Once again, the townsfolk scurried about, but today felt different. A large mustached man, carrying a bucket in each hand, flashed Elisabeth a conspiratorial smile, as if privy to some secret. He then nodded his head respectfully.

The next passerby tipped his hat, displaying a full head of frizzy hair. *"Bonjour."*

"Bonjour," she sang out.

A slow smile spread when noticing Colette ahead. With a wooden sword tucked into her belt, she walked away from a stone well, pulling the little wagon behind her. The head of a ragdoll peeked over the edge, propped into place between two very full water buckets.

Colette's eyes widened when she spotted Elisabeth. She picked up the pace, oblivious to the pails of water sloshing about, soaking her doll, and splashing to the ground. "Whoa. You *really* look like a princess today."

Elisabeth felt for the pearl-encrusted headband in her hair. "I have to admit, I kind of feel like one."

"So, what's it like?" Colette ditched the wagon and bobbed alongside Elisabeth.

"What's what like?"

135

"You know…" As she tilted her head to the side, a huge grin spread across her little face. "I heard your father is richer than King Charles himself."

Elisabeth's brows lifted. "Who said that?"

"My friend, Colin. Is it true he gives you *anything* your heart desires?" she asked as they reached the edge of the village. "You know what I'd ask for if I were you?"

"What would you ask the mighty Lord Cathon for, Colette?"

"A unicorn." She bounced from foot to foot. "Do you have one yet?"

"A unicorn?" Elisabeth let out a belly laugh. "No, I don't have one. They're not real, you know."

Colette gasped. "Of course they're real. Percy said he once saw one and Nellie made a painting and told me *all* about them. They're quick and hard to find, but I was thinking…if your father wants to catch one—for *you*—I can help."

Elisabeth squinted in amusement. "How?"

"Well, when they're wild, they're *really* dangerous." Colette reached for her wooden sword, waving it in the air as she spoke. "Nellie says they can kill an elephant by stabbing it in the stomach with their horn. But, for some reason, little girls…" She sheathed her sword and pointed playfully to herself, "…like *me*…make them docile. So, I was thinking, if your father can fund an expedition deep into the Hercynian Forest, I'll lure one for you. I'm not scared, you know. After the unicorn falls asleep in my lap, the hunters can come closer and capture it for us." Colette bounced on her tiptoes. "That's why we need your father. We need funding and the very best hunters money can buy to bring the unicorn home. Once I tame it, we can keep it in the stable with the horses." She stopped and took a deep breath while shifting back and forth. "What do you think?"

Elisabeth clamped her lips together to keep from laughing. "Well, that's a really great plan, but—"

"No..." Colette grabbed hold of Elisabeth's arm while giggling. "Oh please don't say no yet. Think of all the practical reasons for keeping a unicorn. They're...they're excellent at detecting poison."

"Nobody's trying to poison us."

"Yet..." Colette made strong eye contact. "Last summer, Madame Blavot was hanged for poisoning her husband."

Elisabeth gasped. "Where'd you hear that?"

"Colin." Colette bit down on a smile. "Just think about it. A unicorn. A real live unicorn. I promise to take care of it *entirely* myself. I won't even make Percy do the work." She then came to an abrupt stop once they reached the stone bridge. "I'm not allowed to go any farther *and* I'm supposed to be fetching water for my sister...but think about it," she added with a wide grin. "Really, *really* think about it." With an enthusiastic wave goodbye, she turned around, bouncing back toward her abandoned wagon.

Elisabeth shook her head in amusement before continuing over the bridge, eventually reaching the city gate. She wound her way through the streets of Paris, heading toward Notre Dame, before coming upon Balinus' little bookshop.

Not surprisingly, the front door was wide open. Elisabeth paused in the threshold, watching the master and his new apprentice work side by side at the large table in the center of the room. Her breath stalled, amazed this was real life. They looked like two actors filming a scene in a medieval movie. She listened to several items clink softly when David moved them across the table, followed by the crisp ruffle of pages being fanned as Balinus organized sheets of folded parchment.

David ran a penknife down a wooden triangle used like a ruler, letting out an unforced laugh when Balinus murmured something to him. His posture then straightened as they inspected the sheet of parchment he'd just cut to size. "Is that satisfactory?"

Balinus replied with a crisp nod. "Well done. Now, you need to do the same thing to all the rest, all right?"

With a deep, gratifying sigh, Elisabeth walked inside. "*Salve*. I come bearing supplies for you."

"*Cor meum*." A warm smile spread across David's face when he looked up. "*Quomodo te habes?*"

Elisabeth pulled the strap of the purse over her head and emptied the contents onto the table. "*Satis bene.*"

Balinus paused to examine her. "Close the door behind you, dear. We need to speak in private."

Her eyes widened while shutting the door. "Is everything all right?"

The old man cleared his throat. "Perhaps *you* can answer that question."

Chapter Thirteen

"I am glad you're here," Balinus said in an uncertain tone. "Because I've been awaiting the opportunity to ask what in the world is going on regarding..." His brows furrowed in confusion. *"Lord Cathon?"*

Elisabeth gasped. "Aquarius hasn't told you yet?"

"Told me what?"

David's ears turned red and he cleared his throat. "Last night was rather hectic and then today...here...I've been trying to pay attention and learn everything..."

Elisabeth's hand covered her mouth as she stared at Balinus across the table. "It's Cato."

The old man's head flinched back slightly. *"Who's Cato?"*

"Lord Cathon." She twisted her belt. "Lord Cathon is Cato."

Balinus' eyes narrowed and he turned to David, still standing beside him. "Your *brother*?"

"The one and only," he replied while rubbing his temples.

"How? I don't under—?"

Elisabeth stepped forward, resting her folded hands on the worktable. "When Mount Vesuvius erupted—"

"Refresh an old man's memory, if you please," Balinus said with a slow, disbelieving shake of his head. "I no longer take the elixir so my mind isn't quite as sharp as it once was."

"Sorry." A flush crept across her cheeks. "Before you left Pompeii with Soran and Larisa, you gave me a vial of your elixir so I could save Aquarius' life. He'd been stabbed in the arena and was bleeding to death."

"Yes," he said in a soothing voice. "I do recall that."

"Well, when I returned, Cato realized your elixir was ambrosia, the nectar of the gods. He stole it from me—"

"And left me for dead." David pinched his lips together. "Cato left me for dead."

Elisabeth's heart ached, knowing how betrayed he'd been.

David drew in a slow, steady breath. "My loyalty to those I care about is unwavering, but I warned him. I warned him not to mistake my kindness for a lack of strength. He went too far and we all know it."

Balinus lightly touched David's shoulder.

Elisabeth's brows pulled in. "Cato's older now, but he's obviously been using the elixir's...*benefits*...for centuries. Maybe he's a changed—"

"No. I will never forgive what he did to you," David interrupted with a scathing tone. "Have you forgotten he held a sword to your throat barely four days ago?"

"Of course not." Elisabeth pulled at her ear. "I'm just telling you what he told me; he's trying to make amends to prove he's a changed man."

David snorted.

"He begged for forgiveness. Said he wants to protect us and by playing the role of my father, it will give us a background nobody here will doubt."

With a too-quick smile, David leaned across the table. "We *have* a background here now. I am the nephew and apprentice of a bookmaker."

"You don't think people can change?" she asked quietly. "Perenelle seems to think *Lord Cathon* is a good man with a fine reputation, helping others and—"

"Look, I cannot say if Cato's character remains unchanged, but even if a thousand years have passed, he will *never* be deserving of my friendship again."

Balinus nodded in understanding. "Lord Cathon's *daughter*." A pained smile crossed his face as he glanced across the table at her. "That explains your attire today."

David's eyes widened and he looked at Elisabeth again. "That *stola* is not from Cato, is it?"

Stola? Elisabeth squinted in amusement. *You can take the boy out of Ancient Rome, but...* "Oh, come on..." Her heartbeat quickened as she stared down at the gorgeous gown. "I needed something to wear. The one Isabeau gave me was torn to shreds yesterday, remember? And the blue dress I wore in Pompeii was also—"

David held up a hand. "You know what he's trying to do, don't you?"

"Yeah..." Elisabeth gave a small nod. "Of course I do, but I *literally* have nothing else to wear here." She let out a dejected sigh. "And it's *sooooo* pretty."

David lifted his chin. "I will get you an even finer *stola* myself."

"Aquarius..." Elisabeth shook her head. "That's not the point."

"It *is* the point. Cato cannot buy our forgiveness

because what he did was unforgivable."

"It's *just* a dress." Elisabeth let out a theatrical groan. "Why'd he have to send such pretty ones?"

With an appreciative sigh, David reached across the table and caressed her thumb with his. "We don't need any help from him," he whispered.

"I know." She squeezed his hand. "That's exactly what I told him myself."

"I wonder…" Balinus paused, seeming to weigh his words. "If Cato has been alive all these centuries, the fact our paths never crossed worries me greatly. It suggests Cato took a…a different path. The amount of elixir I left with you would not have lasted this long."

Elisabeth's eyes narrowed. "You mean he's found another way to become immortal?"

"Let's just say there are both light and dark forces of nature. I have always chosen to walk the path in the light and over the centuries have met others who have too." Balinus swallowed a lump in his throat before looking at them with a wrinkled brow.

"What are you implying?" David sounded tense.

"Well, a wise sage once said, 'we can easily forgive a child who is afraid of the dark. The real tragedy of life is when men are afraid of the light.'"

Elisabeth's head flinched back slightly. She glanced over at David, who looked just as concerned.

Balinus leaned forward, his eyes now dark and serious. "There comes a time in every man's life when he must decide—"

The front door suddenly opened. A middle-aged man with receding brown hair walked into the little shop. His dark tunic was made of fine material and embellished with shiny buttons, giving him an air of sophistication.

"We'll continue this conversation afterward," Balinus whispered before looking up at his customer, a wide grin spreading across his face.

When David picked up his penknife and started back to work, Elisabeth grabbed a nearby book, pretending to read it.

"Pizan, tell me what you think so far." Balinus opened a drawer and, with a gleam in his eye, pulled out a palm-sized book, showing off the front and back covers. They looked like aged brown leather. Balinus then rapped a knuckle against it. "I've had it bound in carved wood."

Pizan took it, inspecting the clasps, before flipping through the colorful pages edged in gold leaf. "An exquisite job, as usual, Flamel. Christine will love it." Pizan then turned his head, his eyes narrowing as he watched Elisabeth, who quickly averted her gaze, pretending to read the book in her hands.

"Come back at *vespers* tomorrow," Balinus said, drawing the man's focus back to the manuscript. "It will be finished by then."

"Ahead of schedule. I can always count on you." Pizan puffed his chest out before stealing another glance at Elisabeth, this time with a smile.

Balinus cleared his throat. "Thomas de Pizan, may I introduce you to my *nephew*, David Perrier, and—"

"Lord Cathon's daughter. Lady…?"

She glanced up at the man, swallowing the lump in her throat while shaking her head. "No…"

David's gaze flicked upward.

"Elisabeth. Just plain old Elisabeth," she said with a small laugh.

"Ahh, just plain old Elisabeth." Pizan exchanged a knowing look with her. "I should introduce you to my daughter, Christine. I think you'd have much in common."

Elisabeth flashed him a quick, false smile, unsure how to reply.

He quirked an eyebrow, grinning. "I moved my family here from Venice several years ago, so…not too far from where I assume you grew up. I'm the King's astrologer," he added with a crisp nod. "I had the distinct pleasure of meeting your father at his castle outside of Verona once."

Elisabeth's grip on the book tightened. *Holy cow. How many freaking castles does Cato own?* "What a small world," she said with a tight-lipped smile.

The man's gaze went distant as he nodded at David. "Pleased to meet you." He then turned his attention back to Balinus.

"I should get going," Elisabeth said to David when the men went back to examining the book. A satisfied grin drifted across her face. "I don't want to keep you from your work."

"I'll see you out," he whispered.

Elisabeth discreetly waved goodbye to Balinus, grabbed the blue drawstring purse, and exited the little shop. The clip-clop sound of a horse drew nearer, pulling a cart down the cobblestone street. As people carried on with their daily lives, a man's contagious laugh in the distance caught her attention.

"Well…" She turned around, pulling the purse strap over her head when David shut the door behind them. "You seem to be adjusting *very* well here."

He gave a slow, disbelieving shake of his head and

stepped aside, moving next to the crown glass window. "I can scarcely believe it." He reached for both Elisabeth's hands and pulled her closer. "Days ago I was a slave, a gladiator." His voice was barely a whisper. "In the blink of an eye, I'm an apprentice to a bookmaker. I can actually imagine a future ahead—an incredible one—with *you*."

Elisabeth's brow wrinkled while staring up at him.

David didn't avert his gaze. "Once my apprenticeship with Balinus is complete, I will be a qualified journeyman, like Giovanni." He leaned in. "I'll spend three years and a day as a *paid* dayworker for other bookmakers. Then, I'll be a master, just like the old man. I'll inherit this very shop..." He glanced up at the building and sucked in a quick breath, before looking back at Elisabeth again. "I swear, you'll want for nothing. I'll..."

She lowered her head, shuffling her feet. "It's the best possible scenario for you, living here, learning under Balinus..."

"What's wrong?" His determined tone changed to a calming one now.

Her eyes widened and she looked up. "Nothing. Why?"

"I can tell something weighs heavy on your mind."

"No. Honestly, I am *so* happy for you. You truly deserve all this and more."

"Elisabeth..." His brows drew together. "Tell me what troubles you."

"It's nothing to do with you. It's just...I'm worried this Cato rumor is spinning out of control." A cold chill ran up her spine. "I'm mostly annoyed at myself for not doing more to stop it in the beginning because it already feels too late. It's taking on a life of its own." She paused, lips pursed. "Now, it seems I have no choice but to pretend to be Lord Cathon's daughter while I'm here. At this point, who'd believe me if I said I wasn't? It'd be my word against his and he's the one with all the power. Literally."

"Don't worry about Cato. He'll soon grow bored and move on to some new curiosity. What I worry about is…" He swallowed hard. "…whether or not you will too. Can it *truly* ever be your home here?"

Elisabeth slid her arms around David's waist. "I'll be fine, trust me. It's just a bit of an adjustment." Wrapped in his embrace, she released an appreciative sigh, then bounced on her tippy toes to kiss him goodbye. "As long as you're here, I'm not going anywhere."

David quietly exhaled.

"Well…I mean…I'm going *now*…but I'll see you later." With a goofy giggle, she pulled away. "You know what I mean."

David lowered his chin and raised an eyebrow; a bemused smile on his face as Elisabeth pranced off, glancing over her shoulder and sweetly waving goodbye one more time.

After turning a corner, her walk slowed, realizing how life at home was safe and predictable. With pretty much her entire life planned out, she always did what was expected and proper.

But here?

Here everything was a new and exciting adventure. It was uncharted territory.

And it both thrilled and terrified her.

The truth was…she wanted to be wherever Gaius

Cornelius Aquarius was.

Elisabeth inhaled a warm, savory scent as she strolled past a popular pie shop. It reminded her of Isabeau, which caused a sinking feeling in the pit of her stomach. Skinning and deboning rabbits to cook over an open fire didn't make her heart sing. Elisabeth wanted to stay, but needed something satisfying to fill her days. School seemed out of the question for girls here. Unless one attended a convent school, which is to prepare for marriage and motherhood…or sisterhood.

The sisterhood.

While Elisabeth did want the former someday, right now…she wanted more than a provincial life. She bit down on a smile, resisting the urge to break into song when realizing who that sounded like.

Strolling along the streets, numerous storefronts were decorated with potted flowers, others with hand-painted signs overhead. This section of the city oozed charm. It was the kind of neighborhood you'd dream of opening a little pastel-colored patisserie in.

Elisabeth froze.

How hard would it be to run a small bakery in medieval Paris? She could manage and run the shop while Isabeau did the baking. It could be a lot of fun, *plus* she'd earn her own money here. Elisabeth's heart raced as countless ideas bounced around in her mind.

She then let out a heavy sigh, knowing there was no money to finance any such dream by herself. There was absolutely *no* way she'd go to Cato for help.

After continuing along the crowded cobblestone streets, Elisabeth paused, glancing through the open door of what appeared to be a small tailor or dressmaker's shop. Inside, a nicely dressed woman arranged bolts of fabric.

Elisabeth's shoulders slumped. If she had her jeweled box, everything would be perfect. She could sell the gemstones for money like they'd done in Ancient Rome. But the box had been lost—somewhere near Marmore Falls roughly thirteen-hundred years ago. She had nothing of value anymore. Chin lowered to her chest; Elisabeth shuffled on.

A moment later, she stopped midstride, suddenly knowing what to do. Pulse racing, she darted down a nearby alley. Elisabeth fished the necklace out from behind the neckline of her dress, grabbing hold of the crystal.

Thoughts of home entered her mind.

Home.

Chapter Fourteen

Back in her bedroom, Elisabeth glanced around, trying to remember what day it was. So far, she hadn't done a very good job balancing life between the two timelines. Her brow furrowed. She needed to make more of an effort. A calculus book sat on her desk and she let out a long exhale.

You're not going back until after that test.

She'd put that exam off for…well…centuries, to be perfectly honest.

With the bedroom bathed in moonlight, Elisabeth pulled the blinds shut and removed her medieval dress, hiding it in the closet. After taking the braids out of her hair, she jumped in the shower. The hot water worked its magic, soothing her muscles and seeming to wash every problem away. Afterward, she applied a touch of antibiotic ointment to her scraped chin, dressed in comfy pajamas, parked herself at the desk, and focused on that darn calculus exam.

****

Wednesday morning, Elisabeth smacked the alarm clock beside her bed to turn it off. She bit down on a smile. It was *finally* a fourteenth-century day. She'd stayed home almost a week straight in order to catch up with homework and family life and the truth was, she missed Aquarius terribly. She clamped a hand over her mouth to stifle a squeal before jumping out of bed.

At school yesterday, when the final bell rang, Elisabeth handed in her calculus test and let out a huge sigh of relief. In the corridor, she walked past a bunch of bright-eyed ninth graders taping handmade posters to the walls, advertising auditions for the upcoming school play. Phones dinged and chimed, books thumped as they were tossed into lockers, and a muffled announcement came over the PA system. Elisabeth grabbed her jacket and backpack from the locker and said goodbye to her friends, heading straight to Mrs. Waters' house.

With a wide grin, she ran up the porch steps after spotting the package she'd ordered online waiting beside the welcome mat. Elisabeth grabbed the box and unlocked the front door. As she stepped inside the old mansion and dropped her backpack on the chair, the gears of the clock shifted into place and the bird poked its head out, cuckooing three times.

"*Salve,*" Elisabeth shouted as she put the box on the hall table, slicing the tape with the end of her key to open it.

"*Salve,*" Mrs. Waters sang out from the living room straight ahead. "*Quomodo te habes?*"

Elisabeth's eyes widened.

Inside the box were several bags, each holding an entire pound of whole nutmegs. The little nuts Isabeau told her weighed more than twice their weight in gold were relatively inexpensive and easy to order online.

Now, she could afford almost anything her heart desired in the fourteenth century. "*Maxime!*" Elisabeth replied with a laugh.

Chapter Fifteen

Elisabeth tucked the crystal safely behind the neckline of her parti-colored dress, strolled out of the alleyway, and back onto the main street. She felt for the nutmegs tucked into her drawstring purse, suddenly unsure how to proceed.

Deciding to backtrack to the little tailor's shop, she swallowed a lump in her throat and walked inside. The front of the store appeared to be a simple showroom, where a rainbow of fabrics lined numerous shelves. In the far corner was a tri-folding privacy screen made of carved wood. Flanking an open door leading into the workshop were two dress-form dummies, not so different than those used by tailors today. One displayed a maroon dress with a gray belt. The other held a man's gray tunic embellished with yellow embroidery.

The same woman she'd seen earlier stepped out of the back room. Dressed in sage green, her brown hair was braided and pinned up like two earmuffs. They peeked out from either side of her white headscarf and shoulder-length veil, reminding Elisabeth of Maid Marian from some Robin Hood movie she and Mom had once watched. The woman looked to be in her late twenties and greeted Elisabeth with a polite nod and a warm smile.

"Salve," Elisabeth said while running a hand over

a beautiful blush pink fabric. "Oh, my goodness, this is beautiful."

"To be honest, it's one of my favorites too. Everyone wants vibrant colors but this soft rosy shade is so lovely. The cloth is from Bruges. Dyed with brazilwood, I believe."

Elisabeth continued glancing around the shop. "I'm wondering if you can help me with something."

The woman nodded again while looking Elisabeth's outfit over, her eyes wide with approval. "I will certainly try my best."

"It's a bit of an emergency. I...I need some clothing as quickly as possible. You see, while traveling from Rome, there was a robbery and—"

"Oh!" The woman's head jerked back. "Oh, yes, you must be Lord Cathon's daughter," she said with an understanding nod. "Everyone has heard what happened."

"Gossip travels fast around here, doesn't it?" Elisabeth said with a nervous laugh. "I suppose you also heard all my money was taken?" She pulled a little bag of nutmegs out of her purse, holding it up. "Can you tell me where I can exchange spices for coins first?" Her posture suddenly perked up.

Didn't they barter in the old days?

Well, here she was, smack dab in the middle of the old days.

"Unless you want to trade?" Elisabeth held her breath in anticipation.

The woman moved in closer. "I'd be *more* than happy to make an exchange. What exactly do you need?"

Elisabeth quietly exhaled. That was easier than

expected. "Well, to start…something like that?" She pointed to the display dummy.

"Oh, I see." With a spontaneous laugh, the lady led Elisabeth to an entire wall of fabrics. "I'm Marie, by the way."

Elisabeth smoothed down her dress as she followed Marie across the little shop.

"May I suggest this linen?" She pulled out a bolt of fabric, running her hand along it. "Any other colors in particular? I know you like the light brazilwood pink."

Elisabeth reached for a rich sapphire blue. "I *love* this one."

"Azure, excellent choice." Marie's voice was bubbly. "The wool over here is quite nice too. Five *sous* a yard. Excuse me a moment while I speak to my husband?" With a radiant smile, Marie rushed into the workroom. "Etienne…?" Her voice then became muffled.

A moment later, Marie reappeared, followed by Etienne. He was an imposing man of about thirty, with brown shoulder-length hair, a neatly trimmed beard and mustache. His appearance was more "musketeer" than tailor.

Etienne crossed his arms and leaned against the door frame in an easy-going manner. "I hear you're in a bit of a bind."

"Yes," Elisabeth replied before explaining the situation.

"Not a problem. Leave it with Marie and I. We'll take care of everything," he said with a relaxed smile before returning to his workshop.

Marie spent close to an hour recommending fabrics and styles. "Doublets are very fashionable right now," she explained while showing Elisabeth a rich brown fabric. "Four yards of this cloth will make one with a high collar and puffed sleeves."

Elisabeth bit her lip. *High collar and puffed sleeves?* "No...keep it simple. Nothing too poufy or fancy."

"All right. I think I understand what you want."

"Thank you. You've been incredibly helpful."

A genuine smile lit up the woman's face. "Etienne and I will start right now. If needed, we can do a final adjustment at the very end."

Elisabeth squirmed with excitement.

"Leave it to me, Lady—"

"*Please*, just call me Elisabeth."

"You leave everything to me, Elisabeth."

"Thank you! Should I drop in tomorrow to check how things are going?"

"Mm-hm," Marie said with a crisp nod. "We'll work as fast as possible, without compromising the quality, of course."

"Here..." Elisabeth gave the woman a small bag of nutmegs. "So you know I'm coming back."

"No." Marie handed the bag back, shaking her head. "We are good, honest people here. You can pay us after we take care of everything."

"Really, please..." Elisabeth pressed the nutmegs into the woman's hand again. "Let me pay you now so I don't have to worry about it later." When Marie's mouth dropped, Elisabeth practically bounced out the door on her tippy toes. Bringing spices here to use as currency was the best idea ever!

"Cor meum?" With a bark of laughter, David grabbed her arm.

Elisabeth squealed while spinning playfully around. "Aquarius!" It had been a week since she last saw him. Both arms flew around his neck, eager to hold him tight.

"Well…" Still laughing, David wrapped his arms around Elisabeth in return and kissed the top of her head. "What has *you* so excited?"

"You," she said with a silly grin after pulling away. "I wasn't expecting to see you here."

"Clearly." David turned his head, pausing to glance inside the little shop she'd just walked out of. The display dress was visible from the street. "You're certainly making your way through town at a leisurely pace."

"Yep. I was looking at a bunch of stuff. Everything is so different here." Elisabeth cleared her throat and pulled David by the hand, away from the shop. "Where's Nicolas?" She figured it best to start calling Balinus that in order to avoid a slip-up in public.

David's posture relaxed as they strolled down the street. "He's staying a bit longer to work on his codex."

They soon left the city behind, following the dirt road leading to the little village. With slow, easy breaths, they walked in comfortable silence, listening to songbirds and buzzing insects. Tall grasses and wildflowers in the meadow alongside the road danced in the breeze, dotting the lush green landscape with shades of yellow, orange, purple, and white.

Before long, they came upon a heavy-set man with brown hair and a scruffy beard, leading a chestnut horse by the reins. "Care to buy an old mare?"

Elisabeth let out a shallow sigh. It reminded her of Dandy, the horse she'd come to love in Scotland all those years ago. "She's lovely." Her smile then wavered. Part of her wanted to say *yes*, but she didn't know the first thing about caring for a horse. "Sorry, not today."

"You sure?" A huge smile spread across the man's face. "She's not the kind to keep you up all night."

Her eyes narrowed in confusion. "Do horses normally keep people up all night?"

"Only a real *night*mare," he said with a belly laugh as he continued toward the city.

David and Elisabeth looked at each other wide-eyed before bursting into laughter.

She let out a satisfied sigh as the bubbling stream made its way over rocks, winding through the countryside. "This bridge is so pretty. Look at its reflection on the water. Don't you love how the arch makes a perfect circle?"

David grinned. "Yes, it's…" His brows then squished together and he stopped walking to softly touch her chin. "Your scrapes could not have healed in the short time since you left the bookstore. You've taken the elixir again?"

"No," Elisabeth replied with a hesitant shake of her head. "It healed on its own." She stepped back. "After leaving the bookshop, I went home. I…I've kind of been there for the last week," she said with a grimace.

David offered her a weak smile. "That long?"

"I…" She fumbled for the right words. "I missed you terribly, but I needed to study and write that calculus exam I've been putting off." Elisabeth fidgeted with the Hercules love knot on her wrist. "I'm trying my best to figure out how to balance two different worlds, so promise you won't make me feel guilty about going home because—"

David's shoulders dropped. "If I've *ever* made you feel guilty about going home, I assure you it was unintentional. By the gods, you must know by now I'd...no, it's nothing like that, it's...something isn't right," he said in an uncertain tone.

Elisabeth's head flinched back slightly. "What do you mean?"

Instead of crossing the stone bridge, David left the road. "It will be quieter here than at home. I need to think." Leading the way, he walked down the grassy bank to the water's edge, following the stream a short distance to where it curved.

After passing a handful of oak trees, they stopped beneath the largest. From here, Elisabeth saw it was actually two trees. Their trunks had grown so close they'd entwined together, each one supporting the other while growing into the most majestic oak of them all.

David rubbed the back of his neck, pacing, saying nothing for several long minutes.

"You're freaking me out, Aquarius. What's wrong?"

"I think we've overlooked something." He turned to face her but kept moving about, unable to settle. "Is that your plan? To alternate days between here and—?"

"Yes." She took a deep breath to calm herself. "It was the *only* solution I could come up with...so I could stay here with you." Her hands trembled. "But I didn't want to tell you until I had all the details figured out because I—"

David's arms curled over his head and a look of dread washed over him. His shaking hands then cupped Elisabeth's face. "Please tell me you have access to the elixir?"

Her eyes widened. "I'm trying everything to *stop* you from taking the elixir."

"It's not for me." He gave her a pained stare. "It's for you."

A cold chill ran up Elisabeth's spine. "Why?"

"It won't work." His chest caved in. "*Cor meum*, dividing your time won't work. Not long term."

She rocked slightly. "Wh…what do you mean it won't work?"

David reached for her fingers. "You'll age twice as fast as me," he whispered.

Chapter Sixteen

It felt like she'd been punched in the gut. Elisabeth opened her mouth to say something, but no words came out.

David was right.

It was so obvious.

Although they'd last been together an hour ago at Balinus' bookshop, in reality, she'd been home a week. That meant she'd aged seven days to his one hour.

"If you alternate days…" David's voice quaked. "…in two years, you'll be four years older. In five years, you'll have aged ten."

Elisabeth's breathing slowed, wondering how to fix this dilemma.

Of course, the plan wasn't perfect, she knew that, but still…this was unexpected. David pulled her into a tight hug and she sagged against him, burying her face in his chest. "Everything will be all right," she finally said with a dejected sigh. "We'll think of something."

David slumped down onto the grass, sitting cross-legged. "I think the elixir is the only way."

Elisabeth answered with a small nod. "I can use it to slow down the aging process. I guess we should look on the bright side. At least we *have* that option."

David's gaze darted up at her.

"The irony, eh?" With a nervous laugh, Elisabeth flopped down in front of him. "*Me* taking the elixir may be the only thing that stops *you* from taking it." She leaned in and gave him a half-hearted shrug. "With help from either Nicolas or *future* you, we'll figure this out. I'll do what I have to do, so stop worrying so much." Elisabeth then rose playfully to her knees, wrapped her arms around his neck, and pushed him onto his back, falling on top of him. "You're not getting rid of me that easily, Gaius Cornelius Aquarius."

With a bark of laughter, David twisted around, cradling her head in the crook of his elbow beneath him. "Promise?"

"Promise," Elisabeth whispered in between kisses.

When David stretched out onto his back, one arm still wrapped around Elisabeth, she nestled against him in the soft grass.

"Hey, Romeo…" She let out a heavy sigh. "We've always known this wasn't going to be an easy task…realigning the stars ourselves."

His eyes twinkled with mischief while staring at her. "Romeo?"

A bemused smile spread across Elisabeth's face. "Romeo and Juliet, the most famous star-crossed lovers of them all. I studied the book at school last year."

"Really? How'd *they* realign the stars?"

When Elisabeth looked at David with a pout, he let out an amused snort. "Ah. Say no more."

"Yeah, bad example. Tragic, really."

He raised an eyebrow. "Well, now I'm curious."

"Apparently, it's based on a true story that…" Elisabeth gasped. "…took place in Verona in the fourteenth century." She let out a spontaneous laugh. "Oh my gosh, what are the odds? Same period and where everyone here believes I'm from."

David leaned in, kissing her forehead.

"There's these two feuding families, the Montagues and the Capulets. One night, the Capulets throw a fancy party and some of the young Montague men sneak in. While there, Romeo *Montague* falls head over heels in love with Juliet—"

"Let me guess," he interrupted with a grin. "*Capulet*?"

"Yep." Elisabeth reached out, brushing hair from David's eyes. "Juliet's father has already arranged for her to be married to some rich old guy she doesn't love. But…Juliet's nurse absolutely adores her and *she* arranges for Romeo and Juliet to secretly marry the next day."

"The day after they met?" David asked in an incredulous voice.

"The very next day," she said, nodding her head. "They run away and elope, but later, a fight breaks out on the street between some of the Capulets and Montagues over the fact the Montagues crashed the party. In the scuffle, Juliet's cousin is killed by Romeo."

"That *is* tragic," David whispered while holding his hand out.

Elisabeth lifted her fingers to meet his, their entwined hands then resting against his chest.

"Because of this, Romeo is banished from Verona. Juliet is, of course, beside herself with grief. She loved her cousin, but she's also madly in love with Romeo. She sneaks off to see the friar who just married them, begging for help. He comes up with a plan and tells Juliet to agree to marry the old guy. However, the night before her wedding, she's to drink a potion the friar gives her. It will make her *appear* dead. Afterward, she'll be laid to rest in the family tomb."

David's lips were slightly parted as he listened intently.

"Meanwhile, the friar promises to send word to Romeo. He will come and get Juliet. Then, they'll run away together and live happily ever after."

David raised his eyebrows, hanging on Elisabeth's every word.

"The night before her wedding, Juliet drinks the potion to fake her death. However, Romeo doesn't get the message from the friar in time. Instead, he hears that Juliet has died and, of course, believes it to be true. Romeo rushes to the Capulet crypt and sees her there, seemingly dead. Overcome with grief, he drinks an entire bottle of poison he'd bought from an apothecary along the way."

David's brow furrowed as he scrutinized her with an intense gaze. "And you thought Orpheus and Eurydice's ending was depressing?"

"It was," she said with a playful swat before sitting up, becoming more animated. "Juliet wakes up moments later and sees Romeo…dead from the poison. She grabs his dagger and…" Elisabeth extended her arms, pretending to plunge an imaginary knife into her heart before collapsing onto David, who was stretched out on the grass. "She kills herself," Elisabeth whispered, still flopped over, pretending to be dead. "The end."

"The end?" David said with a high-pitched voice before sitting up and tickling Elisabeth, causing her to burst into giggles. "They're both dead?"

She offered him a bemused smile. "Yep. It's the

most famous love story of them all."

David shook his head while looking at Elisabeth. "I am unmoved by them."

Her eyes widened. "WHAT? Why?"

"When Eurydice died, Orpheus traveled past the gates of hell into the underworld, defeated Cerberus, and came face to face with Pluto, the god of death himself. Then, he begged Pluto to allow him to bring Eurydice back to the world of the living. Moved by the *incredible* act of love, Pluto agreed…albeit conditionally."

"Yes, but…" Elisabeth's tummy fluttered, thinking back to that moonlit night at Aurelius' villa when David entertained her with tales of Orpheus and Eurydice, Cupid and Psyche. "It's totally far-fetched in comparison."

"Perhaps, but it doesn't change the fact that if Romeo had not acted in such an impulsive manner, he'd have realized Juliet was not dead. They took the easy way out…both of them. Orpheus and Eurydice attempted to rearrange the stars. Romeo and Juliet…they foolishly killed themselves in haste."

"But that's *why* it's a tragic love story."

"Do you not think it would have been a thousand times more tragic for Romeo to live an entire lifetime *without* Juliet, as Orpheus did without Eurydice?" David let out a deep sigh. "And so, it is Orpheus who earns my sympathy, not Romeo."

Elisabeth's posture stiffened. "Well, when you put it like that…" Head cocked to the side, for a split-second her breathing was suspended as she imagined David—wandering the earth for centuries, trying to right some tragic wrong.

Her heart sank when that familiar haunting question took over.

Why?

Elisabeth turned away, hiding her face.

Had she finally figured out the reason?

Chapter Seventeen

David stood and stretched before pulling Elisabeth to her feet. "We should get going."

"Did you know Romeo and Juliet were only, like, fourteen or fifteen years old?" After Elisabeth picked colorful wildflowers growing along the bank of the creek, she noticed a huge, overgrown rose bush with arching branches covered in pale pink blooms. "Something like that, anyway."

The fragrance wafted toward her.

Not terribly thorny, Elisabeth managed to bend several canes back and forth to break a few stems off, trying to focus her thoughts before fear took over. She held her bouquet out to David, deciding it was pretty enough to bring home for the dinner table. "Which ones do you like best?"

"What *flowers* do I like best?" David offered Elisabeth an incredulous look that caused her to burst into laughter again. "I can honestly say nobody has ever asked me that before."

"Well…which ones?"

David bit his lips to hide a grin, pondering the question before pointing at the deep purple bellflowers that had been growing in a heap beneath a nearby tree. "Those, I suppose." He paused to examine Elisabeth. "And you?"

"Oh…definitely the roses. That blush pink is my

favorite color."

"I used to have to pick roses for Domina. When they were in season, the oil was used at the fullery to perfume the laundry and…" David put an arm around Elisabeth's shoulder, continuing his story as they made their way home.

"Thank goodness you're back. I've stubbed my toe on that blasted trunk one too many times," Perenelle said as she marched into the screens passage when they walked in the front door. "David, I need you to carry it upstairs right now before I lose my mind." Her gaze darted over his shoulder, onto the street. "Oh, there's Pierre. I'll get him to help you move it." She nudged her way outside, past David and Elisabeth, who stood wide-eyed, watching her chase after a muscular man walking down the street. "Pierre? Yoo-hoo, Pierre," she called out in a sing-song voice.

Pierre, a middle-aged man with non-descript looks, came into the house, grabbed one end of the trunk, and helped David carry it upstairs. He then nodded in acknowledgement when Perenelle thanked him and walked back outside, continuing on his way without having uttered a single word the entire time.

"Not very talkative, was he?" David whispered to Elisabeth with an amused snort after Perenelle marched back into the great hall.

"The strong, silent type." She fidgeted with the flowers in her hand. "Guess I've decided to keep the new clothes."

David's smile wavered. "Well, I suppose you do need *something* to wear." He let out a long, low sigh. "I only wish they hadn't been from Cato."

"I know." Her brows pulled in. "Me too."

"But…it seems everyone already believes you to be his daughter." David shook his head. "You were right. '*Fama, malum qua non aliud velocius ullum*,'" he recited while frowning.

There is no evil that travels faster than a rumor.

At that moment, Colette skipped through the back door. A wide grin spread across her face while looking at David. "You *have* to see what I just found."

His posture perked up. "What did you find?"

"I'll show you." She grabbed David's hand, bouncing backward while dragging him outside. "You are going to be *so* excited once you see."

When Elisabeth started to follow, Colette's head jerked back. "Oh…*you* do not want to see this," she said loudly. "A grass snake just had about fifty babies and they're all squirming around in a big, heaping pile."

David burst into laughter before turning around to give Elisabeth a playful wink.

"Snakes?" She wrinkled her nose. "Yeah, I'll stay here and put these flowers in water instead."

As David and Colette disappeared out back, Elisabeth's smile wavered, thinking back to when she nearly died from the asp bite. A chill ran up her spine recollecting the countless *other* ways she'd cheated death: the encounter with a rabid dog, a witch trial in Stonehaven, arrows hissing by her at Dunnottar, escaping from Hayri's men at Marmore Falls, Cato holding a sword to her throat, trapped in the arena as Mount Vesuvius erupted…

Elisabeth closed her eyes, realizing her luck was probably going to run out eventually. Her chest hitched, thoughts racing back to Mahone Bay—to that encounter with David Perrier in the gazebo before she'd ended up in Ancient Rome.

"For hundreds of years I have lived, but lived in hell. I'm condemned to this prison of my own making until the day everything can be made right again," he had said.

With trembling hands, she laid the bouquet on the sideboard. Was her *death* what he was attempting to undo? Elisabeth squeezed her eyes shut, knowing it made perfect sense.

But wait…

She rubbed her forehead.

Mrs. Waters is alive.

Elisabeth's chest tightened. She reached for her crystal, unable to wait another moment to find out what had happened—or rather, what was *going* to happen.

****

Elisabeth let out an appreciative sigh while peeking out from beneath her umbrella. One of the prettiest sights to behold is a blazing sugar maple in October. Those fleeting few days when the leaves turn shades of orange so bright the entire tree glows as if lit from within, are nothing short of magical. The leaves clinging to the tree on Mrs. Waters' front lawn danced from the branches in the gentle rain. Several let go, floating softly to the ground. They blanketed the brick path from the driveway, coordinating perfectly with the pumpkins decorating the front porch.

Elisabeth paused, taking a moment to appreciate the architecture of the beautiful old house. As picturesque as Mahone Bay was, this home was the loveliest of them all.

The best part?

It was a hidden gem tucked off a quiet side road

that nobody really knew about, even as it discreetly overlooked the harbor.

Painted soft yellow with white gingerbread trim, the attention to detail inside and out was extraordinary. A single glance told you whoever built it did so with love. It had the same romantic characteristics as numerous homes built in the 1800s by seafaring captains for their brides. From the Maritimes to New England, many of them still stand today, often converted into dreamy bed-and-breakfasts.

Elisabeth sucked in a quick breath, suddenly realizing *exactly* who built this house.

Her hand covered her mouth. Mrs. Water's may reside here at present, but David constructed it well over a hundred years ago. He'd said as much but she'd been too overwhelmed to grasp the significance at the time.

Her stomach fluttered, seeing the house, *really* seeing the house, as if for the first time. From the double front doors made of a beautiful dark wood with stained glass inserts, to the cozy wrap-around porch with rocking chairs and wicker furniture. He might have built it over a century ago, but thanks to the steady stream of painters, caretakers, and gardeners Elisabeth had seen over the years tending to the property, it remained in perfect condition.

She ran up the veranda steps two at a time, leaned the umbrella against the buttery yellow clapboard, and fished the house key out of her pocket.

Her eyes narrowed after opening the front door.

The foyer was dark.

The house felt empty.

"*Salve…?*" Elisabeth called out in an uncertain

tone while stepping inside. She dropped her jacket on a chair. "Mrs. Waters?"

Everything was quiet and still.

Elisabeth glanced around.

"Felis?"

She flicked on a light switch, realizing even the cat was nowhere to be found.

When the clock suddenly sprang to life, Elisabeth let out a sharp scream.

Biting her nails, she tiptoed toward the dark living room. "Hello?" Her eyes widened while standing outside the doorway.

The room was filled with strange shadows, looking like ghosts of days gone by. Her heart raced when a boney finger tapped softly at the window pane. Elisabeth shook her head. "It's only a branch," she muttered. The spooky Halloween decorations around town were obviously messing with her. After turning on a nearby lamp to illuminate the room, her posture stiffened. The strange silhouettes were from dust sheets covering the furniture.

"Mrs. Waters?"

Hurrying back to the foyer, she noticed a note on the hall table.

Elisabeth,
Had to dash out.
Nothing to worry about. Felis is with me.
See you tomorrow.
Yours,
Elisabeth—hahahaha

With a shaky laugh, Elisabeth's gaze drifted to the top of the staircase. Her head then tilted to the side, and she walked closer, running fingers along the polished oak banister. The elixir of life was needed, but neither Sissi nor David was present.

Elisabeth climbed to the top of the stairs, slowly opening the first door she came to. Inside the study, she flicked on a lamp while the rain pitter-pattered against the window. Like the rest of the house, the décor in this room was classic, elegant. The dark paneled walls, floor-to-ceiling bookshelves, and leather furniture gave it an air of sophistication. Elisabeth rubbed her bottom lip while heading straight to the desk, rummaging through one drawer after another. She pushed papers and trinkets aside, trying to find a bottle of elixir. Wringing her hands, she looked around the room, noticing a side table between the two leather chairs had a drawer. She hurried over, searching the contents.

Nothing.

She inspected the bookshelves, the coffee table, the fireplace mantle…

Elisabeth's breath burst in and out, realizing Balinus no longer took the elixir. How long would David be gone? Last time, it had been five years.

What if there's no elixir here?

Elisabeth rushed out of the room and down the hallway, dashing into the guest suite where she'd previously showered and changed. She went straight to the nightstand closest to the door.

The drawer was empty.

With a whimper, she checked the opposite bedside table.

Still no elixir.

Elisabeth walked into the hallway. At the end of the long corridor, opposite the way back to the library, a beautifully arranged vignette caught her attention. An antique console table held two lamps, and what looked like a very expensive (and very old) Chinese porcelain bowl as the centerpiece. She crept closer, spotting the now familiar photograph. Her eyes prickled with tears while picking the photo up once again. She let out a subdued laugh. The colorful medieval clothing David wore in the picture finally made sense.

The beautifully candid shot appeared as if David had swept her off her feet the moment before it was snapped. He smiled at her rather than the camera, with a look of complete adoration on his face. Dressed in a blush-colored gown, Elisabeth had one arm around his neck and the other stretched playfully to the side in a moment of excitement. With her head tilted up, she appeared to be in the midst of laughter.

Elisabeth rubbed a hand against her heart, not understanding why the photo made her tummy flutter. She put it back down, gazing out the window, before shuffling closer. The view beckoned.

The gorgeous treed property sloped gently downhill. Houses along the main road backed onto Sissi's land and from where Elisabeth stood, she could see Mahone Harbour spread out before her. It was a completely new vantage point. Her lips parted, watching a fishing vessel sail by, gliding along the narrow waterway, heading home from the open sea. She released an appreciative sigh, eyeing the showy foliage across the bay.

As Elisabeth edged closer to the window, she bumped the table. Something clattered, rolling back and forth rhythmically inside the decorative bowl. When glancing down to see what she'd knocked over, her head jerked back, watching as a tiny vial of elixir came

172

to rest.

With a bark of laughter, Elisabeth picked it up, slipped it into her pocket, and raced back down the corridor. Downstairs, she pulled on her jacket, turned out the lights, and locked the door. After grabbing the umbrella from the porch, Elisabeth ran to her mom's car. She'd let her borrow it today because of the rain. While pulling out of the driveway, a *great* idea popped into her head.

She'd need to stop at the grocery store first.

Chapter Eighteen

The next morning, Elisabeth returned to the fourteenth century with the elixir tucked safely in her drawstring purse. For a moment, her eyes narrowed in confusion. The feeling was similar to when you forget where you left off in a book, but when you pick it up again, you're pulled right back into that world as if you'd never left.

A grin spread across her face, watching as David and Colette disappeared out back.

Colette was bringing him to see baby snakes.

Elisabeth grabbed the flowers she'd placed on the sideboard, making her way into the great hall. "Do you have a vase for these? I thought you might like a bouquet for the table."

Perenelle walked to a hutch, grabbing a pitcher from the shelf. "It's lovely this time of year when everything is blooming, isn't it?"

Elisabeth took a deep, savoring breath. "It sure is."

"Here. I wish I had something fancier. You can get water from the rain barrel at the side of the…" The old woman's eyes bulged, staring at the flowers in Elisabeth's hand. The color drained from her face. "Throw those in the fire at once," she said with a raised voice.

Stunned for a moment, Elisabeth gave her an incredulous stare but immediately did as she was told.

Perenelle watched the fire, making sure the flames consumed the entire bouquet. "Don't you know dwale when you see it?" she snapped.

"What's...?" Elisabeth nervously shook out her hands. "What's dwale?"

Once the bouquet was nothing but ashes, Perenelle let out a huge breath and put the pitcher back. She then looked at her with a pained expression. "Don't be swayed by appearances, my dear. Those pretty purple flowers will kill you as reliably as any sword. Eating one leaf will kill a grown man. Every single part is poisonous."

Elisabeth's breath hitched.

"You didn't find them anywhere around the house, did you?"

"No, but there are *lots* growing by the bridge."

"That's why I don't like Colette over there. The plant later produces plump, juicy dark berries. They look like cherries and taste as sweet. We..." Her bottom lip began to tremble. "We almost lost Colette when she was younger. That child tasted but one before Beau-Beau slapped it out of her hand." She let out a shallow sigh.

"I am *so* sorry." Elisabeth's voice cracked. "I had no idea the flowers were poisonous. I swear, had I known, I'd *never* have picked a bouquet of them."

"I know. It's all right." Perenelle walked closer and hugged Elisabeth. "I apologize for snapping at you, dear."

****

Dressed in a soft white nightgown she'd found in the trunk, Elisabeth's eyelids grew heavy, listening to gentle rain fall while waiting for everyone to drift off to sleep. Earlier, Balinus had mentioned he planned to stay up a bit later to read in his study. This was her chance to speak to him in private—about David.

She lay on the little pallet in the girls' bedroom, surprised by how comfy the makeshift bed was. Overcome with nightmares about Mt. Vesuvius' eruption the previous night here, Elisabeth hadn't even noticed until now.

The mattress was stuffed with straw, cedar shavings, and lavender. Apparently, the latter two items were added to drive insects away. They also provided a welcome scent, toning down the barn-like smell of the hay.

Elisabeth glanced across the dark room when Colette finally stopped tossing and turning. The straw crackled with every movement. A few minutes later, Isabeau's breathing became shallow, suggesting both girls had dozed off.

Elisabeth stole out of bed, grabbing her blue drawstring purse before tiptoeing downstairs. She crept through the great hall, past the fire pit. Embers from the cooking fire glowed in the darkness. She then tapped quietly on the old man's study door.

"Enter," he said in a warm tone.

Elisabeth opened the wooden door and poked her head into the room. Lit with both flickering candles and oil lamps, it was surprisingly cozy. "Can I speak to you for a few minutes?" she whispered.

Balinus, seated at a large desk beneath the shuttered window, looked over his shoulder. A slow smile built. "I do not know. Can you?"

Elisabeth let out an appreciative sigh. "I need to speak to you privately," she said with a grin.

"Of course, my dear. Come in."

The room had white-washed walls and wooden beams. A large rug made of tightly braided rushes filled most of the floor space, adding an element of warmth to the earthen floor. A cluttered work table sat straight ahead, nestled between two overflowing bookshelves.

Elisabeth's eyes widened, noticing the colorful tapestry hanging above the table. On a background of red, blue, and green threads, a white unicorn with a ridiculously long horn sat beside a young girl in a forest. Chuckling, Elisabeth pointed to it as the door slowly swung closed on its own. "That reminds me of Colette."

Balinus let out an amused snort. "That child has *me* half-convinced she's going to find and tame a unicorn someday." He then pulled a wooden stool out from under the table. "Come. Sit."

Elisabeth crossed the room and sat. She closed her eyes and took a deep breath, enjoying the fragrance that filled the space. "Why does it smell *so* good in here?"

Balinus' posture relaxed and he pointed at the rug. "Perenelle insists all the woven mats in the house have lavender and chamomile added. The perfume always seems to linger the longest in here."

She took another deep breath. "I absolutely love it."

Balinus nodded in agreement before tilting his head to the side. "What's on your mind, my dear?"

Her brows squished together and she fished some nutmegs out of the bag, unsure where to begin. She then leaned forward, placing a handful on Balinus' desk. "Can you give these to Aquarius?"

His eyes widened. "Why?"

"Well…I know as an apprentice he earns no money yet…and I just thought it would be nice for him to—"

"These are not needed, my dear girl," the old man said in a soothing voice. "Aquarius has everything he needs to succeed. He's learning a trade, has a roof over his head, food in his belly…and even an adoptive family to love and support him."

Elisabeth placed a hand over her heart. "I know, believe me, I know and am forever grateful, but…" She teared up. "Aquarius has never had *anything* of his own before. Even his clothes are borrowed from Giovanni. I thought if you paid him one time, with these, he'd be able to treat himself to something nice, or save a little nest egg. I don't know what…but he deserves it. These are just spices I brought from home once I discovered how much they're worth here." Elisabeth looked down. "However, I don't want him to know they're from me."

Balinus raised an eyebrow.

"Today, he just seemed so proud of what he's accomplishing. If I swoop in and toss him little things from the future, like I did with the jewels in Ancient Rome, it sort of takes away everything he's working toward. I don't want to be—"

"All right," Balinus interrupted with a small nod. "I understand what you're saying."

She let out a sigh of relief. "You do?"

"Yes…but I will only give him half of this." Balinus set half aside, handing the rest of the nutmegs back. He then cleared his throat. "How many of these do you have?"

A wide grin spread across Elisabeth's face. "Heaps of them! You want any? I've got tons and can easily get more," she added with a snort. "They're completely affordable at home and found in practically every kitchen."

Balinus rubbed his eyebrow. "Restraint, my dear girl. I advise you to use those with restraint. You do not want to draw unwanted attention to yourself. They are…" He paused, seeming to weigh his words. "They are worth a fortune."

"I know, but I don't think me spending or exchanging them will raise any questions…under the circumstances." Elisabeth twisted at her nightgown sleeve. "It seems the entire city already believes I'm Lord Cathon's daughter."

"Still…" His head cocked to the side. "You don't want to step on the toes of the *épiceries*."

Her head flinched back slightly. "Huh?"

"The spicers. My advice, although you did not ask for it, is to use them sparingly."

Elisabeth frowned. "But wouldn't it be *charitable* to spread these around to support little shops and merchants?"

"In theory, yes—"

"They're as good as gold to them."

"And that is the problem." He let out a dejected sigh and leaned back in his chair. "That's just my advice. You may take it or leave it however you see fit."

Elisabeth replied with a hesitant nod and then tugged at her ear. "There's one other reason I needed to talk to you. We've, uh…we've run into a little…*time-travel* problem." She whispered the last part.

The old man's posture perked up while listening.

"My plan was to spend one day here, one day at home, alternating the days. However, it seems that won't work out as intended. I can't believe I didn't see it earlier but…I'm aging twice as fast by doing that. Really, I might even technically be eighteen or nineteen by now! I've no idea."

Balinus' breath caught. "Oh…my…yes. I suppose you're right." He let out a heavy sigh. "If you're asking me if I have some elixir, the answer is no. As you've learned, I no longer take it. But, regardless of my personal…*evolution*, it is now almost impossible to procure. Unfortunately, the elixir is becoming one of those forgotten mysteries, lost over time." His voice suddenly seemed strained. "*That* is in part why I am quite concerned as to how Cato has been obtaining it— or rather, I fear, a version of it."

Elisabeth gasped. "You mean, even *you* can't get it anymore?"

"It was hard to find a thousand years ago. Now…?" His voice trailed off.

"But, you're…" She gave him a dazed look. "You're *Nicolas Flamel*."

The old man's eyebrows squished together. "Is there something I should know…about *myself*?"

She rubbed a hand through her hair, debating whether or not to tell him *who* he was.

Chapter Nineteen

Elisabeth softly shook her head and then leaned closer. "In the future, you're pretty much considered to be the only person who figured out how to make the elixir of life. I mean, if you research the philosopher's stone, it's *your* name that comes up. *Nicolas Flamel*," she said, making air quotes with her fingers. "You're kind of famous."

Balinus opened his mouth to say something, but no words came out.

"Despite all that, *that's* not exactly what I wanted to ask." She offered him a weak smile, pulling the vial out of her purse and handing it to him. "I actually have some. The problem is I have no idea how much to take."

He rubbed his ear, pondering the question, and then put a minuscule amount onto the tip of his baby finger. "In your case, not more than this...approximately every seven days." He scratched his cheek, thinking it over. "Yes, that should be sufficient." With a curt nod, he tapped the red powder back into the vial before returning it to Elisabeth. "You want to *appear* to age at a normal pace, after all."

"Yes, exactly. Thank you." Elisabeth stood up and tucked the elixir into her purse. "Oh, one more thing. Do you happen to have any scraps of parchment I could write on? Paper from home is a bit...different."

Balinus shuffled through the objects on his desk and then glanced around his study. "If you come by the bookshop tomorrow, I'm certain we can find something to your satisfaction there."

Elisabeth leaned in, giving the old man a quick hug. "Thank you so much for everything."

He patted her back. "Happy to help, my dear."

****

Elisabeth did not consider herself to be a late sleeper, yet she was always last to awaken in the Flamel household. Everyone else rose at dawn. While browsing through the chest of clothing, she frowned, realizing David was, no doubt, already long gone for the day with Balinus.

Her posture perked up when slipping into a linen gray dress with blue and yellow embroidery along the scooped neckline. Blue ribbon was laced decoratively along the sleeves, and also down the back, which created the look similar to a corset. The result was an extremely flattering shape. Compared to what everyone else here wore, the dresses Cato sent were on a whole other level. She couldn't help being swept away by them. Surely, they were the medieval equivalent of *haute couture*.

Elisabeth strolled into the great hall. Her gaze wandered over to the workbench, noticing the pie Isabeau had baked for Giovanni still sat there—waiting for him. After helping herself to some bread and honey, plus a small bowl of raspberries, she took a seat at the table to eat breakfast.

"Good morning," Isabeau said, walking in a few minutes later, balancing a basket filled with clusters of delicate white flowers on one hip. Her mouth fell open while glancing at Elisabeth's breakfast. "You eating berries like *that*?"

Elisabeth's head jerked back. "Like what?"

"Raw! You will get sick."

Elisabeth's eyes widened while staring down at the raspberries she'd washed herself. "What?"

Isabeau plunked the flower basket onto the work table, walked over to Elisabeth, and took her bowl of raspberries away. "You should *never* eat raw fruits and vegetables. You bad as Colette." She shook her head.

Elisabeth sat speechless.

"Colette ate half a dwale berry once, thinking it was cherry. Slept through the night and entire day." Isabeau's posture slumped. "Ten will kill a grown man."

"But…" Elisabeth lifted her brows, pointing at the bowl in Isabeau's hand. "Those are just raspberries!"

"I made raspberry compote if you want fruit." She walked out of the great hall and into the pantry.

With a dazed look, Elisabeth watched as Isabeau marched back and placed a spoon, and a small bowl of what looked like raspberry puree, on the table.

As Elisabeth grabbed the spoon, a wide grin spread across her face. "Actually…this looks good."

"It is." Isabeau let out a huge breath and grabbed a bunch of the flowers she'd gathered. "I can't believe you eating raw fruit," she mumbled to herself while pulling the tiny white blooms off the stems, dropping them into a bowl.

"I was wondering…?" Elisabeth leaned forward. "Are you very busy today, because I have a *great* idea?"

Isabeau looked up. "I making *sambocade* this

183

morning. But…" Her voice filled with wonder. "What your idea?"

"I thought you might like to try a new recipe later. It's one of my favourites," she said, licking her spoon of raspberry compote clean.

"Really?"

"Yes, but I need to go out and get the ingredients first because they're *quite* rare." In truth, she was bringing them from home since some were still centuries away from being discovered here—like chocolate.

Isabeau's eyes widened. "Ohhhh…exotic ingredients fit for king?"

Elisabeth let out a belly laugh. "I guess you could say that." She hummed while finishing her breakfast, then grabbed her purse filled with nutmegs, and bid Isabeau farewell, practically dancing out the front door—where she nearly tripped over the wooden wagon.

"Colette?" she called loudly.

The little girl suddenly appeared, holding a tiny kitten under her chin. "Look!" Her voice cracked with emotion.

Elisabeth released an appreciative sigh and moved closer, stroking the kitten's gray head. "Oh my gosh, it's adorable."

"I know!" Colette squealed. "There are three more in Colin's barn."

"Awww, you should probably bring that sweet baby back to its mother, though."

"I will. I want to show Percy first."

"Hey…can I borrow your wagon?"

"That depends." Colette's face radiated with an

unknown thrill as she gazed at Elisabeth. "Will you get me a unicorn?" she asked with a cheeky grin.

Elisabeth offered her a bemused smile. "I'm borrowing your wagon." She grabbed the handle. "You'll be glad I did. Trust me."

"Wait!" With one hand, Colette picked up her wooden sword from the cart, sheathing it behind her belt. She then grabbed the rag doll, tucking it under one arm, all while holding the tiny animal against her chest. "All right, you can use it now." She turned and strolled around the side of the house, toward the stable, murmuring sweet nothings to the kitten.

A rolling mist moved through the quaint village, quickly being burned off by the morning sun. A man drove by in a horse-drawn wagon. The wheels clickety-clacked as he sped along the dirt road, which reminded Elisabeth of the beat to a familiar song.

That song became stuck in her head.

Humming the tune, she reached the bridge, making her way toward the city while being serenaded by birds. Elisabeth took a deep, satisfied breath and looked around. The dirt road was pretty much empty so...she burst into song, stopping only when the heavy-set man, pulling the horse that looked like Dandy, neared her on the road.

"Care to buy an old mare today?" he asked.

Elisabeth stopped to pat the gentle horse, letting out a shallow sigh. "She's really lovely. I'm tempted...but not today. Sorry."

"You sure?" A huge smile spread across the man's bearded face. "She's very sweet-tempered. Never gets depressed."

Elisabeth's brows squished together. "Do horses

185

get depressed?"

"Oh, some horses have a terrible tale of *whoa*," he said with dramatic flair.

She groaned, and then burst into laughter before continuing to the city, pulling the wooden wagon behind her.

Perhaps it *would* be nice to have a horse to ride to town on.

****

"Hello," Elisabeth sang out while entering the bookshop, pulling the little cart inside with her.

David and Balinus, standing side by side, looked up from behind the long work table.

The slow smile building on David's face made her heart skip beats.

"Good day," Balinus said. "Parchment?"

"Please!"

"We'll find you some scraps." The old man put his hand on David's shoulder. "You can show her what you're doing first, if you like."

"I've learned how to make ink."

"Really?" Elisabeth crept closer.

Balinus slipped away, climbing the steps to the little loft. He settled in at the writing desk, dipped a feather quill into a clamshell holding ink, and began writing.

David's attention turned to a small wooden bowl in front of him. Inside was a blueish-green powder.

"What's that?" Elisabeth asked.

"Green vitriol." He walked over to the shelf, selected a small pot, and brought it over to the work table, but then paused to examine it. "I forget what this is for," he said, trying to suppress a grin.

"It's gum Arabic. To make the ink less runny," Balinus answered matter-of-factly without looking up from his work.

"Right. Thank you, Uncle."

Elisabeth and David exchanged secret smiles.

"Next, I take oak galls..." He grabbed what looked like three round nuts, wrapped them in a cloth, smashing them with a small hammer. "...and grind them as finely as I can."

Elisabeth leaned closer, placing both elbows on the table as she watched him work across from her.

David looked up, wide-eyed, "Did you know wasps are hatched from these? They're found on oak tree limbs."

She wrinkled her nose. "Ew. That's kind of gross."

He chuckled while pouring the oak gall contents into a mortar, using a pestle to turn it into a fine powder. "Then, I add rainwater."

"*Rain*water? Is that followed by 'eye of newt and toe of frog?'"

His brows squished together while using a small stick to stir the ingredients. "Eye of newt?"

"I'd swear you're making magic potions in here, not ink," Elisabeth said with an amused snort.

He glanced up and winked playfully, causing her heartbeat to quicken again.

When Elisabeth's cheeks heated, she questioned if he wasn't concocting a *love* potion.

After stirring in green vitriol, the ink immediately blackened. David added the gum to thicken it up. "Now, we leave it for two days." With a satisfied smile, he set it aside and then leaned across the table. His gaze wandered over to Balinus before discreetly reaching for

Elisabeth's fingers. "You need parchment?"

"Yes, please." A silly grin spread across her face as David's thumb caressed the back of her hand. "A small piece will do. I just need to write out a recipe."

He turned around, grabbed a stack of parchment scraps from a nearby shelf, and plopped them on the table. "Come see if there's anything you like over here," he whispered before adding, "*besides me,*" with a mischievous smile.

Walking around the worktable, Elisabeth shook her head in amusement, lips clamped together. The two stood close enough their arms touched while she searched through the scraps of parchment. The velvety sheets were made from stretched animal skin.

After finding a piece the size of an index card, Elisabeth held it up. "This will be perfect." She then called out, "Nicholas?"

He turned around and leaned forward.

"Can I borrow a few things?"

"Like what?"

"Some sacks, a few little bottles...I won't keep them. You can have everything back." Her eyes widened. "And can I write on this parchment with a *real* feather quill and homemade ink?" She held still in expectation.

The old man laughed. "Of course. But, now I'm curious as to what do *you* use to write with?"

"Oh, I'll show you!" Elisabeth scurried about the bookshop, selecting two empty glass bottles from a shelf, a variety of sacks, and some twine. Then, she held her crystal and thought of home.

Home.

****

Elisabeth stood at her desk, rummaging through the bags of groceries bought the previous night to make chocolate chip cookies with Isabeau. She wanted to use the familiar ingredients from home so they'd taste the same, but couldn't exactly bring modern packaging back with her. So, she poured white sugar, brown sugar, white flour, and chocolate chips into the various sacks, tying each closed with the twine. The glass bottles with cork lids looked like something out of an apothecary shop. Using a funnel, she filled one with vanilla extract, the other with baking soda, unsure if the latter was available in the late fourteenth century or not. Everything was then placed into a larger sack, along with mother's chocolate chip cookie recipe, and several ballpoint pens for Balinus.

She positioned the bag over one shoulder and reached for her crystal once again.

****

Both David and Balinus gasped when a sack appeared, as if by magic, over her shoulder.

She couldn't help giggling at their reaction while placing everything into Colette's wooden wagon. "It's most of the ingredients for a recipe I thought you'd like to try." She looked at David. "Remember the night we had chocolate chip cookies in that hilltop garden?"

His grin contained secret knowledge. "When we heard the cuckoo bird?"

With a shy smile, she nodded.

"I remember." David then looked at Balinus. "I promise, you will *love* chocolate."

Elisabeth retrieved the pens and climbed the stairs to the loft, handing them to Balinus. "Here. Keep them."

The old man's eyes widened. He put all but one down, twisting it apart to inspect the inside workings.

Elisabeth returned to the main worktable, reached for the piece of parchment, and placed the recipe card from home beside it. Meanwhile, David sharpened the tip of a feather quill and then poured ink into a clamshell for her.

"Look at you," she said with a bubbly voice. "You're a natural at all this."

With a gleam in his eye, he trimmed the parchment neatly with a penknife and ruler. "Here you go."

"Thank you." Grinning, she took the feather, dipped it into the ink, and squealed while writing the recipe out. "This is *so* cool." After letting the ink dry, she stashed the recipes into her drawstring purse. "I should probably get going now. Thank you both so much. That was actually quite fun."

With a smile, Balinus glanced over. "See you at home. I look forward to trying this chocolate you speak of."

David placed his hand on the small of Elisabeth's back, sending a tingle up her spine. "I'll see you out."

Her posture relaxed as he steered her out the door, away from the entrance of the shop. Then, in one graceful move, he whirled her around, drew her close, and stole a kiss.

When he pulled back, she let out a spontaneous laugh.

His eyes twinkled as both hands wrapped around her waist. "*Gaudium meum.*"

My joy.

Elisabeth's insides were buzzing. She bounced on tippy toes to kiss him goodbye one more time before he sauntered back into the shop, smooth as ever, leaving her standing outside with a goofy grin on her face.

She took a deep, savoring breath.

Heat then rushed to Elisabeth's cheeks. "Oh crap." She slowly re-opened the door after him, feeling like a complete dork. "Forgot the wagon," she whispered while tiptoeing inside, grabbing the handle, and creeping away with it as David shook his head, chuckling.

Chapter Twenty

As Elisabeth headed toward the little tailor shop, a crowded pop-up market in the distance caught her attention. She paused a moment, listening as music played. She then turned, pulling the wagon behind her, detouring toward the action instead of Marie and Etienne's.

Rows and rows of tables filled with produce and goods were set up in a town square, offering seasonal fruits and vegetables as well as handcrafted items. Bright tablecloths fluttered in the breeze, while people haggled over prices with vendors. In one corner, a band of colorfully dressed musicians played a variety of instruments: a small drum, some sort of flute, a weird-looking guitar, and something that looked like a fiddle. Walking by, Elisabeth discreetly dropped a nutmeg into an open case used for collecting coins.

As she made her way through the crowd, someone called her name. Turning, she saw Giovanni. Standing beneath the canvas canopy of a rustic market stall, he gave her a small wave before a customer dropped some coins into his hand, paying for several sausages from a neatly stacked pile.

Elisabeth grinned while walking closer. "You work here?"

"For the day," he replied. "Tomorrow I'll—"

"*Excusez moi,*" an adorable old woman interrupted.

Giovanni smiled at her. "*Oui, ma donna…*"

Elisabeth stepped back, waiting as he politely answered the customer's questions.

All at once, several shoppers descended upon the quaint little stall, requiring his attention.

Elisabeth chuckled. "I'll talk to you later." She then leaned in. "You *are* coming by this evening, aren't you?"

Giovanni's posture perked up while giving someone their change. "Am I supposed to?"

"Merels? Isabeau lost, remember?" Elisabeth lowered her voice. "She spent all yesterday baking you a pie and you never came by for it."

Giovanni's brows squished together in confusion while grabbing two sausages from a stack and handing them to a middle-aged woman. "Our wagers are only in jest," he replied in a hushed tone.

Elisabeth stepped aside as a man shuffled closer, pondering what to purchase. "Well, *Isabeau* doesn't seem to think so."

For a moment, Blondie stood frozen, blinking rapidly. He then bit his lips to hide a grin. "Did she *really* make me a—?"

"Yup," Elisabeth said with a crisp nod before strolling away. "See you tonight," she called over her shoulder.

Another market stall caught her eye and she walked closer. Behind it sat a middle-aged woman selling stick horses. Elisabeth's eyes widened as she admired the toys. "These are absolutely beautiful."

A genuine smile lit up the woman's face and she rose to her feet. "Made them all myself over the winter."

Elisabeth reached out, touching a dark one, admiring it more closely. Mounted on a long wooden stick, the toy horse's head was made from stuffed brown fabric, with black leather for the eyes and nostrils. Black yarn created a glorious mane. An attached bridle and reins became the toy's perfect finishing touch.

With a wide smile, Elisabeth dug into her little purse again. "If you're willing to trade for some spice," —she held up a nutmeg— "I'll definitely take one."

The woman's eyes widened. "That's more than enough to buy the lot of them, Miss."

"I just need one." Elisabeth handed the nutmeg over and placed the stick horse into the wagon. "Thank you," she called out before walking away.

She wandered around the market for a while—long enough to exchange a few more nutmegs. She found a beautifully hand-painted clay vase for Perenelle, a new pair of leather ankle boots for David, a decorative ink pot for Balinus, and a pretty ribbon for Isabeau to weave through her thick braids. She'd noticed several stylish young ladies in Paris wearing their hair that way and it looked quite pretty.

Hopefully, hair ribbon didn't break any sumptuary laws and send the fashion police knocking.

Literally.

Before leaving, she bought two good luck charms. One made of red coral for Giovanni, and a horseshoe for Percival. Then, a folding pocket knife with a leather sheath caught her eye, so she bought that for David as well.

****

A bell over the door of the tailor's shop announced

Elisabeth's arrival as she pulled the little wagon in behind her.

Marie walked out of the back room, a bemused smile lighting her face. "We were just talking about you."

"Uh-oh. Nothing bad I hope."

"Definitely not," she said with a laugh.

Elisabeth feigned a sigh of relief. "I thought I'd check and see how things are going."

"Very well. In fact, if you come back tomorrow at *nones*, we will have everything ready for you."

"Really? That's amazing!"

What time is nones?

With a wide grin, Marie nodded. "The sizing can be adjusted afterward, if needed, but we're almost finished. We've had a journeyman here to help."

"Oh! Do you...by any chance...have seven little scraps of fabric I could have? About this big?" Elisabeth held her hands up to show the size. "I mean, *only* if it's not too much trouble."

"No trouble at all. Give me one moment." The seamstress disappeared into the backroom before returning with an armful of offcuts and handed Elisabeth the scraps. "Etienne just reminded me of something. Would you mind terribly doing *me* a favor as well?"

She placed the colorful fabric remnants into the wagon. "Of course not."

"I forgot to get measurements for another customer. Luckily, she's about the same size as you."

"Oh...sure." Elisabeth stood still while Marie took her measurements using strips of parchment.

She made a bunch of notches in various places,

finishing the job in seconds. "Thank you," Marie said before politely shooing her out the door, eager to get back to work.

Once outside, Elisabeth made her way home. She stopped at the bridge and sat on the grass, taking a few minutes to knot-wrap each gift with the scraps of fabric—all except for the stick horse.

****

"You're home," Colette called out from the threshold, running outside and straight toward Elisabeth.

"Stop!" With a bark of laughter, Elisabeth held up a hand. "Close your eyes. I have a surprise for you."

"*Really*?" She covered her eyes with both hands.

"Now, it's not a unicorn, but...hold your arms out."

Colette complied, squirming with excitement.

Elisabeth placed the toy across her outstretched arms. "All right, you can open them now."

She squealed even before looking. "Oh! I think I know what it is and I've *always* wanted one!"

Elisabeth burst into laughter.

Colette slowly opened one eye at a time and then gasped. "You bought this for *me*?"

"I thought you might like it."

"No...I don't like it." She shook her head theatrically, a huge grin on her face. "I don't like it. I LOVE it! Thank you, thank you, thank you." She then threw one leg over the stick and galloped away on her horse. "Colin! Colin, look what I have..."

With a small laugh, Elisabeth pulled the wagon inside. "I'm back," she announced, continuing into the great hall.

Perenelle walked out of the study, followed by Isabeau.

"Hello, dear." The old woman's brow furrowed while glancing around the room. "Where's Colette?"

"Gone to find Colin," Elisabeth said, unloading all the baking supplies from her wagon onto the work table.

Perenelle's head jerked back. "Gone to find Colin?" Her voice rose in pitch. "She wanted a drink of water. We're in the middle of a mathematics lesson!"

Elisabeth pressed fingers against her lips to keep from laughing. "Sorry. That's my fault. Colette ran outside when she saw me coming. I bought her a stick horse, and she was so excited she galloped off with it."

Perenelle snorted in amusement. "I suppose we were almost finished, anyhow."

A wide grin spread across Isabeau's face, clearly happy to be done with her lesson. "Then…can we begin cooking? Did you find everything needed?"

"Yes." Elisabeth placed the fabric-wrapped gifts she'd bought on a side table. "We can make the cookies right now if you want. They won't take too long and I have everything except butter, eggs, and salt."

Perenelle took a deep, satisfied breath. "I've work to do, but will be right here if you need a taste tester." She winked, propping the door open as she returned to the study.

"Butter, eggs, salt," Isabeau repeated, glancing at the work table. "Salt right here." She dashed out of the great hall, returning a moment later with a bowl of eggs and a crock of butter.

Elisabeth walked to an open hutch, selecting a variety of cups that looked the right size for measuring.

"Oh, we also need two mixing bowls."

Isabeau plopped two large bowls onto the worktable.

Elisabeth flitted about the space, doing her best to measure approximate amounts of each ingredient into individual bowls.

Isabeau looked on, seeming to take mental notes of everything being done.

"All right. The recipe says to take the butter and both sugars and cream them together."

Isabeau bit down on a smile, following every step read to her, mixing the cookie dough by hand at the end.

Although there was no oven, Elisabeth knew Isabeau could work magic with that open fire. "Next, we make little balls and bake them until golden brown and gooey."

Isa flashed a confident smile and grabbed a large black pot. She put it on smoldering embers beside the actual cooking fire and covered the lid with more fiery cinders. "We let get hot, yes?"

Elisabeth raised her brows. It was like preheating an oven. "Yes, definitely let it get hot."

After a few minutes, Isa removed the lid of the pot with a pointy tool. The girls placed the little balls of dough into it and replaced the lid to keep the heat in. It worked the same as an oven and within a short while, golden brown chocolate chip cookies were cooling on the worktable.

"Try one," Elisabeth said after they'd cooled down slightly.

Perenelle reappeared, shuffling closer to check them out.

Isabeau bit into one and then squealed dramatically.

Perenelle's eyes bulged after biting into hers. "Oh my word, these are out of this world. They're unlike anything I've ever tasted in my entire life."

"Well..." Elisabeth's posture straightened. "I was thinking maybe Isabeau and I could sell them."

"Sell them?" A slow smile spread across the old woman's face. "Do you have enough ingredients to make another batch?"

"Yes. We can make *several* more batches. No problem."

Perenelle looked at Isabeau, wide-eyed. "Are you interested?"

"Yes!" she said, quickly setting to work, starting a second round of cookies.

With a wide grin, Elisabeth noticed Isabeau measure and mix everything straight away, the recipe somehow already committed to memory. Since it was no longer needed, Elisabeth slipped the recipe, written on parchment, into her purse.

Several hours later, they had numerous batches of cookies and had used up all the groceries brought from home.

Perenelle lifted a side table. "Here, grab the other end."

Eyes narrowed in confusion, Elisabeth obeyed while Isabeau started cleaning up the mess they'd made.

As Perenelle led the way outside, Elisabeth realized they were setting up a makeshift market table on the street in front of the house—reminiscent of a child's lemonade stand.

"We're selling them here?" Elisabeth's voice filled with surprise. "Now?"

"Why not? 'Idle hands are the devil's workshop.'" Perenelle hurried back inside and returned with a saucer of little bitty sample pieces, in one hand, a platter of warm cookies in the other. "I put a batch aside for all of us to enjoy this evening after…"

A middle-aged woman, with a pretty smile, rushed over immediately. Her brows squished together as she bent closer to stare at the cookies. "What on earth are these, Nellie?"

"Marguerite…the finest little cakes you'll ever taste is what these are," Perenelle replied with a booming laugh. "Try a bite." She handed the woman a tiny piece from the sample plate, a little chocolate chip included.

When the woman gasped, more people began to gather around, eager to try the sample bites Perenelle was handing out freely.

"Did Isabeau make these?" most asked while reaching for a piece.

Elisabeth bit her lip, eager to watch everyone's reaction to trying chocolate for the first time in their lives.

Some yelped.

Postures stiffened.

Others squeezed their eyes shut, savoring the flavors.

"How much?"

"What's the cost?"

"I'll pay a *sous* for the lot!"

"Six for a *denier*," Perenelle answered.

The villagers began slapping coins onto the table.

Elisabeth distributed the cookies to grabby hands as quickly as possible, while Perenelle collected the money, dropping the coins into a little box.

Moments later, the cookies were completely sold out.

Perenelle held the coin box while instructing Elisabeth and Isabeau to carry the table back into the great hall. With a satisfied smile, the old woman then placed the cookie money into Elisabeth's hands. "*'It is the hard-working farmer who ought to have the first share of the crops,'*" she recited.

"Oh!" Elisabeth shook her head. "No, I really don't—"

"It was *your* recipe, *your* ingredients, and *you* did a lot of the work. *You* can decide a fair wage for Isabeau's help."

Elisabeth's shoulders pushed back and she handed the box of coins to Isabeau. "You take them."

Isa's eyes widened and she glanced at Perenelle, unsure of what to do.

The old woman shrugged her shoulders and walked back into the study. "I'll leave it to you two to sort out," she said with a chuckle.

Isabeau looked back at Elisabeth, her chin held high. "I will not take all of it. I take my fair share, not a *denier* more."

Elisabeth's brow furrowed. "How about you take half then? You did most of the actual baking."

Isa bit down on a smile. "Thank you. That still too generous, though." She counted out slightly less than half the coins and handed the rest back.

Elisabeth tiptoed into the study where Perenelle worked and placed the remainder of the coins on the desk. "For you and Nicolas, for your kindness…and I won't take no for an answer." When the old woman stood and tried to hand the coins back while protesting, Elisabeth dashed out of the room, giggling as she ran past Isabeau. "Oh, and Giovanni is coming over to see you tonight," she yelled over her shoulder with a bark of laughter, scurrying out the front door.

Outside, Elisabeth eventually slowed, strolling down the village street, enjoying the late afternoon sunshine. Ahead, she noticed David returning from the city. With an appreciative sigh, she watched as he walked hand in hand with little Colette. He seemed deep in conversation while she listened intently, occasionally wiping her nose with the back of her hand.

As they drew nearer, Elisabeth's head jerked back, realizing the girl's eyes were red and puffy from crying and her hair and dress were completely disheveled. With a wrinkled brow, she sprinted closer, desperate to find out what was wrong.

Chapter Twenty-One

"Awww, what's the matter?" Elisabeth asked, bending down in front of Colette. "Are you all right?" She glanced up at David for answers, but he clamped his lips together, trying not to laugh.

Elisabeth's head tilted to the side in confusion.

"Colin called me a baby."

"Oh…!" Elisabeth's eyes widened and she stood, trying not to look at David for fear of laughing at poor Colette's distress. "Well, that wasn't very nice of him."

"Wait…" David said with a mischievous grin as Elisabeth took the little girl's other hand and the three headed home. "Are you telling us…you *aren't* a baby?"

"No!"

"Then, so what?"

Colette's head flinched back slightly as she looked up at David.

"Who cares what Colin says?"

"Well, Colin also said unicorns aren't real."

"Do you believe unicorns are real?" he asked.

She pressed her lips together. "I *know* they're real."

"Then, so what?"

"But—?"

"No buts." David looked her directly in the eye. "It doesn't matter what Colin or anyone else says. Do you know what I do when someone says something that upsets me?"

She shook her head.

"I just say to myself, so what. So what, so what, so what." His eyes narrowed and Elisabeth noticed he gave Colette's hand a comforting squeeze. "But you weren't crying because he called you a baby, were you?"

Her bottom lip quivered and she shook her head.

Elisabeth's brows squished together. "Then…why were you crying?"

"Because I hit Colin over the head with my sword." She looked down at her feet and started sobbing. "And it broke in half."

When Elisabeth glanced at David, he nodded and wiped at his mouth. She turned away to compose herself. "Colette…" Elisabeth eventually said, "you can't go around hitting people over the head when you're mad at something they said to you."

"Slings work much better," David muttered while plucking at his clothes.

Elisabeth shot him a warning glance, still trying to keep a straight face.

"Where is your sword?" he asked. "Maybe we can fix it."

Colette took a deep breath and led them back to where her broken toy lay abandoned near the well.

****

"You did what?" Perenelle shrieked when Colette showed her the broken sword. She untied her apron, slapped it on the work table, and extended her hand. "Come on. You're going to Colin's house to apologize immediately."

Colette slumped into a slouch as she took Perenelle's hand.

"What did I tell you the last time about…?" The old woman's voice faded away as the two walked into the screens passage and out the front door.

When they left, Elisabeth and Isabeau burst into laughter.

David chuckled while grabbing a pitcher and a cup, before taking a seat at the table.

"Colette can be *so* naughty," Isa said, shaking her head while adding diced onions to a pot.

****

Balinus arrived home moments after Perenelle and Colette returned. The old man's eyes sparkled more than usual as the little girl ran straight into his outstretched arms.

"I missed you," she whispered.

"Oh, alrighty then," he said with a grin, softly adding, "…and I missed you too."

"Can you fix my sword? It broke in half."

The old man nodded. "I'll have a look at it after supper. How did it break?"

"Colin broke it with his head."

"Co-lette…" Perenelle warned.

Elisabeth confined laughter to a snort while setting the table.

Balinus eventually dismissed Colette with a loving pat on the head and walked toward his study, pausing in the doorway. "Nellie, might I have a word with you?" His mouth twitched, attempting to hold back a smile. "In private?"

She paused to examine him. "Of course."

When the door shut, Isabeau's posture perked up while chopping what looked like bacon. She then made a funny face at her little sister. "Maybe they talk about sending *you* to convent for naughty girls," she whispered.

"WHAT?" Colette yelped. "They're not!"

Elisabeth glanced at David. "I wonder what they're talking about."

He cleared his throat and looked away.

She gasped. "You know something, don't you?"

"My lips are sealed." He tilted his head back, downing the remainder of his drink before playfully slamming the cup on the table and standing. "Come, Colette, I'll teach you how to use a sling."

Colette's eyes widened. "Really?"

"Yes, but only if you promise *not* to use it on Colin." He chuckled while strolling out of the room, the little one skipping alongside him.

Elisabeth was about to say something when Perenelle squealed from the other side of the door. It flew open and she hurried out. With a huge smile on her face, she rushed toward Isabeau, prying the knife out of her hand. "Ohhhh, go upstairs and make yourself pretty, my dear. Giovanni is on his way over."

"But…" Isabeau's brow furrowed. "Giovanni *often* come over."

Perenelle put the knife on the table and leaned closer. "Yes, but today is different. Today Giovanni means to make you a bride!"

Isabeau looked down, trying to hide an enormous grin.

Elisabeth gasped.

Happy tears rolled down Perenelle's cheeks. "He stopped by the bookstore late this afternoon to ask Nicolas for permission…and for his blessing. Go! Go get washed up." She clasped both hands beneath her chin. "Ohhh, what a joyous day. A match made in Heaven, to be sure. Elisabeth…help Isabeau, my dear. Leave the supper to me!"

Isabeau whipped off her apron, threw it in the air like confetti, and burst into laughter. She raced into the screens passage and upstairs to the bedroom. "I shall wear new dress you gave me," Isabeau said, closing the door behind them.

Elisabeth's brows pulled in. "Are you going to say *yes* when he proposes?"

Isabeau's head jerked back. "What you mean?"

"It's just…how well do you even *know* Giovanni?"

Her hazel eyes widened.

"Don't get me wrong, I like Giovanni. He's awesome, but…?" Elisabeth grabbed the hair comb from her trunk. "Aren't you both still a bit…*young*?"

"No. Nellie think Giovanni would make excellent husband." Isabeau's smile wavered. She flopped onto the bed causing the straw-filled mattress to crinkle loudly. "And I like him," she added with a heavy sigh. "A lot."

Elisabeth kneeled on the bed behind Isabeau, combing her long auburn hair. "Don't you think you should get to know him a bit more *first*?" she whispered.

"Nellie says it better for couples who form attachment to marry fast. *Before* discovering each other's flaws."

"Seriously?" Elisabeth said with a bark of laughter.

Isa's shoulders slumped, her head hung low, and her posture hunched. "You don't think I should accept proposal?"

"Oh…no…that's not what I'm saying. You have to

make the right decision for *you*. I just know if it was *me*, I'd wait a while longer."

"How long you and David know each other?" she asked, pinching her bottom lip.

Elisabeth's brows pulled in, unsure how to answer. "Quite a while, but still, I've *no* intention of marrying anytime soon. In fact, I've been thinking…" She paused, softly shaking her head.

Isabeau's posture perked up. "What?"

"It's just…" She took a deep breath. "Can you keep a secret?"

"Yes."

"Well, I've been thinking how much fun it would be…if you and I opened an adorable little bakery in Paris."

Isabeau gasped. "You jest."

"No, I'm completely serious," Elisabeth whispered in a hushed, but excited tone while braiding Isa's hair. "Wouldn't it be *amazing*? You could do the baking; I would run the shop. That's why I bought all those fancy ingredients for you to try. I was waiting for the right time to suggest the bakery idea to you. I know this is a tough decision, but I have the money to do this and was going to start looking for a shop. You're so talented; you'd probably become the most famous baker in all of Paris. More sought after than Gallivant himself."

Isabeau's posture stiffened. "Taillevent?"

"Yeah, him. Taillevent. I'm not saying you shouldn't marry Giovanni. I just think if I were you, I'd wait. Have a little *adventure* first."

Isabeau stood and turned around, a sad smile on her face. "But none of this possible. I am not baker."

Elisabeth jumped off the bed. "You most certainly

are! You're one of the most gifted I've ever seen and I'd hate for you to waste your talent by—"

"You don't understand. I was never apprentice to baker. No guild would let—"

"Guild schmild." Elisabeth waved her hand dismissively. "Let me worry about that. My father is Lord Cathon, after all," she added with a grin. "I think if Giovanni *truly* loves you, he'll wait."

Isabeau gave a slow, disbelieving shake of her head. "A bakery?"

Elisabeth gently bit her lip and nodded. "The prettiest bakery in all of Paris. People will come from miles around to buy our creations."

Isabeau tugged at her ear while wandering over to where she kept the garnet-colored dress Elisabeth gave her. After running a hand along it, she turned around, smoothing down the simple tunic she already wore. "I ready. This dress look fine. Now, tell me…" She bit down on a smile, linking her arm through Elisabeth's. "What will name of bakery be?"

Elisabeth bounced onto her tiptoes. "You *have* to keep this a secret until I get everything sorted out, but I was thinking something like…" She waved a hand theatrically in the air, as if it was written in lights. "Elisabeau's.*"

Isabeau looked at her and snorted.

Elisabeth let out a shallow sigh. "I know. I'm still trying to come up with a great name. Just promise me you'll let poor Giovanni down gently."

209

Chapter Twenty-Two

Isabeau cleared her throat after walking into the great hall. "Nellie...? I change my mind."

The old woman's brow furrowed as she looked up from the cooking fire. "Changed your mind? Changed your mind about what?"

"I do not wish to marry Giovanni right now."

Her eyes widened. "Why on earth not?"

Elisabeth stood back, twisting the Hercules love knot on her wrist.

Isabeau looked down. "I...uh...I..."

"Oh, Beau-Beau," Perenelle said in a soothing tone. "Don't be foolish. It's perfectly normal to be nervous. Giovanni is a nice boy with an even temper. He'll make a fine husband. Once you get to know him more you may even—"

"But—"

"And he's a butcher." Perenelle retied her loose apron while heading toward the work table. "You'll never go hungry."

"But, I think—"

"Enough. You will accept Giovanni's proposal *graciously*."

Isabeau let out a theatrical groan and stomped her foot. "Nell-ee. I want to wait. Marry Giovanni *later*."

Perenelle's brows squished together. "WAIT? Wait for what? No." She shook her head. "Certainly not.

Have you lost all sense? He cannot be expected to *wait* for a silly girl to come to her—"

"Then he does not love me."

The old woman let out a heavy sigh. "Although, by the grace of God I believe he does, you are in no position to hold such romantic sensibilities. You will accept Giovanni's proposal and that is final. I do not understand what has changed your once—"

"Nellie, please…" Isabeau gave her a pained stare.

Perenelle's hands flew to her throat as if a thought suddenly occurred to her. She then gave an understanding nod and walked closer, clasping Isabeau's hands within her own. "Your change of heart is nervousness about the…" She lowered her voice to a whisper. "The *wedding night*, isn't it?"

Elisabeth's head jerked back. She then eyed the exit. "Oh, I hear someone calling me." She hurried to the screens passage, toward the back door. "Coming," she shouted to no one, attempting to escape before Perenelle started explaining the birds and the bees.

In the screens passage, both front and back doors were propped wide open, as usual, letting a cross breeze flow through the house.

"Good evening, *ma donna*," Giovanni said as he approached the front door, walking into the screens passage behind Elisabeth.

Her eyes bulged and she spun around. "Giovanni!"

He fiddled nervously with something in his hands.

She let out a bark of laughter. "Erm…uh…" Elisabeth rushed closer, linked her arm through his, rushing him through the passage and outside through the back door.

His brows drew together. "Have I come at a bad

time?"

"What? *Nooo*." With a nervous laugh, her gaze darted all around, searching for David and Colette. "Um…David wanted to…ask you something." She quietly exhaled after hearing Colette's laughter and led Giovanni to the little orchard, toward the tree with the wooden swing.

David sat on the grass, leaning against the trunk while Colette stood nearby—in an archer's stance. She whirled the rope over her shoulder, aimed for a bale of hay, but missed completely.

"Remember; always look where you want the stone to go." David laced his fingers behind his head. "Other than that, you're doing great."

Colette turned around, grinning at David. "Really?"

"Definitely," he said with a crisp nod, watching as she placed another rock in the rope and moved into the proper stance. As she began to spin the rope over her shoulder, David smiled and scrambled to his feet, noticing Elisabeth march toward him, half-dragging Giovanni with her.

While still whirling the sling over her shoulder, a distracted Colette spun around to see what was happening.

"Colette!" Elisabeth screamed, pulling both arms protectively around her head, hoping the little girl's aim was just as bad this time.

With precise movements, David swooped in, leaning across her body to push Colette's arm down before the rock shot out of the sling.

Giovanni let out a huge breath.

"I think that's enough practice for today," David

said with a shaky laugh.

A flush crept across her cheeks. "Sorry."

Elisabeth sat on the swing, using her feet to twist it around and around. "Other than *that*, how's the sling lesson going?"

"Although he won't admit it…" Colette scrunched her nose. "I'm not very good." She handed the rope back to David.

He flashed a satisfied smile, attaching it to his belt. "The more you practice, the better you'll get."

Giovanni cleared his throat and walked toward David. "So, what is it you wish to ask me?"

David's head flinched back. "I wished to—?"

"Yes…*remember*?" Elisabeth shot him a wide-eyed look. "You wanted to ask him about…" She lifted her feet off the ground, letting the swing spin faster and faster as the rope unwound.

"Oh yes…" David rubbed his chin. "I wanted to ask about…?"

"Pigs." When Elisabeth jumped off the swing, she swayed a moment from dizziness. "Whoa…I didn't think it would go that fast," she said with a nervous giggle, making her way drunkenly toward David, planting herself next to him. "What part of the pig do you get bacon from? I say it's from the back, near the tail, but *he* insists it's—?"

"I insist it's from the belly." David swallowed his laughter, shaking his head as he slipped his arm around Elisabeth's shoulders. "I told her bacon cannot possibly come from the rump."

"Well, David is correct. You see…" Giovanni turned his head away, gathering his thoughts. His posture then perked up, noticing Isabeau strolling

213

toward them.

"Beau-Beau's coming. It must be suppertime." Colette looked over at the paddock. "I'll get Percival," she announced before running off to the stable.

Giovanni turned his attention back to David and Elisabeth, swallowing an obvious lump in his throat. "If you'll excuse me…?" He scraped a shaky hand through his hair and walked toward Isabeau.

"Do you want to know a secret?" David leaned closer, a wide grin on his face. "Giovanni is going to propose marriage to her," he whispered. "That's the cause of his nervousness."

Elisabeth let out a heavy sigh as they watched Isabeau greet Giovanni with a warm smile. "She's going to say no."

David's head jerked back. "Why on earth would she say no?" His arm dropped from Elisabeth's shoulders and he turned to face her. "Giovanni is a good man and they've formed an attachment. She's given him *every* indication that his affections are reciprocated."

Elisabeth glanced across the property, watching as Giovanni lovingly put something into Isabeau's hair. "She doesn't want to get married yet. She wants to wait a bit."

"Wait a bit?"

"Yeah." Elisabeth pulled at her ear and looked back at David. "She wants to do stuff first."

"Stuff?" David deliberately lowered his head, eyes narrowing as he stared at Elisabeth. "What kind of *stuff*?"

"Well…I was thinking—"

"*You* were thinking?" He stood tall again and

crossed his arms. "What on earth do *you* have to do with any of this?"

Her lips pinched together.

David shuffled back a step. "Her refusal is *your* doing, isn't it?"

Elisabeth stomped her foot. "I think Isabeau should wait before getting married."

"Wait? Wait for what?" His tone deepened. "Isabeau barely has a dowry, no parents…what do you suggest she *wait* for?"

"Well…she's a talented baker."

His head flinched back slightly. "I do not deny that, but what does it have to do with marriage? Giovanni's offer will provide her a life of stability, yet you would begrudge her that?"

"Begrudge her!" Elisabeth's voice grew more shrill with each spoken word. "If he loves her, he will wait."

David scraped a hand over his face. "Perenelle and Nicolas have managed to secure Isabeau…not only an advantageous marriage, but one in which an attachment and mutual affection has clearly been formed. Why would you *choose* to meddle in that? This was an unwise move, Elisabeth. Giovanni is a superior match in both station and—clearly if Isabeau listened to your advice—in sense."

"They should *both* wait until they're older to get married."

He took a deep breath.

Elisabeth held her chin high. "Isabeau and I are going to open a bakery together in Paris."

David's eyes widened. "*Cor meum*…do you not see how things work here? You two cannot just *open* a bakery."

She pounded a fist against her thigh. "Why not?"

He threw his hands up in the air. "Because there are laws, regulations, guilds…"

"Well, I figured that since Ca—"

"No." David's nostrils flared. "Do *NOT* say Cato."

"Why?" she snapped back. "Everyone already thinks I'm—"

"Everyone thinks you're his daughter because you've done *nothing* to suggest otherwise," he said through clenched teeth. With a frustrated roar, he turned and stormed toward the house.

"Aquarius." Elisabeth let out a theatrical groan, marching after him. "Aquarius!"

Giovanni and Isabeau turned, their eyes wide while watching the lover's quarrel unfold. "Aquarius?" they whispered to each other in confusion.

"It's my pet name for David!" Elisabeth yelled as she stomped past them, wondering why they were holding hands.

Chapter Twenty-Three

Elisabeth rushed in the back door, through the screens passage, and into the great hall. Her posture suddenly stiffened while glancing around. "Where'd David go?"

Balinus looked up from the bench where he sat repairing Colette's wooden sword. "Is he not with you?"

"No." She swiped at tears, trying to hide them.

"He'll show up," the old man said in a soothing tone.

Perenelle, oblivious to Elisabeth's distress at the moment, stirred a pot over the cooking fire. "How does everything appear between Isabeau and Giovanni? I pray Nicolas managed to talk some sense into her."

Elisabeth rubbed the back of her neck and looked at the old man. "What was your advice?"

He kept his head down, still gluing Colette's broken sword. "I told her a wise sage once said, *'Marry or marry not, in either case, you'll regret it.'*"

Perenelle chuckled. "You better *not* have said that to her."

Balinus looked up and winked at Elisabeth.

She snorted, trying to suppress the small smile threatening to form on her face. "I think Isabeau and Giovanni are on their way. So are Colette and Percy. I'll be right back." She walked into the screens passage, climbed the staircase, and knocked on the door to David's room.

No answer.

"Aquarius!" she whispered loudly.

No answer.

She cursed under her breath, cracking open the door to poke her head in.

The room was empty.

Her shoulders hunched and she climbed back down the steep staircase, dashing out the front door.

Perhaps he'd gone for a walk to cool off.

Elisabeth started down the village street, immediately spotting him in the alleyway beside the house, leaning against the wall next to the raspberry bush. He had one leg on the ground, the opposite foot pressed against the wall, and both hands behind his back.

She felt her skin flush and she fidgeted with her sleeve while heading toward him. "There you are."

David turned, holding firm eye contact as she walked closer.

Elisabeth picked a few raspberries, popped all but one into her mouth, and then stood next to him, leaning against the wall as well. "I brought a peace offering," she said softly, holding up the single berry.

David shook his head and chuckled, then let out a long, low sigh. He moved in front of Elisabeth, placing one hand against the wall, just above her head. "A peace offering?"

"Yes. Open your mouth," she said with an amused snort, tossing the berry at his lips.

His reaction time was perfect and he caught it, causing Elisabeth to burst into laughter.

When he moved closer, twirling a lock of her hair around his fingers, she relaxed and wrapped both arms around his waist. "Is this the part where we kiss and make up?" she whispered, leaning forward to give him a quick peck on the lips, before leaning back again, awaiting his reaction.

With a bemused grin, David stared at Elisabeth for a moment. "I think so." He then cupped her face with his hands and moved his head closer. Her tummy fluttered as their lips met in slow, gentle kisses.

Happy noise from within the house drifted outside through an open window.

"I think supper's ready," she murmured, touching her forehead to his before glancing away.

With a small smile, David turned Elisabeth's face back toward him, stealing another lingering kiss. When he pulled back, warmth radiated throughout her body and she looked down, trying to hide a grin. He then reached for Elisabeth's hand and playfully tapped her palm with his fingers.

Her response was immediate, lacing her fingers with his. Together they walked toward the front of the house—until she suddenly froze. Still in the alleyway, Elisabeth's eyes became watery while looking at David. "I never meant to cause Giovanni or Isabeau any—"

"I know," he whispered with a small nod.

"No, I don't think you do." She let out an uncontrollable moan. "I convinced Isabeau to turn down Giovanni's proposal...after somehow convincing Giovanni to propose in the first place."

David gave her an incredulous stare. "What?"

She brought a shaky hand to her forehead. "I ran into Giovanni today after leaving the bookstore. I was talking Isabeau up to him…never imagining he'd *propose*. I figured they'd just date or something."

David's brows squished together. "Date?"

"Yeah, you know…courting? Courtship?"

"Ahhh, yes."

"It never occurred to me he'd show up on bended knee."

David's brows squished together again. "Bended knee?"

Elisabeth's face reddened and she poked him. "Don't make me laugh. I feel horrible."

"I am trying to understand your meaning."

"Well, when a man proposes, he's supposed to get down on one knee."

His eyes narrowed. "Why?"

"It's a romantic tradition, but that's not the point I was making." Elisabeth's chest caved in. "My intentions—although I admit might have been a bit selfish—weren't meant to be cruel. I only want the best for both of them. Where I'm from, not only are they too young to get married; they don't know each other well enough. I'd have given the same advice to *any* of my friends."

"Cor meum…" David put his hands on her waist and pulled her closer. "You cannot apply the norms of *your* time to *this* time."

"You're right." Her voice cracked. "I once read that we've progressed more in the last one hundred years than in the previous two thousand…technologically speaking anyway." She let out a shaky laugh. "Probably another good reason you ended up here instead of at *my* house."

David let out a heavy sigh, wrapped Elisabeth into

his arms, and kissed the top of her head. "You might as well be one of the gods, for all the differences between our worlds."

She leaned her head against his chest. "No, *our* differences complement each other." Elisabeth pulled back and raised her hand, showing David the amulet he'd made by entwining her red ribbon with rope from his primitive sling. "And those differences created something beautiful."

"The Hercules love knot." With slow, languid movements, he ran his thumb across the inside of her wrist, along the bracelet. "It's the strongest knot you can tie."

Her eyes prickled with tears and she nodded. "You said it was a symbol of the unbreakable bond you and I share."

"I remem..." He sniffled and looked away, clearing his throat. "Yes, I remember." He then took hold of her hand, leading her out of the alleyway and toward the front door. "Best to get this over with."

Elisabeth gave David a pained look before following him into the house. "I only hope I can *un*do whatever damage I've done."

Chapter Twenty-Four

Inside the great hall, Colette jumped up and down, holding her arms in the air, doing a victory dance. "Giovanni is to be my brother!"

A smiling Perenelle placed a calming hand on Colette's head. "Settle down, child, before you make him regret asking Beau-Beau. Now, go help your sister."

"Congratulations to the happy couple," Percy said, sliding into his seat.

Elisabeth's lips parted slightly as she made her way across the room to the dining table, taking her usual seat on the bench next to David.

Had Isabeau accepted Giovanni's proposal after all?

Wide-eyed, David glanced at Elisabeth before looking back at Giovanni. "So, she said yes?"

Blondie nodded, flopped into an empty spot at the table, and let out a *huge* sigh of relief, causing David to burst into laughter.

"Well, I wish you a lifetime of marital bliss," he said.

"Yes, congratulations." Elisabeth pressed a palm against her heart. "That's wonderful news."

Balinus put the toy sword aside to dry and took his seat at the head of the table. "It is joyful news, to be sure."

Isabeau's eyes were wide and glossy as she fluttered around the cooking fire. She ladled the contents from a huge kettle into a bowl, which Colette carefully carried to the dining table.

At the work table, Perenelle sprinkled the small white flowers Isabeau had collected that morning onto the top of a large tart. "Elisabeth," the old woman suddenly said with a chuckle, "this isn't one of your father's fancy castles. Come over here and make yourself useful, my dear."

Heat rushed to her cheeks as she jumped up, hurrying to help. "Sorry," she whispered.

Perenelle winked at her. "Do you know how to slice bread?"

With an amused snort, Elisabeth grabbed a sharp knife. "Of course, I know how to slice bread."

"Giovanni?" Balinus slid his chair closer to the table. "I've been meaning to ask if you are going to the trade fair in Provins."

"Yes. Augustin is sending me with a cartload of sausage he wants sold."

"Excellent." Balinus' posture perked up. "I am also going."

"Well, then we must travel together!" Giovanni said with a bark of laughter. "Have you been before?"

"Yes, I make it a—"

Colette squealed. "Can I come too? You will bring me, won't you?"

"Not this time, little one," he said. "But if you're a good girl, perhaps I'll bring you back a bauble." Balinus leaned back in his seat and smiled at David. "I'll put *you* in charge of the shop while I'm gone."

David's eyes widened.

Colette clasped both hands to her chest. "The fair in Provins is the *most* fun. When I was there, we saw musicians, acrobats, stilt walkers..." She paused, distracted by the fabric-wrapped gifts piled on a sideboard. "What are all those?"

Everyone turned to look.

Elisabeth continued slicing the rustic loaf. "Oh, just little trinkets I bought for each of you. I already gave you *your* gift though, Colette."

The little girl slowly carried another bowl to the table, placing it in front of Percy. "She gave me the most beautiful stick horse you've ever seen."

Perenelle's eyes widened. "You bought gifts for *everyone*? Oh, sheesh." She pried the knife from Elisabeth's hand and tried to playfully shoo her away. "Go sit back down, *m'lady.*" Her high-pitched voice caused everyone to burst into laughter.

Elisabeth brought the bread basket to the table and climbed over the bench, settling into her spot across from Isabeau. She cleared her throat, pointing at Isa's auburn hair. "That's pretty."

With everyone seated, talking and laughing amongst—and over—each other, Isabeau's hazel eyes sparkled. "Giovanni give me ivory comb also." She leaned in, turning her head to show it off. "How could I say no after that?" A wide grin spread across her face.

"It's absolutely beautiful. And...I'm glad you said yes."

Isabeau extended her hand across the table and Elisabeth reached out to take it. "I knew you would understand."

She took a deep breath and nodded. "I do." *Now.*

As they both pulled their hands back, David gave a

small yelp. "This is delicious." He gulped down another spoonful of...*something*.

Elisabeth couldn't help giggling. "You'll happily eat anything."

"I'm glad you're enjoying the pottage, nephew," Perenelle said with a smile.

Elisabeth ran a spoon through the thick soup, spotting bacon, peas, and onions in it.

"Isabeau made *sambocade* and there's also Elisabeth's little cakes you must all try." Perenelle glanced over at Balinus while reaching for a slice of bread. "Beau-Beau and Elisabeth spent all afternoon making them. We sold the entire lot in front of the house in a matter of minutes." The old woman's eyes widened. "You should see how much money the girls made."

David stole a glance at Elisabeth, a proud smile on his face.

When everyone finished eating, Colette jumped up from the bench. "Can I hand out the presents now?"

"Sure." After walking to the sideboard, Elisabeth felt the first fabric-wrapped gift. "You can give this one to Nicolas," she whispered.

With a wide grin, Colette carried it to him.

"Oh, alrighty then." After un-wrapping his ink pot, the old man pressed fingers to his smiling lips. "Many thanks, my dear girl. This is exquisite, yet practical. I shall cherish it always."

"Ohhh!" Perenelle shook her head while holding up her new vase. "It's absolutely lovely."

"It's hand-painted," Elisabeth said proudly before feeling her cheeks flush. "Because... how else would it be painted?" she added with a bark of laughter,

225

reminding herself this was the fourteenth century.

Isabeau squealed, holding out hair ribbons for everyone to see.

Percival scraped a hand through his hair before unwrapping the horseshoe.

"If you hang that up, it's supposed to bring you good luck," Elisabeth said.

"Many thanks," he replied quietly.

"*Cor meum...?*" David's voice was emotional as he looked up and quirked a brow.

Elisabeth nodded while smiling at him.

His eyes softened, inspecting the soft leather ankle boots and the folding pocket knife.

She handed Colette the remaining gift. "Last but not least, Giovanni."

Blondie's eyes widened. "For me?"

"I knew you were coming over tonight," she said with a bemused smile. "The man I bought that from said it's made from red coral and is supposed to bring you good luck."

"I'm not one to turn down good luck." Giovanni unwrapped the gift and held it up, showing everyone a little amulet that reminded Elisabeth of a red chilli pepper. "A lucky horn. Many thanks, *ma donna.*"

"You're wel—"

She caught David exchange a knowing glance with Balinus before the two of them burst into laughter.

Her brows squished together while returning to the table. "What's so funny?"

"Nothing," David mumbled, wiping at his mouth.

With wide-eyed looks, everyone stared at the old man.

Balinus cleared his throat. "My nephew seems to

know the *ancient* meaning of the *cornicello*."

Elisabeth's hand touched her mouth. "Is it not for good luck?"

David plucked at his clothes. "Oh, it is. It definitely is."

Perenelle made a face while collecting the dirty dishes. "Do tell."

"May I?" Balinus held out a hand to Giovanni.

"Of course." Blondie placed the trinket into his waiting palm.

"Well, you see...the, uh..." The old man sniffled, still trying not to laugh as he held it up, attempting to explain. "It's amusing—if not ironic—that Giovanni was gifted this on the night of his betrothal...because the phallic shape—"

Perenelle's head jerked back. "Cover your ears, Colette!"

"—is an ancient Greek reference to the god of male fertility, Priapus. As you can guess from the...uh..*horn* shape, Priapus was the protector of the..." Balinus waved his hand in the air indicating the answer should now be obvious to the adults.

Colette tilted her head to the side.

Elisabeth groaned and covered her face with both hands, realizing she'd gifted Giovanni what was once considered a good luck charm for the male...private part.

Everyone burst into laughter and Colette scratched her eyebrow in confusion.

David rubbed Elisabeth's back. His eyes twinkled with mischief as heat rushed to her face. "It's all right. I think you've just wished them many, *many* children in the future."

Giovanni had a bemused smile while taking his lucky horn back from Balinus. Meanwhile, Isabeau's own cheeks flushed and she looked everywhere except at her fiancé.

Chapter Twenty-Five

The next day, Elisabeth bit down on a smile while strolling along the village street, starting the journey toward Marie and Etienne's little shop. Turns out, *nones* is three o'clock in the afternoon. As her body buzzed with anticipation, a line from a favorite book floated into her thoughts.

"Oh, Marilla, looking forward to things is half the pleasure of them."

It was certainly true today. She couldn't wait to see what they'd sewed and stitched with that azure blue fabric.

Behind her, a horse whinnied.

"Care to buy an old mare?" a familiar voice asked.

With a grin, Elisabeth spun around.

The heavy-set man walked closer, leading his sweet horse with a rope halter. Not much taller than a pony, its coat was entirely chestnut, except for a strip of faded white running down the bridge of its nose. Its blonde tail swished gently back and forth while watery brown eyes seemed to study its surroundings.

With an appreciative sigh, Elisabeth stepped closer, stroking the horse's neck. "I am *so* tempted...but not today."

The man's posture drooped. "Well, I thought I'd ask one last time." He let out a heavy sigh. "It seems the only folks with any use for her now are glue-makers. We're heading to one now."

"What do horses have to do with glue?" Elisabeth asked, awaiting the inevitable corny punchline.

He took a shaky breath. "How do you think they *make* glue?"

Elisabeth's brows squished together.

"I always prayed she'd live out the remainder of her days happily grazing some pasture."

"Wait…?" Elisabeth's eyes widened. "You're not serious, are you?"

"I wish I wasn't. Rosamund's of no use to me anymore and I cannot keep her."

"Made into glue?" She winced and then looked at the horse. "Rosamund? That's her name?"

The man wiped his nose. "Yeah. I knew better than to get attached, but she's a *real* sweet mare."

The horse turned and gently nudged Elisabeth.

"Well, look at that," he said with a weak smile. "She likes you."

Elisabeth's chest caved in. "On second thought, I'll take her."

The man swallowed an obvious lump in his throat and nodded. "Really?"

"Yes. Sell her to me. Here…" As she stepped back, digging through her purse, her eyes clouded with tears. "Will you take spices? I can pay you with a nutmeg."

"A nutmeg?"

"It's worth about eleven sous."

The man squeezed his eyes shut.

"There's *no* way you can sell her to be made into glue." Elisabeth shook her head. "Even though I've absolutely no idea how to care for a horse…" she muttered while paying the man. "But I'll learn."

His posture slumped in relief. "You live with the Flamels?"

She nodded.

"Don't worry. Percival will see she's well cared for. He's a fine lad. Loves horses more than people, don't he?" He handed Elisabeth the lead rope. "She's the *perfect* lady's horse. Lovely to ride, doesn't eat too much, and isn't high maintenance. You'll never find a sweeter girl than Rosamund here." He placed a loose fist against his chest and then walked off, through the village, along the road leading to the city gate.

Elisabeth whimpered. "Oh, dear God, what have I done?" With a dejected sigh, she turned around to head back home, leading her new horse down the alley beside the house, past the raspberry patch. The sun shone, birds sang, and the old mare gave the occasional snort as her hooves clip-clopped next to Elisabeth.

The stable was a storey-and-a-half tall, had a thatched roof, rough wooden walls, and a wattle and daub fence surrounding it. Like everything else here, it looked straight out of a fairy-tale. Two horses grazed in the pasture beyond.

The double doors were wide open and inside, a shadowy figure used a pitchfork to move hay into a stall.

Elisabeth opened the gate and entered the paddock. "Percy?"

He leaned his pitchfork against a wall and scratched his chin while walking outside. His brow then furrowed. "That's Rosamund."

Elisabeth opened her mouth, and then closed it again. "Yeah," she finally said.

Percy was already doting on the mare.

"Did you know they were going to make *glue* out of her?"

He nodded, averting his eyes.

Elisabeth's posture sagged. "So, I bought her."

Percy's head jerked back. "You bought her?" A wide grin spread across his face. "Really?"

"Yes, but I know *nothing* about taking care of—"

"Oh, don't worry about that. I'll take good care of her." His face seemed to shine and he took the lead rope. "Come inside. Smokey and Cazador are in the pasture."

Elisabeth followed Percy as he led Rosamund into the spotless stable. It smelled of sweet, fresh hay.

He grabbed a carrot from a bushel and fed it to the mare. "She's a great horse. Everyone 'round here just loves her. I'm, uh...I'm really glad you saved her. Nellie's favourite old gelding, Bayard, died last winter and she's been pining for another ever since. This might convince her to finally buy another for herself as well. There're too many empty stalls in here," he said with a sigh.

Elisabeth glanced around the space. To her left were three simple wooden stalls, with another three on her right; the first one filled with neatly stacked bales of hay. A sunbeam streaking in through the open doors illuminated a large spider web in the rafters. Along the back wall, shelves and hooks were organized with supplies: bridles, halters, saddles, feed bins, and a neatly arranged row of brooms and pitchforks. On the right-hand side, a simple wooden ladder led up to a cozy hayloft under the eaves. From where she stood, Elisabeth could see dust particles floating in the sunlit air thanks to an open window.

"Oh—you have to see the barn sparrows!" Percival climbed the ladder to the loft. "Come here."

As Elisabeth followed, he pointed at a bird's nest in the rafters. It looked like it was made of mud pellets, grass, and feathers.

"Watch this." With a wide grin, Percy walked closer. "Chicka-chick-chick-chick."

All of a sudden, five little beaks popped up and cheeped in reply before falling back down again.

Elisabeth's brows rose and she burst into laughter. "Oh my gosh, that is hilarious."

"I thought you'd find that funny."

As she looked around, a pile of blankets was arranged atop a large heap of straw. Her eyes widened and she pointed at it. "Is this where you sleep?"

Percy nodded. "There's not a comfier or more peaceful spot to be, sleeping in the sweet-smelling hay. I've even got a view of the pasture," he added with a distant, unfocused smile.

Elisabeth poked her head out the window, eying green rolling hills and the small forest beyond. Down below, a kitten was curled up, sound asleep on a haystack pushed against the outer stable wall.

With a slow shake of her head, she looked back at Percy. "It's *so* cozy. Not at all what I imagined." Elisabeth paused to examine him. "How old are you, anyway?"

"Fourteen."

She nodded. "That's about what I thought." When Rosamund whinnied, they climbed back down the ladder. Elisabeth reached out to stroke her and then let out a nervous laugh. "I still can't believe it. There I was, heading to Paris for an appointment, and then…"

She gestured theatrically at Rosamund. "I stopped and bought a freaking horse. A horse!" She looked at Percival wide-eyed and let out a mock scream.

Percy chuckled. "Do you want me to tack her up so you can ride into the city to your appointment?"

Her head jerked back. "Can I?"

He wiped at his mouth, trying not to laugh again. "She's *your* horse."

Elisabeth clasped both hands under her chin and squealed. "All right." She then stepped lightly from foot to foot, watching as the groom brushed the old mare with a brick-size bundle of straw that had been twisted together. He checked each hoof, picking at her feet. "Later, can you teach me how to do all this?"

"Any time," he said with an easy nod, placing a simple, but colorful saddle across the horse's back.

Unlike a typical leather saddle, this one had a wooden saddle tree painted bright red. It was topped with a decorative pillow made of olive-green canvas and had a navy-blue strip around it. Beneath was a greige linen pad from which four leather straps hung down slightly, along with metal stirrups. The entire thing looked handmade and hand-sewn together.

"I have no idea what you're doing," Elisabeth said.

"You'll get the hang of it after you do it enough times." To a leather strap, Percy attached a longer strap. He pulled it under the horse's belly, connected it to the other side of the saddle, holding everything in place. "You want to try the next girth?"

"Sure." Elisabeth followed Percival's instructions, finding the task rather easy.

He walked to a row of wooden pegs and selected a bridle, held it up, inspecting and straightening the straps. "This part is a bit tricky so I'll do it for you." Percy slipped the reins over Rosamund's head. Then, he quickly placed something into the horse's mouth and slipped the bridle over the simple rope halter. "Good girl," he murmured, fixing her forelock. "Ready?"

Elisabeth bit down on a smile and nodded, following him outside.

He knotted the rope through a simple ring of twine sewed to the saddle cushion and pulled, keeping it neatly in place. "When you tie her up, use the lead rope, not the reins, otherwise she could hurt herself if spooked."

Elisabeth leaned in closer to watch what he was doing. "Can you show me how to do that again?"

"Of course." Percy tugged one end of the rope and the entire knot slipped apart. He then slowly made the slip knot again. "Remember, tie her at eye level and arm's length so she's safe."

Elisabeth nodded. "Got it." The horse was small, which made her easy to mount. "Thanks so much for all your help, Percy."

"Happy to help."

She adjusted the reins and gave the horse a gentle nudge with her legs. Rosamund started walking, her head bobbing up and down while clip-clopping rhythmically along. There was something incredibly soothing about the sound of hooves hitting the ground. Elisabeth took a deep, satisfied breath, sitting tall in the saddle, deciding that horseback riding into town was a thousand times more fun than walking alone. A gentle breeze blew through her hair—and Rosamund's mane. Before long, she was whispering sweet nothings to the horse, telling her what a good girl she was.

Once at her destination, Elisabeth dismounted, tying the rope to a metal ring attached to the façade of the building, just as Percy had showed her. "I won't be too long," she whispered softly while stroking Rosamund's side. Then she smoothed down her dress and walked into the shop.

The jingling bell announced Elisabeth's arrival and her posture perked up. The workroom door was closed today, which was a bit odd. But Marie quickly appeared, slipping into the front of the shop, closing the door behind her again.

"Have I come at the wrong time?" Elisabeth asked in an uncertain tone.

Marie's breath hitched. "The wrong time? Heavens no." A wide grin spread across her face while carrying a blush-colored dress in her arms. "It's the perfect time. Everything is ready for you to inspect." She fluttered about, unable to keep still. "I must say, now that I see the doublet complete, the azure blue fabric was a *wonderful* choice. Etienne's doing some last-minute adjustments and will be out shortly to show you." Marie ushered Elisabeth to the privacy screen at the opposite end of the room and lowered her voice. "My husband is going to be cross with me if I don't get this customer's cotehardie finished soon. But, there's something wrong with the seam and you're about the right size so I thought—?"

"You want me to try it on for you?" Elisabeth whispered, recognizing the gorgeous pale pink fabric she'd admired that very first day she came into the shop.

Marie let out a sigh of relief. "You don't mind?"

"Not at all." She walked behind the privacy screen

and changed into the blush gown. Elisabeth took a deep, savoring breath and stepped out to show the seamstress. "This is my all-time favourite color." Her lips parted while smoothing down the soft fabric, admiring everything about the romantic gown, from its scooped neckline to the long, tight sleeves.

Marie's eyes filled with tears as she placed a hand over her heart. "My word, it suits *you* perfectly."

Elisabeth twirled. "Well, it's absolutely gorgeous. I don't think you've done anything wrong at all because it's flawless. Whoever this is for will *love* it."

Marie cocked her head to the side and stepped closer, inspecting and fussing with the dress. "Let me have Etienne look at it. He insists the seam wasn't done correctly." She hurried to the door, throwing it wide open this time. "Etienne? Do you have a moment?" She wiped at her mouth, clearly attempting not to smile.

Etienne walked out, a bemused grin on his face. He then turned around, speaking to someone inside the workroom. "Thank you so much for trying that on. It's just…I thought there was something wrong with one of the seams. You're about the same size as the person it's for and I'd really like Marie to look at it." Etienne then winked at his wife.

Elisabeth's brows squished together in confusion.

"It appears fine to me," David said, glancing down while walking out of the workroom behind Etienne— dressed in a—

Wait…was that the blue doublet…and the rest of the outfit Elisabeth had the tailor make for him? Her eyes widened and she stared at Marie.

The woman's cheeks flushed as she nodded in reply.

Elisabeth's gaze went distant; trying to figure out what the heck was going on.

Chapter Twenty-Six

At that moment, before David looked up, time stood still. Elisabeth felt her cheeks flush while staring at him. He looked dashingly handsome—like Romeo himself. Over a soft white chemise, he wore the azure blue hip-length tunic. It laced halfway up the front, from mid-chest to the neckline. The sleeves were slightly gathered at the top, which accentuated his broad shoulders. Rather than a ridiculously puffy look he would have hated, it was just the right amount of extra fabric. It added an air of sophistication to an outfit befitting the "nephew" and adopted son of a wealthy merchant. A wide leather belt and charcoal gray (she hated to call them tights) *leggings* completed the ensemble, looking perfect with the new leather ankle boots he wore. In his fingers he held a thin cord, fidgeting with it like one of his slings. Elisabeth's eyes narrowed, noticing the cord was dyed a rosy pink—coordinating perfectly with the gown she currently wore.

She gasped, covering her mouth with both hands.

David's head jerked back. A slow, adorable grin then spread across his face as he held firm eye contact.

Marie released an appreciative sigh, watching them with rapt attention.

Etienne cleared his throat. "Wife!"

"Oh!" She jumped and let out a shaky laugh.

"Oh…yes, well…erm…it turns out, you…you've *both* secretly been coming here to have clothing made for each other, unbeknownst to the other."

Etienne, leaning against the doorframe, snorted in amusement.

David and Elisabeth continued staring at each other across the shop, wide-eyed.

When Marie squealed dramatically and clasped both hands beneath her chin, Etienne chuckled. He sauntered over to his wife and grabbed her arm. "Give them a few minutes alone, my dear," he said, drawing her into the backroom with him.

David remained motionless. "Did you really have these garments made for me?"

Elisabeth nodded, and then sashayed back and forth for a moment, showing off the dress. "What do you think?"

David pressed a fist to his mouth as his eyes filled with tears. Suddenly, they both walked quickly across the shop floor, erasing the distance between them.

"You look *so* handsome," she whispered with an enormous smile.

He brushed a hand through her hair. "I did some extra work for the old man and he paid me quite well. Enough that I kept my word of buying you a *stola* even finer than—"

"Aquarius…" Her voice cracked with emotion. "You should have saved that money for yourself." Elisabeth reached for his fingers, feeling the thin rope in one of his hands instead.

"Oh!" David looked down at the rosy cord he still held. "Here…" He wrapped it around Elisabeth's waist and playfully pulled her closer, knotting it before letting the beautiful belt drape down, almost to the floor. "I, uh…" He cleared his throat. "I chose fabric for the gown that was rather expensive and I didn't have quite enough money, so I made the belt for you—from my favorite sling. Marie offered to dye it at no cost so it would be a perfect match." His voice cracked with emotion. "It might not be the fanciest, but I assure you it was made with love."

"WHAT?" Elisabeth's mouth fell open and she stared down at the beautifully braided belt. "When did you make this?"

"At night. When everyone slept, I took the sling apart and—"

Her chest caved in. "That's the sweetest thing I've ever heard." Elisabeth's voice choked with tears and she wrapped both arms around his neck.

When David pulled her into a tight embrace, Marie walked out of the backroom again, clearing her throat.

David's posture stiffened as he pulled away, entwining Elisabeth's fingers with his. He tilted his head toward Marie. "All right, how did all this transpire?" he asked with a smirk.

She bit her lip. "First, please tell me you're not vexed? You both turned out to be so personable that I admit, we might have gotten a little carried—"

"*We?*" Etienne reappeared, leaning against the doorframe. "There's no *we* here. I told you to mind your own business, Marie," he said. The tailor then looked at David and Elisabeth. "That being said, I cannot tell you how enthralled the two of you have kept my wife." He crossed his arms and chuckled. "She was determined to have you pick up the finished clothing at the same time just so she might see your faces."

David exchanged a look with Elisabeth and they both burst into laughter. He then said to Marie, "I assure you we are quite entertained. I can *easily* imagine Elisabeth doing the same thing in your situation."

Marie let out a huge breath. "Well...you see, Elisabeth came in explaining how she needed clothing for *you* after being robbed of everything by bandits. Getting measurements was going to be tricky since she wanted it to be a surprise. But, we figured we'd worry about that later. We could make adjustments afterward if necessary. The next day—" Marie pointed to David, "—*you* came in."

"I saw you *bouncing* out of the shop," he said to Elisabeth, a bemused smile on his face.

She giggled at the memory.

"You were so excited I was certain something in here had caught your eye and was determined to get you *whatever* it was."

Elisabeth's tummy fluttered. "I tried to drag you away so you wouldn't realize I was shopping for *you*."

With a grin, Marie nodded. "David came in, all tongue-tied I might add, trying to explain how he needed...what did he call it? A *stola*?" Marie let out a small laugh.

Elisabeth and David exchanged darting glances, biting down on smiles at his...Roman-ness.

"He needed a *stola* for a certain young lady who'd been robbed of everything by bandits. Two bandit stories in as many days?" She placed a hand over her heart and sighed. "I may have been born at night, but not *last* night. I immediately realized what was happening, especially after he said the fabric had to be the color of soft pink roses in spring. Everyone else wants vibrant colors."

Elisabeth closed her eyes.

"So, I subtly suggested the beautiful fabric she'd been admiring."

David squeezed Elisabeth's hand and she took a slow easy breath.

Etienne let out a belly laugh. "You both even obliged us in getting your very own measurements. I cannot tell you how much we laughed each time one of you left the shop."

After several more minutes of chitchat, a new customer came into the shop. Goodbyes were exchanged, with promises to return. They left, dressed in their new clothing. Etienne had put their other outfits into a small sack for the trip home and handed it to David.

Once outside, Elisabeth's lips clamped together, trying not to laugh while turning around—standing directly in front of Rosamund as she adjusted her purse.

David lowered his head and raised an eyebrow. "I recognize that look."

"What look?"

"That mischievous one."

Elisabeth wiped at her mouth. "All right...so, I came up with a *brilliant* idea."

David shuffled closer.

"I've been bringing spices from home to use as currency here. *That's* how I bought your clothing and the gifts for everyone last night. It's been entertaining and is giving me something fun to do here."

"I assumed the money was from baking you sold with Isabeau."

Her eyes widened. "Oh! Yeah, no."

His head tilted to the side. "Go on…"

"Well, remember that man we ran into? 'Care to buy an old mare?'" she said, deepening her voice, doing her best imitation of him.

David snorted. "Yes…?"

Elisabeth nodded, still standing in front of Rosamund.

He gave her a blank look.

She began plucking at her clothes as if cooling down.

David then glanced over her shoulder, finally noticing the old mare standing there. His eyes bulged and he did a double-take.

Elisabeth burst into giggles. "Meet Rosamund…my new horse."

Chapter Twenty-Seven

David scratched his head. "You bought a horse?"

"Yeah. I can't believe it myself, but the man was so sad because he said he couldn't keep her anymore and was going to have to sell her and she was going to be killed and made into glue, and then before I knew it, I was trying not to cry while digging through my purse so I could give him a nutmeg in exchange for…"

As she rambled on, David let out a spontaneous laugh, placed the cloth bag on Rosamund's saddle, and pulled Elisabeth into a hug. "I love you," he blurted out.

With an enormous grin, she flung her arms around his neck, oblivious to anyone else on the street. "I love you too." Then, David playfully leaned forward, dipping her low. Elisabeth burst into giggles as she curved her back, tipping her head upside down, knowing she was completely safe in his grasp. When he raised her again, his eyes were wide and glowing. She had a smile that couldn't be contained. "You don't think I'm crazy?"

"Oh, I think you're completely mad." He smirked. "But not for buying a horse."

She laughed while swatting at him.

David grabbed the bag from the saddle. "It makes me hopeful."

"Hopeful?" Elisabeth untied Rosamund, holding the lead rope in her hand.

He moved closer. "You wouldn't have bought a horse if you weren't at least *starting* to settle in here."

As she led Rosamund along the cobblestone streets of Paris, her lips parted slightly. "I never thought of it that way."

Outside of the city, before they crossed the stone bridge leading to the village, David flashed Elisabeth a mischievous grin.

A slow smile crept across her face as she followed him off the main road, down the grassy bank. They walked through the trees, close to the water's edge.

Spotting a large fallen branch on the ground, David wandered over, easily pulling the bark from it. Then, they followed the stream a short distance to where it curved, stopping to rest near the largest oak; the one with the entwined trunks.

David sat on the ground, resting both elbows on his raised knees.

Elisabeth let Rosamund drink from the water before tying her to a nearby branch. The grassy meadow was now dotted with daisies and Elisabeth gathered a thick bouquet while David pulled bark fibers apart to make a new sling.

"I spent some time with Percy this afternoon and did you know he's completely *not* shy when he's at the stables? It's like he's a totally different person when talking about horses." She walked over to David, sat cross-legged beside him, and arranged the flower stems neatly on the ground in front of her. "He's going to teach me how to take care of Rosamund."

David bit his lips to keep from smiling as he twisted the bark fibers into rope.

While braiding daisy stems together into a chain,

Elisabeth glanced over at him and then raised an eyebrow. "What are you smiling about?"

He let out a satisfied sigh. "I quite like it here."

Elisabeth nodded in agreement as her gaze wandered, looking beyond the leafy green canopy to fluffy white clouds drifting slowly across the blue sky. "Me too." Nearby, the splashing stream danced and tripped over rocks. A squirrel chittered from a nearby tree. She took a deep breath before tying the ends of her daisy chain together to make a crown. "It smells like sunshine here."

"Sunshine?" David chuckled as he continued twisting the bark fibers into rope.

When a butterfly landed on a nearby bush, Elisabeth's eyes widened, recognizing the dainty purple bellflowers. "I forgot to tell you…the flowers I brought to Perenelle the other night…?" She clamped her lips together while setting the daisy crown on her head and adjusting her hair. "Oh my gosh, I *really* shouldn't laugh but…"

David turned, pausing to examine her.

"Apparently…" Elisabeth wiped at her mouth. "I gave her a poisonous bouquet."

"What?" He let out a spontaneous laugh.

She pointed at the nearby bush. "Do you know that plant is, like, *crazy* poisonous?"

He gave a slow disbelieving shake of his head and tossed the rope aside. "Only you," he said before wrapping his arms around Elisabeth and playfully pulling her flat onto the ground beside him. "Only you."

"Hey, you knocked my crown off." With a soft laugh, she rolled onto her side, curling up against him, and rested her head on his outstretched arm.

David's brow wrinkled and he tucked her hair behind an ear. "First, you burnt your hand with a poisonous plant, and then you gifted a deadly bouquet to Perenelle." David's free arm moved around Elisabeth's waist. "You need to be more careful."

With a bemused smile, she wiggled even closer, touching her lips to his earlobe, lingering there a moment before whispering, "I'll try—"

David's eyes twinkled with mischief, listening to her.

"—not to poison anyone else."

"TRY?" Grinning, he rolled on top of her and she burst into giggles until being hushed with lingering kisses.

Heat radiated through her chest. There was no place in the world she'd rather be.

David propped himself up on one elbow and his brows drew together. "You *must* be more careful, *cor meum*."

She reached up and touched his face as her breathing slowed. "I will. I promise. Apparently, Colette nearly died when she was younger from eating just half a poisonous berry that bush produces when it's done flowering."

His eyes widened and he rolled onto his side. "Really?"

"Yeah. She slept for something like a day and a half."

His brow furrowed.

She released an appreciative sigh. "Don't worry. I'll be more careful with all the different flowers. I honestly had no idea some were *that* deadly." After a few minutes of silence, she let out a small laugh. "I bet that's part of the reason Colette's so obsessed with unicorns."

"Huh?"

Elisabeth sat up. Legs folded beneath her; she leaned over David. "Do you know how many times Colette has asked me for a unicorn?"

He stretched out, clasping both hands behind his head as his blue eyes squinted with amusement. "A unicorn?"

"Yes! She's convinced they're real and told me I should get one because they're great at detecting poison." When the horse suddenly snorted, Elisabeth glanced over at it. "Colette's going to be so disappointed I bought an old mare instead of a unicorn."

"She'll survive," he said, chuckling.

Elisabeth suddenly gasped and jumped up. "I have a *great* idea!"

David shook his head and held up a hand. "Elisabeth, no…" He clamped his lips together trying not to laugh as he scrambled to his feet. "No more of your *great* ideas."

With a throaty laugh, she bounced away from David and grabbed hold of the crystal. "I'll be right back."

"Cor meum…" David warned.

She had thoughts of home on her mind.

Home.

****

Elisabeth tossed her purse on the desk. It contained nutmegs, the cookie recipe written on parchment, and the vial of elixir. She grabbed the smartphone from her dresser, flopped onto the bed, and started shopping online. A wide grin spread across her face after finding exactly what she'd been imagining. The reviews were fabulous so she filled in the online order form.

Colette would lose her mind with excitement.

Elisabeth's shoulders slumped. "Five to seven days for delivery?"

With a dejected sigh, she knew she should probably stay home for a while to see her parents, go to school...do all that *normal* stuff, anyway.

The longer she hung out in the fourteenth century, the stranger it was returning to school. She felt less and less connected to friends and classmates. Elisabeth had an entire life kept hidden from *everyone*—except for Sissi Waters and David Perrier.

Oh, the irony.

The only ones who understood the situation regarding her and David—were *older* her and David.

****

"*Salve!*" Elisabeth called out while shutting the front door.

Felis immediately sauntered into the foyer to greet her.

"In here!" Mrs. Waters replied.

After dropping her coat and backpack at the door, Elisabeth scooped the purring cat into her arms, heading to the living room.

"What do you think?" With a gleam in her eye, Mrs. Waters pulled drop cloths off the furniture. "I had the room repainted."

Elisabeth rubbed her forehead. "It looks *exactly* the same."

"*Nooo*, this color has a touch more cream in it."

"Well, it looks great…just like it did before." She couldn't help chuckling.

The old woman cleared her throat. "Did you find the note I left yesterday? I had to rush Felis to the vet."

"WHAT?" Elisabeth lowered her head and gave the cat Eskimo kisses. "Is everything okay?"

"For the most part. Apparently, he's just getting old." She let out a shallow sigh. "That's the hard part about having pets, isn't it?"

Elisabeth's head jerked back. "I just bought a horse."

Sissi's hand flew to her chest. "Rosamund?"

"Yes." She put the cat on the floor.

"Oh, sweet Rosamund." Mrs. Waters' eyes clouded with tears and she dug into her pocket for a tissue.

Elisabeth held her breath. "There's, uh…there's something I've been meaning to ask you."

The old woman pressed a fist to her lips and shook her head. "No, I don't want to influence any of your decisions."

She leaned in. "Don't you think I have a right to know if I'm going to *die* soon?"

Mrs. Waters clasped Elisabeth's hands in her own. "I'm still here, aren't I?"

****

The day the parcel arrived, Elisabeth scooped it off the front porch. With a huge grin, she dashed up to her room, eager to see it in real life. She held her breath, opening the package, praying it looked as good as the photos online. Bouncing from foot to foot, she wondered if this wasn't more for her than Colette.

Elisabeth's eyes widened, and she squealed dramatically. She reached into the back of her closet, grabbing the pale pink gown. Funny how out of all the dresses recently acquired, it was David's that made her heart sing. She slipped into it, tummy fluttering while knotting the long belt around her waist. Elisabeth left her purse, but grabbed the new items from the bed, arranging everything in her arms.

She let out a throaty laugh and reached for the crystal.

Colette would *finally* get to see a unicorn.

****

David's mouth fell open as Elisabeth seemed to make an armful of flowers materialize out of thin air. His brows squished together. "What in the name of Jupiter…?"

"I'm turning Rosamund into a unicorn," she said with a sing-song voice, bouncing on her tiptoes toward the horse. "For Colette."

With an incredulous look, David watched Elisabeth clip a soft golden horn to a strap on the bridle, arranging Rosamund's forelock around it. The foot-long horn was surrounded with pink silk garden roses, like a crown.

Elisabeth squealed. "Oh my gosh, she looks amazing, doesn't she?"

When she draped a matching floral garland around Rosamund's neck, David covered his mouth with a hand, trying hard not to laugh. "By the gods, *cor meum*…what on *earth* do flowers have to do with unicorns?"

"What do you mean?" Her posture perked up. "They're pretty. It's for Colette."

He gave a slow, disbelieving shake of his head. "I can honestly say I've seen nothing like this before." He shuffled closer. "Diana, the goddess of hunting, had a chariot drawn by eight unicorns. Are you not aware they were ferocious *fighters*?"

"Well…mine isn't," she said with a cheeky grin. She bounced toward David and grabbed his hand, playfully dancing around him before wrapping both arms around his waist. Looking up at him, she took a deep, savoring breath. If only he knew how much he'd been missed while she was home for a week. Elisabeth then jerked her head back. "Wait…" Her eyes squinted with amusement. "Are you saying you believe unicorns were real?"

David offered a bemused smile, kissed the top of her head, and then suddenly bent down, flipping her over his shoulder. Half upside down, she burst into laughter as he walked away from the horse and back to the entwined tree trunks before setting her down again.

When David sat and continued making his sling, Elisabeth grabbed her discarded daisy crown, placed it on her head, and helped by pulling the bark fibers apart for him.

"So…" Elisabeth leaned in. "How should we do it?"

He looked up at her, a blank look on his face. "Do what?"

She gestured toward Rosamund. "Trick Colette into thinking I have a unicorn!"

"Oh, no, no, no." David chuckled as he stood, tucked the new sling into his belt, and grabbed the cloth bag. "I remain uninvolved in *this* scheme, love."

"Oh, come on. Don't be a fun-sucker." She rose, sauntering over to the horse, untying Rosamund with a simple tug.

"Good knot. I'm impressed."

Elisabeth's brows squished together as she led Rosamund back toward David. "Huh?"

He pointed at the lead rope she held in her hand. "I'm surprised you tied the horse *properly*."

She playfully flicked an end of her long rope belt at him. "Percy taught me."

He caught the belt and, with a mischievous smile, pulled her toward him. "Want me to show you a knot *everyone* should know?"

Elisabeth tiptoed closer. "All right."

After draping the cloth bag from the bright red wooden saddle tree, David removed her belt, holding one end of the rosy-colored rope in his hands. "First, make a simple overhand knot like this…" He looped it around and pulled it through until it resembled a pretzel. "Now you have a slip-knot." He moved the knot up and down to demonstrate how it worked. "Then, take this end and tie another overhand knot." David twisted it, pulled it through, and then tightened the loop around his finger, showing how strong it was. "Now see if you can do it." He handed her the end of the belt and took hold of Rosamund's lead rope.

As Elisabeth attempted the knot herself, David walked her through the steps. Within a few minutes, she had it figured out. "I'm *never* going to need to know this, though," she said with a small laugh.

"Oh, really?" Eyes twinkling, he leaned in. "You now know how to tie a *strong* knot if you ever need to….oh, I don't know…fly across a waterfall, escape an arena when a fire mountain is exploding, or if you're trying to rescue *me* after I've fallen into a mine."

Her brows lifted while tying the belt around her

waist once again. "Oh. I guess it *is* kind of useful."

"Very."

They walked back to the main road—with Rosamund dressed as a unicorn—clip-clopping behind them.

"All right, you go on ahead and have Colette wait on the street for me, but don't say anything," Elisabeth insisted as they neared the little bridge.

David shook his head, confined his laughter to a snort, and walked on ahead to the village by himself.

As she watched him disappear in the distance, Elisabeth bit down on a smile, waiting with Rosamund, stalling for time.

She glanced behind, hearing several horses galloping closer.

One neighed loudly.

Her muscles tensed watching five men riding from the direction of Paris, heading toward the village. Dressed in drab colors and moving quickly, something about them sent a shiver up her spine.

As they neared, their hardened faces looked dark and serious.

Elisabeth swallowed a lump in her throat and stepped back, clearing the road for them, trying to appear inconspicuous—with a flower adorned *unicorn* beside her.

The men approached and the leader glanced her way. He looked to be in his early thirties. He had stringy blond hair, calculating eyes, and a long nose that came to a point. He wore an off-white shirt beneath a dark brown, knee-length tunic, black pants, and tall boots.

Elisabeth winced. "Come on, Rosamund," she

whispered, tugging at the rope.

The leader had a harsh squint as he rode by. He then turned his horse around, gesturing to the rest of his posse.

Elisabeth's heart pounded in her chest and she gripped the rope tighter, but in doing so spooked Rosamund.

The men moved into position, blocking the bridge.

Sensing trouble, the old mare whinnied, stomped a front foot, and then reared up, managing to break free. The horse charged through the stream, toward the village.

CRAP!

Pulse racing, Elisabeth pushed both shoulders back and raised her chin, attempting to appear unintimidated. Realizing she still wore the daisy crown, she whipped it off and tossed it aside. "What does my father want *this* time?"

The leader forced a laugh and gestured at his men. "It's her."

Elisabeth's brows squished together.

Wait…? What's going on?

Instinct took over and she backed away with quick, jerky steps. She then turned, bolting along the bank, looking for a spot to cross the stream and head toward the village herself.

Thunderous hooves galloped after her, closing in.

Suddenly, the leader grabbed Elisabeth under the arms, dragged her up onto his large horse, and set her on the saddle in front of him. "Good evening, *milady*," he said through clenched teeth.

The other four men quickly fell in line and the horses sped off, heading away from the village.

And away from Paris.

Chapter Twenty-Eight

The late afternoon sun beat down on Elisabeth. She wiped sweat from her brow, riding side-saddle in front of the robust man. One of his hands gripped the reins; the other her arm. They'd been riding for several hours over the hills of the French countryside. Her stomach growled after they left the dirt road. They were now traveling slowly through a rugged area filled with scrubby growth and half-buried boulders and rocks.

A noisy stream ran alongside them, rushing down through the craggy hillside. The men seemed to be following it as they chatted and conversed with each other in some language Elisabeth didn't recognize, maybe Italian.

When they stopped outside of an abandoned cabin made of field stones, her shoulders tensed. The windowless structure, no bigger than a garden shed, had random boulders stacked around the perimeter. Its wooden apex roof was so primitive that the end of a large log was visible at the peak.

The door opened outward and Elisabeth could see a compacted dirt floor inside the dark, empty room. Her eyes narrowed, trying to figure out the noise. The rushing water she recognized, but there was another, almost rhythmic, mechanical sound quietly emanating from inside.

The men dismounted, the leader pulling Elisabeth

from his horse.

She shook her head in denial and glanced around, needing a weapon.

Anything.

A knife from home?

No. Not yet.

Elisabeth couldn't risk losing her crystal, which was tucked safely beneath her dress.

Dragged to the cabin by the wrist, her pulse raced.

No!

She couldn't let them take her inside to do God knows what!

Her eyes bulged, searching the ground for a rock.

With rasping breaths, Elisabeth tried to break free from his grasp, pressing a foot against the doorframe to stop him from pulling her inside.

The other men chuckled when the leader grabbed Elisabeth in both arms and entered the cabin as if she was nothing but a toddler throwing a temper tantrum.

He then walked back out and slammed the wooden door shut.

Elisabeth heard them grunt, moving a heavy item, barricading her inside.

With an ear to the door, her posture slumped in relief, listening as the men mounted their horses and rode off.

Now in the darkness, she realized that strange, creepy sound was directly behind her. The mechanical noise was unending, as if something was continuously spinning.

Elisabeth's muscles tightened. She felt the color drain from her face and grabbed hold of her crystal.

Thoughts of home entered her mind.

Home.

****

Standing in her room once again, Elisabeth planted her feet in a wide stance. "What do I need?" she mumbled, determined to escape from that cabin before the men returned.

A candle.

Matches.

Maybe an axe...?

Elisabeth pulled a housecoat over her dress as her tummy rumbled. First, she needed some food. It's hard to think your way out of a kidnapping on an empty stomach.

****

Elisabeth struck a match to light a candle, illuminating the small cabin. When she held it up and turned around to see what the rhythmic noise was, her eyes narrowed, trying to figure out what she was looking at.

The back half of the cabin floor dropped down about two feet, creating a rectangular pit. Inside the pit, a heavy stone wheel spun continuously. Over top, a small metal chute was positioned to drop something through a hole in the center of the wheel. While pausing to examine it, Elisabeth listened to the rushing stream. It sounded as if the back of the cabin was built atop it.

She gasped, finally realizing what this place was: an abandoned mill; the spinning stone probably once used for grinding grain.

Mystery solved, Elisabeth placed the candle aside and grabbed the axe, slamming it against the door over and over again. The thick wood became notched with marks but didn't budge.

Whatever blocked it was heavy.

Eventually, Elisabeth's posture slumped and the hacking became less forceful. Her eyes filled with tears, the axe dropped to the ground, and she sat to rest for a moment, leaning against the stone wall.

She rubbed her face and eyes.

Exhaustion was overwhelming.

Elisabeth hugged both knees to her chest and laid her head down.

Eyes closed.

Just for a minute…

"Elisabeth?"

"ELISABETH?"

A horse neighed.

"Elisabeth!"

Gasping, her head flinched back. How long had she been asleep?

The candle appeared to have burned out long ago, but sunlight now streamed through gaps in the roof.

With a slow smile, she scrambled to her feet and let out an appreciative sigh.

She *knew* David would find her.

Elisabeth spun around, banging her fists against the wood. "In here! I'm in here!"

With an ear pressed against the door, her legs felt wobbly, listening as several men pushed the blockade away. The door flew open, and her chest tightened with emotion as she flung both arms around her hero.

"Oh, thank God, we found you," Cato said as he stiffly hugged her in return. "Are you hurt?"

Her mouth fell open and she jerked back, staring into his aging eyes.

He wrapped an arm around her shoulders. "Are you

able to walk, my dear? The carriage is just beyond that hill. Quickly, before the rain starts."

"Yes, I'm...I'm fine," she replied with a dazed look as he helped her across the rugged terrain, accompanied by Crooked Nose and the rest of his men. "How did you know I was...?"

He stared at her for a moment, his eyes turning dark and serious. "Because I just paid your ransom."

She gasped. "Ransom?"

"Come along." His tone was soothing. "I'll bring you home."

Elisabeth followed Cato and his men as they hiked along the stream. Overhead, a gray sky threatened to spill at any moment. When they finally reached the road, her eyes widened, noticing more men on horseback and a luxurious horse-drawn carriage awaiting them.

A footman's posture straightened and he quickly opened the door. "Milady," he said, taking Elisabeth's arm and helping her inside.

She slumped onto the upholstered bench as Cato climbed in, taking the spot across from her.

The footman shut the door and a moment later they sped off.

Cato reached over, lifting a drop-leaf table attached to the side of the carriage between their seats. "I believe you know how to play chess." He pulled an ornate folding game board from a drawer beneath his bench. "It will help pass the time."

She gave a hesitant nod and leaned in closer, watching him place the pieces on red and white squares. "So, I...I was kidnapped for a ransom?"

Cato cleared his throat. "It seems you've played the

role of my daughter quite convincingly." He let out a deep sigh as rain began pitter-pattering on the carriage roof. He pointed at her chess pieces. "White moves first."

Elisabeth felt heat rush to her ears. "Thanks for paying it," she said with a weakened voice, moving a pawn at the edge of the board.

A horse nickered as the carriage bumped along, following a road through the countryside, accompanied by an entire team of men on horseback.

Cato looked at her. "If you had accepted my help when first offered, none of this would have happened. As I told you last time, Aquarius and I were once close as brothers. You and I were once friends. I am no longer a weak...*boy*. I could have protected you." He shook his head and moved her pawn back, pointing at the four squares in the center of the board. "You want to try and take control of these four squares."

"Oh." Elisabeth moved a pawn in the center instead. "I know how to play, but I'm not very good at it."

Cato countered with a similar chess move. "I am not the same person you once knew."

She studied the board. Maybe he *was* being honest.

So far, Cato had done *nothing* to indicate he harbored ill will against either of them. In fact, he'd begged forgiveness, asked how he could help, offered them both protection, sent gifts, and now paid a ransom to rescue her.

Elisabeth let out a long exhale and moved a knight. "Thanks for everything you've done. To be honest, it's actually been really helpful pretending to be your daughter."

He leaned back in his seat, looking her directly in the eye.

"When I don't fit in, or when I say something wrong that might give me away, everyone assumes it's because I've grown up in some gilded castle outside of the real world."

Cato sat silent for a moment and then moved his own knight. "I think it would be wise—not just for your safety, but for Aquarius'—if you stay with me for the time being. Now, the decision is entirely yours of course."

Elisabeth's body tensed as she moved a bishop. "But what about—?"

"It appears you've drawn too much attention to yourself lately. At this point, it would be unwise *not* to live under tightened security."

She opened her mouth to say something, but no words came out.

"Does a king's daughter not require protection?" He took out her pawn.

Elisabeth glanced around the board uneasily, then answered with a small nod. "Yes, of course."

"And what of the king *maker's* daughter?"

"But—"

"I'm not sure you understand the seriousness of the predicament you've gotten yourself into." Cato let out a heavy sigh, watching as she took out his knight. "You've *also* angered the spice guild, and they're not someone you want as an enemy."

Elisabeth covered her face with both hands. Balinus had warned her, but she'd been too stupid to listen.

"I can take care of the guild as well, but it will take

a few days at the very least." He rubbed his brow as if a headache was starting. "Eventually, they'll soon forget they had a quarrel with us."

Us?

Elisabeth's chin quivered. How could she have messed up this badly? "Thank you...again. It seems I'm causing you a lot of problems."

"As a *daughter* sometimes does," he said with a wink before moving another knight across the chess board.

She gazed out the window for a moment, staring at nothing. "Do you have any children?"

"No." His focus was on the board, but his eyes filled with tears. "Not anymore."

Elisabeth gave him an understanding nod. "I'm sorry."

In silence, both lost in their own thoughts, they maneuvered their chess pieces around the squares.

Perhaps she *should* go stay at that beautiful castle until things simmer down. She'd never forgive herself if David, little Colette, or any of the others were inadvertently put in harm's way because of her. Elisabeth's brows pulled in and she glanced up at Cato. "If I stay with you, what about Aquarius? He's going to be worried sick."

"I'll take care of Aquarius," he said in a soothing tone, moving a rook.

She took a deep, pained breath and closed her eyes. "All right. I'll go. It's only for a few days."

Cato gave a crisp nod. "I'll do what I can to help get you out of this predicament you've managed to get yourself into."

"Thanks."

Cato moved his queen and then leaned back in the seat. "Check."

Elisabeth's eyes widened. "Already!"

She stared at the chessboard, trying to figure out what move might possibly save her in this little game they now played.

Chapter Twenty-Nine

Elisabeth climbed out of the carriage after Cato, following him into the courtyard. Her breath stalled while taking in the luxurious surroundings once again, enjoying the soothing sound of splashing water. She let out an appreciative sigh, eying the fountain with the statue of the Roman-looking woman whose pitcher continuously spilled into the basin. "I love that fountain."

"It's Hebe."

"Who?"

"Hebe, the goddess of youth. On Mount Olympus, her job was to serve ambrosia to the other gods in order to keep them young and immortal."

Elisabeth's eyes widened. "So...you're basically telling everyone your little secret, but nobody realizes it."

"It's right in front of their faces." Cato exchanged a knowing glance with her. "You'd be surprised how decidedly *un*curious most people are about the world in which we live." When the colorful bird strutted closer, he bent down, stroking its bright feathers.

As if a child had colored it using every crayon they could find, the bird had a golden-yellow head and scarlet chest, a striped cape of light orange trimmed in black, dark blue wings, a green and yellow back, and a long, flowing tail of brown and black.

Elisabeth stepped closer. "That bird really loves you, doesn't it?"

"It's been nurtured and handled by me long enough that I've earned its trust."

She tilted her head to the side. "I've never seen anything like it."

"That's because it's amongst the rarest and most beautiful ever found; a golden pheasant." Cato led the way along the edge of the courtyard, heading toward a doorway with the bird following close behind. "According to legend, it was originally brought to the known world from Colchis by the Argonauts while on their quest for the Golden Fleece. Probably mistook it for a phoenix."

"The Argonauts?"

"Jason, Hercules, Orpheus—"

Elisabeth's eyes widened. "Orpheus as in Orpheus and Eurydice?"

"The one and the same. Orpheus was an Argonaut. He married Eurydice after his return from the expedition. She then died from the snakebite on their wedding night."

With a slow, disbelieving shake of her head, Elisabeth stared at the colorful creature.

Cato stopped and scooped the lovestruck bird into his arms, stroking the pheasant's plumed head. Its tail feathers flowed majestically toward the floor. "Now, rest and be ready to dine with Guglielmo Tartare this evening. He wields his own sort of power which should prove useful getting you out of this predicament you're in."

"Really?"

Cato gave her an easy nod. "As my daughter, I

suggest you make yourself agreeable to him."

"I'll be as charming as possible," she said with a slow smile. "Thanks *again* for all your help." Elisabeth's posture stiffened while following Cato as he walked into his castle with wide, confident steps. "Also…please, I need to get word to Aquarius that I'm safe. He's going to be worried sick."

Cato turned around and let out an arrogant laugh. "Consider it done. If things turn out the way I suspect, you'll most likely lay your eyes upon him this very night."

Elisabeth glanced around the foyer. Ahead were three stone archways. Beyond that—a grand staircase. The plaster walls were covered with paintings, decorative woodwork, and tapestries; the lobby filled with tall bronze candelabra, their unlit candles awaiting nightfall.

She followed Cato into a room on the left. Like the courtyard outside, it looked more Roman than medieval.

It made sense, considering Cato's origins.

The floors were tiled in an elaborate two-toned pattern and the walls garbed in rich, carved panelling about five feet high. Above that, a decorative bas-relief border was painted green. The remainder of the walls, up to the high ceiling, were painted in a repeating pattern, not unlike wallpaper.

The room was cozier than a typical medieval great room. More intimate. Twelve chairs with leather upholstery and bronze nail heads surrounded the dining table, with a large iron candelabrum in the center.

Scattered throughout were sideboards holding brass serving trays, additional chairs, and several floor candelabra. Right now, sunshine poured into the room through mullion windows made of tiny diamond-shaped panes of glass. She glanced outside, taking in the courtyard's view.

Elisabeth's eyes widened. "Maybe Aquarius can stay here too." She then cleared her throat, knowing David wasn't going to be so quick to forgive. "Never mind."

As Cato chuckled, his attention turned to a servant entering the room.

A petite, fair-skinned woman of about forty walked closer, wearing a blue-black dress and a white wimple in her blonde hair. Her blue eyes seemed warm and friendly.

"Agnès, see that my daughter is rested and ready to join our guest for supper with me this evening."

Agnès gave a respectful nod. "This way, milady," she said, leading her back into the foyer and up the stairs.

Elisabeth grabbed onto a heavy rope that served as a wall-mounted handrail, following the woman to the first landing. Wide planked wooden floors creaked as they walked down the long corridor. When they came upon arched windows, Elisabeth paused, staring at the spectacular view of the lake. On the opposite bank, a rolling hill led to a nearby forest.

At the end of the hallway, they turned left and Elisabeth trailed slowly behind.

Passing an open door, she peeked inside.

She stared incredulously, eyes wide with surprise.

The focal point of the room was a luxurious marble bathtub that looked as if Michelangelo might have sculpted the stone (although he probably wasn't even born yet). The tub had an "Ancient Roman" feel to it, with carved lion heads lining the outside of the tub, holding what looked like swags of fabric in their mouths. On the wall above it, two large bronze faucets protruded.

"Does…does that bathtub have hot and cold running water?" Elisabeth asked with an incredulous voice.

A satisfied smile crossed Agnès' face. "Yes. It does. Your father has always been quite the visionary," she said with a small laugh. "Apparently, Lord Cathon had those installed about twenty years ago. When King Edward found out, he had the same thing installed at Westminster."

"Wow," Elisabeth said with a slow shake of her head. "I can't believe it."

Although she knew—firsthand—there was hot and cold running water to the baths in Ancient Rome, she had *no* idea the extremely wealthy had it in the 1300s. A slight chill ran up her spine as she remained in the doorway. Above the bathtub hung a white canopy, deep green curtains lined the walls, and a fireplace built into the corner added coziness to the space. It seemed as if…

"Milady?"

When she turned around, Agnès opened an ornately carved wooden door across the hall.

Elisabeth's mouth snapped shut after stepping into a large bed chamber. Red floor-to-ceiling curtains lined the walls, and there was an elaborate stone carving over a fireplace mantel. Exquisite furniture was scattered throughout the room, including a canopy bed covered with white netting. The surfaces of tables and chests were decorated with linens, pitchers, and trays filled with display objects. On a dressing table sat a tri-folding vanity mirror made from what looked like polished bronze, along with an ivory comb. Elisabeth's hand covered her mouth realizing that Cato "the kingmaker" probably lived more luxuriously than the medieval kings themselves.

"I suppose your convent school was much humbler," Agnès said.

"Yes. Very much so."

The servant walked across the room to a small serving table. From two pitchers she poured wine and water into a large goblet, setting it beside a plate of dates and what looked like lacy pizzelle cookies. She then politely excused herself from the room.

All alone, Elisabeth let out a spontaneous laugh and reached for the watered-down wine, gulping it down. Her posture relaxed, eying the comfy bed. With a yawn, she shuffled over and climbed in between the luxurious sheets. After last night's ordeal, a little nap might not be a bad idea.

****

"Milady?"

Elisabeth's eyes opened, listening as someone knocked gently on the door.

"Milady?"

"Huh?" She sat up, rubbing her face. "Yeah?"

"Your father requests your presence in his private dining room immediately."

"Oh…all right." She yawned. "I'll be there in a minute."

Elisabeth tumbled out of bed and made her way to the dressing table, running the comb through her hair to look presentable. She smoothed down her dress before heading back downstairs.

As she entered the dining room, Cato was deep in conversation with a blond man, obviously their dinner guest, Guglielmo Tartare, whose back faced the doorway.

"...are the terms of the alliance in which—" Cato glanced up. "Here she is now." He then gestured toward an empty seat as a servant placed a bowl of bread rolls on the table.

Rather than turning to acknowledge her, Guglielmo grabbed a roll.

A servant stepped forward, holding out a bowl of perfumed water and a small towel for Elisabeth to wash her hands.

"You've slept the day away," Cato said, his voice incredulous.

"Really?" She dried her hands and joined the men at the table, taking a seat across from the stranger. "I didn't realize how exhausted—"

Her heart pounded in her chest while staring at Guglielmo Tartare.

The man who'd kidnapped her.

"What's going on?" she asked Cato with a raised voice.

"Tartare, you've already met my daughter, Elisabeth."

As he nodded in reply, a cold chill ran up her spine. Still dressed in the off-white shirt and dark brown tunic, the man reached for another piece of bread, breaking it apart with his fingers while watching Elisabeth.

She gripped the edge of the table.

Guglielmo's eyes narrowed and he popped the

bread into his mouth. He then turned, speaking to Cato. "So, with this alliance, the Purchace Company will…"

Everyone's attention was distracted when a young man, wearing disheveled traveling clothes, rushed into the room, struggling to catch his breath.

Guglielmo's posture stiffened and he leapt to his feet. "Apologies, milord, but I must take my leave."

Cato nodded. "Go. We'll adjust the finer details later, but consider the deal done."

Tartare rushed out the door with the man.

Elisabeth shook her head. "You *do* know that's the man who kidnapped me, right? That you paid the ransom to? Why on earth would you—?"

Cato interrupted with an exaggerated sigh while marching into the foyer and outside to the courtyard. "Oh, do show a little gratitude. I am trying to help and you're acting like a spoiled child. Do you understand how much trouble I've gone through in order to fix what *you* have done?"

Elisabeth's eyes widened and her throat tightened as they walked along the gravel walkway. "How on earth can *he* help?"

Cato watched as the men disappeared around the corner toward the covered portico and front gate. "*He* is the most successful and famous mercenary leader— from Italy to Flanders and beyond."

Mercenary?

Elisabeth gave him a blank look.

Cato took a deep breath, savoring the moment. "And we have just formed a powerful alliance."

"An alliance with…" Her eyes narrowed in confusion. "…a soldier for hire?"

"My dear, Guglielmo Tartare commands an

enormous and powerful *army*. An army for *hire*."

Elisabeth tugged her ear, trying to figure out the significance. "Does that mean I'm now...untouchable?"

When Cato let out a small chuckle, the golden pheasant suddenly appeared, letting out a high-pitched chirp while running over from behind a short hedge. He scooped the bird into his arms, stroking its plumed head. "The truth is, life is nothing but a game of chess. When you have a strategy, can see the bigger picture and think several moves ahead, you can maneuver your pieces and remove your opponents one by one, until you're ultimately the winner."

Elisabeth's brows squished together. "So...you turned around and allied with my kidnapper." A slow smile formed on her face. "That means nobody can touch me now because they'll basically have to deal with an entire army!"

With a deep, gratifying sigh, Cato grinned while caressing the bird's scarlet chest. "Exactly."

Elisabeth let out a shaky laugh. "That's amazing. You...YOU'RE amazing! Oh my gosh, thank you!"

Cato gave her a look that radiated superiority. Still stroking the bird's neck, he suddenly bent its golden-yellow head backward, twisted his hands, and pulled—killing it instantly.

Chapter Thirty

As the golden pheasant fell limp in Cato's arms, Elisabeth gasped and shuffled back a step.

At that moment, a pretty servant walked over. "Milord?"

"Yes, Melisende? What is it?"

"The young man from the bridge...?" She stole a glance at Elisabeth for a split second before lowering her voice. "Sir, he refused to leave and caused such a fuss..."

Elisabeth shook her head, still gawking at the dead bird.

Cato frowned. "Where is he now?"

She openly stared at him. "In the sugar drawer!"

"That's fine. I'll take care of the matter. Oh..." He handed Melisende the colorfully-feathered carcass. "Tell cook we're to feast on pheasant tomorrow evening."

Without flinching, Melisende took it, quickly curtsied, and then hurried toward the servant's entrance.

Elisabeth shook her head in denial. "You killed your bird?"

Cato rolled his eyes. "It's just a bird. Pheasant is a delicacy and this union with Tartare calls for a celebration."

Elisabeth opened and then closed her mouth.

She thought back to Isabeau easily skinning and

deboning a rabbit.

Mom and Dad *always* cooked a big stuffed turkey at Thanksgiving and Christmas.

Elisabeth's brows squished together. Perhaps she was reading too much into it?

"I need to check my sugar drawer." Cato fished a key out of his waist pouch and then walked away. "You're free to come if you like," he called over his shoulder.

"Sugar drawer?" Her voice softened as she hurried after him. "Is that where you store expensive sugars and spices and stuff?"

"Something like that."

She trailed Cato along the parapet, taking in the scenic views of the lake, and sauntered down the familiar stairs behind him. Like last time, the iron gate at the bottom was wide open, leading to the water's edge.

Elisabeth watched a mama duck and her babies waddle into the moat. "Is it very deep?"

"Deep enough. I had it dug out and then the river rerouted here a long, *long* time ago."

Elisabeth's breath caught. "Wow!"

She glanced up at the enormous castle beside her, following Cato as he walked along the pathway to the cellar entrance. He unlocked the heavy door, pushed it wide open, leading the way through an arched passage lined with wine barrels. Numerous storage rooms branched off the main route.

Elisabeth's posture perked up. "Is this whole area, like…a pantry?"

"Yes. Everything from straw to meat to wax is kept here in the cellar."

At the end of the corridor, they turned left and climbed a rough stone staircase. A tiny niche led to another flight of stairs—this one heading back down again.

"Strange place for a sugar drawer," Elisabeth said with a nervous laugh.

At the bottom was a door made of thick, dark wood with enormous hinges and countless steel studs. Cato unlocked it and they entered a large room where lantern sconces flickered eerily.

An icy chill ran up Elisabeth's spine.

This wasn't a pantry.

Ahead of her, Cato's head flinched back. He then let out an impatient sneer and cursed under his breath, pointing toward something. "Behold, my *empty* sugar drawer."

Elisabeth turned slowly, unwillingly, staring at a large metal cage.

The torture device was empty.

Cato's posture perked up while glancing around the dungeon. "Where are you?" he whispered.

Elisabeth's hands trembled.

Although it appeared empty of any prisoners, the torture chamber was lined with shackles along the walls and what looked like a wooden medieval version of a massage table, but with heavy ropes to tie a person down.

Her leg muscles tightened and she eyed the door, ready to run.

Cato walked into a little alcove, stared down at the floor, and shook his head. "My apologies, Aquarius. I was told you were in the sugar drawer, *not* the oubliette. I'd have come sooner, but—"

"Aquarius?" She shook her head in denial, running into the alcove. "Aquarius…"

In a pit, about ten feet below, David gasped. "Cato? I am warning you, *old man*…if you lay a hand on her I'll—"

Cato let out a cocky laugh. "Predictable as always, dear *brother*. Threatening me from the bottom of an inescapable prison cell. Why would I hurt my own daughter?"

David scrubbed a hand over his face and then flashed Elisabeth an incredulous look. "I'd ask in jest if you care to join me down here, love, but last time you did."

"Don't worry. I'm getting you out of there." Glaring at Cato, Elisabeth's nostrils flared. "If your men hurt him, I swear to God, I'll kill them myself," she hissed. "You can't even *imagine* the weapons I have access to in the twenty-first century."

Cato leaned in. "As did the gods of old. Whether you choose to believe it or not, you and I are cut from the same cloth." His voice was steady and low-pitched. "*We* could be the greatest, most powerful father-daughter duo since Jupiter and Minerva, Zeus and Athena."

Elisabeth recoiled in disgust. "I am *nothing* like you."

"Athena was conceived without a mother and emerged fully grown from Zeus' forehead. At least our backstory is far more believable." Cato smirked. "In the meantime, I've no intention of killing either of you. I was only told the fool was down here moments ago. Apparently, he showed up at the castle gate after *you* went missing and refused to leave. I suppose my guards simply had enough." Cato turned and strolled out of the dungeon.

Elisabeth dropped to her knees at the edge of the narrow oubliette, staring down at David. "I'm so sorry, Aquarius." Her voice choked with tears. "This is *all* my fault. I should have listened when you said—"

"*Cor meum.*" David raised an eyebrow. "Your belt."

"Huh?"

"It won't be long enough, but I should be able to jump to reach it."

"Oh." She sprang to her feet, untying the long rope belt he'd made. "Déjà vu." Her gaze then darted around. "There's nothing to tie it to."

"Find a piece of wood, a broom, a spear…"

"Just a sec." Elisabeth sprinted out of the alcove, into the dungeon, spotting chains, shackles, and a variety of wooden and iron torture devices. Her posture slumped in relief, eyeing a long pole leaning against the wall with a pronged, U-shaped end. She grabbed it and ran back to the pit.

"Now remember that knot I showed you?" David called up.

Her brows drew together and she nodded.

As David talked Elisabeth through the steps, she fiddled with the end of her rope belt until it resembled a pretzel.

"Slip the knot onto the end of the pole and pull it tight."

"'Kay," she muttered, and then, with trembling hands, lay the pole across the top of the pit and lowered the rope to David.

"Good job, love," he said with a playful wink. He

then jumped up, reaching it on the first try. Hand over hand he climbed, pulling his knees to his chest, wrapping his feet around the rope, and lifting himself up and out of the oubliette.

Elisabeth's chest caved in and she threw herself into his arms.

He wrapped her in a bear hug. "I was worried sick about you. Your horse returned without you and I didn't know what—"

"I was kidnapped and held in some abandoned mill overnight." She gave a slow, disbelieving shake of her head. "I honestly don't think Cato knew you were in that pit. I was there when he found out *and* he paid my ransom and brought me here to safety."

"*Cato* paid your ransom?" David's eyes narrowed while grabbing her hand. "*Cato?*"

Elisabeth's brows pulled in. "Yes. I've made a huge mess of things and he's been helping—"

"No." David shook his head. "Whatever he's doing…he is untrustworthy. We're getting out of here *right* now." He limped slightly as they rushed toward the exit.

"Your foot…?"

"It's fine. I'll walk it off."

"Wait!" She ran back and quickly untied the belt, attaching it around her waist once again before hurrying back. They climbed the stairs and when reaching the main corridor, she let out a sigh of relief as faint light from the setting sun filtered into the space.

The door remained ajar.

With a fast-paced stride, the young couple exited the cellar and marched back up to the courtyard, straight to the front gate.

"Open it," he snapped at a guard.

"Milady." Crooked Nose suddenly appeared. He held a small coiled rope in one hand. "I'm afraid you're to remain within the castle walls. Your father's orders." His jaw clenched and he glared at David, slamming the sling into his stomach. "I believe this is yours. *You're* free to go and I suggest you do so."

David grunted and shoved the rope sling into his belt. He grabbed Elisabeth's hand. "*We* are leaving."

More of Cato's guards began to congregate. Somewhere nearby, a horse whinnied and stomped its foot.

"Come on…" Elisabeth dragged David away before things escalated. "We'll find another way out," she whispered. "He can't *keep* me here."

Back in the courtyard, in the fading light, David glanced to his right and his breathing became labored.

Elisabeth turned to see what caught his eye.

Through the mullion glass window panes, they watched as Cato ate alone at the large table, surrounded by candlelight.

David's face reddened and he barrelled toward him.

Elisabeth jogged to keep up.

They marched through the foyer and into the dining room.

"CA-TO!"

Cato's head jerked back. He rose from the table as his guards rushed over. "It's fine." He forced a smile, waving them off. "Leave us in privacy."

David stormed closer, gripping the edge of the table. "*You* left me for dead in the rubble."

"That was ages ago."

David's nostrils flared. "Not to me."

"Yet here you are. You rose like a damn phoenix out of the ashes of Pompeii, didn't you?" Cato returned to his seat. The table was filled with more food than he could ever eat on his own. He gestured toward a platter of mushrooms and leeks. "Join me if you wish."

Elisabeth's tummy growled, eyeing golden custard tarts, beans with what looked like pomegranate seeds…

"What game are you playing?" David asked through gritted teeth.

Cato looked up from his meal. "Game?" He shrugged. "Chess, I suppose." He then glanced at Elisabeth. "Checkmate."

Her eyes narrowed in confusion. "Checkmate?"

"You've been out-maneuvered. I've already won our little game." He shoved a handful of green beans into his mouth with his fingers. "I'm just watching the final moves play out now."

A cold chill ran up her spine.

"As my daughter, I have full authority over you."

"She is *not* your daughter," David said in a scathing tone.

"Who on earth would believe she isn't?" He lowered his voice. "Remember, I never forced her into this. She happily played along whenever it suited her. And being the daughter of Lord Cathon *always* suited her. Every move, every choice has been entirely hers, right down to coming home to my castle instead of going home to you."

Elisabeth glanced around the room as if looking for answers.

This was all a game to Cato?

David's hands clenched and unclenched.

"Wait a minute...?" Elisabeth's brows squished together. "*You* had Guglielmo Tartare kidnap me, didn't you? You used me to get your alliance with him and his army."

David squeezed his eyes shut. "What alliance?"

Cato sat back in his chair, crossing his arms. "Figure it out, Aquarius. Why would a *daughter* come in handy when wanting to form a powerful alliance?"

With a guttural roar, David shoved the table aside and lunged for Cato.

"GUARDS!"

Four guards stormed into the room, pulling David off, and holding him back.

"Escort the boy off my property," Cato said with a quick, disgusted snort.

Muscles and veins strained against David's skin. "If you're having her married off, I swear to the gods I will kill you!" he yelled as they dragged him out of the room. "I will kill you!"

Elisabeth shuffled back and then ran after David.

Before reaching the door, two more guards moved into place, blocking the exit.

Cato forced a smile. "Refuse this arranged marriage to Guglielmo Tartare and you'll be locked up until your wedding day."

She planted her feet wide apart. "I will *not* marry Guglielmo Tartare."

"Oh yes, you will, you ungrateful girl." His eyes narrowed as he looked at her. "And do you know why?"

Elisabeth swallowed the lump in her throat.

"I held up my part of the arrangement. Exactly as asked. Not only are you the daughter of Lord Cathon, but the bride-to-be of Guglielmo Tartare. You are now *untouchable*—in more ways than one."

Elisabeth felt light-headed.

"Like I said...*checkmate*. Now go to your room."

With her stomach in knots, she stormed out of the dining room.

"Make sure my daughter does not leave her bed chamber," Cato instructed one of his men.

Her heart pounded in her ears while stomping up the stairs.

The floor creaked as the guard followed at a distance.

Once in her room, Elisabeth slammed the door shut with all of her might.

She might as well have truly been Cato's daughter for all the control he had over her now.

Chapter Thirty-One

Elisabeth pounded both fists against her thighs. "I am *not* marrying Guglielmo Tartare!"

The guard stationed outside the door spoke to someone in a hushed tone.

As she paced the floor, trying to figure out what to do, a plan began to take shape.

Elisabeth softly shook her head.

It was a dumb idea.

She curled both arms over her head, trying to think of another option.

Posture sagged in defeat, she hurried to the window, unlatching and opening it wide.

The sun had set and the glow of twilight filled the sky. It was no longer light outside, but not yet truly dark. The magic hour, as Aurelius had called it. Across the moat, the rooftops of a tiny village peeked up from behind a protective stone wall. Candles and lanterns from the castle twinkled on the surface of the water below, reflecting like a giant mirror. Elisabeth poked her head out, glancing down. From here, her room was about three stories high and overlooked the wide path near the top of the staircase that led to the water's edge. Her body trembled while staring at the small lake.

Could she swim across?

Brow furrowed; she looked around the room.

Her posture perked up, eyeing the red curtains

hanging from the walls. Working quickly, she pulled each one down. Gathering the fabric into a pile in the middle of the room, Elisabeth knotted them together at the corners, forming a makeshift rope to escape from this—

Someone knocked on the door.

Elisabeth's head jerked back.

"Milady?" The handle turned and the door slowly opened.

With a yelp, Elisabeth flew across the room, slamming it shut. "Sorry, I'm…I'm not dressed," she blurted out.

"I've come to undress you for bed, milady," Agnès whispered through the door, her voice incredulous.

Elisabeth cleared her throat. "It's fine. I can manage myself. Thank you, Agnès." She faked a yawn. "I'm going to bed now. Good night."

Ear pressed to the door, she heard Agnès bid the guard a good evening before walking away.

Tiptoeing back to where she'd been working, Elisabeth tied the rest of the curtain panels together. When she peered over the edge, she estimated the rope was long enough to reach the ground. She hurried across the room, knotting one end to the leg of the heavy canopy bed, and then made a second knot—just in case.

Arms overflowing with fabric, she peered out the window once again, this time spotting an archer walking the parapet below. Elisabeth held her breath, waiting for the sentry to make his rounds.

A maid strolled toward him.

Elisabeth tilted her head to the side, trying to get a better look.

It was Melisende, the pretty maid who'd taken the dead pheasant from Cato. When she gave the guard a little wave, he sauntered closer. Their muffled voices drifted up to the open window as Melisende laughed and touched the man's arm.

With a quiet groan, Elisabeth tapped her foot, waiting for the flirting below to finish so she could commence escaping.

Eventually, the guard pulled at his collar and the two strolled away, disappearing toward the courtyard together.

He was clearly more interested in the pretty maid than guarding the fortress.

With the coast now clear, it was finally dark. Elisabeth threw the makeshift rope over the sill and climbed through the open window, straddling the ledge. She gripped the fabric tight in her hands, and lifted her other leg out, lowering into position.

While dangling from the castle window, Elisabeth's breath came out in short, panicked bursts.

She repelled back slightly to plant both feet against the stones, deciding that walking backward down the wall was her best bet.

Slowly, carefully, she made her way down, praying the fabric rope was tied tight enough.

When reaching the ground, her posture slumped in relief. Then, fists clenched, she sprinted along the walkway to the top of the stairs.

After running down the steps, she cursed under her breath.

The metal gate was closed and locked now.

Elisabeth ran back up, taking the stairs two at a time.

She startled at a noise, wringing her hands, trying to figure out how the heck to get to the water's edge below.

Her gaze darted all around, eventually noticing the tree top stretching above the parapet beside her. She leaned over. The wall was only a single storey high in this section. Elisabeth climbed the rampart, grabbed a branch, and maneuvered through the leafy canopy until she was able to jump down.

She raced to the shoreline, darting along the bank to where it was narrowest to swim across.

Keep to the right, she reminded herself. *Keep to the right.*

Because the moat widened into a small lake, if she were to drift too far left, Elisabeth wasn't certain she could make it safely to the other side.

A man cleared his throat. "I'd rethink that if I were you, milady. Nasty things in them waters."

Elisabeth's hands went limp as she spun around.

An archer stood atop the rampart. His arrow notched, but bow lowered. "Besides, I'm certain your father won't take kindly to—"

From behind her, across the moat, Elisabeth heard the familiar whipping noise of a sling before the guard fell to the ground mid-sentence a moment later.

She stared across the narrow part of the channel in time to see David's shadow disappear behind a tree.

Elisabeth's muscles tightened and she dove into the moat, swimming underwater as far and as fast as possible.

She eventually resurfaced, desperate for air.

Treading water quietly while catching her breath, Elisabeth glanced behind. The moonlit castle looked magnificent, illuminated with torches and lamplight. The shadow of the improvised rope hanging out the bedroom window swayed in the darkness. Hopefully it wouldn't be noticed just yet, buying her precious time to get away.

Toward the back of the castle, another guard came into view, watching the moat as he made his rounds.

Elisabeth tried to remain still as possible. She dared not break the surface of the water while struggling to stay afloat.

When the sentinel disappeared over the ramparts, she slowly turned around again, shivering in the inky lake while trying to orient herself. In the night, it was almost impossible to differentiate between water and land. Everything to the tree line was just—darkness.

Crickets chirped and, in the distance, several owls hooted.

Keep to the right.

Something slimy in the water slithered by her leg. Her heart pounded. Were there really nasty things in the water she didn't know about?

A snake?

An eel?

What if it was a catfish? Don't catfish sting?

Her pulse raced.

Oh my God, what if it's blood-sucking leaches?

Are there leeches in here?

What about piranhas?

Panic began to set in.

Her teeth chattered as she tried not to splash the water.

"Cor meum…"

She stopped, listening to David in the darkness.

"Cor meum…"

With a fluttery feeling in her chest, she straightened course, following David's reassuring voice silently across the water.

The distance was farther than anticipated.

Her muscles felt heavy.

Her breathing labored.

When her hands swept through reeds and long grasses growing out of the water, she let out a sigh of relief knowing she was near the opposite shore.

Suddenly, David was there. His outstretched arms reached for her.

Elisabeth looked up, tears welling behind her eyes. As she grabbed onto him, he pulled her from the moat. Then, without uttering a word, they broke into a run. Her legs shook as they raced into the forest beyond Cato's castle. When she eventually slowed to wipe water from her face, twigs snapped ahead.

Someone—or something—had moved.

Elisabeth froze, yanking David back.

"It's all right." He squeezed her fingers. "Look…"

In the moonlight, a familiar chestnut-colored *unicorn* wandered toward her. Elisabeth let out a shaky laugh and reached out to adjust the flowers and horn on Rosamund's head.

"I rode her to Cato's when searching for you yesterday. They treated her better than me," he added with a snort. "Come on." With precise movements, David pulled off his blue jacket and wrapped it around Elisabeth's dripping wet shoulders.

She laughed, wringing water from her long hair. "You came to rescue me with Rosamund still dressed like *a unicorn*?"

With a groan, David put his hands around her waist, helping her onto the horse. "I wasn't thinking straight and am sleep deprived. Obviously."

He led the horse, with Elisabeth atop, through forests and meadows, heading as far away from Cato's as possible, attempting to follow a moonlit trail.

"Do you think anyone knows I'm gone yet?"

"Probably. As soon as the guard who saw you either wakes or is found."

Elisabeth let out an appreciative sigh. "That shot was incredible."

David laughed. "I was at the waterfront, wondering what to do, when…by the grace of the gods, I saw you climb out the window and was able to keep an eye on you."

Elisabeth dismounted, preferring to walk beside David instead.

"What are…?" He yawned and then his thoughts seemed to drift off.

"This looks like a good place to rest," Elisabeth said in a soothing tone, realizing he probably hadn't slept at all since she'd been kidnapped. "I don't think anyone's following us."

David looked behind while rubbing his face and eyes. "All right. I can no longer see the path in the darkness, anyhow." His words slurred and his feet dragged as he lay down in a soft grassy meadow just off the trail. "I'll keep watch while you rest. Just let me lay my head down a minute."

After Elisabeth tied Rosamund to a nearby tree, she lay next to David on the ground, draping his jacket over them like a blanket. When he let out a heavy sigh, drawing her close to his body, she curled up against him and closed her eyes, melting into his arms.

****

Ouch!

In Elisabeth's dream, someone poked her in the shoulder with a tree branch as a thousand songbirds serenaded her in the forest.

Ouch!

A unicorn whinnied and became restless.

Leaves crunched under someone's sandaled foot.

Elisabeth's eyes opened wide.

This wasn't a dream.

Golden sunlight streamed through trees alive with birdsong. She and David were in a field of white clover. The light scent of honey filled her senses.

A tall monk poked David with the end of his long walking staff.

When Elisabeth bolted upright, the man's head jerked back.

"Oh, thank God." He moved into a relaxed stance; his hand gripping the quarterstaff at eye level beside him. "What sound sleepers you are. I was surprised you did not hear me approach so felt the need to check you were still alive."

"We're fine." She nudged David. "We were tired and just resting here for the night."

The monk looked to be in his forties. He had thick dark hair and an even thicker beard. His warm smile and kind eyes immediately put Elisabeth at ease. Dressed in a brown woolen robe with a hood, he stood at least six feet tall. Around his waist was a simple rope belt from which dangled a cross, a rosary, and a pouch.

As David, still half-asleep, scrambled to his feet and instinctively reached for his sling, the monk rotated his quarterstaff, pressing it to David's chest as a gentle warning. "I'm not going to harm you," he said with a smile. "So go ahead and put that sling away."

Elisabeth rose and put a reassuring hand on David's arm. "It's all right. He's a monk."

"A what?"

"A monk," she whispered. "Like…a holy man."

The man nodded, pulling his quarterstaff back, and holding it upright beside him again. "A friar, actually."

Rosamund snorted.

The friar's eyes narrowed and he stared at Elisabeth, as if afraid to look directly at the old mare. "Do my eyes deceive me…or is that a unicorn? In truth, that's the reason I stopped in the first place."

"It's just a horse in costume," Elisabeth said with a bemused smile. "There's a little girl who loves unicorns and I was trying to do something special for her."

"Ah, I see, well…a horse, you say." The man chuckled. "I must admit to being slightly disappointed."

"Me too," Elisabeth said with a small laugh. "Me too."

The friar turned his attention to David while pointing down the lane. "If you're in want of a meal, there's a village not far from here where you'll find a tavern with ale and gruel to fill your bellies."

David offered a wave of thanks before the friar strolled away. He then flashed Elisabeth a strained smile and picked up his jacket, pulling it on over the white chemise. "We are fortunate that wasn't one of Cato's men who found us."

Elisabeth bit her lip while nodding. "I've *really* made a mess of things."

"Cato intends to have you married off."

"To Guglielmo Tartare." Her voice choked with tears. "I don't even want to think about that right now."

David drew in slow, steady breaths. "Well, if he thinks I will stand back and—"

"Aquarius…" She gave him a pained stare. "I don't know what to do. We've been outmaneuvered by Cato. Tartare is in charge of an extremely powerful army for hire. This arrangement not only gives Cato even more influence and control, but it also gives him unlimited soldiers and makes me untouchable…to *you*."

David's hands curled into tight fists. "Then we must leave here. We will run away where Cato cannot find us and—"

Elisabeth's posture sagged. "They're too powerful and their reach too wide. There's no escaping them. Cato made that perfectly clear." Wringing her hands while glancing down the lane, she saw the friar disappear over the horizon. Her posture perked up. "*Unless*…" Elisabeth paused. She rubbed the back of her neck and paced as an idea took shape. "There *might* be a way to get out of this arranged marriage."

David's lips parted slightly. "How?"

Heat rushed to her cheeks and she shuffled her feet. "Never mind. It's a stupid idea."

"*Cor meum*…" He crept closer. "Tell me."

"Well…I was just thinking…" She tilted her head to the side. "I can't be forced to marry someone if I'm already *legally* married to someone else."

His head flinched back. "What! Who?"

Elisabeth's eyes widened. "WHO? What do you mean who?" She looked away, shaking her head. "Unbelievable."

David's posture stiffened. "Wait…" An enormous

grin spread across his face and he reached for her hands, playfully tugging her closer. "Are you suggesting you and I…?"

Unable to meet his eyes, Elisabeth stared down at their entwined fingers and nodded. "I don't see any other way out of this, do you?" She looked up at David again. "Nobody's above the law. Not even Cato, right?" She cleared her throat. "I mean…it won't be a *real* marriage. It's just for legal purposes—on paper—to get out of an arranged marriage to Guglielmo Tartare." Elisabeth's brows pulled in. "But I *really* shouldn't ask you to do this for me."

David cupped the sides of her head. "I'd do anything for you," he whispered.

Elisabeth stepped back and a slow smile spread across her face. She then squealed and threw both arms around his neck. "It just might be crazy enough to work!"

With a booming laugh, David wrapped his arms around Elisabeth's waist, spinning her in a circle. He untied Rosamund, grabbed Elisabeth's hand, and began speed-walking down the lane.

Elisabeth couldn't help giggling. "What's the rush?"

He flashed a cheeky grin. "I need to find someone to marry us before you change your mind."

"The friar can do it!" She then glanced over her shoulder uneasily. "Unless Cato's men find us first."

Chapter Thirty-Two

They hurried along the path, eventually reaching a tiny farming village located at the edge of the forest. Chickens roamed about the dusty road and a handful of ducks waddled toward a small stream. Elisabeth glanced at the rustic buildings made of sticks, straw, and mud.

When noticing the brown robes of the friar disappear through a doorway, she smiled and pointed ahead. "There he is."

David's face lit up as he gazed upon Elisabeth. "Are we *really* doing this?"

She pulled him to a stop, brushed grass from his shoulder, and adjusted the azure blue jacket he wore. "Only if you want to."

He kissed her forehead. "More than you'll ever know."

She released an appreciative sigh and glanced at Rosamund. Then, with a throaty laugh, removed the floral unicorn horn from the horse's bridle.

"Thank goodness you've tired of that ridiculous thing." David chuckled.

Elisabeth gave him a playful nudge and carefully detached the ring of silk roses from the horn. "Sorry, Rosamund, but a bride needs flowers." With a cheeky grin, she re-attached the golden horn to the bridle and then adjusted the crown of pink garden roses into her own dark hair.

David extended his hand after tying the old mare to a fence post around the side of the building. "Ready?"

She smoothed down her gown and reached for his fingers. "I think so."

Hand in hand, they walked into the tavern where the friar was.

Inside, it smelled unbelievably—good.

Elisabeth's eyes widened, realizing the interior looked exactly as you'd imagined a medieval tavern to look: dirt floor, simple tables and stools, wooden barrels stacked in the corner, and a weary-looking woman carrying a jug and a cup to the friar—who appeared to be the tavern's only patron. A small pig roasted on a spit over the open firepit in the middle of the room, the smoke escaping through a hole in the soot-blackened ceiling.

With a bark of laughter, the friar waved them over.

David cleared his throat as he approached the table. "My apologies for bothering you, but we wonder if you might help us. You see..." He paused to grin at Elisabeth. "We wish to be married."

"As soon as possible," she blurted out.

The friar's posture relaxed and he pushed a flickering candle aside. "Good for you. The sacrament of marriage is most virtuous."

Elisabeth tilted her head to the side. "Are *you* able to do it?" She readjusted the crown of flowers in her hair.

"I am authorized to administer the sacraments, yes." With an unforced laugh, he glanced over at David. "And you consent?"

"Yes. Yes, I most certainly consent."

The friar turned to Elisabeth. "And you?"

"Hm-hm. I do too."

"And you are not related, correct?"

They both shook their heads.

The friar clapped. "Excellent. I must admit, you seem to be a match of suitable temperaments."

Elisabeth rubbed her brow and smiled, waiting as the weary-looking woman returned, placed a bowl of what looked like watery oatmeal on the table, and cracked an obvious joke in some form of French before disappearing again.

"If you're hungry, the gruel is quite hardy."

Elisabeth's eyes narrowed. "Thank you, so…um…is it likely we can be married as soon as possible? Today even?"

The man wiped his mouth, trying not to laugh. "It is already done. You've both verbally consented. Oh…" He made a half-hearted sign of the cross in the air in front of them.

Her head jerked back. "That was it? Shouldn't there be more to it? Don't we need witnesses or something?"

"You don't even need *me*." The friar took a deep, gratified sigh and pointed above. "God is your witness."

"I'm afraid you don't understand," Elisabeth said with a shaky voice. "This needs to be *legally* binding."

"My child…" He shoveled a spoonful of gruel into his mouth. "I assure you it is."

David eased onto a stool across from the friar. "We need proof to show her father, Lord Cathon."

The friar's head jerked back. "Lord Cathon?"

Elisabeth's heartbeat raced. "He intends to have me married off to some horrible man in order to gain even *more* power and influence."

"Ahhh." The friar gave an understanding nod and looked at Elisabeth. "So, you two have exchanged vows in *secret,* without your father's knowledge. Rest assured—you *are* married." He then turned to David. "She is legally bound to *you* until death, and you to her."

David shifted back and forth on the stool. "Even if her father is Lord Cathon?"

"Yes, even if her father is Lord Cathon." The friar paused to take a sip from his cup. "Joan of Kent. Currently the Dowager Princess of Wales. Do you know of her?"

"No." Elisabeth tilted her body closer.

"Well, Joan is the King of England's mother. When she was younger…" The friar paused to chuckle. "I should preface this by saying Joan is the granddaughter of both King Edward I of England *and* King Phillip III of France. Joan was—like you— obviously expected to marry someone suitable when she came of age."

Elisabeth nodded slowly.

"However, at thirteen, she *secretly* exchanged vows with a lowly knight, Tom Holland, before he went off to war." The friar twisted the signet ring on his pinky. "Joan and Tom told no one."

David's posture perked up while listening.

"Unfortunately, while Tom was away, Joan's marriage to the Earl of Salisbury, William Montagu, was arranged."

"Montagu?" Elisabeth muttered to herself.

"Afraid for Tom's life, Joan kept her secret marriage, well…a secret. She then proceeded to have a large church wedding to the earl."

Elisabeth gasped. "Really?"

The friar nodded. "A few years later, when Tom returned from war, he revealed his marriage to Joan and insisted Montagu return her to him."

David's eyes widened.

"What happened next?" Elisabeth asked.

"Montagu had Joan locked up to prevent her testifying, but eventually the Church insisted he release her. Under oath, Joan admitted she had, indeed, secretly exchanged vows with Tom Holland. The Pope had no choice but to annul the marriage to Montagu and return her to her rightful husband—Tom."

David's posture perked up and he reached for Elisabeth's hand. "You are *certain* we are legally bound by marriage now and no one, not even Lord Cathon, can undo that?"

The friar nodded. "God is your witness."

Elisabeth gently bit her lip. "*You* are our witness too. I mean, can *you* sign a paper, make a seal or something like that so I have proof to show my father?"

He let out a heavy sigh. "I'd be happy to, under the circumstances. But alas, I have neither paper, ink, nor pen, and I doubt you'll find any here."

As David glanced around the tavern, Elisabeth grabbed his arm.

"We'll be right back!" she said with a wide-eyed grin. Once outside, she pointed at the waddling ducks before pulling out her crystal and heading around the side of the building. "You get a feather. I'll get some parchment and ink from home," she whispered.

"Consider it done," he yelled while sprinting toward the ducks.

****

Elisabeth tucked her necklace away again, now holding her drawstring purse retrieved from home. When David returned, waving a white feather, she let out a spontaneous laugh and grabbed it.

"Excellent." She hurried toward Rosamund. "I think this plan is going to work, Aquarius." Her gaze darted about while stashing the feather away for now. "Nobody's watching us, right?"

David raised his brows and glanced behind. "I believe we are unobserved here."

"Good. This place feels like a ghost town." She pulled out her smartphone grabbed from home and balanced it on a fence post.

David's eyes widened and he leaned in closer. "What is that?"

"I want to take our picture."

He touched the base of his neck. "Our *picture*?"

She turned to look at him, a sweet smile spreading across her face. "I want to capture our image so we always remember this day."

He suddenly became still. "You think I'll *ever* forget the day we eloped?"

Elisabeth let out an appreciative sigh and gave David a quick kiss. She then grabbed his arm, showing him where to stand.

After the timer was set, she scurried back to his side. "Smile for *ten* seconds."

His head flinched back slightly and he turned, staring at her. "Huh?"

The blank look on David's confused face caused Elisabeth to burst into laughter, so he reached over, playfully sweeping her off both feet.

She threw her hands up in surrender, laughing at the ruined photo. "And that was going to be our wedding picture."

"Well..." He walked off with her. "I do not understand what that contraption is."

"Clearly!" she said in a high-pitched voice.

Ahead, they spotted a farmer pushing a wooden wheelbarrow.

David cleared his throat and lowered Elisabeth to her feet again.

"I need to hide that," she whispered with a smile that couldn't be contained. She dashed back to the fence post and pulled the smartphone down while pretending to adjust Rosamund's saddle. The farmer disappeared into a paddock and her posture perked up again. "Come here." She glanced behind at David. "I'll show you what this *contraption* does."

He shuffled closer and leaned over her shoulder to look.

When Elisabeth stared down at the screen, she gasped. Her hand flew up, covering her mouth.

"By the gods..." David's voice was incredulous as he wrapped his arms around her from behind and kissed the side of her head. He then became unnaturally still. "That is our likeness."

"It's called a photograph." Elisabeth's eyes filled with tears and she gave a disbelieving shake of her head. "How did I not notice? How on *earth* did I not notice?"

The blush-colored dress.

The crown of pink garden roses in her dark hair.

David sweeping her off her feet the moment before it was snapped, smiling at her rather than the camera...

Elisabeth's lips parted when she turned around, stepping back to admire David's colorful medieval clothes.

His eyes narrowed. "Is something wrong?"

She stared back down at the familiar photograph and rubbed a hand against her heart. "No, it's just…it's an absolutely beautiful photograph of us." She let out a subdued laugh. "In the future, if you ever need me to travel back in time to save your life, just show me this photo."

David scratched his temple, his gaze going distant.

"Come on…" Elisabeth said when Rosamund whinnied. "We should get back to business." She dropped the smartphone into her purse, and pulled out the feather and a piece of parchment. "Unfortunately, it has the cookie recipe on the back." She flipped it over to show him.

A wide smile spread across his face. "It'll do!"

Elisabeth took out a tube of paint, squeezing a bit onto a rag she'd grabbed. Unable to bring the ballpoint pens or felt tip markers here, it was the only thing she could think of in a rush. "I don't have ink on hand like you might think, but we can water this black paint down. It's my mom's."

She replaced the lid, put the tube back in her purse, and together they hurried into the tavern.

Elisabeth bounced from foot to foot after placing the parchment, blank side up, on the table in front of the friar. "Here you go."

David pulled out his pocket knife and sharpened the tip of the feather before handing it to him.

"My goodness," the man said with a belly laugh as he pulled the paper closer, inspecting the feather quill.

"You're both quite determined to have this in writing, aren't you?"

David's shoulders pushed back and he took the rag from Elisabeth. "We just need a cup for the ink."

The friar's eyes widened as he finished the last drop of his beverage and slid the mug closer.

"I don't travel light," Elisabeth said with a small laugh, fiddling with her bracelet.

"I can see that." His voice was incredulous while thinning the paint with water from a nearby jug.

When he dipped the feather quill into the cup and began to write on the parchment, Elisabeth let out a huge breath.

David glanced over at her, a slow smile spreading across his face.

When the friar finished, David and Elisabeth added their signatures to the document—Elisabeth's in a flowing script and David's with an X.

The friar folded the parchment, dripped wax from the candle onto it, and pressed his signet ring into the seal before holding it out to them with a deep, satisfying sigh. "Keep this safe."

David took it from him. "Believe me, I will guard it with my life."

With a knowing grin, the friar nodded.

Elisabeth bounced on her toes as they headed toward the door. "Thank you for everything…?"

"Jacques. Frère Jacques."

Her eyes widened and she wiped at her mouth, trying desperately not to burst into laughter—or song.

"I promise, we will be *singing* your praises forever, Frère Jacques."

Ding dang dong.
Ding dang dong.

Chapter Thirty-Three

Elisabeth sucked in a quick breath as they left the little farming village behind, following a dirt road that wound its way amongst brush and trees.

She then looked at David and let out a spontaneous laugh. "This little plan to stop Cato marrying me off to Tartare just might work."

"We eloped," he said with a mischievous grin.

****

Isabeau stood out in front of the house, fussing over Giovanni before he climbed onto the seat of a simple horse-drawn cart. He then leaned over to kiss her goodbye. A moment later, Balinus appeared from the alleyway atop a dappled gray horse.

Elisabeth's brow furrowed as she switched Rosamund's lead rope to the opposite hand. "They look like they're going somewhere."

David nodded slowly. "To the trade fair in Provins. I'm to mind the shop for the old man while he's away."

"Oh, yeah. I forgot. Guess we've been a bit preoccupied, huh?"

When noticing David and Elisabeth, Balinus' eyes widened. "You're back!" he shouted.

Both Isabeau and Giovanni's postures perked up.

Colette suddenly appeared in the open doorway. "They're back?" She squealed. "Nellie, they're back with the unicorn!"

Perenelle rushed through the front door, hands clasped together under her chin. "You're home." She pulled them into a tight hug.

Something immediately placed David on guard, and he reached for his sling. "Look who else is here," he muttered.

One by one, everyone turned to see who had caught his attention.

Crooked Nose, atop his dark steed, rode closer. "Milady, you're to return with me immediately. Your father's orders." His eyes narrowed as his attention turned to David. "She is soon to be wed to Guglielmo Tartare, so if you value your—"

"Unfortunately for Guglielmo Tartare..." David sauntered closer with wide, confident steps. "Elisabeth is already wed to *me.*" He stood tall and held strong eye contact with Crooked Nose. "We were married this morning; our union blessed and witnessed by a friar."

Perenelle pressed a palm against her heart while letting out a huge breath.

"It's true." Elisabeth gave a curt nod. "We're married now and there's nothing anyone can do. We even have proof." She nudged David. "Show him."

Crooked Nose turned his head to the side for a moment before looking back at them.

David held the recipe/marriage certificate up. "My *wife* is no longer under Lord Cathon's direct authority, but rather *mine.*"

Giovanni and Isabeau watched the unfolding scene intently.

Perenelle crossed both arms over her chest. "Colette, bring Elisabeth's horse to Percival in the stable, child. She won't be needing it any time soon."

The little girl's eyes widened. "You mean the *unicorn*?"

"Quickly," Perenelle said, taking the lead rope from Elisabeth and thrusting it at Colette.

A wide smile spread across Colette's little face and the adults were unnaturally quiet, watching Rosamund being led toward the alleyway, clip-clopping slowly down the lane.

Still in the saddle, Crooked Nose leaned back. His brow wrinkled while staring at Elisabeth, shaking his head. "Have you two *any* idea what you've done?"

Elisabeth fidgeted with her bracelet.

"Because I'd hate to see such a young *widow*."

She felt the color drain from her face.

Before David could react, Perenelle was already shaking her fist in the air.

"Shame on you!" the old woman said with a raised voice. "Shame on you. Her father can cut her out of his will if he so chooses, but since these two have already wed, there's no use making empty threats. Neither Lord Cathon nor the Lord above can do anything about it now. If her father has something against their union, you have him come talk to *me*."

Crooked Nose shifted in the saddle, nudged his horse, and then rode off without another word.

Elisabeth's hands trembled. "He didn't really mean—?"

"Nooo…" Perenelle shook her head emphatically. "No, he's just trying to frighten you, that's all."

David forced a watery smile into place while pulling Elisabeth into a hug. "Everything will be fine, I promise. There's nothing they can do now and he knows it."

Balinus dismounted, rubbing his eyebrow while approaching David. "That being said...why don't you come to Provins with us? It might not be a terrible idea to get out of town for a few days. The trading fair is the perfect opportunity."

David's posture stooped. "I cannot leave Elisabeth when—"

She grabbed his arm. "No, you should go. Nicolas is right. "You'll be safer in Provins until this blows over."

He glanced around uneasily. "But—?"

Elisabeth's shoulders pushed back. "Excuse us a minute." She reached for David's hand, pulling him into the alleyway at the side of the house for privacy. Once alone, her chest caved in. "Aquarius, you have to go. We didn't stop to think that Cato, or even Guglielmo, might have you *killed* to clear the way for an arranged marriage."

David's jaw clenched. "I will not run and hide like a coward."

She let out a theatrical groan. "You're not being a coward if there's a freaking *army* after you." Her heart was racing. "You *have* to leave. Just give it a few days while I see how they react. I'll be fine here. I'm of no use to Cato dead."

David took a deep breath. "And I'm of no use to him alive."

Elisabeth brought a trembling hand to her forehead. "Promise me you'll go with Giovanni and Nicolas to the trading fair. Hopefully this will all be over in the next few days as word gets out we've eloped. Then, when you come home, everything can go back to the way it was before." She couldn't stop wringing her hands. "Worst-case scenario, I sneak off, find you in Provins…and we run away *together*."

David gave her a pained stare. "When Cato's men return here—and you know they will—what then?"

"Give me the marriage certificate. That's our proof."

With a dejected sigh, he handed the parchment over.

As Elisabeth slipped it into her purse, something at the bottom of the bag caught her eye. She softly shook her head and pulled the object out. "I pray to God you don't need this, but…" She placed the elixir of life into his palm. "If something goes tragically wrong, take the *tiniest* amount of this. No more than what fits onto the tip of your thumb."

"Ambrosia." He glanced up at her, teary-eyed. "Are you sure?"

"No." Elisabeth softly shook her head as her voice broke. "I'm not sure about anything…except that I love you."

He tucked the vial into his belt pouch and then sniffled while pulling her into his arms. "I don't want to leave you," he whispered.

When Balinus cleared his throat, Elisabeth stepped back, brushing away tears.

The old man stood at the end of the alley, on the main street. "If we leave now, we'll reach Provins by tomorrow evening. Go ask Percival to prepare Cazador as quickly as possible."

"All right," David said with a quivering smile before jogging to the stable.

Elisabeth walked back to the street to join the others.

Balinus took a deep breath and put his arm around her shoulders. "A wise sage once said, *'Omnia vincit amor:et nos cedamus amori:'*"

Love conquers all; let us, too, yield to love.

Perenelle let out an impatient snort. "Oh, here we go again; *wise old sage.*" She shook her head and hurried to Elisabeth's side, linking their arms together while shooting Balinus a disapproving look. "It wasn't a *wise old sage* who said that. It was a poet writing about a lovesick man. Even the gods couldn't help him after his love runs away with another, and so he kills himself in the end. You *really* think that's going to make her feel better?"

Elisabeth shot Balinus a wide-eyed look.

"Hmm…" The old man rubbed his chin. "I suppose you're right, wife." He shrugged his shoulders and winked at Elisabeth. "The old brain isn't as sharp as it used to be. I simply meant there is nothing in the world that cannot be overcome by love."

Elisabeth bit down on a smile. "I didn't know the rest, so that's how I took it."

"Oh…well…" Perenelle let out a deep sigh. "I suppose that's all right then."

Sandwiched between the two old folks, Elisabeth's heartbeat quickened. "I love you guys," she said softly.

David reappeared atop a dark brown horse with a flowing black mane. When Elisabeth ran over, he bent down to kiss her goodbye as Balinus' mounted his dappled gray stallion.

Elisabeth bit her lip, watching as they rode away.

Isabeau suddenly linked their arms. "You feel better if I make you something to eat, yes?" she asked in a gentle tone.

Even though fear held strong, Elisabeth let out a small laugh.

****

Isabeau and Colette had long ago drifted off to sleep, but Elisabeth's mind raced as her gaze flittered about the room, imagining every possible scenario. They all seemed to end with Tartare's mercenaries killing David.

Her breathing was shaky, realizing she needed to get to Cato *before* Tartare found out about the elopement.

She had to stop any sort of vengeance against David and reason with Cato.

If all else failed, she had another idea.

Well, it was more like…a last resort.

****

The sun had yet to rise, but Elisabeth was already awake and dressed. Not wanting to attract attention during her solo journey, she pulled a traveling cloak over her gown. However, because it was amongst the clothing Cato had sent, it was a luxurious dark blue fabric that fastened with a silver broach. Hopefully, nobody would get close enough to notice the exquisite quality.

As she tiptoed out of the house, her shoes quickly became wet with dew. Heading straight to the stable in the predawn darkness, Elisabeth double-checked her purse. The only thing in it now was the marriage certificate, and a beeswax wrap from the pantry—the medieval equivalent of plastic wrap.

She slipped into the paddock and the barn door creaked when opening. "Percy?" she whispered.

Hay rustled up in the loft where Percival slept and

he sat up, yawning. "Hmmm?"

"Sorry to wake you. I just want you to know I'm taking Rosamund out for a bit. I, uh…I thought I'd go watch the sunrise."

"I'll be right down to tack her up for you." He slipped a tunic on over his leggings.

"Oh, no…I didn't mean for you to get up. I think I can figure out how to do it."

"I don't mind." He stretched and then climbed down the ladder, leading Rosamund to a patch of moonlight.

"Sorry, but I couldn't sleep," Elisabeth said as he quickly brushed the horse and inspected her hooves.

"Yeah, I don't blame you. I heard what happened." He cleared his throat. "So, the, uh, horn…?"

"Huh?"

"Do you want the unicorn horn today?"

She offered him a bemused smile. "No, that was just for Colette."

He nodded. "I thought so. It was quite amusing. I couldn't bear to tell her the truth so didn't remove the horn from the bridle until after she left."

Elisabeth chuckled. "I'd loved to have seen her face."

Percy confined his laughter to a snort. "It was so funny."

"Well, thank you for everything," Elisabeth said when Rosamund was ready to go.

"Any time. She's such a sweet mare."

"She sure is." Elisabeth leaned forward, stroking Rosamund's withers lovingly after mounting her. "I'm getting quite attached already."

"How can you not? Enjoy your morning ride."

Percy then cleared his throat. "You're, uh…you're not *really* going to watch the sunrise, are you?"

Her chin dipped down. "I have to try and make my father see reason. *Promise* you won't tell anyone where I've gone until later?" she asked while fiddling with the reins.

"I won't." His tone was soothing. "Good luck."

"Thanks."

"Safe travels."

Elisabeth sat tall in the saddle and the horse kept at a slow, steady pace through the village. Crossing the bridge, crickets chirped in the darkness as a soft breeze blew through the tall grasses on either side of the dirt road. She led Rosamund down along the river bank, heading straight toward the entwined trees.

The haze of twilight appeared beneath the horizon and she spotted what she'd come for. The bush that had previously been filled with purple bellflowers was now starting to produce plump, dark berries. Elisabeth took a deep, pained breath and plucked a dwale leaf from a branch, folding it in the beeswax wrap.

It contained enough poison to kill a grown man.

Chapter Thirty-Four

Elisabeth continued on, trying to remember the route to Cato's castle. A handful of passersby traveled along the dusty road, most heading toward Paris. When the walled-in leper colony came into view, she stopped, dismounting to let Rosamund drink from a trickling spring and rest for a while.

Nearby, a wolf howled.

Elisabeth rubbed her arms, looking all around. She mounted the horse again, sallying off toward the enormous gallows perched atop a distant hill. Eventually, the road brought her close enough to see fresh corpses of condemned men and women on display.

The main level of the gibbet was filled to capacity, with two more bodies hanging from nooses on the upper level. With a sinking feeling in her stomach, Elisabeth stared down at her purse, knowing it held deadly poison. She pushed her shoulders back. "It'll never come to that," she reassured herself.

When another wolf howled, Rosamund's ears swiveled back and forth. The horse lifted its head and sped to a canter.

"It's okay," Elisabeth said, her voice shaky while stroking the old mare's withers.

Another wolf howled.

And then another.

She gripped the reins tightly as the horse nickered and began galloping. While bouncing lightly in the saddle, Elisabeth glanced around the fields and meadows uneasily.

Finally, with the gibbet far behind, the horse slowed to a trot.

Wanting to stretch her legs, Elisabeth dismounted and walked Rosamund along a road through the forest, wondering how David's trek to Provins was going. If everything went according to plan, they'd arrive this—

She froze.

Something rustled in the trees and brushwood ahead of her, to the right.

Through tall brush, tree branches walked closer.

Tree branches?

Antlers!

Elisabeth's brows rose, watching an enormous reddish-brown deer step into view and then stop, observing her curiously.

Rosamund seemed either unaware or unbothered.

Sensing no threat, the buck strolled out of the underbrush to get a better look. Elisabeth let out a quiet laugh. She dared not move as the majestic creature studied her. After a few moments, the buck seemed to lose interest, looking left and right before meandering back into the trees.

But—it suddenly stopped and turned, making eye contact one last time.

The deer's gaze then became distracted by something *behind* Elisabeth.

Curious, her posture perked up, turning around to see what caught its attention.

Four wolves stood in the middle of the road

watching her.

Elisabeth's head jerked back and a sudden coldness washed over her. "Oh crap, oh crap, oh crap…"

The underbrush and trees behind her rustled again.

The deer had fled.

Frozen with fear, Elisabeth's heartbeat thrashed in her ears.

The wolves were gray and brown with black tips on their long bushy tails. The largest turned its head away, its posture relaxed as if ignoring Elisabeth. It then looked at her again, lifted its head, and let out a hauntingly beautiful howl.

Elisabeth's eyes widened, watching as the wolf retreated into the forest.

A moment later, the other three playfully followed.

She let out a huge breath. Her knees nearly buckled while forcing herself to turn and press on, praying they wouldn't follow.

Suddenly, a fifth wolf slinked slowly out of the woods, avoiding eye contact as it ventured closer.

Rooted to the spot, Elisabeth's entire body tensed.

With its ears back, posture slumped, the wolf walked right up to her, its tail tucked between its legs.

Elisabeth held her breath.

While smelling the hem of her cloak, the wolf's tail began to wag. It then stared up at her—submissively.

"Oh my gosh…" Elisabeth blinked rapidly.

It seemed more dog than wolf and part of her wanted to reach out and pat it, but she remained still, praying Rosamund stayed calm as well.

The horse, sensing no threat, nibbled at the underbrush.

A moment later, the wolf slunk back into the forest,

heading in the direction the rest of the pack had gone.

With a nervous laugh, Elisabeth mounted Rosamund and rode off, shaking her head in disbelief.

As she continued traveling through the woods, squirrels chattered, zipping and jumping from branch to branch. A brook glistened through the trees, and the air smelled earthy, like decomposing leaves and rotting wood.

Two boys of about twelve dawdled along the road toward her, deep in conversation. One had shaggy brown hair, the other messy blond curls. They each carried a wooden fishing pole and pail.

She pulled the reins to make Rosamund stop and pointed ahead. "Is that the way to Lord Cathon's castle?"

With blank looks on their faces, they stared up at Elisabeth and began speaking rapidly to each other in that strange French dialect.

Elisabeth spoke slowly. "Lord Cathon's…castle?"

The brunet boy's brows squished together. "Cath-on?"

"*Oui!*"

He excitedly blabbered on, gesturing with his hands, pointing forward and backward, while the other boy nodded in agreement at whatever was being said.

"*Merci.*" Elisabeth forced a smile and nudged Rosamund on.

That was useless.

After a few minutes, she shifted in the saddle, unsure if this was the right direction. Once reaching the park-like setting around Cato's castle, it would be recognizable, but for now, nothing looked familiar. Actually, to be more precise, everything looked the *same.*

Elisabeth headed toward a trickling stream to let Rosamund drink and rest. Next to the road was a moss-covered boulder. It almost looked like a gift-wrapped box that had tipped partially onto its side. As they left the road, heading through trees coated in thick moss, she discovered it wasn't a stream—but a boggy area they'd stumbled upon.

Rosamund whinnied.

"Steady…" Elisabeth said in a reassuring tone from the saddle, trying to turn around and head back to the road instead.

The horse snorted as its long, slender legs became stuck in thick mud.

Elisabeth rubbed Rosamund's neck. "Good girl. You can do it. Come on…"

The sweet mare tried to move—but fell.

Elisabeth gasped, scrambling off the fallen horse. As she reached for Rosamund's reins, trying to pull her up, her own feet sank into the mud.

The horse snorted, attempting to stand, now trapped up to the belly.

Elisabeth whipped off the blue cloak and purse, tossing it onto drier ground, trying to free her own feet while sinking to the knees. The cold sticky mud seeped through her shoes, oozed around her legs. She let out an uncontrollable whimper realizing the more they struggled, the more the area liquefied, causing them to sink deeper.

Rosamund's eyes and nostrils were wide with fear. Again, the mare fought to pull herself up, nickering and panting until exhausted—and now chest deep in mud.

Elisabeth choked back tears, trying desperately to

calm the panicked horse. "I'll get you out of here. I promise."

But...the cold mud clamped around Elisabeth's waist, restraining her. It seeped inside her dress, weighing her down. With an uncontrollable cry, she twisted her upper body, grabbing onto a patch of dry ground. Grunting loudly, she pulled with all her might.

It might as well be concrete.

Elisabeth let out a sharp scream. Panic set in.

The old mare nickered, clearly distressed and growing tired as it tried to free itself.

Elisabeth cried out for help. Maybe the boys were within earshot. As she struggled to catch her breath, the horse attempted to get up again, but collapsed, shivering.

Forcing back tears, she reached for Rosamund, doing everything to calm the horse. "Shhh, we're going to get out of this."

Elisabeth tried to wiggle her left foot. With gritted teeth, it took all her strength—but seemed to be working. Lips pinched together, she leaned forward in the mud, breath bursting in and out as she made small movements to free herself, inch by inch. As she focused her attention on the scrubby bush growing on dry land next to her, she realized it was dwale. Her thoughts drifted from the purple flowers and berries, to the wolves she'd encountered, and back to this muddy deathtrap. All reminders that nature was brutal and beautiful in equal measure.

After about an hour of working both legs to the top of the muck, Elisabeth gripped the dry land and pulled herself out while kicking, making the cold sludge wetter in the process.

Elisabeth crawled, gasping, across solid ground to Rosamund, shoveling away the mud with her hands, screaming for help. She shook her head in denial as the exhausted mare attempted to lay her head down. "No! You'll drown!" Elisabeth scrambled to her feet, looking for something to use. The mud clinging to her was so heavy she could barely move. Grabbing the cloak, she bunched it under the horse's head to keep its nose and mouth above the watery sludge.

At that moment, the two boys appeared. They gasped, dropped their fishing poles and pails, running over to help dig Rosamund out.

Elisabeth's chest caved in. "I've been at this for hours. Nothing is working."

The boys babbled to one another rapidly. They looked at Elisabeth, waving their arms in the air, using grand gestures, and then took off running.

Hopefully for help.

Sweet Rosamund, shivering and caked with heavy mud, seemed to have given up. Her glassy brown eyes stared off into space as her head rested on the luxurious blue cloak atop the sludge.

"You are not going to die like this." With manic energy, Elisabeth kept digging mud away from the horse's body. Her arms ached, legs shook, teeth chattered, and tears tumbled.

Eventually, she heard a horse whinny and she glanced behind.

A man rode quickly through the trees.

"Oh, thank God." Elisabeth struggled to stand, holding both hands up, trying to catch her breath. "Careful! My horse is trapped and…" She looked at the man and gasped. "Crooked Nose?"

His eyes narrowed, staring at her covered from head to toe in mud. "Milady?"

"I can't get my horse out." Elisabeth's voice choked with tears. "She's completely stuck."

With a gasp, Crooked Nose dismounted and rushed for the reins, attempting to drag Rosamund out. "The name's Facio, by the way." The poor horse's neck stretched painfully forward as he tugged; her body unable to move. "You're really stuck there, aren't you, old girl?" he said with a grunt. "More men are on the way." He looked at Elisabeth and his brows pulled down. "You look as exhausted as your mare."

Elisabeth gathered dry leaves and brush and constructed a space near Rosamund's head so she could kneel and embrace her, stroking her. "Did two boys send you?"

"Yes. Yvain rode back to get more help." Facio lay flat on the ground, scooping mud away from the horse as quickly as he could. "There's a good girl," he said soothingly, patting Rosamund every now and then.

Elisabeth took deep breaths while watching Crooked Nose.

Facio.

Despite his size and strength, the man seemed to make no progress digging the horse out.

"Why, in the name of God, are you back here?" he asked, his voice strained while continuing to clear the mud away with his bare hands.

"I thought I was leading her to a creek for—"

"No." He looked up, his gaze probing Elisabeth. "I mean *here*, near your father's—"

"Oh." Elisabeth swallowed the lump in her throat. "I thought I could try and reason with him."

"You…" He hesitated a moment. "You and the boy you eloped with should have left when you had the chance." Facio shot her a serious look.

"I can handle my father."

"I'm not talking about your father," he said with a furrowed brow. "I'm talking about Guglielmo Tartare."

Elisabeth flinched and then they both turned their heads, staring through the trees.

It sounded like the entire cavalry was coming.

Crooked Nose hauled himself up and dashed back to the road. "Over here!" he yelled, waving mud-caked arms in the air.

Elisabeth's posture stiffened when about nine men came barrelling through the trees carrying all sorts of supplies. One draped a scratchy blanket around her shoulders before joining the others again.

He looked familiar.

Her eyes widened realizing it was the guard the pretty maid, Melisende, was flirting with.

(Actually, he *was* kind of hot.)

They must be close to Cato's castle after all.

Facio whispered something to one of the men. The man's brows lifted. He quickly glanced at Elisabeth, nodded, and rode off again.

Suddenly, the others were holding spades made of wood and metal, digging the horse out. Moving swiftly, they carefully wound two long ropes around Rosamund's body while navigating the mud.

Then, like a one-sided game of tug-of-war, the men pulled—a tiny bit at a time—easing the horse from the vice-grip of the mud ever so gently.

Elisabeth stood back, holding her stomach.

Rosamund hadn't moved at all while they worked

to rescue her.

The men kept at it, dragging the horse's limp, motionless body onto a wooden plank they'd placed at the edge of the pit with a thick blanket on top.

Elisabeth's chin trembled.

Her chest ached.

The horse, laying on its side, still wasn't moving.

Gulping at air, Elisabeth tried desperately not to wail in front of all the would-be rescuers as tears streamed down her face.

They placed another blanket on top of the mare's torso.

They were too late.

A quiet sob escaped from Elisabeth. "Rosamund..."

Hearing her name, the horse lifted its head, dazed for a moment before struggling to stand up on shaky legs while whinnying.

Elisabeth gasped.

"Easy!" Hottie grabbed the reins, still trying to drape the blanket over Rosamund's torso.

"Your mare will be fine," Facio said with an understanding nod. "She's just exhausted and cold. Not unlike yourself."

Elisabeth shook her head repeatedly. "I thought she was dead. I thought for sure..." She rushed closer and took the reins from Hottie, trying to calm Rosamund. "Thank you." Her voice choked with tears. "Thank you all *so* much for saving my horse."

Rosamund, nuzzled against Elisabeth, seemed to enjoy having her neck scratched.

"Once you wash the mud off the horse, she'll be good as new," Hottie said.

Facio laughed and pointed at a man with curly brown hair. "You mean once *Rogier* washes the mud off the horse."

Rogier's head jerked back. "Me? Why *me*?"

Crooked Nose nodded his head toward Elisabeth. "*That* is Cathon's daughter covered in mud."

There were audible gasps as they all turned to look.

Hottie pointed at Rosamund and then held his hand over his head like a horn. "That's the same horse?"

Facio's lips pinched together and he nodded before everyone burst into laughter.

"Apologies milady." Hottie wiped at his mouth, trying to keep a straight face. "But when that paramour of yours arrived on a *unicorn*—"

Elisabeth waved her hand dismissively. "Yes, yes. I know. Look, it's not his fault. I dressed her up to surprise a little girl, all right?"

"That reminds me…" He glanced at the others. "How's Tristan's head?"

They all burst into laughter again and then gathered their supplies, mounted their horses, and waited on the road.

Facio walked over, holding Elisabeth's purse. "Yours?"

"Yes." Her heartbeat raced as she grabbed it, needing the proof of marriage that remained tucked inside. "Thank you."

Crooked Nose reached for Rosamund's lead rope, guiding them both toward the road. "I'll see your horse safely home."

"No, I'll—"

"The carriage has already been sent for, milady. It will be here any moment."

Her head jerked back. "Really?"

"Yvain left earlier."

"Oh, well, then thank you." With a genuine smile, Elisabeth sat on a small mossy boulder next to the larger one. She was too exhausted to stand, let alone walk to Cato's castle.

Facio's eyes narrowed as he looked at her.

Elisabeth's posture perked up. "What?"

He let out a deep sigh. "It's just…you're nothing like I imagined. I have to give your father credit. He kept you *so* safe, *so* hidden away in a convent, that nobody even knew he had a daughter until recently."

"Well…" She cleared her throat, listening to the sound of approaching horses. "Obviously, we're not close. I'm only returning to show him *proof* of my marriage."

Two dark horses appeared around the bend, cantering along the road, pulling a carriage behind them.

"I cannot be forced to marry Guglielmo Tartare if I'm already married to someone else now, can I?" Elisabeth held her chin high and stood watching as the driver turned the carriage around before coming to a stop. She then looked back at Crooked Nose. "A friar told us that nobody, not even the pope, can do anything about it."

As Facio's mud-caked hand reached out to open the door to the waiting carriage, a grave expression spread across his face. "I'm afraid you underestimate the width and breadth of your father's reach," he whispered while helping her inside.

Elisabeth's brow furrowed, taking a seat upon a blanket someone had set upon the upholstery. "But—?"

"Who do you think helped *put* the pope into power?" he added quietly before shutting the door.

Elisabeth's mouth fell open and she stared out the window at Crooked Nose as he stepped back, still holding Rosamund's lead rope.

"Milady." He bowed his head as the carriage sped off.

Chapter Thirty-Five

Before long, they reached the beautiful park-like setting once again—a sanctuary for swans, peacocks, and mythical-looking birds. The carriage sped past the mausoleum on the right, drove through the romantic ruins of the old barbican, and across the drawbridge into the castle.

Still covered in mud, Elisabeth grabbed her drawstring purse and stepped out of the carriage after a footman opened the door.

She grimaced. "Sorry about the—"

"Oh, heavens above." Agnès pushed toward her, an incredulous look spreading across the blonde woman's pale face.

"I need to speak to my father, *immediately*."

"I'm sure whatever you have to say can wait. I've drawn you a bath."

Elisabeth looked down at her once blush-colored dress and let out a nervous laugh. The mud was drying in lighter patches and hardening. "You think I need a bath?"

Agnès' lips pinched together. "Do not jest, milady. You could have died. It's not like where you've grown up." She led Elisabeth through the courtyard and into the foyer. "The land here and around Paris can be quite marshy. Next time, make sure you stay on the marked roads and paths. How do you think Le Marais got its name?"

The Marsh.

"Oh, I…I didn't realize that." Elisabeth's muddy dress was so heavy and stiff now she could barely climb the stairs. A bath might be a good idea before confronting Cato after all. Besides, Rosamund definitely needed a rest.

"My grand-papa said when he was a boy, *twelve* pilgrims died in the quicksand while heading to the abbey at Mont St. Michel." There was a grim twist to Agnès' mouth. "Eighteen more drowned, still trapped when the tide came in."

Elisabeth gasped. "Are you serious?"

"You're lucky those local boys heard your screams and found Bonifacio and Yvain."

Agnès ushered Elisabeth into the room with the luxurious tub, shutting the door behind them. Sunlight filtered through an ornate window and glowing embers from a fireplace kept the temperature toasty. The intoxicating aroma of roses, combined with musky herbs, swathed her. Eyes closed, she took a deep, satisfying breath.

As the maid peeled the mud-caked dress off, Elisabeth's muscles tensed, realizing the woman intended to stay in the room to wash her.

"I…uh…I prefer to bathe in privacy, if that's all right."

With a half-hearted shrug, Agnès pushed the canopy aside and grabbed Elisabeth's arm, helping her down into the marble tub which was now lined with a white sheet and filled with warm, rose-scented water. "No need to be modest, milady. I won't have your father saying I've not done my job properly."

Elisabeth's eyes widened when she sat upon a bed of sponges arranged beneath the white sheet. Glancing up, the sheets hanging from the ceiling around the bathtub were filled with fragrant flowers and fresh herbs, tied in place by their stems. She let out a spontaneous laugh. "Oh my gosh, you certainly know how to prepare a bath."

Agnès' lips twitched as she gave a crisp nod. "Thank you, milady."

Another maid entered the room, scooping the filthy dress into her arms like it was a pile of rubbish. "Well, this kirtle's seen better days," she said with a chuckle, grabbing the rope belt from the floor as well.

"Actually..." Elisabeth slipped low in the tub. "Can you wash and dry that for me as quickly as possible? I want to wear it again."

The woman lifted her brows.

"It's my favorite."

"Certainly, milady," she said before leaving the room.

With a slow smile, Elisabeth pulled both knees up to her chest, enjoying the steamy perfumed water as Agnès washed her with a soft sponge and rinsed with clean rose water.

Oh boy. This level of pampering was *way* too easy to grow accustomed to.

****

Agnès dressed Elisabeth in a pewter-blue gown with silver and white accents, combed her hair, and then held up a pearl and silver headband. "This one's quite lovely."

"Wow." Elisabeth reached out to touch it. Her lips then pressed together into a slight grimace. "But I'm leaving after I speak to my father so there's no—"

"Leaving?" Agnès' voice rose in pitch. "You're to be wed to Guglielmo Tartare the day after tomorrow."

Elisabeth shook her head emphatically. "No. I'm not marrying Guglielmo Tartare. *Ever*."

Agnès' eyes widened for a moment. "Well...I...I wouldn't get your hopes up too much about that, milady," she said in a soothing tone.

Elisabeth's posture sagged as Agnès fidgeted with the headband and then stepped back, admiring her work.

"Anything else I can do for you?"

"No, thank you. That's..." Elisabeth stared at her reflection in the tri-folding mirror and leaned closer. It might have been a beneficial side-effect from the mud, or perhaps from the rose water bath, but her skin and hair looked positively radiant. "...that's everything."

After the woman departed, Elisabeth grabbed her drawstring purse and left the room to find Cato. Once this matter was settled, she'd find her blush dress, her horse, and leave.

Fists tightened, she marched along the corridor and down the stairs.

"Have you seen my father?" she asked a guard in the foyer.

He pointed behind her.

Elisabeth dug into her purse, pulled the parchment out, and marched toward the door the man had pointed at.

She paused, took a deep breath, and then stormed inside.

The dimly lit room was an office or study, with heavy furniture including several bookshelves. The floor was tiled, the walls richly paneled, and two windows were covered with luxurious red curtains.

Cato lifted his brows while looking up from behind a large desk. On it were an open ledger, a flickering candle, an hourglass, and feather quills in an ornate cup next to an ink pot.

Elisabeth slapped the parchment down in front of him. "There. Read it and weep. Aquarius and I are legally married and there's the proof...not that we need it. As you see, I *cannot* marry Guglielmo Tartare."

Cato's posture perked up and he reached for the paper. Slowly, methodically, he held it up, reading what was written. "One cup of butter. Three-quarter cup—"

Elisabeth let out a frustrated groan. "The other side."

Cato turned the sheet over, glancing at it for several long seconds. "Congratulations." He stood, walked around the desk to shut the door, and then held the parchment over the candle flame. "But this is completely worthless."

As the paper slowly burned, Elisabeth's nails dug into her palms, watching the ashes fall onto the desk.

Cato's eyes narrowed. "Your marriage to Guglielmo Tartare will proceed as scheduled—the day after tomorrow."

Her head jerked back. "No. It won't. Not even the Pope can make..."

With a dismissive glance, Cato returned to his desk and reached for a feather quill.

Elisabeth took a deep breath to calm herself. "Just call off the wedding. Tell Guglielmo you didn't know Aquarius and I had already secretly married. Offer him something else. Don't you have an old castle or something you don't use? I don't care, just leave me and Aquarius out of it. Powerful as you are, you cannot *force* me to marry Guglielmo." She lifted her chin. "I am *legally* married to Aquarius."

"Oh, I am not forcing you. The next move is entirely up to you." Cato put the quill down and leaned closer. "But if this marriage does not take place the day after tomorrow, I will make certain Tartare understands *Aquarius* is personally responsible." He raised his brows and stared at her. "I'd really hate to see you, my beloved daughter, widowed so young. At least I'll take comfort knowing you'll be swiftly *re*married."

Elisabeth swallowed a lump forming in her throat. "You just want me to return to my time and forget Aquarius."

"On the contrary. I'm rather enjoying this." Cato snorted in amusement and picked up the quill again. "You have *no* way out of this. One way or another, I will get my alliance. End of discussion." He dipped the feather in the ink well and began writing in the large ledger.

"THAT'S IT? You *seriously* cannot expect—!"

"END of discussion," he repeated in a steady, lower-pitched voice without looking up from his work.

Elisabeth let out a theatrical groan, kicked his desk, and stormed out of the study—nostrils flaring because now her toes hurt from kicking his stupid desk.

She heard Cato take a deep, gratifying sigh behind her. "Oh…and you will join me for supper this evening."

Her fists clenched and unclenched, stomping upstairs to her room. Once inside, she slammed the door shut and paced the floor. Elisabeth's mind raced, running through possibilities. No matter how you looked at it, Aquarius would be held responsible—and killed—if she didn't marry Tartare and allow Cato to form the alliance he desperately wanted. She bit her nails realizing that even going through with the wedding wasn't an option.

Aquarius would never let that happen.

There's no doubt, when he showed up to claim her as his wife, the result would be pretty much the same—bloodshed.

It seemed the *death* of Aquarius was Cato's endgame.

Elisabeth glanced down at her purse knowing the dwale leaf was still inside. She brushed angry tears away, wondering what to do. If Guglielmo suddenly died, his unwilling bride would be the prime suspect—and she'd undoubtedly hang for the crime. Besides, Cato was the *real* problem.

Cato.

The man had betrayed them more times than she could count and now he just sat there smugly like this was all a game.

Elisabeth stood in the middle of the room, softly shaking her head. With trembling hands, she pulled the beeswax wrap from her purse.

Her heart pounded.

One leaf was all it would take to kill a grown man.

Nobody would suspect Lord Cathon's own daughter.

But…could she *kill* Cato to save Aquarius?

Her muscles tightened realizing the answer.

Someone knocked. "Milady?"

"Yes…?" Elisabeth hid both hands behind her back

as the door opened. "…Agnès, what is it?"

"Your father requests your presence downstairs immediately."

"Thank you. I'm on my way."

When the maid was gone, she tucked the beeswax wrap back into her purse, pushed her shoulders back, and strolled out of the room.

Cato left her no other option.

Chapter Thirty-Six

Elisabeth walked into the dining room, covering her mouth to stifle a yawn. After washing her hands in the bowl of perfumed water, she took a seat across from Cato at the long, empty table, grabbed a cloth napkin, and folded it on her lap. Although hating to admit it, the guy was quite sophisticated.

"It seems to me you live a pretty lonely life." Her voice was subdued. "Don't you have any friends or *loved* ones to eat with?"

Cato let out an arrogant laugh and reached for his cup. "I prefer to dine here, alone with my ungrateful daughter, rather than in the great hall with the plebs and commoners." He took a swig of his drink and gestured toward a servant before looking back at Elisabeth. "So, have you come to terms with the fact your wedding to Guglielmo Tartare will take place the day after tomorrow?"

She let out a quick, disgusted snort and looked away. "What other choice do I have if I want Aquarius to live?" She discreetly moved the beeswax wrap from her purse onto her lap, hiding it under the napkin.

Cato smirked. "How very sensible of you. The…" His voice drifted off as two servants filed into the room, placing a bowl of soup in front of them.

Elisabeth ran a spoon through the broth, spotting leeks, onions, and cabbage. Her eyelids felt heavy as she stared across the table, watching Cato slurp his soup greedily. "You remind me of the day we first met." She glanced at the doorway to make sure they were alone. "You stole money from a drunk, bought food for yourself, and scarfed it all down like you're doing now."

"Is that so?" His posture stiffened for a minute. "I suppose I've always had a ravenous appetite." He pushed his empty bowl back. "I hear there was an incident with your horse today."

She sat with both hands folded in her lap. "Yeah."

Cato glanced at her and raised an eyebrow.

"Look, I'm exhausted and you're the *last* person in the entire world I feel like making polite small talk with."

He confined laughter to a snort. "Suit yourself."

Their bowls were taken away and a second course was brought in—a dish of roasted meat covered in a chunky, bright green sauce. Although it smelled good, like rosemary and sage, Elisabeth's nose scrunched up at the sight.

"I forgot you were a fickle eater. I assure you it's not rat." Cato stabbed a piece of meat with his knife and took a bite. "It's roasted venison with green sauce. A far cry from the *rats* Aquarius hunted to feed you while on the run from Rufus." A bemused smile spread across his face. "I remember you were horrified to discover it wasn't chicken you'd eaten."

Elisabeth's breathing slowed as the memory took over.

"That's the day I realized Aquarius was falling for you—and that your arrival would ruin his life."

Her vision clouded with tears.

"Yet I never dreamt your arrival would provide *me* a future of all this." Cato lifted his chin and glanced around the luxurious space. "I imagine it's the complete opposite of what you'd have intended. You've been a curse to Aquarius and a lucky charm to me." He chuckled and took another swig of his drink. "Imagine that."

Cato was right—and he didn't even know the whole story.

Elisabeth's posture sagged while staring blankly at her dish. She'd never eaten venison before and the sauce spooned on top looked like finely-chopped and mashed herb leaves, similar to the sorrel sauce she'd once prepared. Her body suddenly tensed, realizing this was the perfect dish to hide dwale in.

She cleared her throat and sat taller.

Her heartbeat raced, nearly exploding.

Was she *really* going to go through with this?

As Cato ate, Elisabeth glanced over her shoulder and then back at the dish. With shaking hands, she attempted to tear the poisonous leaf apart to hide it in the green sauce. She'd then offer her meal to Cato. He seemed to eat anything and everything.

Elisabeth's brows pulled in while stalling for time. "If you *must* know, my horse and I became trapped in a muddy bog."

Cato's eyes widened as he looked up. "Oh, you're speaking again? I think I preferred your silence."

"Fine!" she snapped. With clenched teeth, she tried to rip the leaf apart without letting it touch her skin. That might be when it's most toxic.

The task was proving difficult.

Cato wiped his mouth with a napkin and a servant

rushed over to take both their dishes away.

Elisabeth softly shook her head and slipped the dwale back into her purse.

The perfect opportunity was gone—but she'd be better prepared tomorrow.

A wide grin spread across Cato's face as the servers reappeared. "I've been awaiting the next course with great anticipation."

There's more?

Elisabeth cocked her head, trying to make sense of the colorful item being carried across the dining room by two men.

The color drained from her face when an enormous platter was placed in the center of the table—an elaborate meat pie decorated with the golden-yellow severed head and neck of Cato's pet pheasant. Long flowing feathers of scarlet red, soft orange, iridescent blue, and emerald green, were arranged around the pastry so that it created an actual likeness of his dead feathered friend.

Elisabeth threw the napkin on the table and shoved her chair back. "You're despicable," she said through gritted teeth before marching toward the door.

Cato burst into laughter while digging into the pie. "It's just a bird."

"It was your PET!" she yelled back from the foyer. "And it adored you."

****

"Rise and shine, milady." Agnès tiptoed across the dark room, a tray balanced carefully in her arms. She set it on a table before opening the drapes. "It's a busy day today."

As sunlight poured into the space, Elisabeth sat up

in confusion, rubbing sleep out of her eyes. She then let out a heavy sigh. Tomorrow was her wedding day to Guglielmo Tartare. That meant *today* was her last chance to get Cato to ingest the dwale leaf.

It was the *only* way to save Aquarius.

Without Lord Cathon, Tartare had no alliance. That's all either of them cared about—power and money.

She was just a pawn.

Agnès left the room and returned a moment later with the freshly laundered blush-pink dress.

Elisabeth clasped both hands under her chin. "Did the mud come out?"

"Good as new, milady."

"Yay," she said softly.

The maid set the gown aside and picked up the tray, carrying it to the bedside.

"Oh…" As the platter of food was arranged across Elisabeth's lap, she forced a weak smile. Guess she wasn't slipping the poison to Cato across the breakfast table. Elisabeth leaned over the tray, eyeing a freshly-baked raisin bun, two hard-boiled eggs, sliced meat and cheese, and a cup of what looked like milk. Her posture perked up while reaching for the tumbler, breathing in a floral, yet fruity, fragrance. "What is this? It smells *amazing.*"

"Andalusian orange-infused almond milk. Your father drinks it every morning." Agnès let out a small laugh. "Says it keeps him healthy and strong as a Greek god."

Elisabeth's breath hitched. Wide-eyed, she slowly put the cup back down on the tray.

A Greek god.

Cato was immortal now.

He took the elixir of life…ambrosia…the nectar of the gods.

There was *no* way a little dwale leaf was going to slow him down, let alone kill him.

Elisabeth had survived an asp bite with it. David survived what should have been a fatal stab wound. At the first sign of sickness, Cato would take the elixir and heal himself—most likely uncovering her plan to poison him in the process.

Her heartbeat raced.

Crap, crap, crap!

In that case—how *does* one kill a god?

Elisabeth only had one day left to figure that out.

Chapter Thirty-Seven

"Anything else, milady?"

"No." Elisabeth bit her fingernails, trying to think of Plan B. "Thank you."

After Agnès slipped out of the room, Elisabeth pushed the tray aside, climbed out of bed, and paced the floor. When her tummy rumbled, she grabbed the raisin bun, taking huge bites as her mind raced.

There was barely a Plan A, let alone a Plan B!

"Think Elisabeth. Think…"

There *had* to be a way to get out of this. She could *not* enter into an arranged marriage when she was already secretly married to Aquar—

Wait…!

Her mouth fell open as an idea began to take shape.

Elisabeth's gaze darted over to the blush gown. She dressed quickly, scarfed down a hard-boiled egg, and rushed from her room, needing to find Rosamund.

Downstairs, the foyer was buzzing with unusual activity. Head tilted to the side, she followed servants down a main corridor and stumbled into what was obviously the great hall. With unnatural stillness, she stood watching servants scatter fragrant flower petals onto the floor, hang tapestries from the walls, and decorate long tables for an elaborate feast.

A *wedding* feast.

Dashing back down the hallway, Agnès suddenly

appeared in the foyer at the bottom of the stairs. She stood next to a small gray-haired man holding deep purple fabric in his arms. "Milady, time is of the essence. The tailor needs to—"

Elisabeth sucked in a quick breath. "Is this the wedding gown?" She ran her hand over the luxurious silk damask fabric.

The tailor nodded shyly. "Yes. I still need to—"

"I just want to check on my horse and make sure she's all right."

"Oh…" Agnès gave her an understanding nod.

"I'll be back in an hour and then you can have my undivided attention."

Turning to leave, Elisabeth heard Agnès whisper to the tailor, "Terrible incident yesterday. Just horrifying."

"Yes, Henri told me everything," the man replied quietly.

Outside, Elisabeth ran across the courtyard, spotting Crooked Nose ahead of her. "Facio!"

His posture perked up as he turned around. "Milady…?"

"Where's Rosamund?"

His brows squished together. "Who?"

"My horse. I want to check on her."

He snickered and then nodded. "Ah yes. C'mon."

Elisabeth fell in step beside Facio as he strode silently through the barbican and across the drawbridge, leaving the castle behind. To her right, the road weaved its way through the romantic ruins of an old gatehouse; the crumbling walls and arches overtaken by colorful wildflowers and weeds.

"What *was* that?" she asked, pointing at the picturesque structure.

"That's the original barbican from about two hundred years ago." As Facio turned left, he glanced behind, back at the ruins. "Maybe older."

Her eyes widened. "Oh."

The dirt road ran alongside the castle's moat and led straight to the tiny village that Elisabeth could see from her bedroom window. The hamlet was nestled next to another large pond dotted with lily pads and inhabited by both black and white swans. A few feet ahead a mother duck, followed by eight ducklings, waddled slowly across the road. Elisabeth smiled, listening as Mama let out several short, raspy quacks as if telling her babies to stay close. The ducklings responded with high-pitched chirps while trying to keep up.

"They're so cute."

Facio looked at the ducks for a moment before grunting in agreement.

It took less than five minutes to reach the entrance of the tiny hamlet. Crooked Nose pointed to where the road forked and continued to the left. "Next time you ride your mare, this road loops around the entire castle. It's a pleasant route and will bring you right back here to your father's little village."

Elisabeth's eyes narrowed. She glanced up at Facio as they headed toward a long stone building with a thatched roof. "My father's little village?"

"This isn't a *real* village."

Elisabeth's head flinched back slightly, her gaze darting around the charming hamlet. She spotted Rosamund in a nearby field. Sheep grazed outside another tiny farm, while a water wheel turned gently outside of a quaint mill. Rows of neatly planted crops grew beside a chocolate-box cottage, its shuttered windows lined with potted flowers. "What do you mean this isn't a *real* village?"

"The entire thing was built about ten years ago. No villagers live here. It's part of the castle and run by your father's staff. He wanted the day-to-day life of a working castle to be kept separate and out of sight so it's mostly stables, workshops, storage…things like that." Facio pointed to the pond and a little patch of garden. "Although your father will come here on occasion to fish or putter about."

Elisabeth's mouth fell open and she followed Facio through the entranceway of the long fieldstone building, finding herself in the center breezeway of a large stable with a gabled ceiling. The space was spotless, and smelled of sweet fresh hay, with happy-looking horses poking their heads over the stalls to say hello.

"Rogier?" Facio called out.

"Bonifacio, is that you, old turd? Hang on…" he hollered from some unseen location. "By God's nails, you're nev—"

"LADY ELISABETH IS HERE TO CHECK ON HER MARE." Crooked Nose cut him off with a booming voice. He then cleared his throat and glanced at Elisabeth. "Apologies, milady."

Her eyes narrowed in confusion.

"Oh *sard*," she heard Rogier whisper to himself.

With a heavy sigh, Facio shook his head before walking into a nearby stall to collect his (now familiar) dark brown horse.

Rogier, the guy with curly brown hair who'd helped rescue Rosamund, shuffled into view, his cheeks bright red as he fidgeted with a pitchfork. "Apologies, milady. Had I known you were there…I'd…I'd never have used such blasphemy in your presence."

Elisabeth bit her lips to keep from laughing. "It's fine," she said with a snort. "I've heard much worse."

Rogier swallowed hard and nodded while putting his pitchfork aside. "You want me to tack up your horse?"

"How is she?"

"Absolutely fine."

Elisabeth let out a huge breath. "That's *really* good to hear."

****

Before long, Elisabeth was in the saddle of sweet Rosamund, heading back out of the little hamlet and onto the main road—with her babysitter, Crooked Nose, beside her. As they rode under the old portcullis, she could see the mausoleum ahead on her left, built into the hillside.

A cold chill ran up her spine while staring at the ornate doors that led to the crypt. "What would you do if you were me?"

Facio lifted an eyebrow and looked at her. "Milady?"

She cleared her throat. "I mean…you know I'm already secretly married."

He looked down. "My opinion is irrelevant."

"As is my fate," Elisabeth said as her posture slumped. "So, I've consented to marry Tartare."

Facio let out a deep sigh and then gave her an understanding nod.

"No offense, because believe it or not, you're kind of growing on me, but I'd like to be alone for a bit, if that's…*allowed*."

Facio pulled at his ear, as if undecided.

Elisabeth's eyes widened. "Where am I going to go? You always find me, anyhow. I just want some alone time to *mentally* prepare for tomorrow. I won't go far, I promise."

"All right," he finally said. "Stick to the path around the castle. And if you're not back in an hour—"

"I know, I know…" With a theatrical groan, she nudged Rosamund and trotted off. After a few minutes, Elisabeth glanced over her shoulder, watching Crooked Nose ride back across the drawbridge. When he was gone, she sped to a canter, heading along the road and back into the forest, trying to find the muddy bog again.

It took longer than anticipated, but she eventually stumbled upon the spot after finding the large moss-covered rock that looked like a gift-wrapped box. She left Rosamund safely on the main road and hiked back into the trees on foot. Her heart pounded with every step, praying she was on solid ground.

Ahead was the scrubby dwale bush.

Elisabeth's shoulders tightened, trying to skirt around the mud to get closer.

When she finally reached the bush, full of ripe, plump berries, she could hardly breathe. Although eating ten would kill a grown man—eating just half of one put little Colette into a deep sleep for almost two days.

Dwale *must* be what Juliet Capulet had taken.

It *had* to be.

How many berries would it would take to fake my own death?

Unlike a clueless Romeo, Aquarius would figure out her plan.

He would, right?
Yes, of course, he would!

They'd had a whole debate about Romeo vs. Orpheus.

Elisabeth's shoulders slumped and she pulled the beeswax wrap from her purse, tossed the leaf aside, and replaced it with a handful of berries for herself.

This was the only way to outmaneuver Cato.

Her tummy fluttered while going over the plan in her head.

Right now, she needed to hurry back to the castle. She'll consent to marriage with Guglielmo Tartare—then at bedtime eat the berries before going to sleep.

If there's one thing that travels fast around here it's gossip. Everyone from Paris to beyond will hear news that Lord Cathon's daughter had died in the night. After being laid to rest in the mausoleum, Aquarius will arrive and use the elixir to revive her from the death-like sleep.

It was just like Romeo and Juliet...but with a happy ending.

She had no doubt Aquarius would figure out her plan. Then, they'd run away and live happily ever after. Neither Cato or Tartare would ever be the wiser.

With a satisfied smile, she took off the crystal necklace, hiding it in the leaves behind the box-shaped boulder.

She had to admit, her idea was pretty brilliant—

Although Aquarius might not think so.

Chapter Thirty-Eight

Dressed in a flowing, white cotton nightdress, Elisabeth stood alone in her bedchamber, peering out the open window.

Her breathing was slow and even. The sun had set and flaming torch lights from the castle reflected on the lake below. In the distance, someone holding a lantern moved about outside the stables in Cato's little village. Probably Rogier, checking on Rosamund and the other horses, making sure they were tucked away, comfy for the night. The sky above was clear, filled with hundreds...no, *thousands*...of sparkling stars. She sniffled and wiped her nose, wondering if Aquarius was staring up at that same night sky right now.

Elisabeth looked down at the dark berries in her hand, praying she'd calculated the amount correctly to pull off this stunt. She stood taller, pushed her shoulders back, and popped them into her mouth, biting into the sweet, poisonous fruit.

After climbing into bed, Elisabeth arranged the blankets around her while waiting to become sleepy.

When she next awoke, Aquarius would be by her side.

Chapter Thirty-Nine

Elisabeth was in a pitch-black tunnel.

Heartbeat pounding in both ears.

It grew louder and louder until she gasped for air and her eyes shot open.

But—she was still in complete darkness.

The intense fragrance of heady roses filled the space.

Elisabeth pulled a gauzy fabric away from her face and attempted to sit up, grunting in pain after bashing her forehead on stone. She lay back down, sinking into what felt like a silk pillow. Breathing rapidly, she tried to figure out what was going on.

While feeling her throat for the crystal, Elisabeth recalled hiding it in the forest to retrieve it later. The last thing she remembered was waiting for sleep to come after eating the dwale berries. Both hands moved around in the dark, feeling nothing but stone.

It encased her.

"No…" Elisabeth whimpered as her hands fluttered feverishly all around.

She trembled uncontrollably.

"No, no, no, no, no, no…."

With rasping breaths, Elisabeth realized she wasn't laid out on a slab in the middle of the crypt, draped romantically with a gauzy white shroud while awaiting Aquarius.

She was enclosed in a coffin.

Gasping for air, Elisabeth's eyes bulged. "Aquarius!" She pounded both fists on the stone lid, but it neither budged nor made a sound. She let out a primal scream and started sobbing. "Aquarius?"

No answer.

Claustrophobia began to set in and Elisabeth struggled to catch her breath.

"Get it together..." she blubbered, realizing she was on the verge of hyperventilating.

Closing her eyes, she forced herself to take calming breaths.

Breathe.

In and out.

In and out.

She ran both hands over her dress, feeling thorny flower stems and yards of silk fabric.

They must have buried her in the royal purple wedding gown and thrown roses into the coffin.

Elisabeth needed to move the stone lid before running out of oxygen. Hopefully six feet of dirt from a freshly dug grave wouldn't come rushing in from above.

Although weak from being "dead", she pushed her hands against the lid with all her might.

Nothing.

She twisted around, rolling onto her stomach. While knotted and twisted in the full dress, Elisabeth tucked both legs beneath her, rising slowly onto hands and knees, pushing against the stone slab with her back. As her muscles strained in pain, the stone shifted ever so slightly.

With a moan, Elisabeth collapsed again, curling up

with her head on the pillow, struggling to catch her breath.

A crack of light now seeped into the coffin from a nearby wall torch and she let out a sigh of relief.

She was in a crypt.

Her eyes closed as exhaustion took over. After a short rest, she'd try to move the lid some more.

****

"Elisabeth?"

Roused from sleep, her eyes popped open when she heard David's faint, but frantic, whispers.

"Elisabeth?"

"Aquarius?" Turning onto her side, Elisabeth slapped her hand repeatedly against the stone, trying to make as much noise as possible. "Aquarius!"

The light filtering in through the crack flickered for a moment. She then heard David grunting as the heavy stone lid scraped across the base.

When she let out a shaky laugh, his shoulders slumped in relief.

"What took you so long?"

David's head jerked back. "What took me so long?" He pulled her from the partially opened sarcophagus and held out a canteen of water when she became unsteady on her feet. "I traveled as fast as I could from Provins the instant I learned you pulled this ridiculous, asinine, idiotic stunt," he whispered through clenched teeth.

"I figured you'd be angry, but…" Elisabeth paused, gulping down water. She wiped her mouth with the back of her hand and returned the canteen to him to tuck away. "But once you hear the whole story you'll see it was actually a *brilliant* plan."

"I find *that* hard to believe," he said with another grunt while sliding the lid back into place. David then grabbed her hand, leading the way through the crypt.

A satisfied smile spread across her face. "I *knew* you'd figure out I wasn't really dead."

He turned and opened his mouth to say something, but no words came out. Instead, he scrubbed a hand over his face and shook his head before they raced up the stairs.

Outside, a guard was flat on his back, knocked-out cold. In the pre-dawn darkness, it was hard to be certain, but it looked like Hottie.

"Oh sheesh," Elisabeth muttered. "That guy helped save my horse."

David led the way up the hill next to the mausoleum entrance and into a small wooded area where his borrowed horse, Cazador, waited.

"I have to get Rosamund." Elisabeth pointed to the little village. "She's right there in the first building on the left. I'm *not* leaving her with Cato, the bird killer."

David let out a long exhale. "I'll get her. Wait here and stay hidden. We cannot risk you being seen."

"Not even if I pretend to be the *ghost* of Lady Elisabeth?" she whispered with a giggle.

He lowered his chin and raised an eyebrow. "Not funny. Stay. Here."

"Be careful, Aquarius."

"I always am."

Elisabeth nervously crossed and uncrossed her arms, watching David sprint off into the morning twilight. Her purple gown sleeves billowed around her like wings. As she paced, awaiting his return, a dark mood washed over her when the memory of something

Cato said became trapped in her mind.

"You've been a curse to Aquarius and a lucky charm to me."

Taking a deep, pained breath, Elisabeth tried to push the thought away, but her eyes filled with tears instead.

"You've been a curse to Aquarius and a lucky charm to me."

The words ran through her mind, over and over again. She could see Cato's smug face across the dining table in his fairy-tale castle. *"You've been a curse to Aquarius..."*

Elisabeth took drunken steps and sagged against a tree trunk. Her chest caved in knowing Cato was right.

About ten minutes later, David reappeared, this time atop Rosamund.

When he dismounted, Elisabeth smoothed down her dress and averted her gaze, hoping he wouldn't notice her crying eyes in the morning starlight. "Follow me." Her voice cracked as she mounted the horse.

David's brows drew together, reaching for Cazador's reins. *"Cor meum?"*

She sniffled and wiped her nose with the back of her hand before forcing a smile. "It's nothing. I'm fine."

The sun was just below the horizon as they rode off into the forest, looking for the mossy box-shaped rock. With the area now somewhat familiar, she spotted it immediately and dismounted, praying her necklace was still there.

Elisabeth brushed away leaves and let out a sigh of relief.

The necklace was just as she'd left it.

Chin trembling, she stared down at the crystal in her hands, trying to decide between her head and her heart.

"*Cor meum...*" David dismounted. "I can *clearly* see something troubles you."

Elisabeth slipped the chain over her head and tried to smile through tears. "All right, so..." She cleared her throat. "If you travel back along this road, it will eventually take you home."

David's head flinched back slightly.

"And can you tell Percy that I left Rosamund to him in my will...or something like that?"

He released an appreciative sigh while walking toward her.

Elisabeth's posture slumped. "From the day we met, I've been nothing but a curse to you. Everything I do brings you bad luck."

David pulled her into his arms, moving his face close to hers. "What on earth are you talking about?" he whispered.

Her voice choked with tears. "If you leave now, without me, you can go on and lead a nice, comfortable life. You can continue your apprenticeship and make something of yourself. I can't let you give all that up for me. Guglielmo Tartare knows *nothing* of you and thinks I'm dead. You have a second chance at—"

David silenced her with a kiss, making this even more difficult as she melted into his arms.

"*You,*" he whispered, "are not going anywhere."

Elisabeth whimpered. "I don't want to, but—"

"But what?" He ran a hand through her hair and took a deep, savoring breath. "Despite what you may think, you are not the only one with ideas and plans."

She stared up at him and her lips parted slightly.

David gave a slow, disbelieving shake of his head. "When I realized you'd become entangled in Cato's web, Balinus and I began to make arrangements for my apprenticeship to continue in *Ghent*—with a colleague of his."

Elisabeth sucked in a quick breath and pulled back. "Wait....what? Ghent?"

"It's the largest city north of Paris."

As she pieced together his plan, a slow smile formed. "Wait...so...we can get away from Cato *together*...and you'll still get to continue your apprenticeship?"

"Yes." David cupped Elisabeth's face in his hands. "The old man made it perfectly clear that although we'll leave for the time being, I remain the much-loved nephew and adopted son of *Nicolas Flamel.* I'll still inherit his bookshop when the time comes, as long as I continue my training with the guild."

Elisabeth let out an uncontrollable sob. "Your plan was so much better than mine."

David snorted in amusement and wiped a stray tear from her cheek. "Now, come on. We need to hurry home to pack and say goodbye to everyone. Nobody—save for Giovanni and the Flamels—knows you're alive, but we do have a long trek to Ghent and need to leave before Cato's guards discover I'm a grave robber and horse thief. I don't imagine they'll take too kindly to your missing corpse."

After he leaned forward and kissed Elisabeth's forehead, she sagged against him, resting her chin on his chest while playfully looking up into his eyes.

David stared down with a bemused smile, then put

his hands on her neck, kissing her while walking toward the horse.

Startled, she grabbed his arms, giggling in-between kisses, trying not to stumble as she walked backward. "I love you."

"*That* is why I married you." With a cheeky grin, he mounted Cazador.

Heat rushed to her cheeks. "Oh, come on. You know why we had to do that. It's not like we're *really* married."

"Hey…" David held his arms up in surrender and raised an eyebrow. "*You* proposed to *me*."

Elisabeth let out a theatrical groan, trying not to laugh as she mounted Rosamund. "We are *so* getting an annulment," she said as they rode off.

Chapter Forty

When Elisabeth walked into the great hall, the yeasty smell of freshly baked bread caused her stomach to rumble so loudly that Isabeau looked up.

"Sorry, but I'm *dead* hungry." Elisabeth chuckled at her own joke as heat crept across her cheeks.

Isabeau's head jerked back and she grabbed a knife. "Here. Eat." She cut a generous piece from the round loaf, slid it across the work table, and let out a huge sigh. "David was right."

"I'm alive and well." Elisabeth shoved the warm bread into her mouth and let out a slight moan. She covered her lips with a hand while chewing. "But don't let Guglielmo Tartare know."

Isabeau grabbed a pitcher, poured water into a cup, and slid it across the table. "You must drink also."

Perenelle walked into the room, too preoccupied tying her apron to notice Elisabeth. She then looked up, pressed a palm to her bosom, and rushed over with outstretched arms. "Oh, my dear girl, thank God you're all right."

Still trying to swallow the bread, Elisabeth nodded and hugged her in return. She then gulped water to wash down the crumbs.

"Nicolas!" the old woman hollered at the top of her lungs.

As the old man walked out of his study, his posture

slumped in relief. He was followed by a glum-looking Colette.

The moment she noticed Elisabeth, her blue eyes widened. She squealed with delight and ran to her.

Elisabeth crouched down and hugged the little girl.

"Colin said you died of poison, but I knew you didn't because your unicorn would have detected it. Aren't you happy I convinced you to get one? It *truly* saved your life."

Elisabeth playfully tugged Colette's blonde braids. "Guess *you* were right all along."

In the distance, dogs barked and several horses whinnied as the village rumbled to life all around them, like every other morning.

Balinus cleared his throat. "Where's David?"

"I'm here." From the screens passage, he could be heard shutting and securing the front door. "I was bringing the horses to the stable." David walked into the great hall and over to the old man, put his hand on his shoulder, and lowered his voice. "Elisabeth and I need to leave for Flanders as soon as her horse is rested. Unfortunately, there was a guard on watch so I left a...*trail*. It won't be long before they find the empty coffin in the crypt—if they haven't already."

Balinus nodded in understanding and looked at Colette. "Remember what Nellie told you about Elisabeth? To keep her safe?"

Colette nodded. "Yes, but what if—"

Everyone froze, listening as at least a dozen horses came thundering through the village—the clopping hooves stopping right outside the house.

Something banged against the door. "OPEN UP!"

David rushed toward Elisabeth, grabbing an arm as

her gaze darted around the room, wondering where to hide.

Perenelle took a deep breath and gave everyone a reassuring look. "Stay calm. Nicolas and I will—"

The front door was suddenly bashed in.

Perenelle's head jerked back. "MY DOOR! Have you ever heard of KNOCKING?" the old woman yelled, eyes protruding as she stomped toward the action. "Lord Cathon will be replacing that!"

As several men stormed through the screens passage, Colette let out a high-pitched shriek, and Isabeau quickly wrapped her little sister in her arms.

Meanwhile, in one sweeping motion, David thrust Elisabeth into the old man's study, pressed her back against the wall behind the door, and covered her mouth with his hand as she was about to let out an involuntary scream.

The stomping of men's boots echoed through the great hall. Her lips and chin trembled while staring wide-eyed at David.

"*You*. Upstairs. *You*, search for him in there."

On the other side of the door, Perenelle scolded the intruders as they raced up the stairs to her bed chamber, and Balinus could be heard soothing a terrified Colette.

Elisabeth's posture became rigid when heavy footsteps approached the study.

David reached for his sling, wrapping the rope taut between both fists.

"Nobody up here," a man's deep voice shouted from the loft upstairs.

"He's not in here," another voice hollered from the direction of the screens passage.

The door to the study flung open and a large man

marched into the room. He walked to the desk and bent to look underneath.

Beads of sweat formed on Elisabeth's forehead and David's grip on the rope tightened.

Then…the door began to slowly swing closed, exposing them.

A quiet gasp escaped from Elisabeth when it was Crooked Nose who turned around. His eyes widened for a moment, but then he quickly composed himself. "All clear!" He walked out of the study, shutting the door behind him. "Let's go."

Elisabeth turned her head and covered her mouth as David stood there with a dazed look on his face.

"Seal off the city gates in and out of Paris," Facio shouted as they rushed from the house.

A moment later, the sounds of shouting men and galloping horse hooves faded into the distance.

When the coast was clear, David shuffled back a step. "He—he helped us?"

"Facio's actually kind of nice once you get to know him."

David shook his head in disbelief. "Facio?"

"I think they're gone," Balinus whispered as he walked into the study and grabbed some parchment from the desk.

Perenelle and the girls crept in behind him.

David scrubbed a hand over his face. "We need to leave immediately. We shouldn't have returned and put you and your family at risk. I am so sorry."

Colette crept closer, blinking her eyes to keep tears from falling. "*You* are our family too, silly."

David's brows drew together as Colette hugged him tight.

Balinus then handed the parchment to him. "Show these papers to the guild when you arrive in Ghent. Do you remember who to look for?"

"Yes." His voice choked with tears. "Thank you."

Colette's face was puffy from crying as she looked up at David again. "You'll come back to visit us, won't you?"

"Of course," David leaned forward. "Who else is going to finish teaching you how to use a sling?"

Isabeau sniffled. "Giovanni travel to Ghent sometimes. We see each other again. I know it."

Elisabeth's chest ached when Balinus hugged her. "Make Aquarius take my horse for the journey," he whispered. "Keep heading north, away from Paris. When this all settles down, I'll send word to you."

She sniffled and nodded while pulling back.

"Godspeed," Perenelle said softly.

David took a deep breath and led the way through the great hall. At the back door, they glanced outside, making sure none of Cato's guards had stayed behind. He then held his hand out. "Ready?"

Elisabeth took a deep breath and entwined her fingers with his. "Ready."

They sprinted to the stable, unlatched the gate, and hurried across the paddock, hopefully without being seen.

"Percival, change of plans." David's voice was tense as they hurried into the stable.

Percy's shoulders slouched while walking toward them with a pitchfork in his hands. "Your…uhh…your father's here."

Elisabeth's eyes bulged. "What? Where?"

Cato stepped slowly out of the shadows.

Chapter Forty-One

David pulled Elisabeth back, attempting to leave, but Facio appeared in the doorway behind them. He had a stony expression on his face as he stared down at the floor.

"I was right." Cato laughed while entering Rosamund's stall, patting the side of her belly. "It *is* my daughter's horse. I thought I recognized it."

Rosamund made a long snorting sound when he touched her.

Elisabeth marched toward Cato, glaring at him. "Get your hands off my horse."

He held his arms up in mock surrender and stepped out of the stall before turning to Percy. "Would you be so kind as to give me a few moments alone with my daughter?"

Percy nodded, leaned the pitchfork against the stall beside Elisabeth, and crept outside, flashing her a sympathetic look on the way out.

"Bonifacio, we'll be along shortly, but as a precaution—" Cato paused, shooting David a warning glance, "—have word sent to both the king and Dainville that I want troops on each and every road, lane, trail, and deer path from Flanders to Rome immediately. Get me the Swiss Guard if you must. Nobody takes a *puppa* in the forest without my knowledge."

Facio's face was deadpan as he nodded and left the stable, shutting the door on the way out.

Cato turned his attention back to Elisabeth and slowly clapped his hands. "Well played, my dear. Well played indeed. I must admit, I'm impressed. Even Tartare believes you to be dead."

David lowered his brow, a fixed stare on Cato.

Up in the eaves, the barn swallows began chirping and Cato stopped to listen. His gaze darted across the stable, trying to find the nest. He then looked back at David and Elisabeth. "I must say, you've *both* changed rather surprisingly.

David's eyes narrowed and he took slow steps forward. "You don't know me at all anymore."

"Is that so." Cato snorted loudly. "Once carefree and reckless, you're now fearful of anything that might rob you of the first person to ever love you. You're barely a man, in love with love, so you work hard to better yourself in order to convince Elisabeth to stay here with you in your—" he paused to glance around the rustic barn "—pathetically small and inconsequential life."

David lifted his chin.

"Just admit to yourself she'll choose a life of luxury at every turn—a life you can never provide her." A grin spread slowly across Cato's face. "But take heart because I'm here to help you."

Elisabeth's nostrils flared. "None of that means anything to me."

Cato offered her a bemused smile. "We all know that isn't true, *Lady* Elisabeth. You certainly enjoyed the luxurious garments, perks, and prestige you received as my daughter, didn't you?" As he stared, his posture perked up. "But love has changed you too. However, unlike Aquarius, it's made you braver, *more* reckless."

Elisabeth's heartbeat raced.

They all turned around when the door to the stable creaked open and Balinus crept in with a piece of parchment folded in his hand. "Oh wonderful, you're still here."

Cato's eyes widened for a moment. "Good to see you, old man. It's been…a while."

Balinus looked at him and then let out a heavy sigh. "Cato? What are you doing here?"

"Ahh, I'm sure you understand this game by now, Monsieur *Flamel*."

The old man lowered his voice to a whisper. "How have our paths not crossed? You are *not* using the elixir I am familiar with, are you?"

Cato wore a grave expression. "Do *not* ask me questions you do not want to know the answer to."

Balinus recoiled.

"Fond of you as I am, I suggest you leave. Go back to that adorable little family of yours and forget you saw any of us here. You have two adopted daughters now, do you not? What are their names again? Isabeau and…*Colette*?"

Elisabeth did a double-take.

Was that a threat?

David's posture stiffened. "Go back into the house, uncle. We can handle this."

Balinus' shoulders drooped and he started toward the door. "Oh…I almost forgot why I came out here." He turned around and walked back to Elisabeth, handing her the parchment. "Colette forgot to give you this picture she painted." He glanced at Cato. "I am a simple bookmaker now and my wife enjoys making the illuminations. She's been teaching our youngest the craft."

Cato fiddled with his cuffs while nodding. "How quaint."

Elisabeth cleared her throat and unfolded the thick paper. "A unicorn, right?" When she glanced down, her chest tightened for a moment as she tried to make sense of the image she saw. A rush of adrenaline surged through her body, understanding the old man's message. "Tell her thank you. It's beautiful."

He swallowed and nodded before shuffling out of the stable.

"You know..." Cato planted his feet in a wide stance and turned his attention back to Elisabeth. "At first, I was furious you ruined the alliance I'd arranged with Tartare."

Elisabeth stepped beside David, who stood with his arms crossed.

"But on the way here, suspecting you were alive, I realized something—I wasn't thinking *big* enough." Cato pushed his shoulders back and paced in front of them, both hands clasped behind his back. "Right now, at this very moment in time, we have an opportunity others could only dream of. So...I have a plan to propose."

David's eyes narrowed. "I don't care to hear it. We're leaving." He put his hand on Elisabeth's back to lead her away.

Cato let out an arrogant laugh. "Where can you possibly go, Aquarius? I suggest you listen to what I have to say because I'm quite certain *Elisabeth* will take an interest."

Elisabeth froze. The birds began to chirp loudly again. Glancing up at the loft and the open window, her shoulders perked up. She squeezed the paper tight in her hand. Whatever happened, she could *not* lose it.

"As you know, I've lived a rather *long* time." Cato's brows furrowed. "The anger of my youth has evolved into experience and wisdom."

David let out a quick, disgusted snort.

"Right now, society is at a perfect time to be molded into whatever *we* want it to be." With a wide grin, he stepped closer. "I've been alive for over a thousand years. Elisabeth, you have advanced knowledge and tools. Who does that remind you of?"

She felt the color drain from her face when Cato held firm eye contact with her, hoping he didn't realize she'd only been half-listening while trying to come up with an escape plan.

"Do you think we are any different from the gods of old?" he asked.

Elisabeth openly stared at him. "Wait…what?"

"For *centuries*, I've been most generous to the masses. They've no idea the great things I've done for them from the shadows." Cato leaned in closer to her. "It's time to come out of the shadows," he whispered.

An icy shiver crept up her spine.

"As we witnessed in Pompeii, you're able to warn of cataclysmic events. But you also have access to weapons and tools I can only imagine. You can easily pull off being…*magic*. Having magical powers."

Elisabeth's head jerked back. "I am *not* bringing you modern technology, if that's what you're asking for."

"Can you imagine the shocked faces of the people who attended your funeral when they learn you've risen from the grave? Within a generation, I'll have them believing you're not only my daughter, but the daughter of Venus herself, and *that* is a fact. Together, you and I will be an unstoppable force."

Elisabeth reached for David's hand and discreetly tapped her finger against his palm, trying to point to the ladder. When he edged closer and squeezed her fingers, she quietly exhaled, knowing he'd be ready to react.

Cato licked his lips. "We will build a foundation to create the world *we* desire. Why be a king when you can be a king-maker? But why be a king-maker when you can be a god? Riches, power, status…you'll have anything and everything you ever desired."

Elisabeth's breath quickened, wondering—just for a moment—what living like a queen with a fairy-tale castle of her very own would be like. Away from Cato's authority.

She'd have Aquarius by her side.

Plus, a never-ending supply of beautiful clothing.

And jewels.

Tiaras!

Staff to cater to her every whim.

Horse-drawn carriages.

Priceless artwork, exquisite gardens, countless pets, a library filled with books…

She swallowed hard. It was a bit *too* easy to imagine.

Cato held strong eye contact with her. "Neither kings nor paupers will *ever* rise against us. If small factions dare try, we simply create a crisis or war to redirect their attention. It's the ultimate game of chess.

It's what's been done to us since the dawn of time—but this time it's *our* turn to be the gods."

Elisabeth's brows pulled in knowing David deserved the opportunity to live a life of luxury, wanting for nothing.

"And what is *my* role in your twisted game?" David asked.

"Your role?" Cato snorted in amusement. "You're naught but a bargaining chip, *brother*."

With a bitter smile, Elisabeth let go of David's hand and stepped toward Cato. "A deal with you is no better than a deal with the devil."

Cato gave her an incredulous look. "Are you a fool? I am giving you the opportunity to become the wealthiest, most influential, powerful, revered woman in the entire world and you scoff at it like a petulant child? Do not underestimate me." Cato's eyes narrowed and he grabbed hold of her arm. "You are either *with* me or you're *against* me."

Elisabeth yanked free, managing to get closer to the ladder.

Cato's hands curled into tight fists as he turned to face David. "Talk some sense into your *wife*. Think of it. *Everything* has led up to this moment, for *all* of us. We should be celebrating, not bickering. Not only will you be wealthy beyond measure, but worshipped and revered beyond anything you've ever imagined. Neither of you will want for *anything*. All your troubles—gone. ALL of them." He moved closer to David and lowered his voice. "This guarantees you'll have her by your side forevermore—however none of this works without her. We need her on our—"

Elisabeth bundled her skirts into one hand. "You're

right. It *doesn't* work without me." She shoved the parchment into her teeth and raced up the wooden ladder, heart pounding the entire time.

As David sprang closer, Cato lunged, grabbing him into a chokehold, suddenly holding a dagger to his throat.

Elisabeth's muscles tensed as she stared down from the loft.

"Are you a fool?" Cato shouted up at her. "I will destroy the *very* thing you hold most dear, without a moment's hesitation."

David suddenly grabbed Cato's arm with both hands and pulled down. Still holding tight, he twisted under Cato's armpit and stepped behind, freeing himself from the chokehold.

Cato's muscles and veins strained against his skin as he lunged again, the dagger still gripped tight in his fist.

Elisabeth's eyes widened when David ran for the pitchfork Percy had abandoned, barreling toward Cato with a war cry, stabbing it through his boot.

While Cato roared in agony, David scrambled toward the ladder, waving Elisabeth down.

She shook her head, frantically waving him *up*. "Hurry, hurry, hurry…"

Brows squished together, he raced up to the loft as Elisabeth ran to the open window, climbed over the ledge, and jumped—heartbeat pounding as she landed on the haystack below.

As soon as she bounced off, David jumped.

"We need to make it to the old mine entrance before he catches up," she whispered.

He grabbed her hand and they sprinted through the

orchard, beyond the vegetable garden, and down to the small woods behind the property.

"GUARDS!"

When Cato swore and cursed loudly, she glanced over her shoulder in time to see him limping across the paddock, struggling to open the gate.

David pulled her along, racing beyond the saponaria bush, down the hill, and into the woods. Her legs shook so badly she nearly stumbled, but David quickly steadied her. They hadn't a moment to lose as several guards on horseback galloped toward Cato.

"They're heading north! Go around and cut them off," he shouted. "I want the entire area blocked off."

Darting through the soft underbrush of ferns, Elisabeth's breath came in quick gasps. The musty smell of moss still hung in the air and twigs snapped beneath her feet.

The fading light left them surrounded by shadows.

"We're almost there…" David said with a shaky voice.

As they flew toward the boulder, he pulled her to the left and they slowed, looking for the spot.

The clip-clopping of horse hooves grew louder as Cato's men rushed to catch them, seemingly from every direction.

Her gaze darted all around, looking for the hole tucked into the hillside. "Oh, dear God…where is it?"

"Here—" David suddenly grabbed Elisabeth from behind and yanked her against him. Her grip on the parchment tightened as he wrapped her protectively in his arms and then jumped, sliding down into the pit just as dozens of men descended upon the area.

This time, there was no thundering noise from

rocks being displaced as they crash-landed at the bottom of the abandoned mine.

Chapter Forty-Two

From deep within the dark pit, David and Elisabeth hid in the shadows below, trying desperately to hear what was happening above.

"I swear," a guard's voice rose in pitch, "it's like they vanished into thin air, milord."

"Are you certain?"

"They must be somewhere," Facio said. "You two, head to the north. *You*, head back to the city gates. They'll not get far. The entire area is blocked off and sealed."

"You say they disappeared into thin air?" Cato asked again in a carefully controlled tone.

"That's what it seems like, milord, but that's not possible. They're around here somewhere, running like hunted deer. We'll find them."

The sounds of shouting men and horse hooves died down as everyone left—but one person remained, stumbling about in the leaves.

David and Elisabeth stared at each other wide-eyed, listening as Cato let out a guttural roar of defeat.

As they waited in silence, eventually, the only sounds left behind were the birds in the trees, and the squirrels chit-chattering to each other.

Elisabeth's mouth fell open. "Cato thinks we've time-traveled out of here, doesn't he?"

"I believe so." Illuminated by a sunbeam filtering

into the hole, David paced while wringing his hands. "But it doesn't change the fact we'll never get all the way to Ghent undetected."

"Actually, we will, because we're going to Ghent..." Elisabeth pointed toward the black void, where the entrance to the mine was, "...*that* way."

David's brow furrowed. "Do you not remember both Nelly and the old man's warnings? 'Where the mines end the real tunnels begin?'"

"I do, but..." Elisabeth bit down on a smile and slowly unfolded the parchment the old man had given her. "Turns out, this isn't a unicorn painting from Colette."

David lowered his chin and raised an eyebrow. "Then...what is it, love?"

"Well..." She moved the picture into the sunbeam for him to see. "It's an old *map* of the mines down here."

A slow smile spread across his face. "We're going to Ghent?"

Elisabeth let out a spontaneous laugh and threw her arms around his neck. "We're going to Ghent."

To be continued...

Author's Note

The old mines beneath Paris still exist today, quarried since the 1st century by the Romans. City records from 1373 show a woman was authorized to re-open the plaster mine located on her property in Montmartre.

The woman's name?

Dame Perenelle.

By the 18th century, the abandoned mines were so numerous that disastrous cave-ins began to occur along the city streets of Paris, including a quarter-mile stretch of houses.

An additional problem was that, after centuries of use, the Parisian cemeteries were running out of space to bury dead bodies. So, King Louis XVI ordered sections of the mines to be reinforced. For the next twelve years, more than 150 cemeteries were dug up during the night—and the skeletal remains of almost *seven million people* were carted down into the old mines where they remain to this day.

You can tour the catacombs and see the neatly stacked bones and skulls, but the miles and miles of abandoned mines are off-limits and illegal to enter—for obvious reasons.

If you travel to other European cities, such as Maastricht in the Netherlands, you can tour the old limestone mines that once reached Belgium, Germany, and beyond.

However, proceed with caution.

The August 1940 issue of *National Geographic* published an article about the tunnels beneath Malta, a Mediterranean island located just south of Sicily. A teacher and her entire fourth-grade class disappeared during a class trip to the tunnels beneath the city. For several weeks, the families of the missing students insisted they could hear the children sobbing and crying underground. Finally, after weeks of frantic searching with no success, they were all presumed dead. The government blocked off the entrances to stop anyone else from exploring the ancient tunnels.

Of course, some say it's only a legend, used to warn children to keep out.

But you know what they say about legends…

A word about the author...

An adventurer at heart, Tammy has explored ruins in Rome, Pompeii, and Istanbul (Constantinople) with historians and archaeologists.

She's slept in the tower of a 15th century castle in Scotland, climbed down the cramped tunnels of Egyptian pyramids, scaled the Sydney Harbour Bridge, sailed on a tiny raft down the Yulong River in rural China, dined at a Bedouin camp in the Arabian Desert, and escaped from head-hunters in the South Pacific.

I suppose one could say her own childhood wish of time traveling adventures came true...in a roundabout way.

http://www.tammylowe.com

Thank you for purchasing
this publication of The Wild Rose Press, Inc.

For questions or more information
contact us at
info@thewildrosepress.com.

The Wild Rose Press, Inc.
www.thewildrosepress.com